Maya knew Athena's rhymes almost better than her own. . . .

Athena was animated. "By tomorrow I need to be the baddest bitch the rap game has ever seen. Not the one who fell off. Not the *you can take the girl outta da hood but* . . . girl. Not the local one-minute ghetto superstar cheerleading for minimum wage. *The* baddest bitch the game has ever seen."

Luckily, Maya already had her poem for her first show down because preparing for the Rap Olympics was an all-night event: helping Athena pick *the* flygirl outfit with matching hair, makeup and nails; rehearsing dopalicious rhymes over and over again; adding a touch of stage presence and a dance move or four. Should Athena go old skool or new? Serious or slutty? By the time they were finished Maya was even correcting Athena and filling in whenever she skipped a beat.

ABIOLA ABRAMS

POCKET BOOKS
NEW YORK LONDON TORONTO SYDNEY

Pocket Books
A Division of Simon & Schuster, Inc.
1230 Avenue of the Americas
New York, NY 10020

This book is a work of fiction. Names, characters, places, and incidents either are products of the author's imagination or are used fictitiously. Any resemblance to actual events or locales or persons, living or dead, is entirely coincidental.

First Pocket Books trade paperback edition December 2007

POCKET and colophon are registered trademarks of Simon & Schuster, Inc.

For information about special discounts for bulk purchases,
please contact Simon & Schuster Special Sales at 1-800-456-6798
or business@simonandschuster.com.

Designed by Jan Pisciotta

Manufactured in the United States of America

10 9 8 7 6 5 4 3 2 1

ISBN-13: 978-1-4165-4166-0

ACKNOWLEDGMENTS

I have been a writer my entire life, so it is my sincere and humbling pleasure to present *Dare.* As a part of my nightly homework I do a rampage of gratitude. I have to list at least ten things that occurred on the given day for which I feel pure appreciation. It's exciting writing these acknowledgments, as I get to do a public rampage of gratitude to thank those who helped to make this book *and* my charmed life possible.

To my family. From shows and pageants to any kooky scheme your girl can dream up, I thank you for your relentless support. Mommy—thanks for reading my five-hundred-page draft. You woke me up every morning saying "rise and shine," and in your steps I'm doing it. Daddy, thank you for teaching by example how to be your own renaissance. Damali and Ovid, you are a part of me both literally and figuratively. I love the way we all take turns being the older and younger siblings. Walla babies rock on! Quamel—I love you, handsome. Eddie—thank you for making me a fighter. Granny Beryl, I hope to be a matriarch like you one day.

My embarrassment of riches continues. . . . I am blessed to have the most amazing tribe in the world. Thank you for laughing, crying and table dancing with me! In no specific order, y'all are my heart. Kristal Mosley, thank you for holding me down during the writing of this book. Woo-hoo! Moca or Sin Sin? Patranila Jefferson, P. Diddy! Thank you for reading the book in New York and L.A. and giving me your hard-hitting, super-helpful criticism. It was what I needed exactly when I needed it. Crazy black chicks forever! Sonia Malfa Jr., I am so appreciative of your enthusiasm, advice and tireless energy, from home to Lagos and back. Thank you, Sean, for lending her to me. Ibrahim Yilla—*Gracias por todo, papi.* Can't wait to talk about it on the jet. : -) Harry Watson II, I will owe you forever for helping me move out of my old life on a hot summer day. Dr. Daniel Banks, you believed before almost anyone. Thank you for your prayer and songs. I continue to be *your* biggest fan. Dayo Ogunyemi, thank you for listening to my very first reading of *Dare.* T'rah Veal, thank you for taking my favorite pics of me and always offering wisdom. Kwamé Holland, thank you for your musical generosity. I owe you, superhero!! Leslie-licious Lewis Sword, you continue to inspire me in every way. All of you, thanks for holding my hand, patting me on the back, listening to me, laughing with *and* at me and never allowing me to take the divine drama that is Abiola too seriously.

My *Dare* sisters Alexis and Abby—yay! Alexis Hurley—you are the most amazing representative and advocate anyone could hope for. I look forward to a long literary future of us growing together. We did it! Many more deserts to come... Abby Zidle—it was so much fun working with you. Your comments pushed me to do better, and I very much appreciate you swooping in and being a wonder woman. I also give love to my characters for trusting me to tell their stories.

I am grateful for Aunt Wendy and her friends who let a bouncy child in a sunny Guyana sitting room blab on endlessly with her first live solo performance. You listened to me rattle off endless "Marvin" jokes for what seemed like hours and you laughed as if I was really funny. ;-)

Thank you so much to my BET family: Ralph Scott, Sean Joell Johnson, Carmen Vicencio, Felix Augustine and the whole team. I *love* working with you. None of us will be the best-kept secret for long! Chikwenye Ogunyemi at Sarah Lawrence—thank you for giving me the confidence to claim my name and the wisdom to claim my words. Womanists—*yeah*! Frances Taliaferro at Brearley—thanks for gifting me Toni Morrison and changing my life. Eve Ensler, you teach that changing the world is possible. Kim Witherspoon, I appreciate you inviting me into the esteemed Inkwell family. Candice Vadala—thank you so much, big sis, for listening to my dreams. Maggie Crawford and Pocket Books, I am humbled and grateful. For my co-creating sisters Julie, Ilona, Claudine, Pamela, Suki and Sharon, it feels so good to take my hand off the stove! Andie Avila and Selena James, thank you for trusting my talent. Lucy, AJ, Shorn, Alex David, Iman, Smadar, Tasha, TeTe—you are amazing assistants and future stars to beat all! Shine on!

For hip-hop and Dr. Roxanne Shanté: When I first heard your voice I was in my parents' backyard fiddling with the basket on my purple bike. An hour later I had scribbled a poem on a paper plate, my first rap. Good looking out, Ed Lover, for letting a little girl get on the mic at a block party. She hasn't stopped yapping since.

Thank you most of all to my Creator, the Source of all that is.

This is for my great-grandmothers and my unborn granddaughters, for my fans who participate in the Goddess Factory online universe—yes, the blogs and podcasts will keep coming. This is for my writing mothers: Ntozake, Zora, Toni, Alicia, Gloria, Nikki, Amina Baraka; and my family on the other side, Ruby, Pearl, Eve, Shielston, Albert, Alexander and Ma. For the dreamers, believe... DARE... then be!

for my regal angels
ruby, pearl and eve

for those who placed the wings on my shoulders
and the crown on my head
norma & ovid

for those who wear them with me
ovid jr., damali, michelle & adana

and those with whom we share them
quamel, kevin, imani, christopher, tehuti

i pour libations,
i kneel,
i kiss earth,
and i know.

yay!

Notebook of Harmony

THE DARE EXPERIMENT
HIP-HOP UNDERCOVER
BY MAYA GAYLE HOPE

NOTEBOOK OF HARMONY

On the surface, the whole thing seemed to be about the music, but it wasn't. Yeah, it seems like my story begins at a hip-hop concert and all, but it is definitely not about music. It's about the way everybody feels, and as my grandmother Ruby would have said, *allyah and all of we is one so we feelin' nice.*

Sociology is the study of human behavior. Why and how folks do what they do. My practice is not only about social implications, but how those implications affect personal power. In my oath to learn something from every experience, the concert would be easy. So easy, in fact, I decided to write the lesson before I got there.

Music is about harmony. Harmony is about balance. The friendly agreement of notes played or sung together. Yinning as much as you yang. That centeredness that we all are searching for. Flow. Whether it's jazz, rock 'n' roll or even hip-hop. . . . Some would say especially hip-hop. *Flow* is a rapper's ability to lay down rhythm and poetry over an internal beat.

I loved rap music for a hot minute when my best friend, Athena, and I were kids, but by the time I went to college, by the time Salt-n-Pepa and then TLC were played out, so was my affiliation with hip-hop. We couldn't have a one-way love affair. I refused. I wanted to love hip-hop, but it was clear that it no longer loved me. I was ready to grow and be an adult but hip-hop clearly wasn't. So like a bad breakup, I forgot I ever loved it, moved on and never looked back.

Harmony and flow are not just about music. Harmony and

flow describe our ability to be in equilibrium with the ebb and flow of our lives.

HARMONY DECLARATION: (Repeat five times every morning, noon and night to reinforce harmony in your life.)

For every yin, there is a yang. For every flow, there is an ebb. For every hip, there is a hop. For every beat there's a stop. Remember when life spins from slow to fast: this too shall pass.

HARMONY ACTION STEP: *In the interest of balance, consider ways that you might live a more harmonic life.*

Prologue

"You know life is all about expression.
You only live once, and you're not coming back
So express yourself, yeah."
—Salt-n-Pepa

"If you don't know what you looking for, then you ain't gonna find it here," the golden singer crooned, snaking her hypnotic hips in perfect circles while her melodious tones wrapped the audience in black velvet.

"I can't see." Maya moved only her shoulders to the beat. Her vision was blocked by the ginormous Camp Hustla logo emblazoned across the guy's jacket in front of her.

"Then stop chair dancing and join the party!" Maya's best friend, Athena, grooved her whole body, hands up high, to the hit R & B tune.

Maya was probably the only person in the entire arena sitting down. "Why'd they even hold it somewhere with chairs if everybody's gonna stand anyway?!" Not that she wanted to see some ghetto chanteuse shake what her mama gave her, but they were already at the concert so she might as well have a good time. Most folks ignored the No Smoking signs, clouding her contacts with tobacco and weed fumes, but it was a night out with her BFs so she wasn't complaining too much. Athena stood on the chair to Maya's left, puffing a nasty Newport, and Maya's boyfriend, Bobby, stood on the floor to her right, surveying the scene and towering easily over the crowd. The energy was off the meter and despite herself, Maya was loving it. She coughed dramatically, waving away Athena's mentholated smoke, and stood up.

"Sorry, boo!" Athena was still tipsy from the box of white wine they'd "shared" earlier: Maya had a sip and Athena polished off the rest. She hopped down and steered her apology straight into song, singing along with vocalist BaTricia Simone. "But if it ain't here, then it don't exist, I said if it ain't here . . ."

". . . Then it don't exist, ba-a-by." Maya sang the last line in Bobby's face as he did a brothaman head nod to the rhythm. "You think her backup dancers came to the show straight from the strip club?"

"Loosen up! Show him what you working with," Athena whispered. She held Maya's hand up and they bounced their booties on the double beat, laughing at themselves as they swiveled in the songstress's scandalous trademark move.

"Wowww. So it's like *that*, Maya?" Bobby grinned. "All these years and I didn't know!!"

"See?" Athena mouthed.

Maya rolled vowels in her mother's musical accent. "I'm West Indian, baby. Natural motion de in my ocean."

"Well, please Hammer, don't hurt 'em." Bobby touched Maya's nose.

"You're showing your age." Maya bumped her butt on Bobby's leg until she realized that she was the only one still doing that move. The music had changed and Athena and everyone else was doing a lean back instead. Maya straightened up.

"This is a good-looking crowd! Three o'clock." Athena nodded toward a young almost-Denzel snuggled up with his woman. Almost-Denzel smiled over homegirl's head and Athena blew a kiss back.

Maya elbowed her. "Yeah. There must be a bald village in China with all this fake hair." Maya shuffled back and forth in her new green Keds with purple laces. Peeps from the hood—who weren't related to Athena—sometimes made her a wee bit nervous. A guy made his way through the crowd selling bootleg T-shirts and hats; Maya studied the loud ghetto crowd and moved closer to Bobby. Uh-huh. Posturing and fronting in their fur, denim and leather; posing silver as platinum and rhinestones as diamonds; other people's names on their butts and chests; talking urgently on their cell phones to no one.

The female uniform was painted-on jeans with any kinda barely there tank top. The male uniform was a jersey or hoodie with baggy jeans. It was a rap video cliché. Pimps up. Hos down. Maya quickly scoped out Bobby to see which half-naked skeezers were pulling his attention, but he was scrolling through his BlackBerry. Good. She fished a near-empty tube of gloss out of her bright yellow knapsack, handed the bag to Bobby and polished her lips. Bobby was too old and too smart at thirty-one to be somebody's waterboy intern, but that's how it went down in the music biz, he explained.

Concerts happened in Faustus only once in a cool moon and the place buzzed with starving energy. The crowd milled around, half paying attention to the opening act, half handling their own biz: dancing, singing, chatting and having a good time. A family reunion without the food or, surprisingly, fights.

"You betta sang, BaTricia Simone!" a sepia goddess in skintight black jeans shouted.

"Those Chloés cost almost four hundred dollars." Athena tossed her cig, eyeing the chick with envy.

"If I spent four hundred dollars on jeans I would know that somewhere the jeans people were laughing at me." Maya watched as Athena's cigarette fell, its still-lit embers chasing a gum wrapper. She squashed it with her heel. *Girlfriends Rule #3. You can diffuse anyone's beauty by ridiculing them.*

Miss Chloé Jeans' white tube top exposed a six-pack tummy. The girl was petite like Athena, Maya noted, and easy in her skin. Unlike Athena, however, chica sported double-D kazongas, technically the same size as Maya's but somehow able to defy gravity and probably leap tall buildings in a single bound.

"You know those are implants, right?" Maya glanced at Bobby.

"What?" he asked. Bobby was caramel pudding with a footballer's build, long locks and radio smooth voice.

The way Bobby pretended to ignore her jealousy made Maya smirk. As a soon-to-be sociologist she lived to observe people's conversations, expressions and emotions and make snap diagnoses. Athena: extrovert, exhibitionist and latent ADD. Bobby: classic he-man complex and overachiever. The overpacked stadium was a personality gold mine.

Men looking hard and ladies looking harder. Game faces in full effect. It was all good—as much about seeing and being seen as it was the music. Everybody rocked their finest gear, scoping each other out across the stadium, overdosing on Dolce and Phat Farm. Athena and Bobby were in their element. Maya? Not so much.

"Take Athena's hand and climb up on my shoulders." Bobby held his new digital camera, Maya's backpack, Athena's fake graffiti Vuitton and binoculars. Stooped over, he was a small tree bowing.

Maya looked up at him. "Uh, climb?" Cute, cocoa and what the homeboys referred to as "thick," it took a lil' effort to get Maya up in the air.

"Gimme your hand and stop bitching." Athena took her hand and the three of them, a pyramid, hoisted Maya onto Bobby's shoulders, smudging the lip gloss she just put on, her four Pocahontas braids swinging to the side.

Bobby swatted Maya's booty. She pushed his hand down playfully, just glad to be above the melee.

"It takes a village." Maya laughed uncomfortably as she settled onto her man's shoulders.

"You're lucky I love you, Miss Hope." Bobby tried to balance their swag and Maya at the same time.

"Whoa." Maya covered Bobby's eyes as the scantily clad singer thrust her hips at a rapid-fire pace.

"She can't compete with you, bootylicious." He removed her hands, kissed each of them, and smiled up at her. She kissed him on the nose, her sisterlocks forming a veil, and they almost toppled.

"Should I vomit now?" Athena handed Maya a hair elastic and Maya tied it on, sticking her plaits straight up. Athena shook her head, her God-given sapphire eyes trained on the peak of Maya's tower of braids.

Maya caught Athena's look. "What?"

"Nothing." Athena knew that it was pointless to say anything about the jutting flamingo feathers on top of Maya's head. In contrast to Maya's green turtleneck (in June) and matching saggy corduroys (never in style), Athena sported a pink cowboy hat, matching stiletto boots, dark jeans and a fringed vest. Athena didn't care that wearing her hat (cocked to show off her cheekbones) to a concert impeded other people's vision. Unlike Maya, she knew her beauty and loved its power. Her signature look was (a) enough chains to fence off Mexico; (b) tennis shoes that never saw a tennis court; and (c) any color Juicy-alike sweats.

"Yo Big Bob," they heard behind them again and again.

"What's up, my man?" Bobby gave a pound to a dude in a low Yankees hat as he walked by.

"Baby, you know everybody now," Maya observed.

"You jealous 'cause I'm popular?" Bobby reached up and tickled her and she giggled, squirming and trying to avoid being hit by their bags.

A guy with big sideburns coughed into the air without covering his mouth. A borderline germaphobe, Maya folded herself into Bobby's 'fro to dodge the airborne molecules of disease.

Ebony black and Marilyn blonde, in her knee-high crimson boots and tight red corset, BaTricia (impulse control disorder) was trying her darndest to channel Mary. The new self-proclaimed Godmama of R & B belted her remake of Al Green's "For the Good Times." In her version, however, instead of "lay your head on my pillow one more time," she sang out in babysweet harmony "stick your head between my legs one more time" over a drop-it-like-it's-hot beat.

"I can do that." Athena, always in competition, affected a perfect triple-time thrust along with BaTricia Simone. "And people wouldn't be acting like it's intermission during my show." She hit Bobby on the arm. "Check it out, y'all. Next year's Big Summer Slam, it's gonna be me up there."

"Well when it's you, make sure your weave matches your skin tone," Maya shouted over the din.

"Weave? Sorry miss but you must be mistaken." Athena flipped her color #4, eighteen-inch tresses with highlights. "Besides, everything goes with butter brown." Athena insisted on referring to herself as "butter brown" instead of "high yella" to prove that she wasn't overly colorstruck like most of the people in their town, although she secretly was. Folks said that Maya and Athena had gotten each other's hair by mistake. Dark-skinned Maya had wild, curly locks that grazed her middle back and light-skinned Athena had coarse, can't-comb naps that wouldn't grow past three inches.

"I can't believe I'm here!!!" Athena was all moves, her face in video pose/pose/pose mode.

"Neither can I." Maya was in neutral, her face in *over it* mode.

Though BaTricia Simone was certainly a treat, the audience was there for one reason only—They knew it and BaTricia Simone knew it too. Prophet. Hoodlum, genius, convicted rapist and teacher. The man, the myth, the legend, the Teflon MC, the rapper. Contradiction was his name and tonight Thug was gracing the stage for the first time at The Dandridge Pavilion and Convention Center, a huge old venue that housed every major event in Faustus, Ohio. The man had been arrested thirteen times for things he bragged openly about in his songs, served two sentences for stuff he claimed he was innocent of and survived three hospital stays after being shot uncountable times. Maya knew about him from the news, not his music. Still, people worshipped him. This concert was all grown-ass people could talk about for weeks.

BaTricia Simone finished up her set doing her typical "Dip it down low, oh no, oh no . . ." Her finger waves were sweating out and a weave track swung loose on the side of her head. She bowed nose to knees like she'd just completed The Pieta and the arena went dark. Everyone clapped wildly, calling her name and whistling, just happy that she was finished and they could move on to the main event. "Thank you, Faustus!!" She yelled into the blackness.

Silence. Everyone stood quietly in the dark, anticipating what was next. Together, they held their breaths and swallowed. And swallowed again. One person started a whispered chant—"Thug, Thug"—and they all joined in. "Thug! Thug! Thug!" Their chanting soon became yelling, then screaming, until the entire arena quaked with one orgasmic breath. They were one stadium under a groove, vibrating on one beat for a good three minutes before breaking into *Happy Birthday, Thug.*

A screen popped up with *Star Wars*–style text: "IN A GALAXY FAR, FAR AWAY, ONE MAN WITH A MISSION TO SAVE THE HOOD THUNDERED FORTH . . ."

"Thug, Thug," they chanted as a video came up over the scroll, his princely face in profile.

"We love you!!" a woman shrieked. Maya squinted into the dark, quite possibly the only person in Ohio not screaming the rapper's name. The air was dewy with the frenzy of a Sunday revival. The forty-something-year-old woman in front of them was crying. In fact, several people were. She looked down at Bobby. Even his alpha male eyes looked wet. Athena fanned herself with her long fake nails. Was it this damn deep?

Swirling red emergency-style lights. Sirens wailing. Canned smoke. The crowd was insane, hyperventilating as if Thug gave them too much air.

P-POW!! POW!! P-POW!! An explosion of fireworks popped off on the huge stage. Probably not a good idea in this crowd. Many heads hit the floor, thinking that someone was shooting. Gunshots were not an unreasonable fear at a Thug concert. P-POW!!! Another explosion and then the sound of barking as Thug and his trademark crew of ten pit bulls appeared in the middle of the stage. Thug pounded on his black bulletproof vest. The barking pit bulls each had a handler dressed in black and wearing a charcoal hockey mask. The long chains almost let the furious dogs leap off the edge of the stage. Maya, who had a particular fear of dogs, was not entertained by this. The front rows bent back, watching pools of canine saliva form puddles.

P-POW!! Maya crouched deeper into Bobby, peeking out with one eye. She only felt somewhat safe in this crowd for two reasons: (1) They'd come through airport-level security to get in. In fact, the feral dogs on stage were quite possibly the same ones used at the doors. (2) Bobby was there.

"It's okay—look!" Bobby said.

Thug (God complex) held his arms open and formed a living cross. "This is my house tonight!!!!" he shouted and his crowd agreed with him. He was on fire, commanding attention, and folks all over the audience were catching the Holy Ghost. Thug's bald mahogany head, sculpted face, ten-o'clock shadow, dewdrop eyes and impossibly long lashes made him look more like a model or African warrior statue than a common thug. Still, just so that you didn't get it twisted, he had THUG emblazoned on one arm, along with a rabid dog foaming out JAH, FOREVA tattooed on the other muscular arm like a carnival sleeve. With cargo pants, bullets strapped across his chest, gun holsters and a six-inch diamond-encrusted crucifix, he was ready to fight the new Crusades.

"Faustus make some noiiiiiiiiiise!!!!!!!" Thug's disciples happily obliged, screaming, yelling, calling his name until the bass kicked in a party beat. "Right now I'm bringin' my hometown Harlem to Faustus! Life is a mixtape and the black Mecca is anywhere we want it to be. Harlem is a state of mind, baby. I'm home!" he said, and as proof took off his bulletproof vest and tossed it aside.

"Yo Thug! Preach, God. Preach!" Bobby called out, proud that his internship with Dreadz Entertainment earned them eleventh-row tickets and the right to bear witness to this historic moment. He put their bags, camera and crap on the floor between his legs so that he could clap, his big cupped hands echoing a deep heavy sound.

Maya gripped Bobby's shoulders, trying to keep an eye on their stuff. "Whoa." She felt queasy as he swayed his whole body.

"Sorry, babe. Forgot you were up there," he said, eyes straight ahead.

Even Maya had to admit, physically, Thug was straight beautiful. He snapped his head hard to the beat, the dogs barking their affirmation. Still, she hated his hip hype.

She wrestled a pen and a Dirrrty Kentucky Strippas flier someone had handed her from her corduroys and started scribbling: *Loud ghetto trash talking lyrics & dough / Women as bitches and hos / Brothas as niggas and foes / Acting like y'all don't know / When your mama told you so / Mind-dulling weed / Nothing but greed / Violence, violence, silence / Chains, rings and this one way to be black thing / Somewhere the Klan is laughing / It is straight-up embarrassing . . .*

But then again, she got embarrassed watching the news, praying "please don't let him be black" about the latest purse snatcher, gang blaster, hell catcher. She hated this music, but via a sadistic joke of fate, the two people closest to her were both hip-hop heads. So here she was. Maybe being here qualified as a good social experiment. If she could turn this night into a paper, it wouldn't be a complete waste.

LAB REPORT

HIP-HOP: Heroes or Zeroes

A Sociological Analysis

By Maya Hope

OBJECTIVE: To attempt an honest analysis of a field of "music" overrun by corporate sexist materialistic junk.

CRITERIA: Make it through an entire song without barfing.

DATA: Taken by the police as evidence.

VOCABULARY: Limited, at best, shawty.

CONCLUSION: One would best stay far, far, away from this meaningless pap for fear that your brain may turn to *mush.*

"Thug!" All of Athena's naturally hyper energy beamed forward. "Put me on stage. Lemme dance for you. Lemme rhyme for you!" She waved her skinny arms and jumped up and down. For a split second he turned in their direction as if he heard her. Then the music came in louder and he kicked into his signature song, "Assassinator," as the dog handlers exited in a military march. Now only the main man stood center stage.

"Yo. I looked 'thug' up in the dictionary last night." Thug brandished his mic like a sword swiping at demons only he could see. "And you know what it said?"

"Nah, tell us!" shouted a chick in the balcony.

"It said brutal and violent!" Thug paced back and forth now, moving with urgency.

"No," Bobby said in an undertone.

"That dictionary said thug meant a cutthroat, a ruffian, a hoodlum."

"No," the crowd murmured.

"They ain't talking to me!" Thug said.

"NO!" roared the crowd.

Thug had a black power fist held high. "They ain't talking to me 'cause that's the same thing they been sayin' 'bout niggas for years, and they ain't talking to US!" The word *niggas* punched Maya in the face and she flinched.

"T.H.U.G. stands for True Heart Under God," the rapper continued.

"Hollaaaah!" screamed the dude in front of them.

"You ain't ready." Thug seemed to be looking at Maya. "They ain't ready!" Thug said, and with that, launched into lyrics as the crowd went into hysterics:

> *"Black Houdini Thug is on the mic . . .*
> *Man listen, you missin', the ass that you kissin',*
> *Pissin' on my grave 'cause you thinking I'm a slave? Knave.*
> *And when I die, don't blame me for my suicide*
> *And when I die, don't blame me 'cause I had to lie*
> *And when I die, don't blame me 'cause I had to hide*
> *And when I cry, just blame me 'cause I never died . . ."*

Bobby moved his lips to every word, his eyes half closed.

"Where are you?" Maya asked.

"Inside the beat," he yelled back.

It wasn't Motown, Badu or jazz but it wasn't *too* bad. She could kinda see why this was B's thing.

She'd re-met Bobby when he slipped her a "Hey Faustus" note during an undergrad music class at Oberlin. *Oh yeah. Hey. Bobby right?* One of the few other kids of color from the Faustus prep school scene. They were friends first for a few years after graduation, and she was locked ever since. He finally kicked it for real/for real when Maya stuck by him through his turning thirty crisis, in which he dropped out of Harvard B-School and moved back to Over-the-Rhine. He now carried boxes, wrote rhymes and hung posters all over nearby Cincinnati for Dreadz, the hottest urban label in town, while Maya went to school.

" 'Scuse me, dawg, 'scuse me. Damn, *move*, motherfucka!" Mauricio (Napoleon complex) made his way over. Mauricio nodded at Bobby and Bobby gave him a pound. Maya had almost forgotten he was with them.

"Where the hell were you?" Athena got up in Mauricio's face. "You missed BaTricia Simone's whole show." Her angry spit hit his pride.

"I could hear it out front! I had bi'ness to tend to," Mauricio didn't make eye contact with Athena. It was Maya's turn to bite her tongue. Athena was too good for half these jokers she brought home. Maya learned not to get too attached.

"What?" Athena asked her.

"Nada." Maya looked straight ahead at the concert.

"Cheese nachos, y'all?" Mauricio held out a one-person-size paper bowl. Athena and Bobby each took a couple. "Maya?" he asked, winking at her.

"No, thanks." Maya turned her head, disgusted.

Athena rubbed what there was of her behind on Mauricio, performing a standing lap dance as a video ho did the same to Thug. Mama on stage was doing circus tricks, spreading her legs wiiide in a tight red bikini and six-inch heels, then launching into a handstand. "I'm gonna murder ya murderer / Bring death to ya pain."

"Listen close to the words, Maya. It's all metaphor." To listen to Bobby, Thug was the first coming of Christ rather than a convicted felon. Bobby broke it down several times how Thug was different, dissecting his lyrics. She dabbled in poetry so she could get with the need for self-expression, but did everybody have to express the same thing over and over again? Just 'cause you got a story to tell doesn't mean that people need to hear it.

Thug gave a thorough show, performing his eclectic platinum hitlist to the fullest. His catalogue seemed to Maya like a weird combo of ultra positive and ultra negative tunes: "God Is My Nigga"; "I'm Gonna Kill Ya"; "The Stay Strong Song, Death Becomes You"; "Side Chick Blitz"; "Pussy Chaser"; "Fear of a Blackman"; "Supreme Mathematics"; "Predickshunz," and "Straight Thuggin." As the crowd clapped, hooted, saluted and did whatever the notorious Thug suggested—*throw your hands up high and wave 'em side to side*—Maya wondered what it must be like to feel that adored. Having been called Maya Hopeless all through her youth, she was still recovering as a woman and the concept was fascinating.

"Baby . . ." Maya chose her words carefully. "Um, how many songs are left?"

"This should be the last one." Bobby's eyes lived onstage as he spoke although his face smiled up at Maya. He did a subtle stretch. Subtext: His neck was getting numb but knowing Maya's complex about her weight he was trying not to show it.

"Yeah. He did almost everything except 'Black Woman, Black Love.' " Athena snapped her fingers with Mauricio.

"Okayyyy." Maya slid down Bobby's back and he stretched his neck. She took his hands and tried to make eye contact. "Then . . . um . . . Can we go? I mean, we know what's gonna happen. Nigga this, nigga that. Applause, cursing, a bunch of encores, more cursing. And, uh, it's gonna take forever for this many people to exit the—"

"We're not leaving." Bobby gave her the shut down. "Thug is known for his big finishes."

Great. Maya launched into attitude mode, snatching their stuff up off the floor in a huff. She cradled the bags and camera in her arms, staring up into indoor clouds of dust, dry ice and smoke. Oh. A small bluebird was caught in the rafters. "He must've gotten in by accident," she said mostly to herself. The bluebird flew around in smaller and smaller circles, confused.

"'Fore y'all leave, I got something hot. A gift for you on my birthday." Thug's image echoed on multiple screens throughout the pavilion.

"If Lenin had the technology, this is definitely how he would have used it," Maya said.

"Don't look surprised," Thug insisted. "Don't Daddy always come through?"

"Yeahhh, Daddy!" Athena was with Thug one on one. Mauricio cleared his throat.

Thug's hard ghetto façade broke into sunbeams as he smiled with his whole face. "James and Tasha—where you at?" A couple raised their hands, the woman whooping loudly and acting very *Price Is Right*. "Aight, Tasha, what you don't know is that ya boy James hooked somethin' special up for you. Lemme also get Dave and Theresa." Another whoop. "And Cherry, Cherril, uh, Cherilyn and Shakim, Gina and Sean, Jenny and Big Black. There's always some brotha named Big Black." The crowd laughed, buoyant with Thug's lighter mood. "Okay ladies, lemme break it down. Check it. Your man wants to marry you. Tasha, Theresa, Cherilyn, Gina and Jenny, y'all are being proposed to." Somebody from the ground reached up and handed him a piece of paper. "Oh, my bad, we also got Maya and Bobby. So Maya, too. Your man, too."

Maya looked at Bobby, then Mauricio, then Athena, completely confused. Athena was clapping in slow motion.

"Black love, black love. It's a beautiful thing." Thug himself applauded as Bobby, James, Shakim, Big Black, Dave and several other random brothas got down on one knee. "Hold your cellies up. Cellies up. Cell phones up," Thug screamed. "Seize the damn day!" The audience held their phones up, illuminating the building in digital phosphorescence.

"Motherfuckas got to be crazy to pull out diamonds in this piece," said Mauricio.

"I was . . . totally . . . not . . ." Maya burst out crying. Overwhelmed by the beauty of Bobby's gesture and not knowing what else to do, Maya knelt down with her love, her one true love, and held him as all the folks in their section shared their moment.

"Y'all are so cute!" Miss Chloé Jeans called out.

Not seeming at all like a convicted rapist, Thug launched into "Black Women, Black Love." Now folks were tearing up for real/for real. Maya kissed Bobby's plum colored lips. Usually, this many people looking at her would have sent her into an anxiety attack.

"You gonna live in my heart?" Bobby asked.

"I already do." Maya's gaze was all Bobby. He made the world stop. Just for her. He found her glass slipper.

"My black woman, my black love, my Nubian queen . . ." Thug kicked his rhyme.

"So Maya, hello!" Bobby kissed her nose. "What's up? You gonna make an honest man outta me or what?"

"YES!" Athena shouted.

"Of course," Maya whispered, alone with Bobby in the crowd.

Athena was ecstatic. "See Maya—I told you! Your horoscope said Virgos should expect big things today!"

Still kneeling with Bobby, Maya wanted to imprint this moment of perfect happiness in her brain: Wednesday, June 16, 2004, 10:03 P.M.

BAM! A crackling sound. Nobody moved, expecting more pyrogenics. Then CRACK-CRACK-CRACK-BAM. BAM-BAM!!! *They're shooting!* someone screamed. A voice cussed God and all hell broke loose as Thug hit the floor, his perfect chest exploded into wet crimson. Someone scooped Maya up and was carrying her. Bobby.

"Athenaaa!" Maya saw Mauricio dragging Athena by the elbow, her cowgirl hat falling off into the crowd. Pierced by a boot. *RUN!* A guy stepped on another dude's Tims and got punched in his metallic teeth.

Pandemonium. Panic. People. Claustrophobia. Crossing. Cursing. *Run!* Every which way. Their crap fell through Maya's arms until she was only grasping Bobby's camera. *Move*. Folks in every direction. *Get off a me*. Every which way. *Help*. Panic. Wailing. Yelling. *Remain calm!* Guards also running. An exit. Door barred. *What the*—?! The crowd kicked it. Locked. Beat it with bloody knuckles. Stuck. Apocalypse.

"I know the way out." Mauricio pushed Athena by the shoulders like a shopping cart.

"The stage!" yelled Bobby. "It's the safest place 'cause the shooters wanna get lost in the crowd!"

Maya, Bobby, Athena and Mauricio scrambled up to the stage and watched from the wings. Sheer madness. People getting trampled. Barking dogs. Screaming sirens. Madness as several people on the other side carried Thug's bloody, lifeless body away, his music still playing. It was the fiddling on the *Titanic.*

Maya squeezed Bobby's arm. Analysis was dead. Their beautiful night, the night of their engagement, had gone down in cosmic flames, gunshots, blood, death, confusion.

"Y'all gon' laugh at this dawg when y'all is old marrieds," Mauricio said.

"Where's my bag?!" Athena's dark blue eyes faded to gray.

"That's problem number fifty-four," said Bobby, stoically.

"Fake Louis ain't cheap!" Athena barked, pacing in a figure eight.

"Charge it to the game." Mauricio pulled out a pack of Newports. "You think that nigga is finally dead, God?" He looked sideways at Bobby. Bobby stared back like he wanted to end him somehow.

"Shut up!" Athena screamed at the top of her lungs. Mauricio turned his back on her and lit up.

Standing with her peeps and not knowing what else to do, Maya snapped a picture of the wild scene. *Snap.* Several people lay motionless with clusters forming around them. *Snap.* More of the pretty ones in one fell swoop. *Snap.* Standing on the stage allowed them to be removed from the chaos, although they were just a few feet from Thug's flaccid bulletproof vest. *Snap.* Above it all, yet in the center of the action. *Snap. Snap. Snap.* Numb fingers. She looked for the bluebird. He was still there, balancing on a rafter. *Snap.* Bobby pried the camera from her hands and wrapped his love around her. She breathed Bobby in and saw blood on his crisp white T-shirt. She put her hand to her face. Her nose was bleeding.

Notebook of Beauty

THE DARE EXPERIMENT
HIP-HOP UNDERCOVER
BY MAYA GAYLE HOPE

NOTEBOOK OF BEAUTY

There is beauty in the ugliest things.
I have seen ugly, known ugly and loved ugly.
Ugly is as ugly does.

Beauty is an appreciation, and
appreciation meets us where we are.
If we let it.

Seeing beauty and calling her name is the highest form of appreciation. To appreciate—to call beauty's name—is to honor the divine.

BEAUTY DECLARATION: *(Repeat five times every morning, noon and night to reinforce beauty in your life.) I find beauty where she lives. In my life, my loves and my mirror. I honor beauty within and without.*

BEAUTY ACTION STEP: *Treat yourself to a beauty binge. No—it's not what you think. Start from wherever you are, and for the next twenty-four hours, acknowledge beauty wherever you find it. From the grandiose, a gorgeous sunrise, to the minuscule, a beautiful ladybug. The frame of mind that this beauty binge puts you in will have you wanting to seek out beauty everywhere. As appreciation of beauty is our gratitude for the divine, perhaps we should. We readily call out ugliness. What if we made the same effort toward beauty?*

Chapter 1

"HE LOSES BECAUSE HE NEVER UNDERSTOOD THE GAME."

—*Sister Souljah,* Coldest Winter Ever

Maya Gayle Hope stood in front of The Dandridge Pavilion and Convention Center on Three Birds Avenue squinting into the dim daylight. Strains of wayward poems in her head, wind-beaten protest sign in her hands, *"Stop police brutality now"* on her lips; her life was held together by rubber bands.

"Once upon a life when I was sexy / Connected to my sweet me-itude. / What a metamorphosis is this? / Shade / Sweetness / Struggle." She was feeling the beginnings of a new poem's first kiss. They usually came at inconvenient times. There was nowhere to write it down.

"No justice, no peace!" She marched the sidewalk chanting like an evening chick gone wrong. A crumbling gray Thunderbird honked an ungentle greeting as it passed. A police car slowed, trying to determine whether she was a threat or a lone crazy. They decided lone crazy and kept it moving. A corn-colored '70s Beetle rumbled by and the back-seaters, laughing, tossed neon orange soda, even their music cussing her: "I'm gonna rape, rape, rape the game / Make you cream, scream out my name / I'll put it in the front and bust out ya back. / Keep pounding till your momma have a heart attack . . ."

"Yo, Pippi Longstocking. Take your panties off your head!" the mohawked one shouted.

Dumb ass. Good men were slim pickings in Faustus. Sistas felt with the shortage it was time to start sharing, meaning that those freaks were a catch to somebody. No brotha she'd ever met, including her pop, knew how to be good to one woman much less multitask.

While other brown girls strove for this year's version of Moschino ho or Versace hottie, Maya's gear of many layers was what a homeless person might sport if Goodwill shut down. In fact, that was where she shopped in the rare moments when saving the world created some net. Her student loans and Athena's credit card debt made for lean living. La glorious bohème it damn sure wasn't, but with her hazelnut eyes, and triple dark toffee skin she could sometimes get away with it. Curry scarf, lemon coat, pomegranate-red corduroys and vanilla pearl earrings. Maya was viewing everything in terms of food these days. Matching was clearly not on her list of priorities. Her booty coulda made JLo blush and her saggin'-too-soon D+ cups definitely would have been helped by a bra. But you know dudes. They don't care.

She caught her reflection in an old rain puddle. She was two years past the age when most people found looking bootleg acceptable. Although thirty is the new twenty, you still need to have your stuff together. Folks blamed her hyper meta colors on her Trini background. She never mentioned that although her parents walked to Tobago for school holiday, the dirt under her childhood fingernails was Yankee through and through. Ohio's own. Yellow Springs born, Faustus bred.

You know that concave spot in the small of your back that's the first to sweat when you're on the treadmill working it like you promised you would? Right above the booty, deliciously kissable when given half a chance but it usually just languishes as a repository for warm sweat? Ick. Yeah. Ick. Faustus, Ohio, just east of Cincinnati, is exactly like that spot with a large dose of small town pride heaped on top. Three things about The Faust that nobody in the real world gives a damn to know: (1) Faustus is the home of The Midwest Game Fishing Museum, a fantastic place to get some geezer to buy you lunch; (2) the best spot anywhere to get your multiculti grub on is Fillet My Sole—be sure you try the crawfish; and (3) hip-hop music is alive and thriving high in the 513 area code.

Oblivious to only one out of three of these critical facts, Maya stood in the center of the sidewalk with her curly 'fro sweating out into plain ole naps under her pom-pommed pea-green knit cap. Her protest was supposed to be five strong, not one weak. A Dunbar grad and the daughter of Antioch professors, activism was in her blood. The parents had drilled it enough times growing up: being black is political whether you are a political person or not. Too bad she wasn't ever with them long enough to get any concrete advice besides (a) the political thang and (b) *Maya, you have to work ten times as hard as anyone else because blah, blah, blah* . . . The good thing now was that her political protests gave her an alternate identity to the "chick with the wedding that wasn't," and gave her something else to focus on besides her sucky job.

"Hey, hey. Ho, ho. Police brutality's got to go!!!!!" She kicked her pitiful pile of handmade signs. How'd it go again? Stand for something or fall for . . . No rest for the weary. Maya thrust a sign back into the air. "To serve, protect and break a brotha's neck!!"

A lazy shingle freed itself from the old building and crashed to the ground barely missing her. Great. If it wasn't for bad luck, she would have none.

Her cause this week? The FPD gave another Mexican kid a beat-down and everybody moved on to *American Idol* while the teen lay in traction. One by one, the defeated people united offered Maya, their chocolate Norma Rae, a bevy of elaborate excuses: Damali decided to get a two-year jump on her dissertation. Apparently this required MAC Lychee Luxe Lip Glass and new cornrows. *Smooches!* Quamel forgot that he'd signed up for animal rescue. *Later Maya.* Ovid's great-aunt's cousin Dee Dee had come in to town and needed a lift. Who would think that his great-aunt would have a dirty-blonde cousin that looked twenty-one? *Wink-wink.* And Athena just wanted to work on her music. Truth was that Ohio was witnessing an unseasonably warm St. Paddy's Day and her protest crew, a ragtag group of other locals who still cared, was probably off in Harmony Park enjoying global warming.

This was just what she needed on an Ugly Day. You know those days? When that extra five pounds becomes twenty overnight? Everybody has Ugly Days. Hell, Halle has Ugly Days. Now, it doesn't matter what you look like, it's what you feel you look like when you ask the mirror, Who the hell is *that*?! Homegirl must've slept on her face because that child is hid-e-ous. Wasn't nothing worse than being stood up by a crowd of people on an Ugly Day.

"Hey, cheesecake! I wouldn't mind eating you." A businessman who should have been a construction worker blew a kiss.

Maya chanted louder but except for the guys trying to kick it, passersby barely glanced. "Ugh. I'm civic roadkill." She plopped down on the building steps. *So much for Justice for Juan Suarez.*

An old crone who probably felt sorry to see such a young woman talking to herself threw some change, starting a trend. Monkey see, monkey doers tossed coins onto the lame pile of signs and fliers. Maya damn sure wasn't mad at this trend as she and Athena combined earned almost $500 less than their monthly budget and only made ends meet with the ancient art of bill juggling. You know, paying who is most overdue and telling the electric co that they can't cancel service because you have a resident on life support. Someone pressed a few dollars into her hand and Maya looked up.

"You got DSL?"

Well hello. Ebony man alert! Finally, a fine one. Almond and beefy. Even during her dry season she knew a hot prospect. How did flirting go again? She pulled off her cap and tried to toss her tangled 'fro. It knotted further and a dash of sediment from the crumbling roof deposited itself like a barrette.

"DSL? Online?" Maya's face was beginning to smile. He grinned back.

"No. Dick Sucking Lips. You look good. What you doing later, girl?" He threw a couple more singles and laughed. "Get your hair combed."

"I'm not your ho!" she shouted at his back as he strutted down the sidewalk, enjoying her piss-off-ity. Despite herself she loved watching a black man walk. She imagined a Zulu plume on his back. If they were Zulu her family could take possession of at least three goats for that disrespect. Maya scrambled up the change and bills and put them on the steps for someone needier. She noticed a new hole in the back of one of her old green Keds. The laces were filthy. If she didn't do such a good job, her boss would never let her into the office. She started to pack up the fliers, then reconsidered. Maybe someone with a little more gas in their engine might be inspired to take up the cause. Sufficiently humiliated for one bright shiny day, she put on her unattached earphones, hopped on her environmentally friendly purple bike and took off, wrapped in wolf whistles all the way, her helmet still hooked to the handlebars.

"Yo, shawty! You need to smile . . ."

"Baby, you got a big ass . . ."

"Your parents wasn't frontin' when they made you . . ."

"What? You can't speak? You black bitch. Bitch. BITCH!"

You know how brothas get. They didn't care that she was wearing headphones. Oh, you're wondering why she was wearing headphones with no iPod, right? Well, her Discman wore out a chip a while back when she was overdosing on Wayne Dyer's motivational words and earphones were a reasonable form of protection. They cut down the hoots and hollers by at least 60 percent. Proven sociological fact: when most guys think you can't hear them, they shut up. Unfortunately, most is not all. The barbershop TV blared a music vid with a dude and naked chicks rapping about something boring. Maya rode faster.

The fresh smell of buttercream frosting summoned as she tried to pass Desi's Desserts. Well, it was already an Ugly Day, might as well earn it. Desi's wife, Salma, smiled as Maya parked her ride in the front door of the adorable neighborhood hot spot. Salma wore her overdyed auburn hair in a flip and sported short rainbow nails that matched her sweet creations.

"Trini gyal! One Strawberry Supreme, right?" Salma's singsongy lilt felt like home.

"Make it two," Maya answered. She used to jump into her own Trini accent whenever she saw Salma. She hadn't in a while. "How's the baby?"

"Teething already." Salma's eyes filled with new-mom tenderness. "Out with Poppa."

Desi and Salma's relationship had moved quickly and Maya was a witness to it. Desi was Indian from India and Salma was Indian from Trinidad. Maya discovered the sweetshop just before TBB—The Big Breakup. Salma started coming in at the same time and found Desi's every word fascinating. While Desi was a pleasant man, sofa-tan and

5' 7", fascinating he was not. Salma whispered to Maya that she needed to be married before she turned thirty-one or she was dead to her family.

When Maya first found Salma and Desi, she was delightfully engaged herself and about to be married, briefly considering personalized cupcakes instead of the standard tiered cake. Maya loved the word *fiancé* and drove Athena crazy with "my fiancé this" and "my fiancé that" during the engagement. Salma cooed over Maya's ring loudly every time the gentleman behind the counter was in earshot. Months after meeting Salma, Maya was single, the rock was in hock and Salma and Desi were promised. Now Salma was nursing her firstborn and Maya was stuck in the same exact place.

Their eyes met again and Salma put an extra cupcake in the bag. Maya wanted to tell her not to bother. She hated being pitied but the Strawberry Supreme frosting was heavenly and they only had the whipped confection at odd times.

Maya hummed "My Favorite Things" as she rode along, turned on by the sugary cakes burning a hole in her bag. Diabetes in a paper sleeve, her mother would say.

Emmaline Carpenter and Delroy Hope missed meeting each other as kids in Port of Spain, Trinidad. They even managed to miss meeting each other at the University of The West Indies. Both affirmative-actioned into teaching at Antioch, Danceman Delroy and Disco Queen Emmaline met in the 70s and instantly got pregnant. They regretted that they hadn't enjoyed each other alone first before pushing out the kid and tried to remedy that with boarding school. Her father told her once that they were planning to send her to Trinidad to be raised by Granny Ruby when Bob Marley's death made them reevaluate their lives. Instead, they convinced Granny Ruby to sell one of her homes, and they sent Maya to Miss Beardsley's Academy for Young Ladies with the proceeds.

The premature sunshine stroked Maya's face and made her feel as if she were coming out of a nervous breakdown. Hmmm. The funny thing was she didn't realize she'd had one in the first place.

A leggy butterscotch crème in a royal blue parka and miniskirt sashayed across the walk arm-in-arm with her prince. Maya's bike just missed them but they didn't notice. Leggy was a glorious swan. Maya was a shapely baby elephant. In her favorite Dali painting she didn't see *Swans Reflecting Elephants.* She saw swans looking down on elephants. Judging them. Elephants were cute, handy in a pinch, but not the jungle's most desired daughter. Or maybe she was a frog. Either way, she couldn't understand how the same universe could create swans and elephants, butterflies *and* frogs. And if that all-knowing power could make swans and butterflies, then why did it bother with the frogs? *Shade. Sweetness. Struggle.* Ribbit.

Chapter 2

"WHO YOU CALLING A BITCH?"
—Queen Latifah

The upstairs neighbor's radio blared as Maya padlocked her bike to the rickety gate: "DJ Manifesta on the one's and two's coming at you LIVE—Whassup party people!! There's a million stories in the naked hood and this is one of 'em. Like any fairy tale, this one begins with a princess, a couple of toads and some crazy-ass beats. Wannabes get it tight 'cause Shell the Boy Wonder is holding open calls in every city for the next hot act. Life starts now . . ."

By the time Maya made it home to the small tenement town house–turned–apartment building 1869 on Bluestone Road, which ran all along the southern border of Ohio—a few blocks from the river—she was through. She opened her front door to a rap attack. "Your ill na-na is sour / Getting worser by the hour / Lady Athena got the power / I'm the bitch to your Chihuahua . . ." Recently discharged from being a cheerleader, Athena's latest get-famous scheme brought her hustle back to where she started: trying to get put on as a rapper. Athena was about as delicate as a bulldog, raising small riots all over Faustus with her scratchy voice and hectic flow. You definitely heard her before you saw her.

"What up, M?" Athena blurred past. Folks thought that Athena and Maya were too old to still be roommates. Athena had paid most of the bills when Maya was in school. Not with the minimum wages from NFL Cheerleading, but from the party appearances, hosting and promotions the gig made available. Now Maya was returning the favor. Although they were the same age, they took turns being the older sister.

"I feel like I'm coming outta some kinda breakdown. You think I had a nervous breakdown?" Maya called after her.

"Well, yeahhh!" Athena was already in her room. The music blasted pure bass as the door slammed shut.

The apartment was a one bedroom that they'd turned into a two by sacrificing the living room. You entered into a not-painted-yet foyer and then had a choice of following the hallway into the roomy kitchen or one of the bedrooms. Maya put two of the cupcakes on the kitchen counter next to the pile of bills that they never opened and went to her room with the third. After she centered her brain she could make love to the goodies. Maya's appetite was outta control. If she was getting any, any at all, she woulda taken a pregnancy test. The best gift her father ever gave her was a decent metabolism. Not model quick by any means but it kept her from becoming a complete porko.

The bedroom was more shockingly colorful than Maya. Pushing the fuchsia door open made the wooden beads draping the posters swing back and forth. A stack of books served as an end table with lavender pillows here and there. In the couple of years since completing her grad degree, she'd managed to accumulate a ton of crap and was not as neat as she imagined herself to be. She pulled a comforter over the twin mattress on the floor and cleared a small path through the books and papers. She'd always planned to be neater when she moved in with her man.

Maya unwrapped her layers, put on a V-Day tank top and shorts and sat cross-legged in front of her altar that had nothing to do with religion, but everything to do with her sanity. The centerpiece was a glowing green stone Granny Ruby had given her. A yellow Kmart candle illuminated a jar of water from the Ohio River, a small bowl of honey, a handful of feathers and a painted card with the image of a naked, beaded brown woman sitting in a waterfall. Wrapped in a gold scarf and shells, the goddess was reaching for her reflection as Maya was reaching for her meditation.

"Ommmm. Ommmmm." Jumping beats from Athena's room fell in between each of Maya's oms, filling the spaces that she needed empty to be effective. "Om My, *My oh my—am I the baddest rapper—oh am I.* No, you're NOT! AAAAH—Noise pollution! Athena—Athena!

"How could somebody so tiny make so much noise?" Maya wobbled up, grabbed the cupcake and marched over to the room next to hers.

Athena, caught up in the beat, didn't hear her enter. CDs and records were neatly catalogued in every inch of the scarlet space. Athena would buy a vintage record or download a hot new song before she spent money on dinner. She always said she'd learned to be a woman from music. In her adolescence, when En Vogue told her to "*hold on to her love,*" she did. After Bell Biv Devoe said that "*that girl is poison,*" she was. She knew "*she didn't want no scrubs*" either and that everybody was "*down with OPP.*"

"*Meter / Cadence / Prosody / Breath / Word Play / Syncopate / 16 Bars / Def,*" Athena repeated.

Maya yanked off Athena's headphones. "I don't know my stuff but I have yours memorized."

"Kick it then," Athena challenged.

Maya nodded her head Athena-style. "Yes, yes y'all / Lady Athena got the props, y'all / And when it gets dark you know we have a ball / Take it back old school and then we singing y'all / Meter / Cadence / Prosody / Breath—"

"Impressive. Now you gotta put some swerve into it, babygirl." Athena put her hands on Maya's hips and attempted to move her body from side to side.

Maya crossed her eyes. "Shouldn't the music be inside the headphones?"

"How did I sound?" Athena turned up her playback.

Maya yelled like she was speaking to a deaf person to make her point. "LOUD. Are you coming to my show tomorrow?" At Athena and her therapist's encouragement, she had been gearing up to perform her poetry for the past six months. Spoken word. Once Maya conquered stage fright she was even hoping to check out some slams, if she ever left Faustus. She stuffed the cupcake in her mouth and headed for the kitchen.

Athena grabbed her only dress and followed Maya to the heart of the apartment. The kitchen walls were plastered with Athena's glam shots and performance pix and Maya's poems and affirmations.

"Ohhh, so now you want somebody to have your back? Thanks for the rave." Athena shook the empty money jar on the counter. "When's the last time you saw me perform?"

"Oh no. We're outta soy milk." Maya grabbed a lone green pepper and handed it to Athena. "I'll make dinner." Maya sloshed water around in the empty pot just in case the roaches were back, emptied it and then filled it with hot water.

Athena slammed a knife into the pepper.

Maya looked over at her friend. "I'm still in mourning."

"That's what I'm pissed about. That was over twelve months ago. Men come and go. You're too cute to retire your jersey, Maya."

"You think I'm cute?" Maya opened a cabinet lined with wall-to-wall ramen noodles. She adjusted her shorts and looked up to meet Athena's eyes on her belly. "What? I'm having a love affair. With food."

"What does that have to do with you hatin' on my music?" Athena asked.

"I don't do hip-hop," Maya said.

"Hip-hop didn't cheat on you, Maya."

"Uh, let's do the math. Late studio sessions, weed weekends, drunken nights, wannabe hoochie hos at every turn. No offense."

Athena pushed the pepper slashed into four awkward chunks toward Maya.

"Um, none taken. I think." Athena kicked off her shelltop Adidas. "And for the record, I'm standing up more for hip-hop and your need to get a life than Bobby."

"I'm just not feeling it!" Maya screamed. Suddenly the breakdown didn't feel so over.

"What about LL?" Athena asked, smiling.

Maya couldn't resist smiling back. She took Athena's hands. "LL Cool James is . . . a metaphor for something bigger."

"Yeah, something bigger." Athena grabbed her crotch Michael

Jackson style. "How come every time you want to shag somebody they gotta be a metaphor for something bigger? Why can't you just be like, I wanna to jump his bones?" Athena did her best preacher imitation. "I want to screw him. I want to get some. I want to fornicate under consent of the king!"

Maya laughed out loud. "Cigarette?"

"Yeah, if you didn't make me quit." Athena wriggled out of her sweatsuit and tossed it on the floor.

"Look Athena, hip-hop ruined my life. End of story. Spicy mushroom, picanté or cajun style?"

"Uh-uh, ma. Freeze-dried noodles for you, lobster for me. I got a date. A *second* date."

"Congrats. Spicy mushroom it is then for my yummy solo dinner."

Athena pulled the dress over her head.

Maya eyeballed the sweats until Athena picked them up. "What's up with the dress?"

"Classy man. I told you. If you wanna take a walk on the wild side and leave Café Ramen, dude said he has a rich friend."

Maya broke the noodles into the boiling water as Athena mouthed with her. "Glitter does not make gold."

"Well, I'm tired of trying to make a dollar outta fifty cents. From this day forward they gotta pay to play. Slumming isn't a lifestyle choice for me." Athena grew up in Over-the-Rhine, the ghetto's ghetto, in Cincinnati. "And didn't you just eat that cupcake?"

"I know, I know." Maya watched the noodles relax into the bubbling water. She burned her tongue on the hot noodles swallowing a mouthful before they were finished. "Ow. Anyway, isn't this the one who offered you a ride at the bus stop?"

Athena nodded.

"I thought you didn't talk to guys on the street."

"Only 'cause it gives the losers hope. But this is overtime and losers don't drive Toyota Camry Solaras." Unlike in the rest of America, in backwater Faustus Toyotas were rare foreign cars. "Midlife crisis colored. Top down." Athena tossed in her green peppers.

"Midlife crisis colored?" Maya inhaled over the pot like she was smelling white truffle sauce instead of condensed salty spices from a flavor packet.

"Revlon red. It was perfect 'cause I was running late for work."

"As usual."

"Yup. He's the first candidate in my new operation—Gold Digger Test Theory. You should do a report on me." Athena smiled and poked out her small boobies. Maya smiled. "What? More than a mouthful just gets in the way."

Maya ignored the only thing she was sure her friend was insecure about. *Girlfriends Rule #4.*

"So then Toyota dropped me off at the café and took fifteen minutes draping his car with a matching cover."

"No. Athena. Seriously? Wasn't Christianne looking out of the window?"

"Of course. And banging on the bathroom door while I freshened up. Then homeboy sat in the café for three hours yakking and ordering stuff as I went from table to table."

"Tipper?"

"A big ole buck fifty."

"El Cheapo."

"No, Maya—a hundred and fifty. Almost one third of the rent. He's taking me out tonight."

"Copacetic!" They high-fived. "Um, if you met him today, Athena, how is this a second date?"

"Well—the first was at the café this morning. You want him to call his friend?" Athena looked in Maya's pot and shook her head.

"No, thanks. I'm just gonna meditate and get ready for tomorrow." Maya held up a fist.

Athena put her fist to Maya's. "And of course I'll be at your show."

Maya smiled. "You have to. You work in the café."

"So, you meditating with batteries or without tonight?" Athena sauntered out of the kitchen, dressed for her same-day second date. She had talents that made Maya marvel. Like with the sidewalk dudes. Athena just looked them in the eye and walked right through. She didn't cross the street or pretend to be on the phone or nothing. "Call me if you need me, babygirl," Athena called out.

"Likewise," Maya yelled back, listening to make sure she heard the door lock.

They were instant fam when they met way back in third grade at Miss Beardsley's. Maya was so happy to see another ebony face that she immediately took the new kid who was said to be super smart under her wing to show her the ropes of the sleepaway school she'd inhabited since first grade. That is, until the student eclipsed the teacher about twenty-four hours after Athena's arrival.

Athena's popularity was legendary. To this day, fifteen years since high school graduation, the kids probably knew who Athena Wagner was. *Oh, the girl who told Miss Ellie to shut up. Uh-huh, the head cheerleader who lettered in track—there's her trophy. Yeah, the scholarship kid who screwed Mr. Davis in the boiler room.* Legendary. Maya and Athena's friendship existed somewhere in the chasm between them. When Maya moved in, those who didn't get it said that they'd kill each other. They hadn't. Yet.

Maya looked out of the kitchen window at a bluejay sitting on the ledge. The tree above their window sported a nest. On the windowsill next to a wilting lucky jade plant was the little jumping broom that was her rehearsal dinner favor. Her gown and a lot of other bridal crap still lingered in the attic of her parents' crib in Yellow Springs. Her mother never mentioned the heap or pressured her to get rid of it, but somehow one of the tiny red, black and green brooms that she'd spent hours finding online found its way post-disaster into her jeans pocket and she couldn't bear to toss it out. So it sat alone and dusty on the dirty sill keeping the blue birds company.

Maya put the tiny broom in the trash, glad that she wasn't bitter. She washed her hands. Then she fished it out.

Chapter 3

"I CAN'T EVEN LOOK IN YOUR FACE WITHOUT
WANTING TO SLAP YOU. DAMN.
I THANK GOD I AIN'T GET THAT TATTOO."
—*Trina*

The hot shower washed the sidewalk dude's guttural mocking off of her skin. *Dick Sucking Lips.* She watched his words roll down the drain, felt momentarily better and then, unfortunately, stepped on the scale. *Weighing in at 155 pounds, ladies and gentleman, even standing on one foot!* Maya toweled off and put on her undies. She oiled her scalp with coconut cream and plaited her short, thick 'fro into four big old school braids that stuck up like horns. Sacrilegious, folks said, when she cut off her almost-waist-length tresses. Black as she was, cuttin' off all that pretty hair. Much as sistas went through to catch an inch of growth—greasing, braiding, pressing, curling, weaving, extending, relaxing, saving every strand—and she cut her blessings off.

Maya's naps were an epic controversy in Faustus. The good African American residents of Faustus didn't want folks with 'fros, braids, or dreads reminding the decent white people of Faustus that they were black. And now her hair kept trying to lock. A day or two without Maya giving it some love and the hairs hugged onto each other in tight balls. She snapped the knots off with her fingers, splitting the strands up to the shaft. She was a hot mess.

"I love playin' in your jungle," Bobby used to say, tangling his fingers through it. After he was gone the forest was wasteland. She sat on the toilet one day with a dull knife and no mirror. When Athena found her hacking away with teeny bits of fuzz jutting out in patches from her scalp, she screamed "Maya, you're a Chia pet!" before she regained the composure and low tones reserved for a friend who has clearly lost it. Maya stared, comatose on the toilet, as Athena picked up handfuls of waves and held them up to her head—briefly considering using Maya's hair for her next weave. Then she put Maya to bed and held her while Maya tried to explain that she just couldn't find the scissors.

Now Maya sat naked in front of her computer. She had posted another personal ad on craigslist yesterday. A sociological experiment, she told herself, since she never had the cojonés to reply to the responders. Interesting the kinds of guys who e-mailed if she said sex NSA—no strings attached—vs. LTR—long-term relationships. Every once in a while one sounded like the ex. *Local Ivy League Educated Black Man seeks* . . . but he probably fancied himself too cool to post ads. "Ass," she said randomly. Screw him for making her unable to date even losers.

The front door creaked open, closed and locked. Two voices. *Knock, knock, knock.* Three knocks on her door as Athena and dude walked by. Their signal for man-on-board. Well, Athena's signal, since Maya never had the opportunity to use it. Toyota was getting lucky. He had heavy footsteps. A good sign for Athena.

Music on. Maya worried about the old bat downstairs. That Methuselah hag (agoraphobic) was quick to dime them out to the landlord for the smallest infraction so they weren't his favorite tenants right now. They were usually able to drag up the rent but in his book single women were trouble. He didn't respond to smiles, flirting or any of the usual gags they used to get over. Mr. Anderson (compulsive hoarder) just wanted his cash money on the first. Athena figured Methuselah was just jealous cause their titties hadn't dropped yet. Nah. It was because they were still dumb enough to be bubbling over with dimples and hope. "Blasting music and chattering like magpies," Methuselah yelled out the window one winter night. "Wait till you learn that even faith rapes you."

Women Seeking Men. "Sociologist recently out of a failed relationship seeks her one true love. Be smart, attractive, fit, healthy, drink/drug/disease free. Be the one." It's a wonder that men weren't beating a path to her door. She checked her secret screen name, PsychoQT, for responses. Nil. Great. She was even a loser in cyberspace.

Maya stood in front of the full-length mirror and did a 360 to assess the situation. Wild bush. Belly and thighs. She felt guilty looking at her nakedness. *Hmm.* Maybe Marilyn Monroe's figure was too fat for post-millennial white boys but the brick house was still in effect for most men of color. Right? *Right?*

Charlie Parker thundered from her computer to block out the moans and dull hip-hop already pouring in from Athena's room. After neo-soul and Motown generation R & B, jazz was Maya's music. The Ex turned her on to jazz—syncopation, swing and blue notes—Monk, 'Trane and them. Bebop, polyrhythms, call and response. Bebop, polyrhythms, call and response. Bebop, polyrhythms . . .

Jazz was how they played the tough instrument of their love. The Ex had turned her on to jazz, then abandoned them both. Then she became a solo sung by Billie at her worst. Monk, Coltrane and Billie were personal. The Ex switched up the beat. Monkey wrenched the flow. Hip-hop was Miles—not early Miles but Miles when it was over. Miles by the end belonged to everybody. He was too commercial, common and wearing a ratty wig to boot. The Blackerati never wanted to hear honest comments about their own so she mostly just kept her opinions between herself and Athena.

Maya dimmed the lights. She fired up her Nag Champa incense with a red candle and remade the bed with her banana satins. Her cotton panties indicated that it was Tuesday. She rubbed cocoa butter on her body and perfumed her pulse points with vanilla essence with all of the importance of a sacred ritual. Mmmm. The room smelled divine.

She brought out the silk. Ever since she was thirteen she pleasured herself through a silk scarf. Less dirty that way. The silk scarf was a method picked up at fat camp. You wouldn't think being away at a boarding school all year that her parents would still let her go to summer camp, but there she was. When everyone was asleep, it was time for the silk scarf. Muffy Bryant showed a group of them how.

Although there wasn't a relationship to speak of, she transferred all of her prior relationship feelings onto her therapist, Dr. Akawaaba, and practically stalked the man, overinterpreting every glance and forgetting that she was paying him to listen.

"You are under extreme stress, Maya. You have to change the story you're telling yourself. That's my diagnosis. You are insecure for no reason. You should loosen up." This after only four visits.

Maya wasn't sure which one of them crossed the line, but she knew that it was the scarves that did it. He asked her to bring them in. They made out and then screwed on his brown leather sofa. He wasn't bad. Afterward, he recommended that she "perhaps should find support elsewhere."

She crawled onto her mattress, stretched out her reddish brown legs and tried to remember the last time she shaved. She stroked her inner thighs and saw the ex's face. Mmmm. "Maya. My Queen Maya," he would say over and again. She touched herself through the cloth. "Maya, I would never leave you." Ohhh. She felt her breasts. "Maya, I know you like to riiide," he used to whisper. Bird was screaming now.

"Yeah," she whispered back. She rubbed herself furiously. Oh. Ahh. Ooooooh. He would kiss her nouns. Yeahhh. And touch her verbs. Aaaaaaaaaa! Yeah! Telling her not to be afraid, it's just words. She turned into the pillow to avoid screaming. Whooo! Whew. Woo. She was good. Mm. She would have used a vibrator if she had the courage to order one.

Maya sat up alone in the dark. She had been with a total of five penises, although on the record she would cop to just three. This was a source of pride. A man knew that when he was with her it was a privilege. Special. Athena was her sister but Maya secretly thought that she was a slut.

"Do I dare disturb the universe?" In her fantasy life, her man would read her poetry. Maybe from the Song of Songs: "You are altogether beautiful, my love. / There is no flaw in you. / Come with me from Lebanon, my bride."

The Ex didn't read poetry. He rapped it. "Aztechian Queen of my

African dreams / My Papaya Maya / My desire Maya . . ." She didn't miss him. She just missed having someone who knew her for real/for real. She went through real physical withdrawal—shaking, anxiety, insomnia, jitters—when they were over. She broke into ten gazillion jagged glass bits on the floor and got lost in the rug when he . . .

Disambiguation. A glossy Master's degree word meaning she wasn't enough. She climaxed again and cried herself almost to sleep. At least it wasn't crying anymore, just wet eyes. For months it had been snotty wailing like the chest-thumping women of the Middle East did over the bodies of their sons.

Maya took a cotton scarf from under her pillow and tied it over her mini pigtails. She remembered when she discovered that he was auditory, a hearer. She was kinesthetic, a feeler. Meaning that she processed life through touch and he processed everything through sound. Feeler meets Hearer. A mixed relationship. They were off zone—yes—that was the problem! She revised her whole way of speaking, replacing "I feel you" with "I hear that," "That sounds right" and other nonsense to improve communication. The relationship was in rigor mortis at that point, the sound of being alone together tugging on her teardrums.

Lonely. It's a weird sense of familiarity when you realize, or remember, that you are truly alone. That the love of your parents, your friends, your man—are all conditional.

Maya wrapped her sheets around her. Alone or not, she felt horny. And hungry. Before this current period of unasked-for celibacy Maya would never have described herself as a sexual person. Hey—she enjoyed a session as much as the next person with her beloved's sweat drizzling onto her body, but what were those stats again? Men think about sex every three minutes, or was it fifteen seconds? Whatever it was, she could compete with them now.

Alone. What an awful word. Social psychologists know that human touch is so important that children who aren't coddled can die. Especially if they're kinesthetic. *Shade. Sweetness. Struggle.* Something had to change.

Maya sat up and scribbled in her notebook:

judge/mental
you promised me you'd water my tree
why did it have to die?
girlfriend doubted her grandmother's face.
doubted her grandmother's face
in the 19th century mahogany medicine cabinet mirror.
she became fixated on her kente cloth foster mother,
dusty royalty myths and marble illusions of sacred females.
why didn't none of that indian in her break loose and shine through?

Dude and Athena were mid-stroke. Maya didn't have to listen to overhear. This one was a moaner. Last week's was a yelper. Three weeks before that, a damn near yodeler. Athena and her love acrobatics.

At least somebody was having fun. She felt like she'd been masturbating with a jagged knife.

LAB REPORT

Likelihood That Maya Hopeless
Will Find Her One True Love
A Sociological Analysis

PURPOSE: To ride off into the sunset with Prince Charming. After getting a life and finding him first.

PREMISE: Life shouldn't be this boring.

METHODS: The general plan is to alternate between seeking out losers, dating losers, avoiding losers and being verbally assaulted by losers on the street.

MATERIALS: Various forms of the species Idiotus Manus; social deviants like malpracticing therapists and abandoners especially welcome.

DATA COLLECTED: None. Subject lacks courage to leave house.

FLAWS IN DATA COLLECTION: The fallibility of human nature and the inability of the female of the species in particular to think with the head and not just with the heart.

COMPLICATIONS: The subject's compete inability to dare to make sensible decisions in own best interest.

RESULTS: Tragic. Tears. Often.

CONCLUSION: Inconclusive. Untallied. Subject strongly considering becoming a reclusive mad scientist with a spinning wheel and a lump of coal in an edible gingerbread house. Delicious.

Chapter 4

"MUST I SAY IT AGAIN, I SAID IT BEFORE
MOVE OUT THE WAY WHEN I'M COMIN' THROUGH THE DOOR"
—*MC Lyte*

It was two months since Athena started working at Pearl's Café, a small cabaret spot. Since the Purgatorex Research Corporation was only five blocks away, Maya walked over for lunch whenever possible. Although Athena having to take this gig was a setback, Maya appreciated being able to break up the monotony of corporate research with a quick gabfest. Three months ago, Athena was a veteran member of Cincinnati's flashy Ben-Gals, the cheerleading squad for the Bengals football team. After a small scandal involving a cornerback, Athena was asked to leave. Maya was proud at how quickly Athena brushed herself off, regrouped, and started working at Pearl's with no shame in her game. Maya was taking a bit longer to recover from her own public humiliation.

Maya made her way over to Athena in the snoozing Pearl's. They both sported tragic brown uniforms—Athena's was an apron; Maya's was a scratchy suit jacket thrown over her usual garb. The only midday customers were two laptop dudes nursing exotic coffee concoctions. Well, exotic for Faustus. Athena, who had been on since breakfast call, redid her "hair" after every tryst and was now a redheaded Medusa.

"Soooo Chaka Khan. How was your date? I tried to wake up early enough for a recap but you were already gone." Maya sat behind the table that Athena was cleaning.

"Cool." Athena moved to another table, unusually tight-lipped.

"Yeah?" Maya followed. She never had to probe for details. Something was wrong. "And the afterparty?"

"You know, Maya, they don't all make it to the promised land." Athena grabbed her rag and cleaning spray and moved to another table.

Maya was quiet. They both knew what she'd heard last night. "Okayyy." Maya sat down at Athena's current table. She tried to catch her eyes and when she did Athena's resistance was dead.

"Basically I fell asleep afterward. And when I woke up he was already gone."

"Oh, Athena. I'm sorry."

"Left a business card on my pillow with 'Call you dot dot dot.' " Athena laughed out loud. "The ones who leave in the middle of the night never do. Another keeper."

"Athena . . . He probably has a woman."

"So what? I'm not the girl you bring home to a meat loaf dinner with Mom. I'm okay with that. Meat loaf makes me hurl."

"I'm just saying . . ."

"I know. One his mother probably adores. One he told he was out with the fellas when he was begging me to lick my kitty cat. One who bored him out of his mind enough to send him looking for me. Know what?" Athena sang the Beyoncé lyric, "He must not know 'bout me, he must not know 'bout me," as she soaked the table.

Maya knew that Athena wasn't the girl guys wanted to leave alone chatting with their cousin Playa Paul at the family reunion. *"If Athena would just apply herself. . ."* Athena was the kid who wasted great opportunities. The one who was braniac enough to win a scholarship to that fancy prep school, but it didn't take. Still Maya would defend her to the death.

"You know what, Athena? His woman is probably a stringy white girl named Amy." *Girlfriends Rule #2:* It is mandatory to dog anyone out in defense of your friend's honor, even when you think she has none.

"Well you know what? I smudged a ninety-nine-cent Dark Cherry lipstick kiss onto the back of his collar where an idiot man would never notice. Let him explain that to Amy. Dickwad."

"You shoulda gotten all *For Colored Girls* Lady in Red and not let him fall asleep." Maya adopted a snooty accent. "I can't possibly wake up with a strange man in my bed. You must go."

Athena picked up the accent and 'tude: "Look, my man, grab some coffee from the kitchen on your way out. Word. That woulda showed him." They cracked up laughing. "I shoulda did that." But she hadn't. One of the laptop guys looked up to summon a waitress but changed his mind and decided to just listen in instead.

"We'll probably be in his next novel," Maya said.

Athena's phone played the theme from *Sex and the City* inside her apron just as Christianne (personality-challenged/human-phobic), the multipierced, tattooed manager, emerged from the storage room. She usually felt the need to flex after stealing sex with the boss on business time.

Christianne's hawk eyes darted around the room. "What's happening? Protocols, people!" She clapped her hands for emphasis.

"All clean." Athena said as she dashed off to the ladies' room. A young blond couple from the cover of *Polo Match* walked in.

Maya looked at the clock and ordered a salad at the counter.

Athena bounced out of the ladies' room a completely changed woman. "Maya! Guess who got called to audition for Shell the Boy Wonder!"

Maya kept one eye on Christianne, who was chatting up a cute patron. "Shell the Boy who?"

"Shell the Boy Wonder, Maya. Camp Hustla? Please tell me you know who that is."

Maya shrugged. "Yeah, yeah, yeah. Of course I do. The rap producer guy, right? Out of LA?"

Athena sat on a bar stool. "No, that's Dr. Dre. Shell the Boy Wonder is the post–Puff Daddy Diddy of the current music scene."

"What?"

Christianne rushed over. "What's happening?"

"Refilling ketchup," Athena called out. Eddie, the short-order cook who was sweet on her, put a can of no-frills ketchup and six empty Heinz bottles on the counter. He winked at Athena, glad to stick it to "the man," and Christianne, "the man," went into the office. Athena sat on the stool next to Maya as Eddie put a cheeseburger order out. Athena shook her head. Still talking. He took it back.

"Shell's the hottest music mogul ever," Athena said, taking the ketchup off the ledge.

"Yeahhhh. That guy is everywhere. I've never heard any of his stuff though." Maya kept an eye on the office door.

"He out-Kanyes Kanye. Turn on the radio—every hit comes from Camp Hustla." Athena pointed to the café speakers as lyrics sputtered forth. "See?! Bam—that's his boys, Black Death."

"Ohhh. Okay. Shell's the one that organized the concert we went to. Where Thug got killed."

"Exactly. MTV, BET, every video you see is feeding him. The man is unstoppable."

"You're happy. I'm happy. Congrats, babe!" She hugged Athena. "You're the hottest rapper out there. Male or female. When's the audition?"

"Tomorrow," Athena managed. Clearly a little sooner than she would have hoped. "He's searching the country for his next hot act."

"Tomorrow?" Maya tried not to let her poker face crack into her worry face. "Cool!"

"I'm good. It's time to lose myself. I've been prepping for this since . . ."

"Your whole life, boo. I was there," Maya chimed in. "I think that Daddy Shell—"

"Shell the Boy Wonder."

"Whoever—I think he'll see how much you bring to the table."

Athena was animated. "By tomorrow I need to be the baddest chick the rap game has ever seen. Not the one who fell off. Not you can take the girl outta the hood but . . . Not the local one-minute ghetto superstar cheerleading for minimum wage. *The* baddest. Lotta false starts but I'm gonna be a star. I got goals, baby!" Athena practically danced over to Laptop Guy, now waving his arm frantically.

Maya felt fed by Athena's energy. She stretched, saluting the sun streaking in through the back window, and focused on the small café stage where, Goddess willing, she would have her first poetry performance tomorrow.

Goals. Good for Athena for being so clear. How old was too old to make it in music anyway? Maya knew that she was destined to make a dent in the planet, but she wasn't sure how. Activism was inspiring. Sociology made her buzz. Poetry was her fave but you couldn't do anything with it. Scattered, although in a very focused kind of way. She couldn't even make up her mind what degrees she needed. Puzzle pieces of her were scattered over three campuses. At one point she was even pre-law. She envied Athena's knowingness even if her calling was to the absurd world of hip-hop.

There's something about wanting to make it—no, needing to make it. People try to capture the need to succeed in lyrics like "to dream the impossible dream" and "I believe I can fly" and "greatest love of all," but for Athena and Maya it was more than that. "Get rich or die trying." Now that described it. One hundred percent plus ten. Extra credit. No choice although obviously they wouldn't die for money. Just "it." Arriving. Acknowledgment. Making it was water. Making it was air.

Luckily, Maya already had the poem for her first show down cold because preparing for the Rap Olympics was an all-night event: helping Athena pick *the* flygirl outfit with matching hair, makeup and nails, rehearsing dopalicious rhymes over and over and over again, adding a touch of stage presence and a dance move or four. Should Athena go old skool or new? Serious or slutty? By the time they were finished Maya was even correcting Athena and filling in whenever she skipped a beat. Her verses weren't that technically impressive to Maya's formal poet's ears, but nobody could touch Athena when it came to total flair.

The next morning Athena was a semi-star. She danced into the kitchen sporting a tight green tracksuit and super-curly hair. "Ready to go," she announced as Maya prepped her honey oats cereal.

Maya held a spoon as a mic.

"And the Grammy goes to Lady Athena!" Maya handed Athena the spoon and the mic became an award.

Athena feigned tears. "I'd like to thank all of the haters that told me get a real job."

"Athena's gonna knock them out. Mama said knock them out!" Maya flexed. "We are doing it!"

"Oh—good luck with your first show, Maya. What time is it?"

"I'm gonna head to the open mic night after work. Use my affirmations if you get nervous," Maya said. "You are a magnificent creature."

"Don't need 'em. I'm the one and only, queen of the mic / I wreck old school to the new / I am a Christian Muslim Jew . . ."

Maya chimed in with Athena's next verse. "Timeless Confess physical brawls hold true."

"Look at you knowing my songs." Athena stuck her thumb in her mouth like she did sometimes when she was nervous. "A bitch is fly."

"Told you I'm your biggest fan, Lady Athena, and a bitch is a female dog."

"When I make it . . ." Rap's next starlet walked out of the kitchen toward her destiny.

Maya called after her, "We'll make it!" Their motto since seventh grade track. Athena made it that year. Maya didn't.

Chapter 5

"CHECK THE BOOTY, YO IT'S KINDA SOFT AND
IF YOU TOUCH IT, YOU LIVIN IN A COFFIN;
WORD TO MOTHER!"
—*Yo Yo*

Except for Maya's messy desk and a wall calendar, her dark-blue cubicle was bare, unfilled with the things that people put up to remind themselves who they are. She didn't want to make herself too much at home, but she'd already been with the company for almost three years. The office was empty. Maya sat at her desk literally pencil pushing. She tapped out her own jazzy drum beat with the eraser as she pumped herself up for her show. She refused to buy any of those silly desk toys, so she created her own time-wasting games.

Purgatorex, a private research institute that conducted sociological studies for businesses and government agencies, recruited Maya immediately after grad school with promises of an exciting experimental career. She imagined herself as a superhero sociologist going undercover as an ex con, perhaps to expose prejudicial hiring practices, or studying voting habits that would determine the nation's political future and unearthing evidence of the full impact of African American culture on the globe. Instead, she was a sociological researcher with her principal client base being paper product concerns. Her research skills were impeccable, but she had no success in bringing in new contracts as this required wheeling, dealing and schmoozing. As a result, her salary was locked at twenty-two thousand dollars a year, and Maya spent her days delving into such meaty matters as whether the average two-income household consumer prefers two-ply toilet tissue over three, and how stationery size affects the average snail mail letter reader.

"Get outta here!" Dirk Gittens (depersonalization disorder) leaned over Maya's desk, startling her as his lazy eye threatened to give out and close altogether. "It's six-thirty, Maya."

"Well . . ." Maya cocked her head to the side, deciding whether to let Dirk in on her secret. She pursed her lips like she might burst if she didn't say something. "I'm performing tonight at Pearl's. Open mic."

"Get outta here! Singing? You?" Dirk's eyebrows went up almost into to his comb-over.

"No, poetry. My first time." Somehow, saying this out loud to Dirk made Maya more nervous than she thought she was.

Dirk grinned broadly. "Why didn't ya say something? We coulda gotten a group up to support ya."

Maya smiled back and shrugged. "I didn't really invite anybody."

Dirk nodded. "Gotcha. I'm a lil' shy myself. Maybe you'll self-publish a lil' poetry book or something so people can see your work."

Hm. That was a thought.

Dirk peered ahead as if he had to start an engine to move forward. "Well, here we go. Another night in traffic." In Faustus this meant about fifteen cars on the road. "Have fun."

"Will do," Maya said. "Night, Dirk."

"Oh and don't forget to adjust the data on the business cards report," Dirk called over his shoulder, walking out. "UV coating will not cause consumers to hold on to standard cards longer, as I first hypothesized. Fascinating, huh?"

Maya's eyes met Dirk's as he gave her one last look before he stepped into the stairwell. He really was, well, fascinated. That by itself was a wondrous thing. Pondering UV coating on business cards made Maya want to impale herself on the official mechanical pencil she was holding. Good for Dirk that he should find his calling. She put the pencil down and took a gulp of lukewarm chamomile tea, hoping that it wouldn't make her appear sleepy on stage.

She stood up and rubbed her nervous belly. "What happens to a queen deferred?" She said the first line of her poem out loud. She had tried to perform twice before and completely chickened out, but tonight she was ready.

• • •

The audition line from The Dandridge Pavilion spilled into the street and rounded the corner. Athena and four hundred and ninety-nine other prescreened Midwest wannabes practiced vicious rhymes and looking gangsta. They were each hoping that Shell the Boy Wonder would find something magical in them and hand them a contract to stardom. Eight hours of standing and now just a coupla heads ahead of her. Athena was almost in.

"Next up, #863! Stanley Herbert AKA One Killa."

"'Scuse me." Someone was tapping on her shoulder. Auditioners purposely tried to break each other's concentration. Athena turned her head. Some Asian chick.

"Yes?" Athena put her CD and picture under her arm so that girlfriend couldn't scope them out.

"Is it weird if I wear this?" Homegirl held up a pile of green tissue paper. "It's an avant-garde skirt. Art." Athena shrugged and turned her back. *Ass.* One Killa sounded dangerous through the door. Maybe Shell would take two artists.

Athena repeated in her head: "I am a magnificent creature." Her phone buzzed. Who would call at a time like this? Oh. Who else? Athena's oldest brother Supreme had been the biggest drug dealer in the Nasti Nati—until he started using his product and things fell apart.

"Hello, 'Preme? Lemme call you back. Your baby sis is about to change all of our lives." A half-naked woman practiced a booty-shaking dance with severe gravitas. 'Preme's words registered . . .

"Oh, my God. I'll be right there." Athena dialed Maya.

Pearl's Café looked intimidating at night. Maya peeped out the stage. Although it was just a sleepy café in a forgotten town, she would feel like a griot, a storyteller, a star on that stage, and the poem she came to share was one of her best. People were gonna change their minds about Maya Gayle Hope after they saw her perform. Not that anyone knew who she was, so maybe she'd just change her mind about herself.

Hopefully there would be a bigger crowd coming to witness Maya's inaugural performance, because the current room was pathetic. A serious man with messy hair and a table full of soiled mugs worked on his computer while two giggly girls made paper airplanes and picked at a shared salad. A woman dozed in the corner. Maya saw a few of the regular poets over by the sandwich bar. A good group usually gathered as the night went on.

"Maya?"

She turned around.

"I thought that was you." The woman behind her was Sherry Gabriel (coercive power complex), a classmate of Maya's from undergrad. Also black and in her early thirties, she was the kind of person who found it acceptable to comment on the details of everyone else's personal life.

"Sherry. Hi."

"Maya, hello. Michelangelo, you remember *Maya Hope.*" Sherry said her name as if the husband would have some inside knowledge of Maya. It figured. When she last ran into them she was planning the wedding that wasn't. Maya quickly offered the requisite niceties so as to get back to the business of her show.

"We got a sitter for the night," Sherry said. "Now that we just had our second little one, we've got her on speed dial."

Michelangelo chuckled and rubbed Sherry's arm. Although they were the same age, Maya noticed that Sherry already looked old. She had creases in the corners of her eye and even a couple of gray hairs.

Maya nodded toward the stage. "I'm doing a poem tonight."

"You?" Sherry asked. She looked down at Maya's dirty sneakers and sniffed. "Michelangelo and I were saying how lucky that some people never really have to grow up. How long have you been doing *this?*" Sherry gestured toward the stage.

"Well, I'll let you find your seats," Maya said, excusing and sparing herself.

Before they could reply, she pushed herself over to Christianne, who stood near the front with a clipboard and was dressed like the grim reaper in an all-black one-piece with a hood. "Hey Christianne. I signed up a couple of weeks ago." *Okay good. Checking in. This was further than she got on any previous attempt.*

Christianne looked at Maya as if she hadn't seen her come in almost every day for lunch for the past two months, or every week to watch poets perform for the past two years. "You are who?" Christianne asked.

Maya stifled an urge to mock her. "Uh, Maya Hope. Athena's friend."

Christianne ticked off Maya's name from her list in an official fashion. "Got it. You're up first. We start soon." Just her luck.

"It's my first time, Christianne. Can I go maybe fourth or something like that?"

"Nope. Priority goes to the regulars."

Maya looked over at the group of poets—a mix of colorful yarns and old backpacks—who already seemed to be having a better time than the budding audience. "Well . . . How about if one of the regulars agrees to switch with me?"

Christianne moved her shoulders back, loving her power. "Nope. Protocols, people. Unless you don't want to perform . . ." Christianne let her voice trail off for dramatic effect.

"Fine." Maya closed her eyes for a brief moment of calm. She'd fought saying that she was a poet for a long time, insisting that she was a social scientist and *not* an artist, although she'd been obsessed with words since grade four.

"I need you to sit down," Christianne said, pushing her arm.

Maya opened her eyes and jerked her arm away. "Okay," she said, letting the knot in her chest go. Maya took a seat in the back. This was no time for beef.

Christianne took the stage. "Letha, our regular host, is out sick tonight, so I'll be emceeing." Her voice was a monotone drawl.

Oh no. Maya raised her hand like she was in class. When Christianne ignored her, she called out, "It's too early! Letha usually waits 'til eight-thirty to get a good crowd."

Christianne barely turned her way. "As I said, Letha is not here. First up, Maya Hope." And with that unspectacular intro Christianne stepped aside, leaving the stage empty, expectant and glaring for Maya's opening night. Fine. It's the emotion in the room, not the size of the audience, right?

The "audience" gave Maya a sort of one-handed clap prompting the sleeping woman in the corner to pop up and loudly gather her paperwork. The serious man exaggerated a yawn and slurped of his coffee. The giggly girls threw a paper plane which circled over Maya's head as she stood. The other poets tried to look supportive when clearly they were each worried about their own thang. Sherry Gabriel elbowed her husband.

All things are possible. All things are possible, Maya repeated in her head, grandly approaching the stage. As she passed the bar, she misjudged a turn and knocked over a stack of paper cups. Laughter wafted over her and into her skin. Christianne gestured for her to move it along.

Keep going, she told herself. Maya made it to the mic and then stopped abruptly. All eyes on her. She looked down at her dirty sneaks. "I'm sorry," she said to no one in particular, turned and walked quickly to the back, grabbing her bag and suit jacket on the way out. She heard Sherry Gabriel call her name as she exited. A dude opened the door to enter just as Maya approached it.

"'Scuse me," she said, pushing past him.

"Hey . . . Maya, right?" a voice said. It was deep, foreboding and seductive.

She turned around in the wispy Faustus air. A kind but prickly face she recognized as the Open Mic Night DJ came into focus. The albino wore an army green triangular Robin Hood hat perched on the front of his head with a matching T-shirt. He held out a hand and then reconsidered and cupped Maya's shoulder, as if he knew she hated to shake hands.

"Scratch," she said. "Yeah. I remember you." She waited the obligatory polite beat before turning to leave. "Well, okay . . ."

"Thought you were gonna give it a go this week." Scratch adjusted his sunglasses in the darkness. He looked even paler than usual, although somehow enticing.

Maya faced him and shook her head. "The vibe was off."

Scratch smiled. "Ahhh. Too bad. You seem like you'd be good."

They both looked through the glass door at a heavyset male poet center stage with his lips moving furiously.

Scratch looked back at Maya. "So, yo, you really wanna do this thing or what?" He sounded like he might actually care.

"That's why I came," Maya said, starting to get angry at herself. She was right there on stage. What the hell was her problem? She was a total failure. A total failure with bad luck, no career, no money, no man, no love, no balls, no nothing. And she was over it.

Scratch put his hands in his pocket and rocked back on his heels. "Why?"

"Why?" Why was she a loser? Maya wasn't in the mood to be questioned by some random dude on the sidewalk but felt strangely held by his gaze.

"Why do you wanna do this?" Scratch asked, moving closer to Maya than strangers should be.

For some reason she wanted to give him a good answer. She thought for a moment. "There's something about the jazz of the rhythms when you pull the words from the page and speak them. Perform them. Share them. Words. And nobody's saying what I'm saying, Scratch. I was born to share that, I think. Maybe even make a difference."

"Damn." Scratch rubbed his tight blonde naps under his hat. "I was gonna say only do it if you got to, but I think you answered that, sis." He chuckled. "Goddamn. Guess that's why fear of being on stage tops death. You sound like you would sell your beautiful soul if you could just do the damn thing." Scratch looked like the joker grinning in the streetlights.

"Yeah," Maya said. "I would. Without a doubt. It hasn't gotten me anywhere. I'd trade my soul for a sandwich."

"How 'bout some luck instead?" Scratch asked, laughing. "You know exactly what you want. You'll be fine." The early moonlight through the trees made a spotted pattern on Scratch's almost translucent face and a stray dog somewhere howled.

In that instant Maya's purpose became more clear, and talking to

Scratch made her feel a little less loser-ish. She draped her jacket over her arm. "Thanks, Scratch."

"No, Maya, thank you," he said, seeming lifted by the conversation as well. "Thanks for the vibe and the soul." Scratch was interrupted by Maya's phone, playing "Wake Me Up Before You Go-Go." He gripped her shoulder, his skin looking healthier now in the glare of the passing headlights. "You are a star, Maya. You got this," he said, staring into her eyes for an extremely convincing beat before he went inside.

Maya felt renewed and momentarily invincible as she answered her phone. "Yay! Athena, hello? Are you finished?"

Athena could barely speak. "My mother had a heart attack."

"Oh my goddess! Is she okay?" Maya headed down the block.

"I don't know. I'm gonna catch a bus up to Grace Hospital right now."

"I'll meet you there!"

"Actually, Maya, how long would it take you to get to the Dandridge?"

"Five minutes—I just left Pearl's."

"Okay. Listen." Athena was overenunciating and speaking quickly at the same time. It made Maya nervous. "Somebody like Shell the Boy Wonder only makes it to Ohio once in a lifetime."

"I know."

"And Faustus never. I worked hard to get this shot—I need you to go in there and get me a second audition."

Maya hustled down Coretta Street. "I'm almost there. I'll give him your CD."

"But Maya—you know the rhymes."

"Next up, number 864! Cherrell Lashawna aka Big Bonze." The girl in front of Athena went in.

"What are you saying, Athena?"

"I'm saying you need to rip it, Maya."

The line outside The Pavilion was crazy. Maya followed the trail of wannabes to The Shriner Room in the basement. She spotted Athena down in the front and made her way over. "Rip what?"

"There's no time for debate. I gotta go see about my moms. Give them my CD and perform it live, Maya—that's all these people read."

"Perform your raps? C'mon, Athena. Me?" Maya and Athena, face-to-face, realized they were still talking on the phone and hung up. "Go see about Miss Evelyn—I'll give them your package."

"But Maya, you know what I've been through. I'm next. What are you gonna do?" Seeing Athena crying was terrifying. Athena was rarely this emotional. There was no time.

Maya took the package and hugged her. "I always said I'd drive your white Bronco."

"When I make it . . ." Tears.

"Go." Maya watched her friend run out. "I'll say a prayer for your mom!"

Maya checked out the gum-smackin', posturing ghetto crowd. Big Bonze, though muffled through the door, sounded like she invented rap. A half-naked woman wore a gun holster. Maya pulled her backpack closer. A gun holster?! She looked around at the leather, big jewelry and furs and then down at her India.Arie look circa 2002. She considered the café audience. Time was up.

"Next! Number 865—Athena Wagner aka Lady Athena . . ." Maybe she should bolt. Yeah. Just hand in the package and be out. The auditioner stepped into the hallway. "Athena . . . Athena Wagner? Last call . . ." White Bronco. Maya inhaled deeply and stepped up. She followed the woman into a room. BOOM. The doors slammed behind her. Darkness. Her eyes widened and focused. FLASH. An intern-looking kid snapped a photo.

"I'm Luci." A plus-sized sista, beigy with a shortish bob, stood up. Her dress style was business provocative. Diagnosis? Narcissist.

"Luci, uh, good to meet you." Maya's eyes darted in the dusky light. She hoped that she didn't have to shake any germy palms. A beefy bodyguard and other handlers shuffled about trying to look busy.

Luci sat down next to a coffee-colored young man in a had-to-be-Italian suit, black sneaks and a humongous diamond Shell the Boy Wonder pendant. Subtle. It was a scene right out of reality TV. Maya adjusted her floor-length skirt.

Shell (megalomaniac) stared at Maya then held his head in his hands. "This? We shoulda stuck with the coasts. The Midwest gold is already mined and reigning on the scene. All that's left is the wood."

Maya realized that she was on a stage. So much for stage fright. Courage in small things first. That's what Dr. Angelou, her namesake godmother in her head, would say. Being at boarding school caused one to make up family members. Take it for the team. "Alrighty. Hi there. My name is May, Maya—name is . . ."

"We got your name, Lady uh . . ." Shell scrambled through a pile of papers on the desk.

"Lady Athena." Luci leaned back and glared.

"Whatever. Well?" Shell replied.

"Impress us." Luci held an arm out and inspected her French-manicured nails.

"Uh . . ." Maya reminded herself that she was there to rep her friend.

The intern-looking guy sat on the edge of the table. "Stupid tax!" Shell yelled at him and the kid grabbed some files. "Deduct fifty bucks from his check."

"But Shell, we don't pay him," someone in the back said.

Maya's survival instincts kicked in. Kinda. "Well, I'm an Ohio native, like the model Sahara and Dave Chapelle as you may know. Drew Carey also . . ."

"Jumpin' Jiminy Crickets Mary Poppins!" Shell shook his head and everyone laughed. "Thanks to *Idol* every hick in the sticks thinks they're the next hot thing. No—'well' means are you rhyming to Beat A or Beat B?"

Her mind went blank. "She didn't tell me!"

"Who didn't tell you?" The woman—what did she say her name was?—stood up more interrogator stern than diva saucy. "I told everybody."

"Well," repeated Shell, already exasperated. "I don't have time for this." He put his head back in his hands.

Maya panicked. "Uhhh. I am a goddess," she mumbled. She felt a nervous nosebleed trying to come on. Anxiety attack. She couldn't remember a verse. A rhyme. A word. Nothing. Not one of Athena's lyrics. No thing. Frozen. Literally. Maybe if she didn't move, something, anything, any song that Athena had kicked in the past ten years would come back to her.

Shell's phone rang. "What up, dawg?" He answered on speaker and began a conversation. Luci lost interest in Maya and rearranged the desk. Intern boy brought them a pitcher of water and some mugs. This was bad. Really. Really. Bad. Maya had to change the energy. Athena was counting on her. Okay. What . . . would . . . LL . . . do? Maya was in *Krush Groove* trying to impress Blair Underwood, uh, Russell Simmons, one of her three rap references. She heard the albino Scratch's words: *you got this.*

"Beat!" Maya thundered and surprised herself. Shell looked up.

"Boy Wonder complete," he told the person on the phone and hung up. "Now we talking!" Shell gave a signal and the music came up.

Maya opened her mouth wishing and praying for words. All that could come out was her own poetry, not Athena's, rapped instead of spoken:

> *"What happens to a queen deferred?*
> *Black woman I am*
> *Blue black yella tan*
> *She of the bangles and burgundy lips*
> *She of quadrangles and full weeping hips*
> *Hottentot stop strut*
> *You lookin at my butt?*
> *You thinkin I'm a slut?*
> *You made me a mutt*
> *F.U.C.—What? Me??*
> *See. The center of my energy is power.*
> *Yes, I am the woman of every hour.*
> *Dare me & I'll do it*
> *Dis me & you blew it*
> *I say the words that you fear to hear.*

Climbed the pyramids 'cause they were there
Follow da leader & the leader is me
Essence of Maya, uh . . . Athena??? H.O.T.
Whoop! Here I am. Bam! It's my world
So kneel down at my gown like the boss Miss Ross
Sam is not my uncle & Jemima ain't my aunt!"

Maya absolutely *ripped it.* Her Trini-ness came in handy: *Thrust-up-back-forth-thrust-up.* Athena would have been proud. For ninety seconds it was GREAT. Fun, even. Her debut, premiere, opening night, inaugural show. She was Queen Latifah! Awesome. Shell's face wanted to smile. She was MC Lyte. Shell nodded. Not half bad. She was . . .

"Thank you," Shell said.

She was a home/girl interrupted. Maya smiled brightly, curtsied and continued, finally remembering a verse of Athena's lyrics.

"I'm Lady Athena . . ."

"NO! Thank you means stop!" Shell screamed. "Did Geffen have to deal with this?!"

Maya hesitated, confused. Luci stood up. "I'll bring in the next person." Maya kept moving, doing the Moribayasa dance, backing that thang up into a Watusi. *Thrust-up-back-forth-thrust-up* . . . She was performing more for herself than Athena or anyone else.

Shell stood. "Enough. Cease and desist!"

Maya froze for ten loooong seconds, jarred back to reality only by the sound of Luci at the door. "Number 866. Caitlin Wagner AKA Callisto! NEXT!" Being rejected again so soon after the café mess shook Maya to the core. Shell was Bobby and everybody else disposing of her, kicking her to the curb.

"Fine! You're welcome!" she shrieked. Maya started to leave as the Asian woman wearing the tissue paper skirt came in.

"I'm Callisto, winner of The Buckeye State Rap Diva Competition." Callisto smoothed down the flapping green paper, and then appeared to be . . . stripping and beat boxing?

Aw, man! Athena was better than this, and so was she. Maya turned around and slammed Athena's CD on the table in front of Shell. He jumped.

"This is the CD of the best rapper there is." Maya saw her spit hit his nose but her mouth kept talking. "Male or female." She threw the business card and Athena's headshot, her face obscured by a Kangol hat, on the desk. "And if you are truly some sort of Wonder Boy—"

"Boy Wonder," Shell and everyone else in the room including Callisto corrected. The beefy guard closed in. Shell held up a hand.

"Whatever." Maya's brain disconnected from her mouth. She had full body Tourette's. "You'll call her." Maya stormed out, heading back down the hall to the stairs. Some friggin' nerve! How could Athena want to be down with people like that?

Maya was no stranger to humiliation. After all, she'd been . . . she'd been kicked to the curb the night before her wedding. So for her to feel that this was the worst humiliation ever was no small thing. Her dignity fell to the floor in clumps as she rushed forward, but she had no energy left to pick it up. In the periphery the wannabes prayed that whatever happened to her wasn't their fate. She wiped her eyes and beelined for the exit.

"Athena, please wait!" Maya kept moving. Someone ran up behind her and tapped her on the shoulder. "Lady Athena!!!"

"Oh . . ." Her surrogate name. *What the hell?* "Yes!"

"I'm Luci." She was huffing like she ran a marathon. She extended a hand and reintroduced herself. Maya awkwardly shook it. "Lady Athena, Shell wants to put you on."

"What?" Slang changed meaning from minute to minute so Maya never bothered to stay up on it.

"I said you were absolutely *marv.*" Luci handed Maya back Athena's demo CD and package.

"What does that mean again exactly?"

"It means you got a deal, baby." Luci was excited. "It means we came here to find YOU. Nobody EVER talks to Shell like that. He said that if a bitch got cojonés to stand up to him like that, then that's a bitch we need to be in business with. Screaming on Shell?! That's hip-hop, yo. Ripe hip-hop! Gangsta!"

The listening-in line of prospective rappers looked at Maya's twirly skirt and knotted hair in disbelief.

"And your lyrics were cool, too," Luci added. "Girl, you must be lucky."

Maya was speechless. The wall-of-man security guard from the audition room caught up with them and hustled Luci and Maya back through the crowd. He guarded Maya like precious cargo, carving an immediate and distinctive space between her and those waiting to audition.

CAMP HUSTLA'S NATIONWIDE MC SEARCH SCORE SHEET

(Confidential: Internal Document)

SCORING based upon a 100 point scale using the categories below

CONTESTANTS	Scale	One Killa #863	Big Bonze #864	Lady Athena #865	Callisto #866
Gender	M/F	M	F	F	F
Looks	25	18	0	15	100
Musicianship: Technique, Rhythm & Flow	10	10	10	5	0
Lyrics	20	10	25	20	0
Stage Presence	20	10	20	15	20
Attitude & Street Cred	25	25	25	~~2~~ 100	NA
Advance to Final Round?	Y/N	Y	N	~~N~~ Y	Y!

Chapter 6

"It's finally my turn to rock the mic
Because my devastating beats I know you will like"
—JJ Fad

Athena and Maya danced around the kitchen to the music thumping in their souls, toasting with tap water. Athena's mom was doing fine. Thankfully it was just a scare.

"Play it again, Sam!" Maya said. They had already used up seventeen anytime minutes replaying Shell's thirty-two-second message. Athena had made Maya describe Shell in deep detail over and over down to the black-nail-polished pinkies he wore for his lost homies.

Athena pushed Speaker on her phone. They repeated with the message. "So here's the art of the deal, Lady Athena. I move fast when I know whassup. I've called off my emcee search and I'm moving you, the winner, immediately to the Big Apple to prep your new album. Thirty Gs cash for the tour to test your audience cred. Your flight leaves Sunday. We bringing NY back, baby! Gangsta!"

"Sunday!" the real Lady Athena repeated for good measure.

"I'm happy for you." Maya was proud of herself, too.

"Thank you, Maya! Camp Hustla, baby!! I did it. My lyrics did it. My demo did it. We did it."

Maya hugged Athena for the hundredth time that day, vowing never to tell her that she didn't kick her lyrics or that they hadn't listened to her demo. They treaded softly on each other's dreams and as thrilling as the performance had been, this victory was Athena's. "Soooo when do we tell him that I'm not Lady Athena?"

"Maya, you're smoking crack, right?"

"We'll just tell the truth. As Orwell said, in times of universal deceit, the truth is a revolutionary act."

"Yeah? Well, as another president said, it depends on what the meaning of *is* is." Athena pretended to dial a phone. "212-Musical-Genius. Hello, Shell the Boy Wonder? Yeah, it's Athena. The real Lady Athena."

"Perfect," agreed Maya.

"See, the chick you met was not me but my best friend, a sociologist. I know that you pride yourself on being the man, but you've been bamboozled. That was her first rap performance. Ever. And she used my lyrics."

"Don't forget to throw in how much I hate his music."

Athena threw her hands up. "Thanks for the thirty thousand bucks and the promise of fame and glory but we're going to pass. There goes springing for pizza."

"So what do we do?"

Athena gave Maya a hard stare, not finding the answers in her face. "We do what worked, boo! Stay on mission. You're going to be a bug in his ear telling him all about me, that I wrote your rhymes and everything, after you're signed. Meanwhile, I'll be your hype man."

"Translation?" Maya took her food and walked to her room.

Athena followed. "The hype man is like . . . a backup singer."

"No. I see where this is going and this is crazy, Athena, big idea crazy. Ralph Kramden–Lucy Ricardo–lemme 'splain crazy." Maya braced herself for the hard sell.

"Come on, Maya—just take a risk." Athena made a puppy dog face.

"A risk?"

"Yeah. You talk so much yin yang—all things are possible and such—and now you slammin' the door on opportunity?"

"Every opportunity is not the right opportunity."

"You're ruining my life right now."

"As long as you're not being too dramatic or anything. Athena—you're the star. Call and tell them. Hell, if they liked me they'll be kvelling over you!"

"It's not that simple!"

Maya took a forkful of noodles.

Athena was quiet. "Okay, Maya. Okay. Ready? I dare you."

They stood silently looking at each other. Athena pulled up a pillow and Maya sat down. They looked at the floor and back at each other. Since childhood, the dare was something of heavy meaning between them. It was only reserved for emergencies.

"I double-dare you, Maya."

"You double-dare me? Aw, Athena. We're grown-ass women now."

Grown-ass women or not, Maya had dared Athena to leave the hellish job at the "strictly" massage parlor. Athena had dared Maya to leave the bed after the Bobby debacle and to finally get up on stage and try performing. "I dare you" had weight. In fifth grade Athena dared Maya to throw the dodge ball directly at Michelle, a husky French-Irish bully, and then ran away and left Maya to get pummeled by Michelle's working class anger. Then, Maya had escaped with a broken nose. In hip-hop, they played with guns.

Maya inhaled. "You should use your powers for good. What are the consequences if I choose not to accept this mission?"

"If you don't take the dare . . ." Athena chose her words with care. "If you don't take the dare you have to call Bobby and see how he's doing. Tell him you still love him and that he wins. Tell him the truth. That you've had difficulty moving on. Your choice."

Maya buried her face in her lap.

"You the one always talking that be positive crap. 'Be a goddess,' " Athena mimicked in a whiny voice. "I knew it was bull."

"Reverse psych. Thanks for the refresher."

"This is the first yes for us. Ever. You're a pussy, Maya." Athena waited for Maya's reaction.

Maya made her sour lemon face. "Lovely."

"And a punk. You are a punk pussy punk. And you've always been a punk pussy punk. What is it you say every time I invite you somewhere fun? It's better to be chicken . . ."

"It's better to be a live chicken than a dead duck."

"Ugh. It's not better to be a loser," Athena said and immediately regretted it. "Sorry."

"Athena, you think I'm a *loser*?"

"Of course not, Maya, but . . ."

"Would you tell me if you did?"

Athena looked at the floor. "Absolutely." Her words picked up pace. "Think about this. Shell never fails. He's a hit factory. What would you dare to do if you couldn't fail?"

Maya was dangling from her thin grasp on excuses. "But I have a job."

"That you hate. Forever analyzing. At some point you gotta start living it, Maya."

Hmmm. Harsh but true. *Live life? Live life.* She thought about her cause of the week posters. Had she really made any difference? She stretched out a leg and hit a pile of books left from what she was studying four years ago. She was a live chicken. And a scaredy-cat. And a punk pussy punk. And she wanted out. As Dr. Phil might say, "And how's that working out for you?" It wasn't. Life didn't make a good spectator sport.

"It's only a few weeks. Three, four max, then we make the switch," Athena said.

"Oh! Only a few weeks." Maya smiled. *You got this.* "I guess there's a whole lot that we can do to help with the money and publicity," she said finally. "I'll take a short leave of absence."

Athena tried to read Maya's face. "Really?"

Maya covered her face with her hands. "No. Yeah. No. Really. Fine. Taking one for the team." Maya's nerves were transparent, but she was for real.

"For real / for real?" Athena asked.

"For real / for real," Maya said.

"Yes!" Athena jumped up and started pacing. "Fifteen Gs apiece! Life just got way better. Okay. The only thing you need now is a different name."

"Whoa—slow. Slow down. Why do I need a different name?"

"'Cause there is only one Lady Athena, baby. And my momma named her."

"So I'll be Lady Maya. It's only temporary . . ."

"Nahhh, we'll think of something, black queen. I'm going to pack."

"Wow. Okay." Maya grinned at Athena like a madwoman. "Yeah."

"What?"

"I got it." Maya had just swallowed somebody's canary.

"Got what?"

"My name. Black Queen Cleopatra! What's up? I am Cleopatra."

"Maya—that's off the chain! MC Cleopatra. I love it."

"Me too!" Maya remembered from biology that frogs are an indicator species, the first to react to changes in the environment. She was born a frog. But for the first time in her life, she was not just reacting. She was taking action. She was a lion! Well almost. A gazelle perhaps?

Maya held her head up and walked like an Egyptian. Athena joined her and they Egypt-walked around the tiny apartment. Cleopatra. Yay.

Chapter 7

"I GOT IT HEMMED.
MAD METHODS TO MICROPHONE MECHANISM
FROM INNER CITY CURRICULUM."
—*Bahamadia*

Athena sat cross-legged with Maya on her bedroom floor to partake in their Official Good-bye Faustus ritual, proposed by Maya of course. Athena was down for anything to keep Maya on track and get her on that plane in the morning. Athena took a drag of a joint as they sat watching the smoke of sage incense climb the air.

Athena wanted to listen to Bob Marley but Maya just couldn't. Bob was the music of her childhood. One note of "Redemption Song," "Rastaman Vibration" or "Uprising" and she was a solo child tripping on secondhand ganja smoke and Big Bird in an interracial room full of high adults talking politics in an American hippie town. Tonight's soundtrack was a mellow neo-soul mix of Aya, Erykah, Jill, Corrine, Lina and Goapale.

Maya had a scarf on her hair and wore a purple pajama set. In a rare moment Athena's real hair had come out to play. She sported brownish naps, never seen outside the home, primed for her next weave. But even in this "before" scenario, she looked like an "after."

"What's it like being pretty?" Maya asked out of the blue.

"You should know, silly." Athena read Maya's homemade affirmation index cards. "I am a magnificent creature. I am always in harmony with the Universe. I am filled with the Love of the Universal Divine Truth. I am free to be me. Everything I touch returns riches to me. I have more power than I ever thought possible . . ."

"I don't doubt you but nobody knows that but me and you. What's it like being beautiful in a—you know, in an obvious way?"

"Maya . . . Just like Dr. Feelgood said, you're insecure for no reason."

"Remember sixth grade? Ugly black duckling? I was Chimney. African Booty Scratcher. Tar Baby. Buckwheat. And that was from the black kids."

"So what, Maya? I grew up being called high yella. Redbone. White girl. And everything else."

"But at least you knew that no matter what jealous people called you, society still saw you as beautiful."

"Society?! When you're a kid, you don't know nothing about no society. I'm not competing with you to see who suffered worse, Maya. Every kid is teased."

"But you watched TV and saw even Smurfette or Miss Piggy with blonde hair. Or all the pretty black girls with darn near white skin like yours. How does that feel?"

"Fine. Pretty, I guess."

" 'Maya's so black she could leave a handprint in charcoal.' Remember that?"

"Aw, Maya, we were twelve."

"But you do remember. Maya's so black she gotta wear white gloves to eat Tootsie Rolls so she don't eat her fingers."

Athena chuckled. "Maya Hopeless is so black, when she jumps in a hot bath it makes instant cocoa."

"Maya's so black the teacher marked her absent."

Athena released her ashes. "You left out the part that makes the whole joke. Maya Hopeless is so black the teacher marked her absent at night school. I got one. Maya's so fat she jumped in the ocean and people thought it was an oil spill."

"So fat, Athena?"

"No, I said so black."

"You said so fat."

"Oh." Athena made a little pile with the affirmation cards.

"Athena, you were size zero before it was in. You have blue eyes. Blue eyes! Naturally. That's whitefolks' holy grail."

"I know. Then there's black-ass me with blue eyes. That'll learn 'em." Athena laughed.

"Did you always feel pretty?"

"Well, when I don't, I don't tell anybody. My momma used to say fake it till you make it. So that's what I do mostly. Look. I don't like my freckles. Bleaching creams don't work. That's why I wear an inch of makeup. But they're still there."

Maya inspected her face. "Your freckles are cute."

"Okay. Don't tell anybody I ever said this, Maya. If you do I'll deny it. But I feel like my beauty is a gift that I have to work at and share with people. Everybody hungers for beauty. So when I . . . when I smile it's like sharing a little piece of it." She took a deep drag of the joint. "When I'm kind to people, I feel benevolent. 'Cause they don't expect me to be. Nice, I mean. And they act like I'm being benevolent right back. Like . . . grateful. That's why I don't think being famous is gonna be hard. People already stare at me. They wanna be my friend already. But when I feel ugly I just pretend."

Maya wanted to reveal something back in solidarity. It was Girlfriends' Rule #5. *If your friend reveals something intimate . . .*

"We're not going to New York," Athena said. "We're going to hip-hop."

Maya nodded. "If we were living in the eighteenth century, I'd drink tea and read my poetry all day."

"If we were living in the eighteenth century, we'd be slaves."

Maya insisted that they chant the affirmations. So they did. Athena insisted that they listen to her favorite affirmation, the song "Hate Me Now" by Nas, her third favorite MC behind Thug and Rakim. An anthem against hateration. They spent the last hour of their ritual dancing around and rapping, "You can hate me now/ but I won't stop now."

Athena and Maya listened to the howling wind knock about on the windows while they looked through Maya's crazy scrapbook. The news said that a tornado was coming. Hopefully the bluejays would be all right in the storm. They closed the book when they got to the snapshots of the folks trampled on her deadly engagement night.

Maya was in a writing mood. She drafted a handwritten letter to snail mail to her folks in Yellow Springs. They appreciated gestures like that, and it made her feel like she was working at the relationship.

When she was finished, Maya wrote on a clean page:

> Things I'd Dare to Do If I Could Not Fail: 1. Skydive, bungee jump or ride a motorcycle. 2. Perform in front of a real audience, like 50 people. 3. Speak my mind. Tell folks what I really think and feel all the time & cuss people out if they deserve it without worrying about their feelings. 4. Strip for fun. :) 5. Make love in a private public place. 6. Try meat or fish. Just a taste! 7. Wear a bikini. 8. Tell a guy I like him. 9. Dance in a club AND NOT FEEL SHY. 10. Love again. Hard.

Chapter 8

"CHICKENHEAD ENVY IS NOT A PRETTY THING."
—Joan Morgan

There was no means for a private jet to fly out of Faustus, so Shell, or rather, Shell's people sent a car to pick up Maya and Athena and drive them to Cincinnati's airport, which by some cruel joke was located in northern Kentucky. The dynamic duo kept vacillating between bringing everything but the kitchen sink and bringing nothing, as nothing in their old life might fit into this proposed new one. They ended up going for the kitchen sink option, keeping the car waiting for forty-five minutes.

The driver of the long black limo blasted the satellite radio at Athena's request. The female DJ sounded amped but Maya and Athena were even more thrilled than she was because the DJ was referring to them: "DJ Manifesta on the mic, y'all. So my peoples in the know say that Big Shell is calling off his search for America's next top emcees. Seems like he found somebody in Ohio, of all places. His new act is headed for the Bigger Apple as we speak! Just what we need; more rap from the boonies. BX where you at? BK where you at? Queens?!? NY stand up!!"

"We don't have to go through security?" Maya asked the driver as they pulled up on the tarmac about twenty-five feet from the plane at 3:15 P.M. Their flight was scheduled to take off at 3:18.

"Not unless one of you is a terrorist." The driver popped the trunk and waved over a team of baggage carriers.

Maya jumped out. "Hurry up, Athena!" Maya quickly counted up their bags. "Three minutes to go and you're lollygagging."

"Chill with our names! And it's impossible to be late 'cause we're the only passengers," Athena had been a wee bit sulky over some dude during the decadent peach yogurt and waffles limo breakfast. Somebody didn't call when he should have or called when he shouldn't have. Maya lost track. At any rate, by the time the car arrived at the airport the rat bastard and his issues were history.

It was drizzling. A Midwest twister was predicted for later that evening, but they should be safely in NYC by then. Four big men bounded over to load their luggage and boxes into the Gulfstream jet with "Camp Hustla" emblazoned on the side in green. Their hodgepodge of pinned and tied suitcases left over from various family members suddenly felt embarrassing here. Maya noticed scuffs invisible back in their apartment on Bluestone Road. She felt her bra for her $500 in cash savings just in case this was some wild-goose chase.

"Help you onto the plane, miss?" a cute skycap asked Maya.

Athena took his hand like they were the prom queen and king and pranced up the stairs. "I could get used to this! See, this is why they call it a runway."

"No, I'm fine," Maya told their backs as she grasped the banister and made her way up. She was wearing new rain boots, a splurge from Payless.

"Oh no!" Maya turned and made her way quickly back down the wet stairs.

"What is it?" Athena called over her shoulder.

"My good luck rock from my altar. My green stone. I left it in the limo." The tiny green iridescent stone that Maya's grandmother Ruby in Trinidad gave her as a kid was shiny then but now was dull, practically gray. She didn't carry it around normally because she was afraid she'd lose it. She checked between the backseats and all over the floor. Gone. It wasn't in the car, meaning that of course the first time she carried it with her, she lost it. Maya gave up and trudged back up the steps to the plane.

"Wow. Mama let me upgrade you." Athena made a beeline for a recliner with a gold silk cover.

"It's a real private jet." Maya stood in the doorway taking it all in as John Coltrane's horn piped in "Ascension." Mmmm. Soft leather seats with dark wood paneling. Muted lighting like a sexy lounge. Six Parsons chairs around a rosewood table. Maya tuned her brain into Trane's notes and relaxed. Was she really doing this? She took a seat as an attendant entered and floated between the sax's soprano.

"Darlins, hello! I'm Belle." Bouffant Belle's voice oozed Southern hospitality. She smiled with big white teeth (inferiority complex).

"Hi, Belle!" Maya and Athena sounded like an AA or Weight Watchers meeting.

"Welcome to the Camp Hustla biz jet. I'll be your in-flight attendant today. A quick tour. This is the stateroom. You can sleep out here but there is a lover-ly bedroom in the back. The new satellite gives us Internet and cable. Chef Ty just dropped off lunch and I'll serve it as soon as we hit cruising altitude, unless either of you is on a diet that requires you eat sooner." Belle spotted Athena's leatherette heels on the silk seating. "Oh. Also Miss Athena, Miss Maya. Let me take your shoes."

Under her jacket Maya wore a faded Free Mumia tee and sweatpants, in stark contrast to Athena's walking shorts and fake Versace top. It used to say "Versage" until she scratched out the *G* and made it a *C* so that Donatella herself wouldn't know the difference. Belle handed them each a small gray wool case imprinted with the Prada logo.

Athena quickly unzipped hers. "Slippers!"

Maya worked off her rubber boots and Belle removed them like toxic waste as she moved into her new footgear. Heaven.

A kindly male voice, also Southern, boomed through the loudspeakers. "Miss Athena and Miss Maya, welcome to *The Hustle*, the private plane of Shell the Boy Wonder. My name is Kapp and I am your *el capitan* today. Get it? Kapp the Captain." He chuckled.

Maya rubbed her feet up and down the floor trying for static sparks. "I hope that his flying is better than his comedy."

"Oh it is, Miss Athena. He flies smooooth," oozed Belle behind the nearby curtain.

Captain Kapp continued. "I am assisted by first officer Harry Truman. Say hi, Harry."

"Hi Harry. Back to you, Kapp."

"Our flight today from CVG Airport to JFK in New York City should take only two hours and thirty-eight minutes. Please sit back, relax and . . ."

"Copy that." Listening to a headset, Belle unlatched the main door to the cabin.

"You know how wasteful this is?" Maya leaned her elbow on a wooden side table.

"Who cares?" Athena was in the DVD cabinet.

"I read that private jets use ten times the amount of fuel per person. That's the equivalent of driving a Hummer across the country twice."

"That also sounds like fun," Athena said, holding up a DVD with a cornrowed guy on the cover.

Maya pointed and flexed her feet again and again in her soft, new Prada slippers. She could perhaps get used to these.

The main cabin door flew back and a twenty-foot-tall photo-ready goddess in huge Jackie O sunglasses flurried in; a real-life Egyptian queen. Cheekbones that could cut glass, long glossy legs as tall as Athena clad in the shortest orange material that could still be legally considered a dress, a royal blue ostrich Birkin bag, large diamond hoops and tawny skin that glowed like full body makeup although you knew it wasn't.

Maya sat up. Who dresses like this in a tornado? Then Maya's eyes focused into recognition. Sahara? Yup—*the* Sahara. As in Iman, Beverly, Roshumba, Naomi, Tyra and now Sahara. Victoria's Secret cover girl Dior Sahara.

"What a day!" The reigning African American supermodel plopped down on the buttery leather sofa that matched her skin and immediately looked like a perfume ad. Maya folded her hands. Perfection. Sahara (superiority complex) tossed her $17,000 waiting-list bag on the floor. Nine diamond tennis bracelets dangled from her tiny wrist.

"Belle. Parched." Sahara spoke in a whiny, clipped, almost British accent although she was from Cincinnati. "Stew-pid paparazzi don't give you a minute's pree-vacy."

"Water, Miss Sahara?" Belle asked. Did she just do a mini curtsy?

"Good God, no. My best friend Jack." Sahara removed her Chanel sunglasses and held them out.

"Right away." Belle removed a white silk kerchief from her waistband, laid it on a side table, placed the sunglasses on top of it and then hustled out.

"I think that's a Cavalli." Why Athena was whispering was a mystery. Unless Sahara was deaf she could easily hear as they were sitting just across from her.

"A what?" Maya whispered back.

Sahara turned around and noticed Maya and Athena, who were both agog. "Cavalli. Roberto made it for me after Milan. Did Shell tell you I was hitching a ride?" Clearly not waiting for an answer, Sahara put her feet up. Belle reappeared with a Jack Daniels bottle and a bejeweled pimp cup—the ugliest thing ever. Big, clumsy red and green stones jutted out awkwardly all over it. Belle clunked it down on the side table. "Hurrahhh," Sahara sang. She reached into her bag and pulled out pink ballet shoes emblazoned with interlocking Cs. She looked down at Maya and Athena's Prada footwear. "Haven't seen those since last year. Are they still comfy?" She held up her Chanel slippers. "The *only* way to go."

"I hear that." Athena propped her head up on her hands and watched Sahara like an eight-year-old watching Saturday morning TV. All she needed was a bowl of cereal. Sahara gathered her silky bone-straight weave and let it drape off the sofa.

Athena whispered to Maya lower now, through gritted teeth. She was like a ventriloquist channeling herself. "DJ Manifesta's been saying for weeks that Sahara is Shell's side chick but Sahara said in *Bonfire* magazine that she barely heard of him 'cause she doesn't follow rap."

The velvet-draped window showed the tornado whipping itself into a frenzy now. Leaves and bits of things spun in twisted curlicues. Maya's stomach did push-ups. Talk about ripped from the headlines. Sahara? This was real/for real. Maya looked around. No vomit bag. "Uh, bathroom, Belle?"

"Are you okay?" Athena put a hand on Maya's forehead. "Clammy." Maya removed Athena's hand.

"Be right back." Maya stood up abruptly and tried to settle herself as though the plane were already taxiing down the runway. It wasn't. "Are we moving?"

Belle didn't skip a beat. She was used to prima donna and pre–prima donna antics. "I have air sickness medication, Dramamine and scopolamine."

"She doesn't do pills, not even aspirin. She used to be terrified of flying so maybe it's that," Athena explained as Maya gripped the seat, unable to explain that she had lavender in her suitcase.

Belle seemed regretful at the rejection of her wares. "Well, there are two ladies' rooms. Yours for today is right this way, Miss Athena." She waved for Maya to follow her.

Miss Athena? Athena and Maya exchanged looks. Belle took off through the silk curtain and Maya aka "Miss Athena" followed on her heels.

Maya closed the door to the loo behind her. A folding half door like any airplane bathroom. Give or take a marble arch. Objective? Hyperventilate. Indulge in a mild nervous breakdown and then return to her seat. She found planned mini anxiety attacks to be more efficient as of late. Whoa. A gilded gold throne toilet, gold bidet and gold fixtures. Definitely not MidWest Airlines. The bathroom was bigger than her bedroom and completely mirrored. Mahogany shelves fully stocked with a selection of men's and women's scents: Armani's Code, Belami, Calvin Klein's scents, Tubereuse Indiana, Mugler's Alien, Lagerfeld's KL, Carolina Herrera's Chic—and, of course, Shell's own signature scent: Despicable.

Talk about an upgrade. She had never flown first class, much less on a personal plane. Nice. A black leather picture frame near the sink announced, "Welcome Athena & Maya." Nicer. A basket of M.A.C. makeup in her colors, Carol's Daughter skincare stuff, plush hand towels, and the smell of patchouli. Cool! It seemed like there should be an attendant with hot towels. She caught her reflection in the over-buffed sink and was relieved that she looked like herself. Smart and a bit unkempt. She slid to the floor and melted into the plush wall-to-wall white carpet. White carpet in a public bathroom? Practical. She put her head back.

Ahhh. This was all she needed. A quiet moment to process. To think. Just a second to . . . *Gonna gimme head, gonna gimme head* . . . Music flooded the bathroom. She looked up into ceiling speakers. Surround sound. Great. Oh. Black velvet curtains. She pulled them back looking for a wizard. Close enough. A walk-in shower. Maybe she could hide in there. She shoved her hand into her jeans pocket and fingered the tiny wedding broom she'd grabbed as the driver beeped outside their apartment. Something old. A security blanket. The bristles pricked her fingers as she remembered.

How cheery the jumping broom favors were, standing at attention at each place setting as Maya, her mother Emmaline and Athena gave the salmonpink and applegreen-themed Kelly Hall the once-over. Emmaline, a copper-colored Maya, wore her graying waves in a severe bun. Like the reformed whores in the front row of her church, Emmaline's past was invisible. Freedom-loving, naked-dancing, counterculture flowerchild begone! She defined elegance in a peach pantsuit and soft pearls as Delroy, Maya's dad, and the tulips arrived right on the rehearsal dinner schedule. Emmaline checked them off on her clipboard. Twenty-five minutes before the guests arrived. Satin chair covers? Check. His-and-hers cakes? Check. Groom?

With Kelly Hall flooded with pink peonies it was still the summer of love. The rehearsal went off without a hitch. Bobby calmed Maya's nerves with a kiss on the nose and then headed to the Yellow Springs Bed & Breakfast to take a nap. The overdone formal rehearsal dinner in her mom's Alpha Kappa Alpha colors was the event for their parents and then in the morning the tiny barefoot wedding would be for them. Bobby's brother and the three members of his rap group The Force represented as his groomsmen while Maya would be attended to by Athena and the rest of her makeshift party—her cousin Amen, Camille from school and her advisor Darcy. As she had no real best buds besides Athena, she took who she could get.

Humming merrily, Emmaline went around the table rearranging

Maya's settings. Clockwise. Noon, 1 P.M., 2 P.M., 3 P.M. . . . Napkin, fork, favor, water, wine . . .

Twenty-four weeks of planning. She'd never imagined herself as a Cinderella wedding girl, but there she was. Until he hacked her heart to bits and sold it on eBay.

Maya was unsure how long she sat on the bathroom floor doing yoga breaths but they worked. "Get over it," she said out loud and stood up. They still weren't flying. Hopefully everything was okay. She did her thing on the luxurious throne, freshened up and exited, bubbling over with her own big idea. She couldn't wait to tell Athena.

"Now that Miss Athena is ready, we're ready," came the captain's voice over the PA.

"He was waiting for *me*?" Maya asked incredulously. Athena was sprawled out on one of the sofas munching walnuts and reading *Glamour.*

"Waiting for you is our job, darlin'." Belle buckled Maya into her seat and then disappeared behind the curtain.

"Check me out." Sahara nodded in the direction of the magazine. She was on the cover. "More in my bag. Party favors, too."

"Like balloons?" Maya asked.

"Balloons? Do I look like a Mexican coke mule? No. Just a vial or two." Sahara leaned back and put a hand on her large regal forehead like explaining simple things to stupid people was exhausting. She lit a cigarette and foul smoke filled the small cabin.

Trying not to cough too much, Maya pulled a box of Cheez-Its from her carry-on. Athena lay back on the adjoining chaise, trying to mimic Sahara's perfect repose.

Brain clearly percolating, Maya took out her notebook and scribbled furiously until Sahara passed out from too much Jack Daniel's.

Cheez-Its in hand, Maya whispered to Athena. "Guess what? I had a life-changing idea in the bathroom."

"Overdose on baby powder and Eternity?" Athena asked.

"Ha ha. No . . ." Maya looked around. Belle was still behind the curtain. Maya lowered her voice. "This is the best thing that's ever happened to me."

"That's what I've been tryin' to tell you."

"No, it's not what you think. This whole thing is going to be an experiment."

"Okay. Go on." Athena had seen Maya do all kinds of mini social experiments on her own to counteract the boredom of her job—testing out how folks would react if she cut them in line (poorly), documenting whether people would comment if she went into a church wearing a mini skirt (yes), investigating whether people would help her if she pretended to be homeless (sometimes) and stuff like that.

Maya nodded. "This whole thing is now an infiltration. I'm going undercover as a rapper. I'm gonna research the life and share the lessons I learn. The impact of hip-hop on the self. *And* I get to do it on somebody else's dime. There's a lot of analysis in this area, but I can come at it from the inside. Write up a sociological paper, get it published, become a star in my industry, and get my words and thoughts out there."

"That's hot, May—" Athena stopped herself before she said her name. "Hot."

"I'm already gonna be there, thanks to you. And I'm glad to hook you up, but I might as well get something out of it. Give folks something to think about."

Athena put her magazine down. "So fifteen thousand bucks to pay off your loans is not getting something out of it?"

Maya was almost bursting. "I'm so excited. For the next three weeks I am going to study this game, roll with it, become the bling-bling."

"Well for starters, if you really wanna be down, don't say *bling-bling.*"

Maya laughed. "I'm a good student. I'll get it."

"Just teasing. Sounds like a very Mayalicious plan."

Chapter 9

"It's my beat."
—*Sweet Tee*

According to MapQuest there are 631.97 miles between Bluestone Road in Faustus, Ohio, and The Heretix Hotel Times Square in New York City. A seventeen-hour drive and a less-than-three-hour flight. Maya and Athena had tried to visit New York once before with a ragtag carload of Athena's friends and stayed with someone's aunt in Jersey on what turned out, unbeknownst to them, to be a drug run. They never left New Jersey so they had never seen this . . . gloss.

After gray Faustus, New York City was in Technicolor. The sun was happier. The people looked just a little better, like everybody was a part-time soap opera star, and were surprisingly polite. Everyone was on their way to somewhere fab and more important. Accountants, street sweepers, everybody. The Big Apple was flash, dash and about being 'bout it, but this time, Athena and Maya would not be left with the seedy core. The true distance between Faustus, Ohio, and New York City—180 degrees.

"I swear that I've seen that check-in girl on the cover of *Cosmo*," Athena said.

The hotel room was a swank white study in fabulosity. Designed by Dolce & Gabbana, a plaque informed them. They sat in a corner on their stacked suitcases. They wanted to scream. They wanted to dance. They were way out of their element. They were . . . too nervous to move. They discussed their flight like strangers discuss the weather. "Not too bad" and "How much Botox did Belle have anyway?" They were waiting for Shell. Maya looked at her lime green plastic Swatch. The Boy Wonder was forty-four minutes late.

"This is wild." Maya was anxious about pulling the whole thing off. Nonetheless, this was the most exciting thing ever. It was a rush. A rush. "A rush!" She looked over at Athena, who was unusually quiet. "What's up?"

"This is real, Maya. We haven't lived in the real." Athena figured she might as well come with it. "I'm hot for the niggas and wiggas at home, but am I hot for New York? Am I hot for real?"

"Nice, Athena." Maya, self-proclaimed expert at diagnoses, never imagined that Athena might be worried.

"Well, what am I supposed to call them? Negroes and Wegroes?" Athena shook her head. "What if you choke and blow our wad before Shell tastes my talent? I gotta tell you something."

"What, you've been masquerading as a sociologist?"

"Ha ha. No. Um . . . remember when I said it would only be a couple of weeks before we wean Shell offa you and get him into Lady Athena?"

"Yes?" Maya fidgeted with the Swatch.

"Well, it's probably gonna take a little longer." Athena braced herself against the wall.

"Like days longer or weeks longer?" Maya asked.

"Uh. Possibly months longer."

Maya looked closer. Was she joking? She wasn't. "Oh, Athena, come on."

"We gotta play this thing right, Maya, or we'll lose everything."

Before Maya could address all kinds of things in that statement the door opened. The newly minted rapper and her "hype wo-man" stood up. A massive beefy bodyguard escorted Shell and his curvaceous partner from the audition—what was her name again?—into the hotel suite. They wore matching pinstriped suits. Maya wondered if it was on purpose.

"It's on, ladies!" Shell had a toothpick hanging out of the corner of his power smile. He handed Athena and Maya cigars.

"Real Cubans," Shell's homegirl pointed out.

Maya didn't know what they were supposed to do with them. "Shell, hi. Welcome. Or I guess we're welcome. The flight was great." She looked toward Athena for a cue or a clue.

Athena was all about Shell. She'd changed into brown knee-high leather boots and a new taupe minidress bought with the cash they hadn't received yet. Her current hair was reddish black and cascaded off her right shoulder.

Shell didn't notice. He was all about Maya. "You're not in Kansas no more." He kissed Maya's hand.

"Ohio," corrected Maya, and Shell and La Diva laughed like there was no difference. Maya tried to catch their vibe, study their movements. After all, they were there to be down.

Maya adjusted her tight black outfit and massive silver jewelry, their Faustus version of sexy. In fact, her hoops had the SEXY spelled out right in the center. Her natural hair was super-gelled, twisted and slicked up with a stylish add-on bun. Athena had re-dressed her on the plane as Sahara napped.

Shell sized Maya up. "We are a part of the Rhythm Nation, right?" The bodyguard snickered. Athena bit her lip. Those earrings were her faves. "Welcome to NYC. Luci, I know you remember the hottest new star on the Camp Hustla label, Jezebel."

Luci thrust out a hand and Maya unwillingly shook it.

"Who?" Maya asked. Athena gave a hesitant smile.

"How could I forget Jezebel?" Luci hugged Maya like they'd been BFFs for years. "I'm your publicist."

The rush of insta-intimacy was a bit much. Maya put some distance between them. She could wash her hands after they left. "Howdy, how are you? Good to see you again. Lucia?"

"Luci. Luci Mefisto."

"Ah. What kinda name is Mefisto?" Maya asked.

"I'm half Italian. My father, but I don't identify." Luci looked at Shell to make sure she wasn't overtalking.

"Give her a pound, girl." Shell was looking at Maya. "You in the game now, baby." Maya looked at him like he was crazy. He didn't notice. He finally looked at Athena. "This must be Jezebel's assistant, Maya, right?"

Maya and Athena realized on the plane that they would need to come clean about the name switch at least. It was too confusing, and IDs are always required to sign contracts and other legal documents.

"Actually *my* name is Maya and *her* name is Athena," Maya said.

"Maya?" Luci looked confused.

"Name snafu," Maya clarified. "She made my audition appointment for me."

Luci's eyes darted back and forth between Maya and Athena. Maybe she was on to them.

"I don't give a damn about government names. Live in the now," Shell told Luci. "Her name is Jezebel." He seemed too agitated at being out of the loop to dwell on something as insignificant as a name.

Maya mouthed, "Jezebel?"

Athena shrugged. She gave Luci a pound. "Hey whassup?"

"The big man is Ill Verge," Shell pointed out. Did Ill Verge (bouts of depression) flex a muscle to accentuate his intro? Okay. Whatever.

This was definitely not Maya's scene, but she was taking mental notes. Ugh. She had to expedite her way out and Athena's way in. "Athena is a rapper too. You should hear—"

"We don't interrupt." Shell was not a man who wasted time. He ignored Maya's *no he didn't* look. "There are many phases to our boot-camp style of breaking and re-making an artist. You're going to live Camp Hustla. Mind, body and soul, baby. Contract."

The bodyguard opened a box and handed a diamond-encrusted fountain pen and a leather folder to Shell. Shell handed Maya the pen along with her contract. She took it with two hands. It was a phone book. Uncle Steve was a lawyer and his number one rule was never sign anything without reading it. Maya looked at Athena. Athena nodded.

"Well, I have nothing to lose." Maya laughed uneasily by herself. Everyone in the room was dead serious. She signed. What could they sue her for? Her futon? The dark ink looked crimson in the cool hotel light.

"Good! Now you live forever. You got this. Fame is eternal life." Shell handed the folder to Sasquatch and continued with all of the importance of the Gettysburg Address. "When you were a child, you spoke as a child, behaved as a child, thought as a child. Now you are a woman. Now you're Jezebel." Maya handed him back the diamond pen. He shook his head. "Visconti limited edition. Ten thousand bucks. Keep it."

Maya squeezed Athena's hand. Hard. Too much was happening in their heads to explain that her new "tag" was Cleopatra, not Jezebel.

"Are you a believer?" Shell asked Maya.

Maya was unclear what the correct answer could be.

Shell nodded at Luci. "You will be. This wallet contains your bank card."

"I picked out the wallet just for you, Jezebel." Luci handed Maya a cigar-sized orange box. "Hope you think it's marv."

"Thank you, Luci." Maya untied a black ribbon that said Hermés in white print and opened the box. Delicate tissue paper over a baby blue leather wallet. She opened it, looked at the bank card with her name on it, then closed it.

"That's lizardskin," Athena said. Maya imagined poor baby blue lizards trying to escape a chi-chi bag wrangler.

"If you don't like it we can exchange it." Luci beamed. "They love me over there."

Shell circled Maya. "What you need to realize is that I peeped you as a paper poet. Your lyrics were well written but poorly executed. It's all good, though. With practice you'll be tight. You're a natural performer, you just suck right now. But make no mistake, it's your balls that got you here, not your style or your swagger."

Maya almost let a laugh escape at the thought that her nerve, which she never knew she had until she practically cussed out Shell in defense of her friend, had gotten her somewhere. The bodyguard popped open a bottle of Cristal and handed it to Shell. He poured a libation on the carpet, guzzled the champagne and passed the bottle to Maya. He leaned in close to her face.

"Remember this . . ." Shell's breath was a fresh summer garden.

"Life is a mixtape. The greatest emcee of all times, my brothaman Thug, said that. May God rest his immortal soul." He looked at Ill Verge and nodded. "Boy Wonder complete." Shell walked to the door with Ill Verge shadowing him. Ill Verge moved like a tremendous bear with something stuck in his claw, maintaining an even distance. Maya stifled a snicker.

"Shell don't like folks all up on him," Ill Verge whispered to Maya.

"Dude, is it that serious?" Maya asked Athena under her breath.

"Shut up." Athena's teeth were gritted. "They're still here."

"People are dying of cancer. AIDS." Athena gave her a look. Maya continued, lower now. "Why do I feel like I sold my soul to the devil—for cheap?" She smoothed the back of her gelled-up 'fro anxiously. "And don't you have to be present to open your own bank account?"

Luci looked over at Maya and smiled. "Yo Shell, any notes?"

Shell snapped back around and circled Maya again, inspecting her like a prize horse.

He spoke only to Luci. His new thoroughbred was invisible. "Just a couple. Overall she's pretty for a dark-skinned girl but her hair looks like Jill Scott threw up; the natural woman is played. Clean up the nails and skin; tell her that if you have to wear items that say sexy you're not; and have her lose about fifteen pounds by next Friday, fifteen more the following week. That's about it. If she works out we can do a titty lift later. Oh, and maybe get her a puppy named Peaches. Celebrity pets are *huge*."

Luci scrambled to write it all down with her own diamond pen.

Maya the non-drinker grabbed a glass from the breakfront and took a swig of the champagne. Dutch courage. Athena, heated, mouthed the words "on mission." After all, Shell had now directly insulted her most hip-hop makeover.

Shell held up his index finger. "We'll be back in one hour, sharp, to introduce you to more fam. No leaving the hotel." And then the Boy Wonder was out.

"Later, Jezebel." Luci squeezed Maya's arm. "It's all uphill from here. Smooth sailing."

"You mean downhill," Maya said.

Luci hugged Maya again and walked out.

"Aaaaaaaaaaaaaaaaaaaahhh!" Athena and Maya screamed the second the fleet sailed out the door.

"This is really real!" Maya said. "So, months now, Athena? Now you're saying months?"

"Do you understand that the loot that we just picked up today already is worth almost twenty Gs?!" Athena fingered the Hermès wallet.

"How long do I have to keep up this farce, Athena? Why don't we just let Shell listen to you rhyme and then I can be *your* hype woman. And still get my research."

"Come on, Maya. This is a music mogul. We tell him he made a mistake and he'll send us packing. I'm sorry I lied, but I had to get you on that plane. You're getting a life. And your experiment."

"So how long, Athena?"

"Well, in hip-hop protocol, I can't directly address him because you are the talent, first in command. So whenever we finally get in the studio, I'll kick some rhymes, and Shell's team will see how hot I am. He was digging my verses. He just hated your delivery."

"I don't think he said that, but how long?"

"He seems reasonable. I guess whenever he and his team decide you're ready for the studio, Maya. We'll feel it out. Meanwhile, drop hints and big me up to Shell, Luci, whoever as much as possible."

"Actually, before Shell completely insulted me, he actually did seem reasonable. And decent. Not what I expected. I guess I'm glad that my best friend, Lady Athena, is a backstabbing liar."

"I love you too."

"Should I take off the earrings?" Maya turned her head to the side. The problem with lying to a friend is you can't stay mad when they lie to you.

"Hell no. We're bringing sexy back. You know, Maya, maybe . . . maybe you should go for Shell. I'd make the sacrifice and give him to you." Athena smiled graciously.

"Me? Go for Shell? Ugh . . . No thanks." Maya took off the "sexy" earrings and put them in a sleek white post-post-modern tray.

"Well, fine. If you don't want him then Shell's gonna be my baby daddy. He's shorter than I thought he would be, but no less magnifico."

"Oh, your family would looove that. What does your mother say? We're poor, baby—"

"Not ghetto and not stupid. I know. But child, please, if I came home to Over-the-Rhine with Shell the Boy Wonder there would be a parade in my honor. I didn't even tell them I was coming here 'cause I didn't want to get their hopes up again."

Maya put down the ten G pen. "This is ridiculous. Shell's ridiculous. The whole thing is . . ."

"Ridiculous? C'mon, Maya. Loosen up. Mayyybe flirt with him."

"He's not really my type, Athena. Hip-hop ruined my life."

"Uh, backsliding. Shell's not hip-hop. He's a man. Damn."

"You get screwed over at the altar and see how quickly you bounce back."

"Get over it!" Athena screamed.

"I can't!" Maya screamed back.

"You're like a one-hit wonder!"

Maya pulled a peanut butter cup from her backpack and unwrapped it.

Athena dropped to her knees dramatically. "Please have sex. Just so that you can stop eating us out of house and home!"

Maya took a bite and shoved the sweet treat back into her bag. "Ha ha ha. Very funny."

Athena walked over to the wall of windows overlooking the city. "Wow. So . . . We, uh, have some time to ourselves."

Maya joined her. They looked out onto Times Square. Incredible. "You thinking what I'm thinking?"

"Yup." Athena was putting on her jacket.

Maya entertained the angel and devil on her shoulders. "Shell said not to leave the hotel room . . . but he couldn't be serious—we're in New York City, for goddess sake."

They snuck down the hallway and broke into a run like kids, giggling all the way. The wearing all black too cool for school classic

NY couple in the elevator gave them a smile, seeing the Midwest on their faces.

"I can't wait to go shopping," Athena said as they practically skipped through the lobby.

"We gotta check out the museums too. Let's not spend anything yet, Athena. Just in case."

"Just in case what?"

"Just in case we wake up and this is a continuation of the cosmic joke that's been our lives until now."

The concierge turned up his nose like he smelled the Ohio River when they walked by.

Athena sucked her teeth. "Asshole."

"No, he's playing his part. Isn't that what he's supposed to do? It's New York!"

The doorman, however, was pleasant as he opened the door. "Good afternoon, ladies."

Then, something changed the moment their feet hit the street. They looked at each other. No need to say what they already knew. "It." This *was* "it." They both inhaled deeply, happy to cough from the luscious big city exhaust. They scanned Broadway. The glam quotient was crazy. Passersby shoved past, annoyed that tourists would presume to stop on a public sidewalk. A fat man made hot dogs that smelled like feet. They peeped their fellow tourists immediately. Then they looked up. Above the Virgin Megastore, diagonally from their hotel, was a million-foot-tall billboard with Shell's face on it. Yup. Their Shell. They looked at each other. No words. They walked into the hotel and back upstairs, minds stretched, expanded beyond belief. Possibilities.

Maya couldn't believe that she was doing this but she was. "I'm proud of myself for taking a chance." A risk. Crash and burn or fly? This was for real. Back in the room, she sat down to catch her breath. A blue velvet envelope emblazoned with a gold "CH" was on her bed. "Oooh—Tyra Mail!"

Athena ran over, picked up the envelope and put it to her nose. "It smells like success." She checked the envelope. "Your new lyrics!" Athena ripped apart the package. "How long you think before we can convince Shell to put me on?" she asked, scanning through the file of papers. "Uh-oh."

"Oh, no. What?" Maya asked.

Athena slowly handed her the top page. The name of the song was "Suck It Up." Maya read it out loud:

"I'll shoot you in the face.
Spray your MOMS with MACE.
Cut off your man's DICK
And erase him like he's waste!"

Maya turned the pages over and back again like they would transform themselves. She continued to read:

"You niggas ain't shit.
'Cause my pussy is legit!"

Athena snatched the pages back. "I'm sure it's just a mix-up."

"Mix-up?" Maya looked at Athena. "I knew something like this was going down. It better be a mix-up or we are outta here. Immediately. At least I am, anyway . . ."

"We'll talk to Shell about it," Athena assured her. "He's a Capricorn. He'll understand."

Maya stood up, then sat back down again; stood up, then sat back down again. "I need to think." Maya pulled out a small yellow candle and her Oshun goddess card from her backpack. She set them up next to the vial of riverwater she'd also brought with her. Granny Ruby taught her that when in doubt, make room for your ancestors—although she doubted that her ancestors wanted to see her shake her groove thang. Athena handed over a lighter and Maya calmed down.

"Ugh. Okaaay. Okay. I trust you, Athena. I trust the universe. This also says he's bringing our road manager by in like ten minutes ago. I guess rock star time is even later than Colored People's Time."

"You mean your road manager."

"I mean *our* road manager, Athena. I think ten minutes equals six hours in Shell time. It says he's bringing another artist too."

"Are you serious? Maya—it could be 50 or Em or anybody!!" The hotel door opened.

As Shell entered, Maya pulled a sheet around her although she was fully dressed. "Excuse you!"

Athena struck a sweaty pose. "Oh, Shell, hi! I was just going to take a looong, hot shower."

Maya involuntarily rolled her eyes. It was like Athena wanted to suck his jones right there.

Athena wanted to suck him all right, but not for what Maya thought. "Shell—I have so many questions for you. Like was Summer Jam in '95 really that crazy? And how are the old-school playas?" Verbal diarrhea. Athena wanted to suck him for stories, for experiences, for hip-hop—then she remembered protocol.

He smiled. "Our keys open the whole floor," he explained. Still, that didn't excuse his just entering someone else's room without knocking. "I foot the bill," he said, answering Maya's thoughts. "Two players you need to meet, ladies. Safe to enter, y'all."

A hardcore pretty boy came in with Ill Verge. Athena gasped as Shell began, "Allow me to introduce—"

"P.I.M.P.!" Athena abandoned all efforts to play it cool. Maya looked at her, completely clueless.

"No doubt." Pimp (alpha dog) eyeballed Athena, used to chicks screaming his name, but still catching a chuckle out of it. His hair was braided with a white scarf tied askew around it, and he wore the tank that Athena liked to refer to as the "husband beater" with dark jeans. All visible skin on his arms was covered in tattoos, with one in the shape of a small gun on his left cheek.

"Pimp from Black Death! The platinum-est rapper of oh-three," Athena exclaimed, half for Maya's benefit and half to quench her own nerves. Pimp puffed out his chest.

Maya had never seen Athena this jittery, but since she didn't know who dude was, she had the advantage of not being nervous in the slightest. It wasn't like he was Michael Moore or Barack Obama or something.

"I'm too dirty to be washed up." Pimp was peeved at the thought.

"Good to meet you. Pimp, was it?" Maya asked.

"Poised for a magnanimous comeback," Shell chimed in. "Yo Ill Verge, get Big Rob off the phone so that he can meet his new charge, man."

Ill Verge ambled out into the hallway.

"I think I smell a samich." Pimp sniffed as he checked out Maya and Athena. "You a P.O. or po-po?" he asked Maya. His diamond-covered teeth gave him a funny lisp.

"Parole officer or police," Athena translated.

Maya glared at Athena, repulsed and fascinated. Hip-hop. Athena shrugged with her eyes. But when Ill Verge came back in with Big Rob, they both froze as Shell launched into another intro.

"Time to get official," Big Rob started to say as the tall, caramel brotha with a head of short curls walked in. Then he stopped, too.

"This is Big Rob, your A&R peoples-slash-manager-slash-everything. Big Rob, this is Jezebel and her sidekick," Shell said.

" 'Big Rob'?" The name burst from Maya's throat. She was in her worst nightmare. She tasted bile bubbling up from the pit of her stomach. Big Rob and Maya stared at each other as Athena mouthed the word "sidekick."

Air. Gone. Now.

"Jezebel?" Big Rob sputtered. Clearly this wasn't his favorite dream either.

"Y'all know each other?" Shell asked. "Don't tell me these broads are groupies."

"That's what's up," Pimp piped in. "Tricks get around."

Athena looked over at Maya again to make sure she was still standing. Maya tried to look at Athena but couldn't.

Air. Air. Air. Gone.

"Noo . . ." Athena clarified. "Maya, uh, Jezebel studies the players in the game. So cool, um, why don't we leave Jezebel alone with her new manager so that they can plan the tour and stuff."

Air. Gone. Now. Gasping.

"Good idea," Shell answered. "Ten cities are kinda hectic for a virgin. We're having a little dinner and bowling get-together, Jez, to welcome you. Your car'll meet you downstairs."

"Bowling? We do that." Athena knew that Maya—Jez, apparently—was unable to hear anything Shell was saying, so she spoke and heard for both of them.

"I'm flying out to Dubai later, but we'll catch up." Shell was glad to have an excuse to leave. He stage-whispered to Big Rob, "Yo, keep an eye out. The new chick is makin me anxious. But I mean, they all do 'fore I stamp CH on 'em. Nahmean, God?" They slapped palms.

"I'm going to jump into that hot shower while they talk, Shell. Dubai 'bye!" Athena tried to affect bedroom eyes and cracked up over her own joke.

Shell doubled back. "Oh. Yo. Don't unpack." He looked at Maya, then Athena, then back at Maya like he was trying to decide who the troublemaker was. "I told y'all not to leave the hotel. Right? Right?" He stroked his hairless chin. "I'm moving y'all to the Heretix Uptown so that we can keep an extra eye on you. Boy Wonder complete," he offered by way of good-bye.

"Peace out, bitches!" Pimp left, following Shell and Ill Verge. Athena and Maya could only deal with one crisis at a time so they didn't respond.

Maya and "Big Rob" stood looking at each other. Maya gripped the bedpost. Air. Gone. Now gasping.

Breathe.

"Hell is empty and all the motherfucking devils are here," Maya said. It could have been out loud or in her head. She couldn't tell. She felt as faint as . . . as faint as a cast-off wedding gown. She'd tried on thirty-three gowns to find "the one." Ivory with spaghetti straps. "You look like Cinderella," the blue-haired lady in Bridal City said. Then Prince Charming took the pumpkin and bounced. Rapunzel shaved herself bald and Sleeping Beauty turned back into a freaking frog.

Breathe.

Athena smashed the silence. "Bobby, what the fuck?"

"What the fuck?" Big Rob/Bobby asked. His eyes were turning red.

The man with the football player's build paced back and forth. "If anybody is asking what the fuck, it should be me!" His massive arms were stuck in the air. Or maybe everything was just moving in slowww motion.

"Don't curse at me, Bobby!" Maya screamed. "How is this happening? What are you doing here?" It was the man who broke off the best bit of her heart, shoved it into his back pocket and sidled away.

After Bobby proposed to Maya at the deadly Thug concert in Faustus three years ago, they quickly made moves toward tying the knot. All was smooth. Maya was not only marrying the man of her dreams right on deadline of hitting the big three-o, but she was also getting her final grad school credit for it. *Sociological Mission: Analyze How a Modern Girl Does an Ancient Ritual.* Her parents were not offering a cow or goat. There wasn't a dowry or exchange of property. So why bother? Ahhhh. Because she could live in the crook of his smile.

She was both graduating and getting married at last. The night before the wedding was super busy—a rehearsal dinner and then their respective bachelor and bachelorette parties. Bobby, known for being a good-time guy, was having a blowout with his boys and Maya was having a grown-woman slumber party.

It was midnight when she had the brilliant idea of crashing the bachelor party. She knew that it would be strippersville, but who cared? She was secure enough at this point that the sight of her man dancing with a tasseled woman wouldn't undo her. However, when she, Athena and her girls barged into Bobby's hotel suite and pushed past his boys expecting laughs and giggles, the sight of her drunken man in a back bedroom, pants-down with a naked stripper was cataclysmic.

"What am I doing here?" Big Rob/Bobby asked now. "Working! This is my *job.* Luckily I was able to find one after you got me fired. What are you doing here? Settin' me up again?"

It was him. The Ex. The man who wasn't supposed to even exist A.B.B. (After the Big Breakup). But here he was. He who deferred her dream. Interrupting. Interrupting "it." This was uninvited fusion. This was bad synchronicity. Sucky syncopation. Dissonance. This was Miles Davis' "You're Under Arrest."

"Fired? I don't know what you're talking about," Maya said. "Jackass."

"Yeah, right," whatever-his-name-was-now said. "This is ridiculous. I feel like I'm in some comedy flick. How did you move from peace poems to Hustla?"

"First of all, Maya's business ain't your business," Athena said.

"Thank you." Maya could count on her girl to have her back.

"Second of all, Maya doesn't know you got fired. That was a gift from me."

"What are you talking about, Athena?" Maya asked.

"A lil' maid of honor revenge. That's driving your white Bronco, Maya—all over his smug face. I called his bosses at Dreadz Entertainment and told them that I had a tip that he was planning to rob them."

"Athena!" Maya sank onto the bed.

"Get it rob, Big Rob." Athena laughed sadistically.

"I don't have time for these games. It took me a long time to get my career back." He looked over at Maya. "Lucy, call off Ethel, please, so we can talk."

"What is there to talk about?" Maya and Athena asked almost in simulcast.

"Two sides, Maya. You hate me? Well, you know what? I hate you too!"

"Twelve," Maya said. "The number of weeks I stayed in my bed too humiliated to see anybody." He was mathematical. She needed to speak his frigging language.

"Don't do this, Maya." He hated a scene.

"Eight. The number of layers on the deluxe red velvet cake that my parents shipped all the way from Tobago." Maya stood up.

"Your parents hated me from jump. Seriously, Maya. You didn't really want to marry me." Rob looked at Maya without looking into her eyes.

"I'm not letting you off the hook. Everybody said to confront you, but I didn't want to hear your dumb-ass whys, Bobby."

"Confront me? Maya, I tried to call you for six months. You never once even answered."

"For what? It's not like you were gonna say, 'I'm a complete dickhead.' " Men never said that. Nobody did. Instead their actions shouted: You do not complete me. You didn't have me at hello. I'm not that into you. And women still kept going. Women like Athena. And her mother. Women like Maya. And her mother. Casting pearls before swine. She hadn't needed to hear his whys. Until now. "Why did you do it?"

"Maya, I don't know what happened. I was drunk and . . ."

"That made it okay for a stripper to give you a blow job at your bachelor party the night before our wedding?"

"Maya, I just . . ." he began again, not looking at all like he could finally explain.

"Seven—the number of words in your enlightened explanation when I busted your lame ass on the spot," Maya continued.

Athena counted out on her fingers: "I'm/just/sorry/Maya/what/can/I/say. Eight. Eight words."

"Scars or scabs, Maya?" he asked.

"Three," Maya said. "The number of bridesmaids who asked me to pay them back."

"Maya, you claimed you loved me but you treated my music, my art, my soul, like it was a hobby I needed to outgrow—and now you're here doing this? You did nothing but disrespect my whole flow."

"So it's my fault?" Maya couldn't believe her ears. "That's what you waited all this time to say?"

"But you didn't even give me a chance. Yeah, I screwed up, but you treated me like I was the devil."

Maya shook her head. "Wrong. I would have more respect for the devil. At least he would be straight up."

"Y'all both have the same martyr complex." Athena sat on the bed.

"Oh—I'm sorry," Maya, said. "I didn't realize you went to Harvard to become a grimy rapper. I didn't realize your stupid plan until I'd already wasted three years."

"Wasted? Oh yeah, we definitely should have gotten married. And you spent four years at Oberlin and every other school in Ohio to become Jezebitch?"

Maya, who never wanted to hurt a living thing, could not move an inch or she would have punched him directly in his big effing nose.

"Okay. Okay. Stop!" Athena didn't like the road this was taking. "We're not gonna blow our big break behind some Bobby mess. We're here for the same reason you are, my man. To do the damn thing and to get paid."

Rob patted his pockets like he was looking for something. "Maya, did my leaving you drive you to this?"

"You arrogant, cowardly . . ." Maya searched for the right word.

"Dickhead?" Athena volunteered.

"What happened to wanting to make a difference?" he asked.

"Don't worry. *We* have a plan," Maya said.

Athena was over the whole soap opera. "So you gonna snitch or not, B?"

"This is ridiculous. How am I supposed to manage Little Miss Muffet as a rapper?"

Low blow. Maya hated being doubted by anyone, most of all this bastard. "I got the contract, right? You doubting Shell's word? Could hip-hop be wrong?" she asked, trying to add a little Jezebel to her flow.

Athena held her hands up in her rap stance.

"The road from poetry to hip-hop is a short one, loser
Poor baby Bobby is scared of Maya 'cause he used her
Now Maya's living large and she's on top
Playing this game we call hip-hop—HEY!"

She threw her hands into Bobby's face.

"She needs to be the one with the deal," Rob said.

"Thank you, Bobby. She got the deal with my lyrics." The words escaped before Athena could stifle them. Maya cut her with her eyes.

"Big Rob," he corrected. "Shell was just looking for a reason to cancel that garbage competition anyway because it was all Ozzie Marvelous' idea."

"You know what, Bobby?" Maya asked. "You want to tell Shell? Go for it! I dare you. I double dare you!"

"Good. I will." He was still standing there.

"You evicted me from my life." Might as well get it all out now. She would probably never see him again. "We were supposed to live happily ever after, you prick. Ass." She was running out of curses and she wanted to use them all.

"Fine. Run home to your perfect parents and lament about how that grimy rapper ruined your life."

"Again," Maya completed as Rob stormed out. He tried to slam the door, but hotel doors are weighted and it took its sweet time closing as Maya yelled curses through the crack.

"Are you crazy?" Athena asked. "On mission. We need to stay on mission." Athena was right. Like it or not, the stupid path this life diverged through could lead them to more than anything they could find back home.

Athena went to the door. "Bobby!"

"Big Rob," Maya reminded her

"I mean, Big Rob! Maya says come back. Please." Athena ran down the hall, pulled Rob back in and elbowed Maya.

"You're right." Maya spoke in a monotone. "Athena should have a deal. Not me. We're working on it. The plan is for Shell to see her performing as my hype woman and in the studio. Please." Apologizing to him, even pseudo apologizing, was making her physically ill. How cool would it be if she threw up on him? He had shaved his locks. She looked at his face. He had the nerve to still be handsome. When people did ugly things the acts should carve mementos right on their faces.

"She's eatin', we all eatin'," Athena pointed out.

Rob looked at Maya and tried not to soften. "You're still beautiful. Even in that costume." He took off his crisp blue Yankees baseball cap and sat on the bed. "You know, Maya," he began.

"Cleopatra," she corrected.

"Cleopatra? Jezebel? Maya, this is crazy. This is not the life for somebody like you. Hip-hop is gully. Sex, thugs and rock and roll."

" 'This ain't me, it's what you made me. Now I'm slapping you back with the same crap you gave me.' Salt-n-Pepa," Maya said. Athena was impressed. Rob was not. He wasn't one to let a fight die. Problem #17 in their relationship.

"Same crap you gave me, Maya."

"Cleopatra, Bobby."

"Big Rob, Cleopatra," he said. They shook on it and abruptly dropped hands. "Cleopatra?"

"That's the name I came up with. I never heard of Jezebel until today."

Rob studied her face. "You're definitely not what I pictured when we created Jezebel."

"Exactly," Athena added her two cents, startling both Maya and Rob, who had forgotten she was there.

Rob straightened up. "Well, we can't change it. Shell has plans in place for branding and imaging. And they were great ideas until it turned out our Jezebel is you." Rob knocked on his head with both fists. He looked like a madman. "I can't believe this. Okay. Give us three, four months of Jezebel. Then we'll announce that you're changing your name and your image to Queen Cleopatra. That'll be hot and we can put out the kinda work I'm sure we all wanna make."

"I don't know what three months of Jezebel means," Maya said. She hated that he still was not *seeing* her.

Rob turned and pressed both palms against the window like he was considering jumping. He spoke to the skyline. "You need to be up on this. Your album is dropping in three months."

Her album. Maya hadn't considered the fact that she could have an album.

"Look—we're meeting tomorrow to discuss this anyway," he said.

"Tomorrow? No one gave me a schedule." Maya tried to make him look at her by sheer will. Now, unleashed, she wanted to force him to deal with her.

Rob spoke to the wall. "All of your time is ours. That little check card you received today says so."

"Oh. So, uh, you don't rap anymore?" Maya was suddenly curious about his life.

"Nah. I figured it was time to grow up. I'm just managing acts now." Rob wasn't prepared to stroll down memory lane. "Fine—fuck it! Let's play charades!" he said suddenly.

"Fine! And stop fucking cursing!" Maya screamed.

Athena put her fist up. This was where she wanted to get them to.

Maya put her fist to Athena's.

Rob added his. "One slipup. You so much as stutter or trip on stage and I'm going straight to Shell. No lip-synching on my team. This is real life for me. Not some school play."

Maya was making a deal with her true devil. She closed her eyes and took a breath. She felt like a stray poodle.

"You know, it was messed up that Pimp called y'all bitches. And he doesn't even know you. But because I do know you, I can say with true candor, *bitches*!"

"Fuuuuck you!" Maya screamed, giving him an old-fashioned playground eye roll and double middle fingers that she hadn't picked up from the fancy school until Athena got there. She had never yelled that hard. Her eyeballs hurt but it felt good. He walked out on her and slammed the door to her heart. Again.

Breathe.

Breathe.

Breathe.

"That went well," said Athena.

Maya looked at her like she was crazy.

"Keep your enemies closer," she explained.

This anger was inspiring something new in Maya. "Aaaaaaaaaaaaaah!" She screamed again. She was no longer the wounded bird who spent months bawling. "Aaaaaaaaaaaaaah!" The caged bird too scared to audition for *Princess Ida* in eighth grade. "Aaaaaaaaaaaaaah!" She was no longer the toad glad to bask in his glow. Or anyone's.

"I never wanted to be this!" Maya massaged her temples.

"Be what?" Athena sat on the bed, reaching for the tissue box. Maya shook her head no. She didn't need it. She wasn't crying.

"An angry black bitch. I avoided this like the plague my whole life." But here she was. Angry, black and bitchy. It was redundant. And it was a relief. A release. Catharsis. If anger was the laxative needed to get rid of Bobby's crap, so be it. "You know what? Let's play this charade out," the newly angry black bitch said. "I'm killing two birds with one beautiful stone. After what he did he has the nerve to have an attitude with me?"

"Word!" Athena needed no new incentive to be angry or bitchy.

"Mofo talking 'bout *he* hates *me?!*"

"Word!" Athena was a one-woman amen choir.

"You know what?!" Preacher Maya stood up.

"What?" Athena knew that this was gonna be good.

"I'm going to make him fall back in love with me. It'll keep him from snitching *and* teach him a lesson," Maya announced. Athena was quiet. Drinking it all in. This was good. And big. And huge. And right.

"Ooooooh. Justice. Now you talking, Shirley!" Athena high-fived the new chick in the room with her.

"But wait, there's more . . ."

"Ginsu knives?" Athena was digging this shift in Mayan energy.

"The minute he says I love you, I'm going to say I'm/just/sorry/Bobby/what/can/I/say?"

"I'm/just/sorry/Bobby/what/can/I/say?"

"I'm/just/sorry/Bobby/what/can/I/say! Eight words."

"You're a genius, Maya. Sorry I ever doubted you."

"When did you doubt me?"

Athena shrugged.

"Love just comes down to his social psychology, really. Question—What does Bobby want? Answer—I fill that hole and *bam* he's in love with me."

"Forget all that. You got the queen of making a man fall in love right here. I'll be your love coach. I may not know how to keep 'em, but hell, I do know how to catch 'em. Ooh—maybe you can even fill another hole."

"Lovely," Maya said. "I need to call my job."

"You said the brother was packing. And you haven't had none since . . ."

"I haven't had any since December 4, 2006, 3:43 P.M. Ugh."

"I'd tell you to get help, but that's what I said last time. I still think you should sue that shrink for breach of ethics."

"Yeah well the last thing I want to do is go to court and explain how I got caught up in an affair with my therapist after my fiancé left me at the altar." Maya's nose started bleeding and Athena handed her a tissue from the box she was holding.

"We gotta catch Shell before he breaks for Dubai, Maya. Ready to bowl?"

"Don't you mean Cleopatra, Miss Thang? Pimp was okay-looking too. Too bad he was an asshole."

"Go 'head. Branch out, girl. He's definitely not your usual cup of tea."

"Assholes are not a branch out for me." Maya went to her suitcase.

"And maybe the rumors aren't true. He didn't look that pink."

"Pink?" Maya found her brush and tried to work it through her hair.

"Yeah. Brokeback. That's what brought him down. Manifesta said he was homo-thuggin it on the radio."

"Mm. If he was homo-thuggin it, it wasn't on the radio." Maya caught a glimpse of herself and she liked what she saw. Maybe it was all the deal-cutting of the past few days. Maybe it was the dim hotel lighting. "I am a magnificent creature," she said and for the first time, she kinda believed it. "No more sleepwalking. I got this." She would stop being a queen deferred. There had to be a space somewhere where she was enough. Freed from the cage of her own making, it was time to sing.

"Let's party." Maya said. "I hope the music is loud."

Notebook

of

Moxie

THE DARE EXPERIMENT
HIP-HOP UNDERCOVER
BY MAYA GAYLE HOPE

NOTEBOOK OF MOXIE

Moxie is courage. In hip-hop they sometimes call it "ballin' " or "being 'bout it."

Moxie means facing adversity with spirit. If male-warrior energy is about slaying the dragon, then female-warrior energy can be about taking the bull by the horns. Both genders should indulge in both energies.

Truth or Dare is the perfect metaphor for life. When we dare to live our truth, we are unafraid of the consequences of our choices. The dare challenges us to live bigger, to be bigger.

I AM MOXIE

I am a fifth-century warrior who will dress in drag as a man,
This is my plan,
Sword first in bloody battles to represent my ailing father.
And together, we go farther. I am.

I am a queen who can single-handedly run Egypt,
Properly equipped,
To keep two Roman rulers at bay to protect my people.
No need to ask if I'm your equal. I am.

I am a small woman with a smaller gun—
And yes I have already won—
I run a people railroad and bust a shot in anybody's ass who will block my
Freedom. Freedom. Freedom. An army of one. I am.

I am a unibrowed, multisexual, multitalented, artist—
Yo, you didn't start this—
Who is not afraid to be ahead of my time and yours.
I open closed doors. I am.

I am a Like a Virgin, but not really gal—
With, uh, MANY pals—who struts my stuff forcing you to
Deal with my attitude, sexuality and controversial version of the truth.
I taught you more than Dr. Ruth. I am.

I am a billionaire who did not allow too black, too fat, too much
As such
To stand in the way of me creating a quiet riot in living rooms worldwide.
Come and stand by my side. I am.

MOXIE DECLARATION: (Repeat five times every morning, noon and night to reinforce your moxie.) *In this moment, I have the moxie required to embrace a life of possibilities.* I have the moxie to live my truth. Not my mother's truth, not my father's truth, not my mate's truth, not my friends' truth or my boss's truth, but *my* truth. *Today I dare to take risks. I dare to step outside of my boundaries. Today I dare to become the me that I have always known myself to be, and I dare to dream bigger than I ever thought possible. Anything can happen, so I dare.*

MOXIE ACTION STEP: *Speak up or stand up for yourself immediately whenever you feel violated. SO many times we don't want to hurt the other person's feelings. Give yourself the same care and consideration.*

Chapter 10

"WHEN A NEW FRIEND ASKED THE OTHER DAY
IF I'D EVER BEEN IN LOVE, I SAID WITHOUT HESITATION,
NO. 'CUZ YOU KNOW? FUCK HIM.
AND HIS FUCKING MIRRORS AND SMOKE.
DOES HE DESERVE A PLACE IN MY HISTORY?"
—*dream hampton*

Where are we headed?" Maya asked Legba (complicated bereavement), their driver(!).

"Uppa Uppa Uppa West Side." About eighty blocks later the sixty-something West Indian gentleman pulled up in front of an unmarked, polished blue-and-gray glass high rise on 122nd Street. No signs. Legba, who it seemed gave info only on a need-to-know basis, explained, "Dis is the uptown Heretix Hotel and Residence, ya punishment for leaving the room downtown." And with that, the curt and kindly grandfather snapped his head back around face front to finish parking the ride, a sizzling onyx Bentley with a burgundy interior.

Athena explained the nouveau riche politics of the car. "You don't get it, Maya. This is big BALLIN!"

"The Flying B. I get it." Maya pressed her face against the illegally tinted glass like a six-year-old. No better way to shake off the shock of seeing Bobby than the newness of luxury. "This is Harlem?"

"Ya mon. What you tink? Dis is Harlem." Legba was completely exasperated although this was the first time Maya had asked the question. He was already through with her when she mistakenly guessed that his accent was Jamaican rather than Guyanese. "No Caribbean wants to be Jamaican except Jamaicans," he said.

"If this is punishment, then why do anything right?" Athena asked and rightfully so as several smartly dressed male handlers in tailored dark gray uniforms emerged from the boutique hotel to welcome them and their bags.

"More supermodels," Maya noted. "Except these are chocolate."

"And tasty," added Athena.

"The Heretix Uptown looks even better than Heretix Times Square!" The double doors formed a golden glowing super-sexy entry "H," and its sidewalk was even paved with gold-colored bricks. Before Maya and Athena could gather themselves, Legba made it from his seat to open their door on the opposite side with the spryness of a much younger man.

"Thanks, Legba." Maya stepped out of the car to orchestrate the bag handlers.

"At home all you ever hear about Harlem is that it's not the place to be caught with your purse open," Athena said.

"And that in the twenties and thirties there was an artistic renaissance," Maya explained to a polite-faced young man who wore the placid look of a servant who couldn't care less what you might have to say but wanted to preserve his tip.

"Yes, ma'am!" Polite Face exclaimed.

"Dis is the new Harlem," Legba announced and adjusted the crisp lapels on his driver's uniform.

Polite Face explained that Maya and Athena would be kicking it one level below the penthouse suite overlooking Morningside Park, which "looks like crap in person but is mad elegant from thirty-three stories up."

Maya counted bags and handlers to make sure it all matched up. "We'll be right back, Legba." She leaned in to Athena, "You have singles? Fodor's said that overtipping in New York is a must."

"Gratuities have been taken care of, miss." Legba moved closer to the car. "Let's get going."

"Yeah but we just need to freshen up before the parteeee," Athena said as if she were already there and on her fifth tequila. She danced her flat butt on the Bentley to accent her favorite word. "Parteee!"

"No time now, miss. Thirty-five full minutes I wait for you two at Heretix midtown. There is a schedule."

"We'll be fast, Legba. Just a quick spin in the mirror," Maya said.

Legba opened the back door and held it. "I'm sorry, miss." That was that. Maya cast Athena a dirty look and Athena made her apology face. They were headed forward in their new ride with their driver. *Their driver.*

The thought of it was so absurd that Maya looked at Athena and they both let a good laugh rip. Maya leaned into Athena again with serious eyebrows. "Pardon me, miss, but do you have any Grey Poupon?"

"No," Athena replied, falling right in, "but are those Bugle Boy jeans that you're wearing?"

"Onward, Jeeves!" Maya made a flourish with her hand and they burst into another fit of giggling.

"Excuse me, miss?" Legba adjusted his review mirror.

Maya straightened up. "Uh, nothing, sir. Thank you, Legba—Mr. Legba." Even though she was in her thirties, good West Indian girls didn't call an elder full-mouthed like that.

Legba nodded. He'd seen this before.

"Athena, are you sure we're not overdressed for bowling?" Maya picked out her freshly washed 'fro with her hands, checking for matts and wannabe dreads.

"Perfecto." Athena powdered her face then Maya's on the short ride.

Maya and Athena were both wearing tight jeans and tank tops. Athena's white top was a bit skimpier than Maya's. Athena never wanted to look like she was trying too hard, so her beauty rule was either full makeup with casual clothes *or* full diva clothes with a "natural" face—foundation, powder, eyes and cheeks only. What? That *was* natural for Athena. Maya's top was navy with wider straps and worn over a bright green turtleneck with a granny flower pin for accent. They both carried Athena's fake Dior bags, the Gaucho Calfskin and the Gaucho Python. Real version: $4,535 for the python alone at Neiman Marcus. Athena's versions: Sixty-two buckeroos and a date with Davio the local bootlegger.

"Harlem Lanes," a banner announced as they pulled up to 126th Street and Adam Clayton Powell Boulevard. "Anything else is just bowling." Another sign threatened, "*Glow in the Dark Extreme Bowling.*" New Harlem. Epic style. Athena gave herself and Maya the once-over as they rode up in the nondescript elevator.

"I can hang with bowling. It's the one sport I'm actually good at. I just hope I can get a good crouch in these jeans." Maya bounced and squatted, showing off her bowling arm.

"Oh yeah. Weren't you and Bobby in a league?" Athena looked up from her compact to see why Maya wasn't responding.

The elevator doors had opened to reveal bowling unlike any they'd ever experienced. Shell's "little get-together" to welcome Maya turned out to be practically a red carpet event. Who knew what this bowling alley usually looked like, but tonight the place was a lush indoor garden with hot pink accents. Tea candles everywhere illuminated a gorgeous rainbow of faces as a beat kept the crowd rocking. Jeez.

In the Faustus, Ohio, Bowlerama, as in the rest of the world, bowling meant polyester and other nonbreathable fabrics, lighting the color of boogers, butt crack exposure of the un-appealing sort, smelly shoes that were a hotbed for athlete's foot, Cheez Doodle breath and ambiguous hot dogs made from Grade D meats. Not in New Harlem. Here, bowling had the ambitious face of *Black Vogue*. Post-hip leather couches. A zillion flat-screen TVs. The female DJ from that music TV show spinning a medley of Camp Hustla's greatest hits. Posturing dudes doing the flyboy lean and gyrating girls gone wild. Mod model chicks in high-heel bowling shoes. High-heel bowling shoes?! There were about twenty-four competition-ready lanes that people just stood in or danced around. Two men dressed in loincloths opened faux gates.

Maya elbowed Athena. "This is sacrilegious to the sport!"

"I'm glad we added a little shine!" Athena did her cleavage adjustment thing. Her padded push-up filled out the sides with cushioning so that you could front with your scant boobies in the middle.

Maya laughed nervously. "I'm bowled over." She made a gun with her thumb and index finger and fired it at her head. "Pow."

As it was billed by Shell as "a little dinner and bowling," Maya had wanted to keep her look simple. Then, considering her seduce Bobby/ Rob plan, she went with Athena's make-an-entrance strategy. Thank the goddess.

"Maya, isn't that the guy from—"

"Yup," answered Maya as the handsome young star known for helping homegirl get her groove back danced by with his equally stunning wife. Maya and Athena hesitated by the entrance checking out the beautiful people from the worlds of music, TV and film.

Sahara glided by in a gaggle of other ten-foot-tall beauties. "Ohh. Hey—Sahara!" Athena called. "Sahara!"

Sahara looked back and squinted like she had never seen Maya or Athena before in her life. She looked extra bored and threw them a generic greeting obviously reserved for her fans—"Toodles!"—as she held up a peace sign.

"Toodles," Maya and Athena echoed but Sahara was already across the room talking to that troll-faced rapper turned reality star.

"This is crazy. What are we supposed to do?"

"I got your back," Athena said.

"Look." Maya nodded toward a flock of people with cameras. Photographers were sprinkled throughout the spot, and a clump of them hung in one area.

"Don't worry, dude. We look cute. You got your own style. I watch entertainment TV. I got us." Athena waved at one of the reporters. He smiled and waved back. "See?"

"Yes! This is a grand adventure. It's all just an experiment," Maya told herself very loudly.

"Yeah. And aren't you a magnificent creature?" Athena rubbed Maya's back like a cat. She arched.

"Bonjour, buongiorno, hola!" Luci circled through Maya and Athena like they were a two-person *Soul Train* line. "Welcome to Hollyhood!" Luci's multi-lingual greeting sounded so cosmopolitan. She wore a very un-bowling bright green flouncy cocktail dress with a matching flower in her short hair. She kissed Maya graciously on each cheek and then acknowledged Athena with a head nod. "Hey! Here's the woman

of the hour, everybody. Jezebel!" she announced kind of generally. Folks in the immediate vicinity turned around for a moment then kept on doing whatever chic thing they were doing.

Maya checked to see if the elevator was waiting. It wasn't. "This is how you bowl in New York?"

"You're stomping with the big dogs now, but don't let the glitterati scare you." Luci took Maya by the crook of her arm. Athena followed, eyeing Luci suspiciously. "Let's do your step and repeat before you sit down. I'm surprised Big Rob didn't meet you at the door. That's not like him." Luci looked toward the back. He was nowhere in sight.

"Yeah, well . . . What's step and repeat?" Maya asked as Luci steered them over to the clump of photogs. Maya noticed that the men couldn't take their eyes off of Luci.

Luci moved her arm up and down in front of Maya. "Your outfit?"

Maya wasn't sure if this was a question or a statement. "Yes?"

"I dressed her." Athena overenunciated like she was teaching Luci manners.

"You did the best you could so don't worry about it, Agatha."

"Athena," Athena and Maya corrected. Luci smoothed Maya's hair and adjusted her top. Athena pursed her lips.

"Well, from now on, when your stylist isn't here I'm in charge of your look." Luci deposited Maya in front of a Camp Hustla–logoed wallpaper wall and red carpet photo area, leaving Athena on the sidelines. She pulled a little folder of rice papers out of her green Chanel lambskin clutch and blotted Maya's face. "Flawless," she said. "Absolutely beautiful. And with no professional makeup or anything. Most stars can't say that."

This was the sweetest thing Maya could remember anyone ever saying to her. "Thank you, Luci. I needed that."

"Well, it's true. Nervous?"

Maya nodded.

"Remember, it's your party—you can cry if you want to," Luke said.

Maya gave Luci a big hug. "Whew. It's hot."

"Heat hot or Hilton hot?" Luci asked.

"Heat hot."

"Lights. Usually, we'd test your outfit to make sure it's flash-proof . . . among other things. Suck it in," Luci added and stepped back. "Jezebel!" she announced. For about sixty seconds, Maya was literally a deer in headlights, er, flashbulbs. *Click. Click. Click.* Awkward, silly and glamorous. *Click. Click. Click.* Dazzling. Lame-o poses. Pretentious and vain. *Click. Click. Click.* I'm too sexy for my shirt. Too sexy for my shirt. So sexy it hurts. She tried not to chuckle. *Très difficile* when you're sucking in.

"Marvelous. Give us tough, Jezebel," called out Luci. Maya felt like the least tough sista on the planet. Luci scowled and flexed as an example. Okay, maybe she was the second least gangsta, Maya crossed her arms like an old Run-D.M.C. poster and heard Athena's voice laughing back.

"Oh! Athena, come on . . ." Maya pulled Athena's hand.

Luci spun around. "W-wait. What's going on?" She had moved her eyes for one second to flirt with a handsome white photographer. She seemed annoyed with herself that she'd let her new charge out of her focus for one minute.

"Oh, Athena's my hype woman so I thought it would be cool for us to get some pictures together."

"This is press. Not some family album. They don't care about . . . entourage." Luci looked Athena up, down, then up again. Athena sucked in, poked out her mini boobs and smiled. "No."

"Bitch," Athena said under her breath.

"Pardon?" asked Luci.

"Delish, I said."

"Be right back." Luci stepped out and into a conversation.

Athena looked around and quickly stepped in. "Let's do it, Maya." Athena took Maya's hand and they pose, pose, posed up a storm. "I was born for this," whispered Athena. "We were born for this. Remember the winter formal?"

"Yes! The Roger Rabbit." Maya did a silly shimmy and tripped on her heels. Athena turned her butt to the camera.

Luci gave a little yelp. She stepped back in and held up a hand. "Thank you. That'll be all today." Luci again took Maya by the crook of the arm.

"Sorry," said Maya.

Luci gave Athena a stern look. "Just a cold run. We won't even release those. How much fun was that?"

"I know. Athena is a natural." Maya turned around. "Athena?" Athena was following behind.

"Don't worry. We'll work on your poses and everything. Shell and Big Rob like baptism by fire," Luci said. They approached a brightly lit, elevated area enclosed by velvet ropes. Luci nodded and a peon dressed in black opened the station. "Your seat, milady." Maya, then Athena stepped up into the banquette. "Oh—there's Big Rob," Rob, Shell and Pimp stood together. "The trinity of cool," Luci declared.

Maya bit her tongue.

"I'm so glad you're here, Jezebel. Be right back." Luci smoothed her scant bangs back.

"Wait, Luci, shouldn't we go say hello to Shell?" Athena asked.

Luci directed her answer to Maya. "No dear heart, we will all come to you. Let me grab Rob. Tardy, tardy. Not a good look for a manager." Luci scampered off. Rob saw her approaching and smiled.

"Bitch," Athena said again, tucking her legs underneath her.

"Aw, I think she's sweet." Maya saw Bob—er, Big Rob—distinctly not notice her. Sitting with flamboyant Athena in the too-tight pants in a too-big, too-bright VIP booth, the only way not to notice her was on purpose. Luci embraced him as Shell and Pimp left them alone. "You think they're screwing?" Maya asked.

"Definitely." Athena looked at Maya. "Sorry."

"I think that the three of us are wearing more clothes than anyone here." Maya took a Bellini from a waiter reaching up into their area. She downed it as Athena was still taking hers off of his gold tray.

"You drinking?" asked Athena.

"Absolutely," said Maya. "In fact, I could use another drink."

"Who you telling?" Athena agreed as they grabbed two backup

Cosmos from another server. A waitress or Playboy Bunny, depending on who you asked, walked by with a tray of chocolate strawberries.

"Wait!!" called Maya in a way she was sure was very gauche. A couple of boho types looked over like they had just heard the yelp of a fishwife. However, her blood sugar was crashing and she didn't care. "More please." Maya and Athena gathered all of the gourmet berries from the server's tray and put them on the napkins on their table.

Chica rolled her eyes. "We make several rounds you know."

Maya popped a whole berry into her mouth. "To us," she toasted, mouth full. They watched that annoying sitcom buffoon and his equally untalented brother slap the bunny-ish waitress on the ass. "Member *Let's Make a Deal*?"

Athena sat up on her heels to see all the drama better. It made her tank top rise up in the front. She smiled at the unexpected benefit. "I think so."

"I'm living it. Next, the champagne girl is gonna show me door number three, asking deal or no deal."

"So make a deal with yourself then. A promise just for Maya."

"Hmmm. There's a thought. No more arrangements, assurances, agreements, pacts, pledges, promises, dares, deals, covenants, contracts, transactions or treaties." For the next twenty-four she was not gonna think about the dare that became a pact with Athena and how she somehow *still* ended up facing its dreaded consequence. She was not going to meditate on the assurance they'd be here only a few days that would turn into months. Her mind couldn't even go near the development deal she'd inked in blood with Shell. She especially didn't wanna touch the treaty she'd shook on with Bobby—his promise that he'd eventually trade Jezebel for Cleopatra—and her diabolical vow to make him fall back in love with her.

Maya rubbed her strawberry-stained fingers on a matching napkin. "Okay. I promise myself that for the next twenty-four hours my only objective is fun. Fun. The word even tastes good." Of all the pledges she'd made in the past few days, she struck her favorite bargain as the tart berry juice embraced her tongue.

"Bet. Well, I promise me that I'm going to couple with some of

New York's finest." Athena leaned back and crossed her legs as they watched two fiiine brothas walk by. "Not them. Married. Wanna bet?"

"Girl, I dunno. No more negotiating or figuring anything out. Or betting. My only goal is to eat another chocolate strawberry. I'm taking a break from the divine comedy of my life." Maya held up another berry.

"Here here." Athena clinked her berry to Maya's. "Girl, look where we are. From my words. My hard work. Finally."

"Yeah . . . I know! You're gifted, Athena." Maya thought about the fact that Athena's words had nothing to do with it.

"Thank you, babygirl." Athena made smooth movements to pay tribute to Maya's dancing. "It was a team effort. Damn. What if . . . what if this is it? No more struggling."

"We are at a party with Pimp and Shell the Boy Wonder on their dime, chilling. Better get ready. This *is* it." Maya sounded surer than she was. "Hello, life. I'm Maya. Great to meet you."

"Yeah. It's been a while. I can't wait to get in the studio. Oh no, Maya. Behind you."

Several hoodlum types were grandstanding: doing cartwheels, crashing into things and causing a ruckus. Pimp was with them and the photogs were loving it. Maya turned back around. "Takes all kinds."

"That's Pimp's group, Black Death—you know, Thug's old crew. The hottest group on your label. They all met when they were kids in group home."

"The one with the goatee is cute too."

"He's not one of them. He must be part of BD Fam, their affiliates."

"*They* have affiliates? Pimp looks like the most sane one. Why was he locked up again?"

"He was hopped up on something and tried to rob a drugstore with a toy gun."

"Nice."

"The twins, Nigg and Gunz; Kronic; plus Pimp makes up Black Death."

"You can say that again. Literally." Rob was finally checking Maya out. He stood solo near an empty lane. She kicked Athena.

"Stick out your breasts and hike up your skirt. Show him what you working with."

"I'm wearing jeans."

"Exactly. Treat your jeans like you're wearing a skirt. He'll see what you want him to see."

"You're right. With Bobby's psychological profile, he wants a woman he can rescue. Especially from being immoral."

"Psychological profile, Maya? All men want a lady in the street and a freak in the bed. Flaunt that booty!" Athena tossed her napkin to the floor and Maya bent down to pick it up, accidentally knocking her purse onto the floor. As the music went low Maya crawled around trying to recapture her junk: lip goo, loose change, airplane ticket stubs, tampon, antibacterial wipes and hand cleanser.

A spotlight went up on the female DJ dressed in head-to-toe Eddie Murphy '80s red leather. "Here ye, here ye, people. Y'all havin a good time?"

"Yeah!" the crowd shouted.

"Taking hip-hop back to hip-hop, DJ Manifesta's on the ones and twos. I'm shoutin' out the lady of the hour."

"Uh-oh, Maya, I think . . ." Athena tapped Maya on the back.

"What?" Maya was under the table chasing a quarter.

"The latest MC on the Camp Hustla label," Manifesta continued.

"Maya." Athena tapped her again.

"What? Gimme a sec!" Maya hated to be rushed.

"The lethal, the lovely Jezebel!" finished Manifesta.

The Klieg spotlight swung around just in time to catch Maya, ass up, scrambling after a tampon. A laugh went around the room as she caught what was happening and tried to hoist herself quickly back up to the bench. She sat down, squashing a choco-berry, and crossed her legs. A video camera captured the whole thing, for posterity. Maya waved Grace Kelly style, the only thing she could think to do. The Klieg and table brights shut off abruptly, leaving her and Athena sitting in pink candlelight.

"Nice. More like Jeze-Ass. Great." Maya touched her face to see if it was actually as hot as she felt.

"I don't think anybody noticed." Athena saw Bobby looking in their direction. He was either laughing or grimacing. "Except your ex." Athena wet a napkin in the drink on the table and handed it to Maya who tried unsuccessfully to scrape the brownish reddish blotch from the right cheek of her jeans with the alcohol.

Maya took a chocolate stick from another passing bunny and gave it a slow blow job, staring at Rob. She took a hard bite and he definitely grimaced. She threw the stick on the table.

Athena laughed. "Bad girl, Maya!"

Spotlight back on DJ Manifesta: "It's all good, Jezebel. I know y'all remember this from back in the day . . ." The music came up loud. "Doin the butt, sexy, sexy . . ." Laughter traveled around the room as people gyrated their backsides to the retro hit.

"Great," said Maya.

"DJ Manifesta's word is law. If she says it's all good, it's all good."

Pimp approached and waved the video camera back over. "Pimp," he declared. He spoke more to the cam than to them. "Glad y'all bitches could make it."

"Uh, I'm not a bitch," said Maya.

Athena smiled at Pimp. "That's right, she's your label-mate. A man as fine as you shouldn't even come off like that." Athena's charismatic finesse softened Pimp around the edges.

"Aw baby, don't take it like that." He actually looked hurt.

A tall, light-skinned dude with freckles and ruddy gray hair walked up holding two martini glasses. His face was much younger than his premature gray. "More Cosmos?" The male Athena deposited the drinks on the table. "I'm Rocky Justice, entertainment attorney."

Pimp gave him the crooked eye. "You sound like an infomercial. Justice Wallace. Entertainment Attorney. Truth. Cash and Lies. Ha-ha."

Dude cracked a smile. "Wassup Pimp. Glad to see you back in Black Death, man. After Thug, you were my favorite."

Pimp gave him a pound and nodded. "Thanks, God."

Mr. Entertainment Attorney (deservability issues) was wearing a blue pinstriped shirt with a blue-black-blue tie, blacker jeans and whiter socks. Ugh. Athena leaned over and whispered to Maya. "Don't worry. I'll take him shopping later."

The lawyer kissed Maya's hand and then looked at Athena. "Wanna dance?" He held out his hand like a footman standing next to a pumpkin coach.

Athena looked at Maya and mouthed "Okay?" Maya kind of shrugged while mentally processing. Athena walked away with dude, already chatting up a storm before Maya could reply.

"Athena!" Maya found herself alone with Pimp and the camera. He glared at her. Great. Time for small talk. This should be informative. "So what did your mother name you, Pimp?" Maya tried to channel her inner Jezebel.

"You mean my government name?" Pimp curled his lips up at the corners.

"Okay. No. I mean, what did your mother name you?"

"I killed my moms in a freak accident when I was ten. So what's your thing?" Pimp stepped up into the booth and stood over Maya.

"Poetry, I guess."

Pimp smiled and he somehow didn't seem as predatory. "Yeah? Me too. I used to scribble in the joint. You ain't what I pictured for Jezebel." Pimp took Maya's hand, pulled her up and started grinding on her. Ewwww. WTF? He looked over at the camera. She started to shove him away when she noticed Rob rushing over. Ah. She held Pimp tight to play up the show. "That's right," he said. "Come to Daddy."

Big Rob tapped Pimp on the shoulder. "Yo Pimp—Maybe we better get ready. Tomorrow's a long day."

"Nah, chief, we good. Right, Jezebel?" She liked the sound of Jezebel coming from Pimp's too black for his brown color lips. Jezebel sounded like a very bad girl.

"Yeah, we good. If we need any managing we'll text you, Big Rob."

"C'mon, dance for me, baby." Pimp put his hands on Maya's hips. She felt like a fish on a bicycle.

Just for the benefit of playing Bobby, and for her experiment, she wanted to play her position but she couldn't. She took a step back with her hands on Pimp's shoulders. They looked like they were learning to waltz. Rob smirked.

"I don't dance," Maya whispered to Pimp.

"Word? So you want to come to my room?" Pimp asked, looking at the video camera. Maya giggled suggestively, eyeing you-know-who. Rob gave the camera a cut signal and walked away with the camera person following.

Maya dropped her arms. "No thanks, Pimp."

"Cool, Jez," Pimp said, falling back. He walked over to where the camera was and danced with the paper skirt girl from the audition. Groupie. How'd she get here?

Okayyy. Maybe this was a great opportunity to meet new people and think about her infiltration. Except for the fact that no one looked remotely interested in getting to know her. In her real life, she eschewed these "tastemakers" as shallow, superficial and materialistic. Here it was all gravy. The Shallows were chatting it up by the café while looking over each other's shoulder to see who might be more interesting. The Superficials, mesmerized by their own images, were adjusting their look in any and every shiny surface. The Materialistics were speaking the loudest to draw attention to their designer threads and luxury car key rings, still in hand. Maya wondered which group Bobby now fit into because the guy she was engaged to would never have even been at this soiree. Then again, neither would she.

Maya filed a mental report of the Top 5 Things You Do When You're Alone at a Club to Indicate That You're Not a Total Loser: (1) Pretend you're on the phone; (2) call people you haven't spoken to in six months; (3) type urgent text messages; (4) scribble the great American novel on a napkin; (5) do an aggressive head nod to the beat.

Athena and homeboy were nowhere in sight. She sat down, found her diamond pen in her faux Dior and scribbled—not the great American novel, poetry or lyrics, but twenty-five tiny squares. *Hip-Hop Party Bingo.* She used to volunteer to call the numbers for the weekly game at Faustus Home for the Aged. And what could be more apropos in a bowling alley?

HIP-HOP PARTY BINGO				
B	I	N	G	O
Ill-Fitting Pants	Massive Cleavage	Reality TV Star	Has Shot Someone	Collagen Overload
One-Hit Wonder	Visible Pantylines	Natural God Given Hair	Aspiring Pimp	Has Been Shot
Platinum Recording Star	Gaudy Jewelry	Needs a Nose Job	Breast Implants	Visible Designer Labels
Skipped High School	Studio Singer	Has a Nose Job	Aspiring Ho	Fake Nails
May Be Carrying a Gun	Big Butt	Blonde Weave	Part-Time Stripper	Natural God Given Face

She easily ticked off the boxes for Blonde Weave, May Be Carrying a Gun and Visible Designer Labels categories. It was the Natural Hair and Natural Face boxes that she was finding challenging.

Maya spied a traffic-free lane. *I'm in a bowling alley. I'll bowl.* That good-looking actress that black people consider Latin and Latinos consider black struck up a convo with that cutie pie soft-spoken Oscar contender. Maya couldn't wait to start her report, Hip-Hop Undercover: The Dare Diaries. It would be rich. She put the napkin in her pocket, cruised the balls and settled for a dusky yellow one with medium weight and good finger holes.

Size up the lane. Align on the last line. Check out the pins. Stance. Eyes on the floor guides. One step, two steps, three steps, crouch and BOWL!

"Jezebel, *what* are you *doing*!" Luci was coming toward her at the same speed that the ball was barreling down the lane.

"Ohhh!" Maya's ball only lopped two pins off the side. "Uh, bowling?"

Luci was aghast. "Why on earth are you doing *that*?"

"Because this is a bowling alley?"

"Um, let's sit down right now."

"Why?"

"Because someone might see us. See you. Bowling. That can't be good for your nails either."

"I don't have any nails." Maya nodded toward a group of fourteen-year-old hipsters. "And look. They're bowling."

"Those juvenile celebutards are not our kind of people. See the guy over there with Shell?" It was an older white guy. "That's Ozzie Marvelous. The wizard behind this whole thing. You, me, Shell's whole empire. How do you think he would feel if he saw you . . ." Luci could barely get the word out. "Bowling."

Maya looked over. Ozzie Marvelous turned his head expectantly like Maya had called his name and raised a glass in her direction. He had grooves in the shape of a W on his forehead. The W moved up and down as he laughed. Maya turned back to Luci. "I'm sorry. I just . . . Maybe I should meet him now anyway. There were some issues with—"

"Meet him? You don't just meet Ozzie Marvelous. He won't be interested in meeting you until he feels that you've made some real contribution."

Rob walked up, sans camera. He flexed his bowling arm. "How's that handicap, Jezebel?"

"Rob. Just in time. Perhaps you should keep a better eye out. She was *bowling*." Luci whispered the word as if Maya had been busted publicly masturbating.

"In a bowling alley, egads, Luci. Shocking. Anyway, Shell was looking for you. CEO, AfroDitie, Criminal and the whole Syndicated Music team is here."

"Poseurs. Who invited them?" Luci gave Maya another look. "We need to discuss protocol and image ASAP." Luci trotted off. "MC AfroDitie! Hellooo. Girlfriend, you look marv!" she screamed across the room.

Great. Alone with the Ex.

Rob looked at his glittering watch. "Maya, check out the freaky little corner on the side." Pimp and that paper skirt chick were practically having sex in the middle of the party.

"Ugh. So?" The Bobby she knew would never wear an ice-ice-baby watch like that.

"No, not Pimp. Further back." Rob pointed with two fingers like a politician. Maya leaned in. Athena and the infomercial lawyer were getting freaky. She was dancing on his lap and people were cheering them on.

"Oh no!" Maya started to rush over, then stopped. Athena would never forgive her for being that uncool. She paced in a circle, then pulled out her phone. Text: "U R bugging. Ready 2 go." Maya watched Athena stop grinding just long enough to type a message and dive back onto the guy's bump.

"Meet U L8r," came the reply. Athena wasn't the most conservative person in the world, but Maya had never known her to dry hump a Just Met.

"Oh no." Maya looked for Luci. Nowhere. The only person to talk to was the Ex. Frig it. "Bobby—Rob—are these drinks laced with something?" Maya re-sent her original text. No reply.

"Yes!" Rob gripped Maya's arm like they were in a horror film.

"Oh my goddess—Athena—I knew it! What's in them?"

"Money, fame and power, baby girl. It's a long way from Faustus." Rob took a ball and bowled it down the lane. Strike! He made a victory fist and pulled it toward his waist. "Yes! Time to get official. This is a game of gods and monsters. Still think you can hang?"

A spotlight came up on Luci, who was holding a microphone. "Attention, attention everyone."

"Oh, yeah. That's what I came over to tell you." Rob looked sideways at Maya and smiled. Suspicious.

"What?"

Rob nodded toward Luci and Shell as the music went down low.

Shell also had a mic and was standing on a platform. "Yo. Thanks for coming out to informally meet our new artist, Jezebel. Where she at?"

Big Rob waved and a spotlight gleamed their way. Maya smiled, learning to perfect her insta-grin, and waved in a kind of weird salute.

"You gonna kick it right now for us, Jezebel?" Shell asked.

Maya's hand hovered in wave formation. She looked up at it and then registered Shell's words. "Kick it right now?" She shook her head "no" and stomped on Rob's foot. Hard. He winced and shook his head at Shell.

"She was begging me to perform tonight," Shell continued. "But we gotta get her beats in place. That's why she gave us all a big kiss my ass earlier. She's crazy. Off the chain. You'll see her spit soon, though. In fact, you can watch the whole thing unfold in a few months on our hit reality special, *Making of a Star*. Check it out!"

"Reality special?" Maya whispered to Rob. He held out his arms and raised his shoulders.

"Shell." A reporter raised a hand. "Page Six. How can you call a show a hit before it's even shot?"

"You in the world of Camp Hustla, baby. I got the Midas touch." Shell snapped his fingers like the Fonz and both spotlights went out.

Maya crossed her arms. "Reality special? Hellooo. Nobody mentioned that. I'm not sure I'm down with that." She did admire Shell's can't-fail attitude, though.

"Not sure you're down with that? You didn't read your contract?" Rob uncrossed his arms.

Contract? Damn. He always said that she was too hasty. Must request copy of contract. "Oh, that's right!" Maya tried to shrug casually. She didn't want to give Rob the satisfaction of her stupidity.

"Maybe you should just go ahead and quit now, Maya. Cut your losses so we can get somebody with real talent." Rob walked away with a sinister smile. *Game point.*

Where was the exit? She *was* going to quit while she was ahead—the party, not the gig. People eyed her as she jostled her way through the spot in that look but don't look, laughing behind your back way. Just before she hit the elevator a hand grabbed her shoulder. Maya turned around. DJ Manifesta.

"Yo. What up, Jezebel?" Manifesta spoke like a hard dude.

"Hey, Manifesta, thanks for the shout-out. Nice to meet—"

"Nah, chick. Check it. I just gave you a little gloss outta love for Shell and Big Rob and them. New emcees I never heard of gets no respect 'til they prove themselves. And you a female so I'ma be tougher on you."

"Well, I—" Maya started.

"No. Listen up. Don't think you coming on my show or any mic I'm in control of 'til I know what you about. I'm sick of these studio bitches. It ain't about having a pretty face and a man writing your rhymes and your checks. If that's how you rollin' you need to quit right now."

Before Maya could think of what to say Manifesta walked away.

Did she say a pretty face?

Quit?! Maya rushed into The Heretix like someone was chasing her. Or something. Maybe it was her rememory. Whatever it was, she didn't want it catching up. A million thoughts knocked up against each other at the same time.

"It's our largest non-suite room, miss," the guy at the front desk explained as he punched up her key. Behind him seven clocks gave the time in Harlem, Paris, London, Dubai, Bangkok, Oaxaca and Cape Town. "Since this will be home for a while, would you like a tour?" the clerk asked. The lighted check-in desk had an actual lawn growing right on top of it. It weirded Maya out too much to take him up on his offer.

Quit? As she took the floating glass elevator up she tried to feel like at least a temporary princess. No, a queen. Nay, a king. They were more in control, weren't they? Queens were usually virginal or beheaded. Rob must be remembering the scared young chick he abandoned. That's not who she was anymore. She could never quit.

She entered her room, turned on the light and then leaned her head against the closed door. Okay. Much better. What a lovely calming vase of orange tulips. That's right. A new room! With orange tulips everywhere.

Mega-stylish. Instead of drapes, an artsy array of brambles covered each of the floor-to-ceiling windows. Two queen-size beds with the space of almost three beds between them were separated by a breezy tangerine chiffon curtain that could be pulled either way. Ooh. Crisp gold sheets, and goose-down comforters.

She sat down at the desk behind the laptop. The place that she felt most comfortable. Ahhh. She checked her e-mail. A couple of well-wishers, folks from work, and a joint e-mail from her parents sent from her father's account.

To: MayaHope@purgatorex.com
From: Delroy.Hope@antioch.faculty.edu
Subject: Missing you already
Our Darling Daughter,
We are writing to send you love, and of course, hope on this your latest venture. Like Alice, enjoy your time in the rabbit hole, but beware of the vortices in Gotham. We hear that they are everywhere. Do write and tell us of your experiences.
Love,
Delroy & Emmaline

To: Delroy.Hope@antioch.faculty.edu,
Emmaline.Hope@antioch.faculty.edu
From: MayaHope@purgatorex.com
Subject: RE: Life is beautiful . . .
Dear People Who Made Me!
Hey! New York is fantastic. Yes, there are many vortices but there is also the possibility of having (gasp) a good time. Something that I realize was missing from my former life. I'll be longer than originally planned. I will write (infrequently) and call (on occasion) and think of you both (often). Thank you for life, breath and everything else.
All My Love,
Maya

Maya held her hands in the prayer position under a hot shower stream that felt like rain in the exquisite lemon + sage Bliss bath suds. It was almost as good as her homemade stuff. Then she slipped into the ultra-soft NFF African robe hanging behind the door. She took up repose on a velveteen chaise longue and put a small bag of calming lavender leaves over her eyes. Hopefully Athena wouldn't be too long.

Dream. Rain forest. Running from a million pairs of red-soled shoes. Doorway inside a tree. Athena running off with teddy bear. Flying. Naked. People. Laughing.

She was awakened by the sound of the slide lock, but before she could greet Athena she heard two voices.

Athena: "You're not a serial killer right?"

Some Guy: "Nah baby, I'm not a serial killer."

Athena: "Good. I'm dead sober and I could kick a brotha's ass."

Some Guy: "Watch out now. Don't take advantage."

Athena: "Well, I know you were just trying to impress me outta my panties, Mr. Ferrari, but I enjoyed the ride."

"Mission almost accomplished then."

Mr. Ferrari? Who in the hell is Mr. Ferrari?

Athena knocked thrice on Maya's bed as they tiptoed to Athena's side of the room. "Sleeps like a rock."

Yeah—usually. Maya didn't want to open her eyes and see too much. Ferrari must be the lawyer guy. How could Athena bring this Just Met back to the room?

He chuckled. "So what kind of soundtrack does this night deserve?"

"One that won't wake Maya." Too late.

"You got any R. Kelly?" he asked.

"Oh, you making requests? Forward," Athena joked. "And Kelly? Not on my computer we don't. I had you figured for a basic Barry Whiter."

"What about Cube's 'You Can Do It'?"

Athena was not to be outdone. "Is that the one where he says *put your ass into it?*" Maya knew that Athena was giving her booty dance as a demonstration.

"Perfect," the lawyer said, probably grinning.

"Yeah. I got that." Athena hit the song, super low, and Maya heard kissing.

This is not happening. Fall asleep please.

Maya heard Athena lean over and pull the privacy panel across to separate the room. Why shut the barn when the cow's already playing in traffic? More sounds of kissing, sucking, slurping and licking. Great.

"Oh Ferrari. You driving me to someplace else," Athena whispered. "Tell me what you like, baby."

Sleep, where are you?!

"No, Athena." Someone was undressing. "Tell me what you like. I want to please you." Sounds of a good old-fashioned hickey. "In my circles I don't meet women as alive as you."

Ice Cube faded into Mariah's "Vision of Love":

> *"Sweet destiny-ee*
> *Carried me through desperation*
> *to the one that was waiting for me-ee . . ."*

Finally, before knowing way more about her BFF than she cared to, Maya drifted back off to sleep.

Chapter 11

"I HAVE 'EM COMING BACK
KNOCKING ON MY DOOR LIKE JEHOVAHS."
—Charli Baltimore

BEEP. BEEP. BEEP. BEEP . . .

"Wake up, Jezebel. Told you it was an early morning."

Maya peeled one eyelid back to see Rob standing over her bed holding a beeping alarm clock. The clock blinked 5:30 A.M. "Isn't there any privacy in hip-hop? You said ten!"

"I lied." Rob pulled the covers off her. "We have a meeting."

Athena turned over on her bed. "I've seen this episode of *Making Da Band.* Original. Turn that thing off!"

Rob ignored her. "We want advance buzz by next Friday. I see you still wear purple jammies, huh, Jezebel?" *BEEP. BEEP. BEEP. BEEP.*

Maya threw her sleeping mask. It wilted halfway across the bed. "Why is the window open?! Also, we don't feel safe with some guy having our room key!"

"You have to earn the right to privacy. I told you this wasn't playtime. If you're not up for it, quit. Otherwise it is what it is." Rob leaned in and whispered with the beeping clock near her head, "Your panties still say the day of the week on them?" *Beep. Beep. Beep.*

Maya held up her middle finger. "Torture is illegal."

"All jokes aside, Legba is gonna bring you to my office. See you at quarter to ten." Rob turned off the beeping alarm.

"Thank you," Athena grumbled from under her blanket.

"Jokes?" Maya wrapped her down comforter tighter around her. "Where's your office?"

"Harlem."

"So if you need us at ten, why are you waking me up at five-thirty?"

"Discipline. Plus you gotta get ready. As you saw from last night, you can't walk around looking like Faustus. Thirdly, it's not we. Just you."

Athena sat up. "Why just her? We're here to blow me up. You know the deal."

"So do you. Just Maya."

"But Athena is gonna be my hype woman."

"Sorry, but the sideman thing doesn't require all that hands-on stuff. Athena can be your assistant if she wants all-access but that's up to y'all." Rob turned like some kind of wannabe general and opened the door. "Oh, check out The Hip-Hop Wire before you break out. Get official, Jezebel."

Maya picked up the alarm clock he left on her bed and threw it at the door as he left. *BAM.* It didn't break. "Are we having fun yet?"

"I am," sputtered Athena.

"What's a hip-hop wire?" Maya asked.

"A news site."

Maya reached for her laptop. "What did I ever see in him?"

"Girrrrrrl. Probably those arms. Did he used to work out?"

"I don't recall, Athena—what's up with bringing old boy here last night? That wasn't cool."

"Oh Maya. Don't be dramatic. It was just a lil' entertainment." Athena stuck her head under her pillow.

"For all three of us? And 'don't be dramatic'? This is the big city. What makes you think I wanna listen to Skinemax when I'm trying to sleep?"

Athena got out of bed, reached through the bramble curtains and slammed the window shut. "See? I even aired out the bedussy smell." She got back in bed.

"Well, just please don't do it again."

"So you know how corporate types always want a show, right?"

"Not really." Maya was typing up notes on her first night undercover.

"Well, they do but he was totally different. I didn't want to get my total freak on right away and scare him off. Otherwise I woulda played Prince's 'Sexy MF.' Maya—you're not listening."

Maya put her computer to the side. "As much as I'm starving? I'm all in. So what was the game plan?"

"I sat on the bed, trying to think of convo that might lead to his name. Then I put my hand between his legs and holy wow, Batman. He was packin'! I'm not a size queen, but—"

"What do you mean trying to think of his name?"

Athena didn't say anything.

Maya jumped up. "Athena! What's his name?"

Athena covered her face in a very un-Athenalike gesture. "I don't know! I was hoping you would remember."

"What do you mean you don't know? Athena, you had sex with the man."

Athena shook her head. "I know. Nobody had ever kissed me like that and it's rare that I see new tricks. What's-his-name was impressive!"

"Athena. We have to remember his name right now. Stone, right? Or something something Granite? Coal?"

"Something like that. Don't stress. Please. Half the time when these dudes are cooing on the celly talking 'bout 'What's up baby, sweetness, precious' it's because they don't want to slip and call you out your name." Athena stretched out her legs and pointed and flexed her toes.

"Well, if you knew you were gonna do all that, why didn't you go back to his place?"

"I don't know that man! He had to be like six six."

Maya got back in bed. "Six!"

"Okay. Maybe I was hallucinating 'cause I felt that firmness. I was gonna pull out my travel rubbers but didn't want to seem too easy. So I was like, maybe Maya will have one."

"Chances are greater that Hillary and Condi would form a rap super-group."

"Exactly. Then he was like I'm going to make you scream my name, and I'm thinking, uh, that could be a problem."

"Damn! You should write erotica."

"Since I'm your assistant now, you're the boss of me so yes, ma'am." Athena rolled her eyes.

"Oh, brother. You'll have your own deal in a minute. You wanna do this or not?" Maya crossed her arms.

"Of course, babygirl. My lyrics got us here." They did their stare at each other to see who blinks first thing and then started laughing.

Athena turned on the TV and spun through the channels. "Only demerit is no WPHT." WPHT: Weave Protocol Home Training. "He reached for my hair. My yaki straight, sixteen inches, color number six hair."

"Aw, man. Come on, brotha." Maya massaged her 'fro.

"Soooo, what are you wearing to this romantic meeting?"

"Romantic?"

"Yeah, girl, why do you think he wants you to come alone?" Athena made kissy sounds.

Maya went to the bathroom door. "I didn't even think of that. I better get cute for the Ex. I'm/just/sorry/Rob/what/can/I/say?"

FW: from hiphopwire.com

For Immediate Release . . .

RAP CHICK TO NATIONAL PRESS "KISS MY ASS"

New "Head Bitch in Charge" at Camp Hustla Tells Press to Kiss Her Ass.

NEW YORK CITY, NY—Last night at Harlem Lanes, music mogul Shell the Boy Wonder threw a glitzy party to present his newest artiste Jezebel to the media—but the young raptress had other ideas. As she was introduced by the high-powered media genius and DJ Manifesta aka Margarete Jean, Jezebel stuck her rear end in the air, practically mooning the crowd. When Shell and business partner Ozzie Marvelous invited her to perform, the new artist refused, saying her beats weren't quite right. Wearing a granny outfit to comment on how stale she felt things were getting in the biz, Jezebel was also spotted wildly lobbing a bowling ball in anger, which thankfully didn't hit anyone. She was also found in a compromising position with rapper Pimp, recently home from yet another stay in prison. Pimp incidentally has recently reunited with his former group, Black Death, currently pumping their new release "Bottom Bitch."

Will this new artist prove too much for even Camp Hustla to handle? "She makes both Foxy Brown and Lil' Kim look like choirgirls," remarked label head Shell the Boy Wonder. "The wonderful thing is that she has the talent and the solid hood cred to back it up. I found her on our worldwide search. Pure ghetto. I was impressed by her skills even though she jumped over a table and practically punched me in the face. A little anger management and she'll be steady."

Check out her music when her album drops soon. Also in the works later this year for this young artist is her own reality TV special, *Making of a Star*, which is currently in a bidding war with several networks. Can we say divatude?

Contact Luci Mefisto: LMefisto@CampHustla.com

Chapter 12

"I PULLS UP IN MY STRETCH
LET MY HOMEGIRLS FLEX"
—Missy Elliott

Maya smoothed down the front of her green corduroy jumper dress. Legba pulled up in front of the subway on 125th Street and St. Nicholas at 9:45 A.M. Black, brown, yellow and beige folks of every hue were hustling off to work or school, or just plain hustling. Harlemworld.

"Legba, this is practically around the corner. If you woulda told me that, I coulda just walked. I'm a tourist. I wanna see the neighborhood."

"Orders." Legba was continuing his whole man-of-few-words thing.

"Okay. Where's Rob's office? I see everything from fried chicken to fried hair but no office buildings. Maybe he works next door to Bill Clinton?" Maya looked for an office worthy of a former Commander in Chief.

"Clinton ain't been here since they cut the ribbon." Legba leaned back and pointed to the entrance of the subway, overflowing with people.

"Okay. Cool. So am I taking the train, then?" Maya waited for a response. It would be easier to have a conversation with a mime.

"Token booth. Mr. Big Rob will find you." Legba's cryptic nature, though endearing yesterday, was getting on Maya's nerves with only four hours of sleep.

"Fine. Thank you." Maya jumped out of the car before Legba could make it to her side and slammed the door.

"Braid your hair for you, miss?" Two African women wearing colorful gele headwraps approached Maya, hands outstretched with business cards. Yellow, green and red. Wow. No one looked like that in Faustus. It was so beautifully . . . *National Geographic.*

"No thanks, but where'd you get your wraps?" she asked, but upon hearing her "no," they were already all over a smartly dressed businesswoman with neat twists who was one of the few people exiting the subway. "Hair braiding for you, lady?"

"Newports, Newports," whispered a man before Maya could hit the stairs.

"I don't smoke," she explained to the man's back. Maya descended the steps of the New York City subway system for the first time with a diverse throng who were mostly huffing, puffing and acting like she was moving too slowly; navigating through what smelled like urine but looked like glue; and trying not to step on a broken bottle. When she finally entered the station, all she could see was people, people and more people.

"Yo. Swipe?" A short Latin brotha in a black hoodie moved in close.

"Excuse me?" asked Maya loudly.

"Swipe you?" He looked around like Maya was breaking procedure.

"Oh. Okay, thanks."

"Dollar." He flashed a yellow MetroCard in his palm.

"Oh no I need the token booth," said Maya, suddenly nervous.

The guy nodded over her head.

"That way?" Maya pointed behind her.

"Don't point!" He moved away, no longer looking at her. She was in front of the token booth the whole time.

Rob emerged from the other side of the booth carrying a dull brown Louis Vuitton backpack and a newspaper. He looked fine in a puffy jacket, jeans and Timberland boots. He looked at his watch. Early. "Impressive, Maya. Good morning."

"Where are we going?" Maya asked cordially.

He swiped a card through the turnstile. "After you."

Maya went through the chrome entry and Rob entered behind her. Wow. Elegant photo murals of blackfolks from the turn of the century. She followed him downstairs to another level marked UPTOWN ABCD. Rob moved with ease through the crowded platform, a lion making his way through his jungle. Maya was just trying to keep up.

"Why don't you watch where you are going?" asked a humongous woman still wearing a bulky winter coat with fur around the collar in the spring.

Maya couldn't reply, "Because you're so fat that you're taking up the walkway," so she said sorry.

A man with a toupee and wire-rimmed glasses elbowed Maya. She was losing sight of Rob. She held her bag closer. He was a shark, moving forward without looking back. She felt herself turning to a pillar of salt. "Rob!" He turned around, noticed that she was still caught up in the swarm and smiled. She expected him to come back to save her but he only stood there watching her fight her way through a teen with a bricklayer's backpack and an armful of books, a lady with preadolescent twin brats, some dude with an oddly angled bike and a man selling handfuls of gum. When she got closer, Rob turned around and continued walking. Idiot.

He made his way to a bench at the end of the platform just as the train arrived. A woman got up and he patted the seat next to him. Maya plunked down and tried to catch her breath. She left a two-person space between them.

"Welcome to my office," he said as the crowd on the platform exchanged itself for the multitude exiting the train.

"What do you mean?" Maya spotted a homeless woman setting up camp.

Rob held out his arms. "The platform. This is my office."

"The subway platform? I thought Camp Hustla was about floss and ice and—"

Rob interrupted like something she said irked him. "I know what Camp Hustla is about. I'm about dollars, too, but I keep it real, and my team needs to be about keeping it real. I'm not chicken noodle souping it. That's why Shell digs me. This is more fun. More real. The people's office."

"Okayyyy . . . whatever. So what's the plan?"

"Glad you're so cooperative. This should be a blast." Rob folded his newspaper into a tight rectangle.

"Well." She spotted something moving out of the corner of her eye.

"So what we need to do is outline the next year of your life." Rob shoved the paper into his bag.

"Oh my goddess!" Maya jumped up on her seat, pointing at the tracks. "A rat! rat! I just saw a rat!" Maya looked around. She was the only person in the subway reacting. Two kids with their mother laughed. Rob looked up at Maya with no expression and she sat down, a little closer to him this time, and fanned herself with her hand.

"Like I said, this is the people's office, Maya. No drama. We're just about the people's business. Making good music, loving life and keeping it real."

"I'm sure. You're such a people person. Oh look, there's your kind of people now." Maya nodded her head toward three cackling big-boobed, short-skirted chicks stealing not so subtle glances at Rob. It was strange sitting with him and not chitchatting about them and everybody else. People watching was a sport that they enjoyed together. Weirdo Watching, Rob called it, although Maya argued that sociologically there was no such thing as a weirdo. However, now she was the odd man out and quite possibly even more of a weirdo here than she was back home. Many things weren't being said.

Rob looked at the chicks then back at Maya. "Look. I need to win." Rob looked into Maya's eyes for the first time since their unlikely reunion. "I have to win," he repeated. "Your big break is my big break. I gotta make you succeed, so can we try to get along please?" He touched her shoulder and she instinctively moved back.

"No worries, Bobby."

"In the game we're not Maya and Bobby." Rob reached for her shoulder again. This time he let his hand hover above her before bringing it down slowly and making extremely awkward contact.

Maya looked at his hand touching her body. It repulsed her. She numbed herself so that she couldn't feel it. "That's funny 'cause we sure look like Maya and Bobby."

Rob dropped his hand. "Can I get a sentence out? Damn. In the game we're not Bobby and Maya. We're manager and artist. Big Rob and Jezebel."

"Cleopatra."

"What's the difference?" Rob gripped his hands into tight balls and then released them.

"Well, obviously Jezebel sounds like trash. Cleopatra is a queen in a Nikki Giovanni poem. I'd rather be in a Giovanni poem than trash."

"Good. Then earn the right to be Cleopatra. Now you have something to strive for." Clearly Rob thought that he was Larry Fishburne in *The Matrix*.

"You promised. And trust me, I have plenty to strive for." Maya wasn't swallowing red pills, blue pills *or* Kool-Aid.

"I know, Maya. Okay." Rob paused like he was reminding himself of something. "I like to start each new artist with an interview . . . to get to know them, but as I, uh, know you already . . . Although the Maya I knew wouldn't be here . . ."

Maya bit her lip. Make him fall in love. Make him fall in love. Then kick him to the curb. Wasn't that the objective? She threw a rough smile up on her face. "So then let's start from scratch."

"Well, almost scratch." Rob stood as an A train thundered into the station, its bright blue A streeeeeeeeeeaking by. Maya covered her ears. "Let's step into my conference room! Rush hour's over!" he yelled over the noise.

The train screeched to a stop and the doors opened. A much smaller mob than before exited. Maya and Rob got on. There were about ten people scattered throughout the car. Lots of empty seats. He sat in a two-seat corner. Maya hesitated.

"I don't bite," he said. No alternative such as the sky swallowing them both whole presented itself so she squeezed in. She forgot how much room he took up.

"The New York City subway. You know this is my first time in a train?"

Rob was all about business although there was a smile somewhere in his face. "So . . . I have a list of about twenty questions that I ask new artists. I can't believe I'm saying this, but anyway . . . These questions allow me to assess you, figure you out, you know, so that I can do the best to develop your image and market you. Select the right producers, that kinda thing."

"The subway is not as grimy as I thought it would be." Maya shared a smile with a wrinkled old lady.

Rob opened a folder. "So I usually begin with where you're from, family background, et cetera, but in this case I am familiar. Do your people know you're here? I'm sure Madame Emmaline must be freaking out."

The rocking of the subway and the bizarre nature of being there with Rob made Maya feel like she was hovering somewhere near the ceiling. She saw herself up there near the flickering fluorescent lights watching the conversation. She wanted to swoop down and slap him for mentioning her mother in a mocking tone but they needed to get along. "I told them I was coming to New York to perform my poetry."

"That's about right." Rob stroked the words on his list of questions with his thumb. It had a platinum ring on it. He never used to be the kind of guy to wear jewelry.

"And my fellow researchers don't interact with the world of cheap pop culture so it's all good." Maya was glad for the opportunity to get a dig in.

"Yeah. I remember. Number two. Any interesting anecdotes, you know, stories, from your past?"

"Interesting anecdotes, Bobby? You must be kidding me! Pass."

"Okay. Moving on. Issues. Problems. Things like imprisonments. Scandals . . . The public craves dirt. The graph we work with is that human nature wants to build you up, then you fall from grace, then you make it a comeback. But obviously you have nothing scandalous so . . ."

"I fucked my therapist." Scandal that. Maya wanted to take a deep breath but she didn't. "Does that count?"

"What?!" Rob stood up.

Maya, the now recovering good girl, spoke a mile a minute. "After you did what you did, I kinda flipped out. And I. Fucked. My. Therapist." Maya noticed that Bobby was turning red. Wow. Red anger plus brown skin makes purple. Like overripe boiled beets. "Over and over again. He was African. And the rumors are true."

Rob pulled a harsh noise from his gut that made everyone in the subway car turn around. "Gaaaarrrrrrr!" It was almost a growl. "I'll kill him!"

"Why?" Maya smiled. Deal with that.

Why? Bobby looked like he wanted to slam his thumbs into his eyes. *Why?* He had no reason. None. Zero. Zip. Nada. So he sat down and continued. Gruffer now. "Four," he choked out. "Uh, how, uh, old will you be when you die, you think?" He looked like he hoped it might be soon.

"A hundred. I'll curl up with my man and we'll die together. Romantic, old and satisfied. Mmmm." Maya closed her eyes and leaned her head back to exaggerate her dream romance.

Rob's flat tone took it back to business. "Okay. Good. That means you're an optimist. Pessimists think they can go at any time."

"Hm. I like that exercise. I'll have to use that." Maya opened her eyes.

"Moving on. Who would you like to meet? Gimme three people. Living or dead. Your dream dinner party."

"Oh wow. Well . . . Maya Angelou, my fake godmother, of course . . ."

"Of course."

"Then John Coltrane, I mean, wow, or maybe I would swap Trane out for Wynton Marsalis."

Rob's face came alive. "Nah . . . Trane or Marsalis over Monk or Miles?"

"Is this my party or yours?"

"I figured as your rep I'd at least score an invite." Rob took out a packet of green gum from his pocket.

"I wouldn't invite you, Rob, 'cause you might screw me over the night before."

Silence. Except for the kid circling round and round the pole across from them and yelling "Mandy Pandy Mandy Pandy," whatever that meant. Then a miracle happened. Both Maya and Rob were . . . laughing. Yes, they were laughing. Hard. Cracking up. Hahahahaha . . . Looking at each other and cracking up. The guy sitting across from them in the NYU sweatshirt looked up from reading *In Search of Lost Time* and smiled. Hehehehehe . . . Then—*bam!* The Mandy Pandy kid tripped and slammed his face into the pole. His mother pounced on him before he could scream, trying to make it all seem like an enjoyable part of the game but it didn't work and he was bawling. The wind changed and Maya, it seemed, was also . . . tearing up. Rob laughed for a couple of beats more before he saw that they were on different pages.

"I'm sorry, Maya, I just . . ." He didn't want to seem like he was apologizing for what had happened in Faustus so long ago so he kept it moving. "I'm sorry, I just wanted to show you . . . This is 207th Street. Last stop in Manhattan. Now the train cycles back down the other way. The historic A is the fastest train in the city," he said softly.

They looked out the window. Someone was actually humming Duke Ellington's "Take the A Train." Loud. A disheveled man stood at the end of the car gathering his things and his words to launch into some kind of pitch. "So sorry to disturb you good people but I am homeless and hungry . . ." He was remarkably well spoken. The mother clutched her son to her lap and NYU guy turned up his iPod, blasting Lenny Kravitz's "Believe." *"I am you and you are me,"* Lenny sang as the homeless man continued, "I was in a shelter but six months ago . . ."

"Fascinating," Maya said.

"Oh perfect, Maya. Next question. Do we help him?"

How did this become some kind of therapy session about her

ethics? She looked at dude's dirty coat and muddy house slippers with dingy socks. "Why not? He says he's hungry."

"Right, but there's shelters and free soup kitchens all over the city. Maybe he wants to get high."

"Maybe. But he obviously needs help." The man was making his way through the subway car. Most people ignored him. A Catholic school girl dropped a couple of coins into his paper cup.

"But do *you* help him?" Rob pointed to a poster across from them. It said help the homeless by giving to charity not individuals.

Maybe the poster was right but what about Aminata Sow Fall's book where the beggars went on strike? Folks lost their right to heaven *and* earthly rewards because there was no one to give to. She looked up. The bum was upon them. He stank of week-old rum. "Yes," she said. Upon hearing the sound of Maya's purse click open, the homeless man whipped around. He was Pavlov's dog with his paw out. While Maya fished around in her bag, Rob pressed several bills into the man's palm.

"Thank you, friend," the man said. "Yous make a mighty handsome couple."

Rob grumbled something that sounded like thanks. Maya handed Rob her coins. He put them in his pocket. They sat trying to feel the benevolent superiority you feel after you give to the less fortunate but it wouldn't come on. Rob surprised Maya by grumbling, "Freeloader."

"How much more, Bobby? I'm tired and hungry. My blood sugar is crashing."

Rob didn't correct her on his name. "It's twenty questions. I need to get them answered today. And I already took your BS into account."

"My BS?"

"Blood sugar." He gave a slight smile. "We're getting off at 59th to meet Athena and Luci. Prearranged. You up to a few more?"

Maya nodded. This therapy session/human resources/reunion was taking its toll. It was hard to look at him without seeing a stripper's head between his legs.

"What do you want, Maya?"

"Excuse me?"

"Money, fame, power or love?" Rob held out the pack of gum.

"Are those the only choices?" She looked down at her sneakers. Even her dirty old high-tops looked much hipper in NYC. "That's easy."

"Is it?"

"Love." She took the gum. She'd wanted to see how long he'd hold it there, but maybe she had bad breath and she didn't want to subject even him to that.

Rob shifted back and forth in his seat. "Why?"

"I want to know that the someone or the someones who love me know me completely and still love me anyway. Unconditionally." She bent over to tighten her laces although they were fine.

"But if you were wealthy people would love you unconditionally anyway, Maya."

"No, they wouldn't. The condition would be the money. The same with the fame. The same with the power."

"Same with the love. The condition is that you love them back."

Hm. Interesting considering the source.

"DVDs. DVDs?" A young Asian woman made her way through the shaking subway car with two handfuls of bootleg movies. Instead of holding on she balanced herself by crouching down whenever turbulence got the best of them. "*Pursuit of Happyness*?" she suggested to either or both of them.

Rob shook his head no and the woman moved on, offering happiness to a more viable customer. "Cool. Next. Ms. Maya Hope. Why are you on the planet?"

"That's an easy one. To fight for oppressed people. To sing their song. To give that man on the subway a quarter."

Rob pointed up at the subway map. "Next stop. See how quick we're zipping from 125th to 59th Street? You'll see when you do this in a car. The traffic is insane. The subway is the best way to go every time. Okay. What's your favorite memory?"

"Ever?"

"Ever."

Maya sat back at the thought of it. "That's easy. When . . . when we were driving to go visit your father in Denver and we stopped at the Grand Canyon."

"If I recall correctly we had a huge fight because you didn't wanna even *see* the Grand Canyon because you had already seen a couple of other canyons." Rob stood up and gripped the bar above her seat.

"I did wanna see the Canyon but I knew if we went there you were gonna try to make me hike it."

"Hiking is good for you, Maya!"

"That's that white blood in you!" She looked up at him and wanted to wink but couldn't.

"Wowww. Nah, baby, I'm a pure African king." Rob pounded his chest.

"Anyway. I still say that looking into the Grand Canyon was . . . It's the face of God. Or the goddess. Or whoever." Maya remembered when she first said this and Rob, ever the pragmatist, laughed at her.

"It is the face of God," he agreed. "If it isn't, then what is?"

Maya was shocked, pleasantly, by his response. Hmmm. "Rob, can I just type the rest of these up? I'm sure I'm more literate than most of the people you deal with." Maya stood up.

The train stopped short. Both Maya and Rob lurched forward, almost tumbling. He caught her and the doors opened as she pushed free.

Chapter 13

"HER BLACKNESS IS FINE, THE BLACKNESS OF HER SKIN
THE BLACKNESS OF HER MIND.
HER BEAUTY CANNOT BE MEASURED
WITH STANDARDS OF A COLONIZED MIND."
—*Me'Shell Ndegeocello*

As Maya and Rob walked together from west to east on Manhattan's tony 57th Street, he felt no need to be a polite tour guide, and she certainly was not going to be the one to ask him for anything. So they walked along in silence. Alone together. It was strange not to hold his hand. She shoved her fists deep into her too-small pockets and followed Rob into the Le Parker Meridien Hotel. Grand mirrors. Roman columns. Cathedral-style lobby. Marble floors. Posh. Like a museum. The art over the reception area resembled a demented graph. *Likelihood that Maya Hopeless won't snap before the day is out. Leading indicators say . . .*

"I thought we'd crawl into a hovel somewhere and forage for food. This doesn't seem like you, Mr. Keep It Real."

"It isn't." Rob made a beeline for a red curtain at the back of the posh lobby.

To Maya's surprise they stepped behind the seductive curtain to find a no-frills burger joint. With its handwritten menu, dark, old-school paneling and un-comfy vinyl seating, the spot felt more like a truck stop than a New York eatery in the lobby of a plush hotel. It was . . . a shack. Maya was confused. "This is the kind of place they used to shuck clams in along the Ohio!"

Athena and Luci sat at a bench booth in the back corner. Neither was speaking. Uh-oh. Luci looked up and spotted Maya. Her almond-shaped eyes widened like she'd won the lottery. "Hey you—over here!"

"Maya!" Athena stood up and waved her skinny arms.

Maya and Rob made their way over and sat on opposite sides of the tight booth.

"How cute is this?" Luci had a half-eaten blood-rare burger in front of her. They both looked like Maya and Rob were rescuing them from something dreadful. Luci wore a chocolate brown catsuit with her hair all swooped forward like one of the Beatles. Athena was wearing a dark blue sweatsuit and blondish waves. Now they were matching each other with cheerleading energy pound for pound. It was too much for Maya on an empty stomach.

"How was your morning, babygirl?" Athena took another bite of her well-done burger. "This is sooo good," she said, talking with her mouth full.

"One minute, ladies. I think Jezebel is mid–blood sugar crash. She needs to order," said Rob.

Maya looked at him, grateful for his sudden kindness, and stood up as Athena's phone rang.

"Helloooo, Ferrari," Athena said.

"Wait, I'll walk you through it." Rob stood to literally walk Maya to the counter.

Maya looked him in his face. "I know that you're used to dealing with imbeciles but I think that I know how to order food." Was that Jezebel or Maya talking?

"Okeydokey." Rob smiled at Luci and she winked back.

Maya stepped up to the counter. Industrial-size cans of ketchup and prepackaged buns lined the shelves. The two guys working the joint traded between order-taking and chef duties in an open kitchen. Maya stepped through three women waiting to pick up their orders.

"Line," said a stylish white girl with big green eyes.

"Oh, sorry." Maya got behind four other people and avoided looking over at the booth. She felt Rob gloating at her line-cutting mishap. She counted the number of people on phones to pass the time. *Twenty-*

three patrons. Thirteen cell phone talkers including Athena. Seventeen if you included texters.

The man behind Maya tapped her on the shoulder. "Okay! Next."

"Oh. Uhhh . . ." Maya stepped up and scanned the menu on the wall. Only four items. "Do you have veggie burgers?"

"Now she looks at the menu," the guy behind shouted. Maya was afraid to turn around.

"Does it say we have veggie burgers?" The cute brother behind the small counter in a gray Brooklyn tee pointed to a sign. IF YOU DON'T SEE IT, WE DON'T HAVE IT. Another sign said CASH, CASH AND CASH ONLY. "No."

"Okay. I was just—" Maya started.

Counter Guy shook his head. "It says burgers, fries, beer and milk shakes. That's it. And yes, brownies. Got that, everyone? Burgers, fries, beer and milk shakes." He turned to a woman in a Burger Joint T-shirt who had just joined them behind the counter. "These are the same people who've been going to McDonald's for the past thirty years and still don't know what they want. It's the same menu."

"I'm a vegetarian," Maya said. But the burgers did smell good.

"Oh, come on!" Counter Guy threw up his hands and the guy on the line guffawed.

"Remember the Soup Nazi?" Athena joined Maya at the order area to rescue her. "These are the Burger Nazis. It's great. Everybody waits for a table. And look at the signatures on the walls. Missy Elliott, Ashton Kutcher, everyone."

Maya was near starving and too mentally exhausted to see the excitement in a scrawl that said *Ashton Kutcher Rules*. "So fine. I'll have a triple order of fries. And bottled water with a brownie." She turned around and cast the man muttering behind her a dirty look.

"And what's your name?" asked Counter Guy.

"Hi. I'm Maya." Maya looked at Athena for further instructions.

"Great," he said as if speaking to a child on the special short bus. "We'll call you when your order is ready, Maya. Next."

Maya doubled back. "No. Jezebel. Put down Jezebel."

"You sure now? Because there's still time to choose an additional secret identity," Counter Guy asked, curling up his lips in the wry way a lot of New Yorkers seemed to do.

"No. I'm committed." Maya bathed her hands in antiseptic gel and held them out to air dry.

"Let it ride," Athena said. Homeboy rolled his eyes. Athena rolled hers right back.

"It's ghetto chic," proclaimed Luci as they sat back down. "So. Princess is coming later. Warning. She's an image consultant and she has a total 'tude. You know, the kind of person who has no problem telling total strangers that their clothes don't match? But she is the best at what she does. Only the best for you, sweetheart."

"Only the best for you, sweetie-heart." Rob mocked Luci and she hit him on the arm. Athena kicked Maya under the table. There was a lot of shrouded violence going on.

"I don't understand why it's so exciting in New York to be treated like crapola in a shoddy restaurant," Maya said.

"She's so cute," Luci said to Rob. "She doesn't get it."

Rob flipped back into question mode. "So Maya, I always ask everybody, when did you first fall in love with hip-hop?"

Maya looped arms with Athena. "Oh, I almost forgot, Athena. Rob and I were in the middle of an inquisition."

"Sounds like fun," Athena said.

"As long as you don't exaggerate too much." Rob took a french fry from Athena's plate.

"I'm sorry, I mean an interrogation." Maya took another fry from Athena's plate, then so did Rob. That's right. His weight complex. He would never order for himself but would just keep eating off everyone else's plate. The curse of growing up a fat kid.

"Feel free," said Athena.

"Jezebel," called the stringy haired dude at the counter. "Jezebel!"

"Oh." Maya waved at the guy, who looked at her like she was the missing link.

"You have to go get it yourself," said Luci. "Isn't that a hoot?"

Rob handed Maya fifteen dollars and she hesitated. "Per diem," he said.

Maya still wasn't sure why this was "a hoot." Especially since it was much less service than she offered at Pearl's in Faustus. Faustus. It spun farther away by the second. Like it only existed now in black-and-white. Maya went to the counter and retrieved a greasy waxed-paper-wrapped mound of thin fries in a brown paper bag. She sat down and immediately stuck a forkful in her mouth. Oh. Delicious. Really tasty. Her blood sugar quickly leveled off. The colors returned. Even Rob didn't seem so annoying.

"Okay. Cool," she said. "So when did I fall in love with hip-hop? Like in *Brown Sugar*?"

"Yes. Although usually the people I'm talking to actually do love hip-hop." Rob reached for one of Maya's fries and then drew his hand back.

Maya pretended not to notice as Luci put a fry in his mouth. Competition. All good—she had home team advantage. She thought for a beat before she gave one of her usual anti-rap answers. "You know what I love? Words. I love words. Language. Rhythm. Poetry. It used to fascinate me the way that you could find so many cool ways to say something simple. You were a good writer, Rob." Take that, Luci.

"Words." Rob squeezed a pat of ketchup onto the corner of Maya's napkin for her to dip in. "Word."

"Oh. You know what else? Storytelling. That's what sociology is about. The stories we tell ourselves about ourselves. That's my favorite kind of music too. Music that tells my story."

"Interesting." Rob adjusted his seat, trying to get comfortable in the small area.

"What?" Maya sat back, trying to subtly mirror his body language, a trick for making people love you she remembered from relationship psych.

"You get it." He scooted forward.

"Get what?" Maya scooted forward.

"What you said, Maya, makes you more hip-hop than ninety percent of the artists who are out there today. The words. Back to the basics. True school. That's where I wanna take it. Back to the grass roots. That's our roots." Rob took another fry.

"Exactly!" exclaimed Athena. "Let's take it back to De La Soul and them."

"Roots? We're from Ohio." Maya dipped a fry in the ketchup.

"You're all from the same place?" asked Luci.

Maya said yes and Rob and Athena said no.

"Nah, baby. We're from the soul." Rob looked at Maya. His new respect for her showed on his face. "Are you committed?"

"I do. I am. Stop asking. Let's make it work already." Maya shoved several fries into her mouth and chewed hard.

"For the love of hip-hop." Rob pulled a package out from his folder.

"For the love of storytelling." Maya took another big bite of fries. Love was easier than she remembered.

Rob looked back to make sure no one was in their business. "Okay, so here's the story. Your name is Jezebel Johnson. You were born in a brothel. You never graduated from fifth grade—that way no one can trace you. Ever." He slid over a black envelope. Maya and Athena looked inside. New IDs: birth certificate, driver's license, passport, Social Security card.

"Is this standard?" Maya asked.

"How do you think Naomi Campbell is still thirty-something?" Luci asked.

"I *was* wondering," said Athena.

"What happened to keeping it real?" Maya pulled out the passport and SS card.

Rob put his hand over the IDs. "Play the game, Maya. You gotta be listened to to be heard. It ain't just parties and bullshit."

Luci bobbed her head up and down.

"Okayyy." Maya slipped her new identity back into the paper envelope.

Rob reached back into his backpack. "I put together this study book and music for you. All the major players—Rakim, Nas, Pac, Biggie, Jay-Z, KRS-One and Thug—are on this iPod." Rob put a binder in front of her with an iPod and three books. "*The Art of Emceeing* by Dead Prez, *Dead Emcee Scrolls* and Thug's poetry book." Rob placed a fist on top of the books.

"Thug's book is slammin'," Athena said.

Luci was cruising the room with her eyes. Rob looked over at her.

This might be a good time to attempt flirting. Maya moved her shoulders back and crossed her legs. "So, Bob uh, Rob—how have you been?"

Rob shoved the pile closer to Maya. "Commit these to memory."

His phone rang.

"*Mi amor*! Hold on . . . Excuse me." Rob walked away.

"*Mi amor?*" Maya asked.

"No sulking." Athena said.

"Sulking?" asked Luci, tuning back in. "Do tell. No in-camp secrets. Do you have a crush on Big Rob?"

Maya looked at Luci and said nothing.

Luci showed teeth. "Oh, don't be shy. Everyone does."

The curtain pulled back and a fashionable thirty-something dark-skinned chick with waist-length micro braids breezed in. She wore a ton of gold jewelry—bangles, earrings, necklace—and a short green baby doll dress. "*Ciao ciao,*" she said to someone on the phone and hung up.

"Princess!!" exclaimed Luci, her voice happier than her face.

"Kiss kiss," said Princess, descending upon the table and sitting down in Rob's spot.

"Back atcha love!" Luci kissed the space next to Princess' well made-up cheek.

"Princess," said Rob, returning to the table even more guarded than usual. He closed his phone and went on a chair hunt.

"Kiss kiss, Big Rob," said Princess. "And you, Jezebel."

Maya put her hands in her lap. "Hey Princess. This is Athena."

"Kiss kiss, Athena. So, Jezebel, I observed you, uh, at the party. Let's consult my assessment report." Princess rifled through the same Birkin Sahara had, but in black.

"Report?" Athena asked.

Rob pulled up a chair.

"Watching me?" Maya looked panicked. "Oh, no, see, I wasn't—"

"Here." Princess handed out copies of her thick report. "Talent, Publicist, Manager." She didn't have one for Athena.

"Assistant," explained Rob with more relish than was necessary.

"Oh? She can take mine then. She needs to help our star stay in the know. Booyah!" Princess slapped a report down in front of Athena. "See that she's up on this when we're not around."

"Thanks." Athena cupped her left hand over her mouth like she was trying to keep the wrong words from slipping out.

Style File.

THE JEZEBEL REPORT
Cover Sheet
by Princess

OBJECTIVE: Fill massive gap in talent's personal style to begin her evolution to Jezebel.
OVERALL LOOK: Seems to strangely prize comfort over fashion.
PROS: Big Butt, Big Lips, Goodish but Nappy Hair.
CONS: Too Colorful, Too Nappy, Too Fat, Too Big Butt, Too Much.
FIX: A style hook, like Samuel L. Jackson's Kangol.
RECOMMENDATION: Complete overhaul.

Princess clasped her hands on the table like she was Kofi Annan calling the UN to order. She looked at Rob, then Maya, then Athena. Luci was already engrossed in the report. Princess cleared her throat until Luci looked up. "My report. Jezebel—we hear the name and this sounds like a chick with an itchy trigger finger ready to bust a cap in somebody's ass, right? And then Mary Sunshine shows up in somebody's grandmother's turtleneck handing out anti-war daisies. It's confusing. The only thing that this chick looks like she'd bust is a blood vessel. Her lyrics are mad hard, then . . ."

Maya raised her eyebrows at Athena. *Was this happening?* Athena nodded. It was.

"Actually, I wanted to talk about lyrics." Maya fished a notebook out of her bag. "Since I was woken up extremely early this morning, I had time to try something."

"Wait 'til you hear this. It's cute," Athena said.

"Well, this was not on the agenda . . ." Princess looked at Rob like this interruption was somehow his fault.

"Go ahead," Rob said.

Maya placed her notebook in the center of the table. This was a good time to test her new hip-hop personality. She scowled, trying to feel tough. As Athena banged out a beat, the touristy-looking folks in the restaurant turned around. The New Yorkers kept doing whatever they were doing.

With a slight growl, Maya read/rapped:

Who's that girl?
Living in your world?
Knotty curls
She of bangles and a gang o' lips feeding swine her pearls?
A queen she could be
Is she me?
Hard to see
'Cause my eyes are getting cloudy
Trying to find my personality
Trading love for lays
My nights for days
My heart for your ways
Now I'm wasting away
My soul flew open
I just wasted a day

Just wasted a minute
My life won't begin it
Your neck I would skin it
I am back in the clinic
But before I begin it
I start to win it
I start to spin it . . ."

"Whoa—Hold up. Athena did you write this?" Rob interrupted.

"Um . . ." Athena held up a hand to cut him off. "That don't sound like me. I write party anthems."

Maya was speaking to her notebook. "What the hell, *Big Rob*? I just said—"

"You're right. My bad, Maya. My bad," said Rob. "It's just that . . . That was really good. I completely get the Cleopatra thing now."

"Me too," Maya said.

Luci hated feeling out of the loop. "Yes, Rob, we got your text about the Cleopatra bomb. Hot to death. But let's be where we're at, like Shell says. It was marv, but is that particular rhyme a Jezebel rhyme?"

"Not really," said Rob.

Athena shook her head.

"No," said Princess. "Most def not. Trust. I'm not just a stylist. I am an image consultant, and those words are not what we're going for at the present time—although the bite-his-head-off attitude at the end was right on." Princess reached over to close the notebook. "We've got to sex things up. Consumers of black culture want sexy."

Athena put her hand on Maya's back.

"Okay," Maya said quietly.

"Sooo, back to my report. And Rob, you called our artist 'Maya.' A no-no. Maya is dead."

Maya put one foot on top of the other. Hmmm. She didn't feel dead.

Princess continued. "Let's never hear that name again. Okay. So, my professional assessment? Overall score on a scale of one to ten. Four. Not a *complete* disaster."

Overall score on the humiliation scale? Twelve.

"Hair. Nappy hair says I'm tightly wound. Uptight. Straight hair says I'm relaxed. I'm easy. I'm beautiful. She has kind of good hair. Let's use that to our advantage. I have a sketch. Page two." Everyone turned to a sketch in the report that looked surprisingly like a Swedish woman.

"You know her hair used to be almost waist length?" Athena smoothed Maya's Afro puffs.

"Thanks!" Maya removed her hand.

Luci leaned forward. "Me too!"

"I thought naps said strong, unbreakable," Maya said.

Princess buffed a huge pink stone ring on Rob's sleeve. "Moving forward. As for makeup, beauty is in triangles. A triangular face is the most stunning. Jezebel's face is unfortunately round. And dark brown girls haven't been in since . . . a while."

Maya rubbed her unfortunately round cheeks.

"What about the Williams sisters?" asked Athena.

"Of course you got your Williamses, your cute big-lipped chick from *Girlfriends* whose leaving killed the show, but racially ambiguous is the way to go these days." Princess turned toward Athena. "You woulda been perfect, honey."

"Tell me about it," said Athena. Maya and Rob both shot her a look.

Princess took some kind of deep Zen cleansing breath and tapped the middle of her forehead, "But as Shell says, deal in the now. Deal in the now."

"Exactly," said Luci. "Let's think light and bright in terms of hair color, makeup, wardrobe, everything. We want to bring to her skin a more golden glow."

Maya looked at her cocoa-colored arm.

"Yes," agreed Princess. "Tough, sexy and golden. If we see some cleavage, we'll be less conscious of how"—Princess moved her hands in a basketball shape—"she is."

Rob burst out laughing, then steadied himself. "So who exactly would be your ideal woman, Princess?"

"Well, my ideal woman, Big Rob, would probably be the same as yours." Princess looked at Luci.

Maya choked on her water and Athena slapped her on the back.

"Are you okay?" asked Luci.

"Fine," said Maya, dabbing her face with a napkin.

"Since you ask," Rob said. "My ideal woman would have a brain."

"The ideal woman has Beyoncé's eyes, Halle's smile and Salma Hayek's tits," Luci answered way too quickly to have just thought it up.

"That's a good start," said Princess. "I would add Tyra's hair . . ."

"Oh yeah," said Athena. "She's completely replaced Janet as my weave role model."

Rob's phone rang again. "Saved by the bell." He walked toward the door.

"The Secretary of State's brain. Although I'd do kinder, gentler things with it," said Maya. "She's an evil genius."

"Word," said Athena, who had heard enough of Maya's speeches to be a policy expert herself. "How about a big, fun and generous Elton John personality?"

"Oh, that's good," said Luci. "And a faux mole!"

Luci, Athena and Maya started giggling.

"Okay, okay." Princess knocked on the table, perturbed that she'd let things run so amok. "Unfortunately, we are not dealing with our ideal woman. We're dealing with Jezebel, so let's stick to that." Her words landed with a thud.

Luci put her hand on Maya's to cushion the blow. "I get what you're saying; basically, we want to keep it on the new."

"Fresh," said Rob as he sat back down.

Princess turned to a clothing sketch. Next to it were magazine cut-outs of clothes and body parts glued together to form one woman. "Let's do a soft and sexy meets tough for wardrobe. Janet's belly and behind."

"But I don't have Janet's belly." Maya ran her fingers on the tight flat abs in the picture.

Princess nodded her head toward the rest of Maya's greasy fries and handsome fudgy brownie, begging to be devoured. "Well then, chop-chop, Jezebel. Anyhoo, I have to run. Got a meeting with that break-down-prone singer we all used to love. Trying to recapture her nineties glory days, but I did pull wardrobe for you. Page thirteen. See my sister N'Zinga at Glam Squad. Hair, Makeup and Fitness will meet you there. Luci. You have the bible."

Great. The wicked witch had a sister. Maybe a house would land on Maya and squash her before they got there for another round of Operation Humiliation.

Chapter 14

"I WEAR TIGHT CLOTHING AND HIGH HEEL SHOES
THAT DON'T MEAN THAT I'M A PROSTITUTE."

—*En Vogue*

After lunch, Legba picked them up at Le Parker Meridien and they dropped Rob off to catch his "conference room" across town to meet Pimp, Gunz, Nigg and Kronic at the studio. Athena sat bopping to the advance Black Death track Rob slipped them while Luci chatted and texted up a nonstop storm on her two phones, one for biz, the other personal. Maya was obsessed with The Jezebel Report. *Basically, we've compiled one hundred pages of data to explain that you suck, times ten.* Was she really that heinous? Princess's report was proof that she needed a new life.

"Now that we've sent Big Rob packing, it's just us girls." Luci took a phone break to give Maya a squeeze while Athena gave Luci the crooked eye. Luci snatched the booklet out of Maya's hands. "Oh honey. You don't need to keep looking at that. We know what we have to do so we'll do it. We're a sorority now."

"Thanks, Luci," Maya said.

"And if you ever think I'm too much, just let me know. I went to all-girls schools my whole life so I tend to have fewer boundaries than most people." Luci's phone dinged and she typed a reply.

"Are you serious? So did we. Athena and I went to Miss Beardsley's. It's an all-girls boarding school in Ohio. That's so funny!" Maya looked to Athena for confirmation on what a great coincidence this was. Athena was nonplussed.

"I knew there was a reason we felt so familiar," exclaimed Luci. "I went to Brearley from kindergarten to twelfth grade here in the city, then Smith."

"So we know exactly where you're coming from. Right, Athena?"

Athena looked out the window. "Uh, yeah. Maya, you said that before we go shopping we need to have a private business meeting to decide how much we're spending."

"Well, what were you thinking about?" asked Luci.

"A *private* meeting," repeated Athena.

"The thing is, Luci, we haven't been shopping in forever. I'm scared to splurge," Maya confided.

Athena gave Maya a look.

"Oh! You don't know?" Luci raised an eyebrow.

Athena didn't trust Luci more than she could throw her. "Know what, Luci?"

Luci drummed her fingers on her purse. "Oh, I wish we had glasses so that we could make a toast. That's the only thing that The Burger Joint lacks."

"Glasses?" asked Maya.

"Booze," said Luci.

"No, we don't know *what*, Luci?" Athena was past annoyed.

"I have my private." Luci flashed a red leather flask in her bag, "But no glasses. We'll buy some. Legba. Fifty-seventh and Fifth. Tiffany and Company, please."

"Right away, Miss Luci."

Maya was incredulous. "We're going to Tiffany's right now to buy wineglasses?"

Athena pointed up at a street sign that said Avenue of the Americas 6th Avenue. "You said Fifth. We're just a block away, right?"

"Yes," said Luci. "*Breakfast at Tiffany's* is my favorite movie."

"Well we can walk it," Maya said.

"Walk it?" Luci flexed her red-soled stilettos and looked aghast. She said nothing as they spent about half an hour trying to get back the other way. Legba explained that Fifth Avenue only moved south and Sixth Avenue only moved north and that translated into insanity at four o'clock in the afternoon on a weekday. "It's all good," Luci said as they finally pulled up on the block. "Let's go."

"Into Tiffany's?" Maya asked.

"Well, the crystal won't come to us!" Luci inspected her teeth in a compact.

Maya wasn't sure what she felt. It was a new, strange feeling. She was either changing, growing or just getting to know herself. Oh. She was *scared.* Scared of not being good enough to go into Tiffany's. Ugh. Athena wasn't budging either.

Maya looked down at her jumper dress. "If I knew we were coming here, Luci, I would have . . ."

"What? Dressed differently? As you're about to see, Jez, we are always on. Pull up right in front, Legba."

Legba double parked and Maya and Athena exchanged looks.

"I thought we were going in." Athena shifted her bag from side to side.

"We are," said Luci. "When Legba is finished, he'll open the door."

"Okayyy. And we can't open it ourselves because . . . ? " asked Maya.

"I get it!" Athena connected with Luci for the first time. "Because we don't have to."

"Exactly." Luci watched as Legba opened the curbside door of the Bentley. "See, when we do this in a few months, Jez, there's gonna be a crowd of reporters and photographers right outside the door, checkin' for what you're gonna do next. So when we open the door the curtain is up. Have you thought about who Jezebel is?" Luci swung both of her legs around from the car to the sidewalk in one motion.

Athena copied Luci and Maya stepped out tumbling, and missed Legba's hand.

"Ya all right, Miss Maya?" Legba helped Maya to her feet.

"I'm chilling, Legba. You can call me Jez," she said and they walked toward the entrance of Tiffany's. "It looks just like the movie!"

"Absolutely." Luci's eyes glazed over. The mothership was calling her home.

Athena elbowed Maya. "This is hot, Maya."

"Now, Athena . . ." This was the first time that Luci had addressed

Athena directly, unsolicited and on purpose. "No more Maya. It's Jezebel, or even Cleopatra. We need to be uniform on this."

Athena bit her lip.

A guy with a Secret Service earpiece greeted them as they revolved in through the spinning door. "Afternoon. Afternoon, ladies." He could have been auditioning to play the next Bond. James Bond. Maya, Luci and Athena waited while a gaggle of chattering salespeople took their sweet time pulling themselves from one another. Clearly, Maya & Co. were not high on the store's priority customer list.

"Yes?" A pinched female face was coming toward them.

"Good afternoon. We need the perfect crystal goblets for a party," Luci told the woman, who definitely had an anvil shoved up her butt.

"Is this a registry?" Pinched Face asked, looking over the top of her glasses. The woman's nasal voice and Boston accent made her sound like a whinnying horse.

Luci raised her voice ever so slightly along with her left eyebrow. "I'm certain that I would have requested registry assistance if that's what I meant."

Pinched Face snapped to attention. "Sorry, miss, I—"

"Now listen very closely. We need four of your finest crystal goblets. The ones that make the wine taste better." Luci stood up to her full five-ten height (six-three with her heels) as if she were above the whole experience.

"Right away, madame," Pinched Face whinnied.

"Actually, we'd like a set of four of the *black* crystal wineglasses. And give me four of the matching *black*, jet-*black*, crystal tumblers while you're at it." Each time Luci emphasized the word black. "And two flasks. We're celebrating."

"Congrats," managed Pinched Face.

"The lady in the jumper just inked a million dollar recording deal with Camp Hustla. You know, Shell the Boy Wonder."

"The party guy. Ah yes, he comes here all the time!" Pinched Face rubbed her hands together like she could feel the memory of Shell's money between her fingers. "Really?"

"Yes. Really. You're about to see her face everywhere."

In record time the famous Tiffany blue boxes sat on the counter in front of them and Luci was handing over plastic. Maya felt the sheer power in the items of the Tiffany store. Things shouldn't have so much power, but they did. Looking around at all of the shiny, expensive toys, she could start to see why everyone in hip-hop was so ice crazy. She was not some naïve bumpkin who could be easily brainwashed by logos and brands and the personality shorthand they offered. She was an adult who worked in the field of studying how and why people get so caught up. A girl's best friend should be her mind. The baubles and rocks in Tiffany's were mostly just expensive carbon. She knew this. Nonetheless, she promised herself that she *would* love again, and the next man would come bearing a blue box (conflict-free, of course), and her answer would be an undeniable yes.

Back in the car it was revelry time.

"That was great, Luci!" Maya bubbled.

Luci nodded. "Hell yeah, girl. You got to fake it 'til you make it."

"That's our theme song," said Athena. "Fake it, baby, 'til you make it, baby."

"I like it," said Maya. "But I think it should be rapped." She demonstrated: *"Yo you gotta fake it, yo, 'til you make it, yo."*

"That's hot, Maya," said Luci.

"Jezebel!" said Athena, smiling.

Maya was in her groove. "Yo you gotta fake it, yo, 'til you make it, yo." She snapped on beat.

"Oh, I almost forgot. Pop the boot, Legba!" Luci knocked on the seat in front of her.

"Yes, miss." Legba swerved over onto a street corner.

"Ladies, unwrap the glasses." This time Luci popped out before Legba could open his own door. She went around to the back of the car and came back with two bottles of wine. "Vintage. There's a cellar in the trunk."

Maya unwrapped the glasses, carefully saving the paper.

Luci filled each glass. "Legba"—she held one up in the air—"a toasting glass for you?"

"No thank you, Miss Luci, I have to drive," he said.

"Party pooper. Okay, here we go! We're toasting the fact, Madame Jezebel, that you have an unlimited credit line against your future earnings." Luci swirled the wine in her glass.

"Are you serious?!" Athena looked like she might kiss Luci.

"What does that mean?" asked Maya.

"It means, dear heart, that you can spend anything you want." Luci took a swig for punctuation. "Whatever. Whenever. Wherever. How marv is that?"

Athena's eyes did a ka-ching.

Maya was moved. "Shell believes in me that much?"

"Come on now," said Luci. "Shell believes in himself. He's a hit-maker. Failproof." Was that sarcasm in Luci's voice? "Spend away."

"Wowww. It's on!" said Athena.

"It is sooo on," echoed Maya.

Shopping was incredible. Maya had forgotten what a rush there could be in handing over an unassuming piece of colored plastic and walking out with bags of clothes, shoes and accessories. And this was just for her everyday look. They were supposed to see Princess' sister for performance and appearance clothing. She felt . . . free. The last time she had been shopping like this was for her wedding with her gift money. Maya, Athena and Luci hit the Manhattan hot spots with a vengeance: Saks Fifth Avenue, Jimmy Choos, Plein Sud, Bond No. 9. It was crazy walking past her old splurge H&M. Maya felt like linking arms with Athena and Luci and skipping down the sidewalk. She would have if either of them was the kind of chick to go for it.

"Our next stop," Luci explained, "is Princess's brownstone in Harlem. Glam Squad. You're not allowed to call or ring the bell."

As they arrived, a light brown fashionista in summer fur shimmered out and into a waiting white Rolls-Royce. A stately woman welcomed them as Luci did intros all around.

"Hello, Jezebel, I'm N'Zinga. Come in." N'Zinga was amber-colored, in her early forties and wore a huge round Afro that Maya was grateful to see. Her orange-toned dashiki dress complemented her slight frame. Princess and N'Zinga were night and day. She took Maya's face in her hands. "Princess sent me your Polaroid. Gorgeous. We're going to get along swimmingly." Maya didn't remember posing for a Polaroid.

"I feel like I'm in *Mahogany*," Athena said.

The Glam Squad showroom was a spacious Mediterranean-style suite with colorful fabrics everywhere. It looked like a gallery and smelled of lavender. Floor-to-ceiling paintings of black women with Shakespearian quotes scrawled across them by artist Ophelia Bard graced every wall. I Am Too Much in the Sun was inked under a blue-colored woman with thick locks in a gold frame.

N'Zinga took Maya's measurements and then wrote them in red ink on Princess' report and circled them. Ugh. Maya felt like she was looking at a huge red F. This wouldn't do.

"What are our immediate concerns?" N'Zinga asked Luci.

Luci looked down at the numbers. "Besides this? Her music vid, photo shoots, press junkets and VH-1 in a coupla weeks."

"What?" This was the first time Maya had heard of any of this.

"VH-1? That's what's up!" said Athena.

"VH-1? What show?" Maya didn't like being uninformed as to her own comings and goings.

"Later, okay, Jez?" Luci said, and that was that.

N'Zinga smiled, grooving between the lines of the whole exchange. "This one isn't comfortable being talent yet."

She rang a bell and two subordinates pushed out a clothing rack. It looked like a lot of denim from what Maya could see, but cute stuff. Luci looked quickly through the rack and gave a thumbs-up.

"I'm open," Maya declared.

"Oh brother," said Athena.

Maya, N'Zinga, Athena and Luci settled into the deep sofa for a private fashion show. They sipped green tea as the lean and lovely models stomped out two at a time. N'Zinga had them grouped by General Appearances, Newspaper, Magazine & Radio Interviews, Television and Red Carpets.

"Why would she need special looks for radio?" Athena asked.

"Because people are vicious. From now on, Jez is on twenty-four-seven," said Luci. After the fashion show Luci and N'Zinga exchanged notes. Athena got up to check out the rest of the gallery.

"Hello?" Luci went to take yet another call.

"Try this on." N'Zinga handed Maya a furry red minidress.

"On where? My big toe?"

"Let's just see what we're working with." N'Zinga draped her measuring tape around her neck.

Maya held out the band of cloth. "Fine. Where should I change?"

"Right here. If there are things on your body to be ashamed of, then you need to do something about them, right?"

N'Zinga and her two male assistants were arranging clothing. Luci was yapping on her phone and Athena was using the (Glam Squad) My Model Shopping Approach—choose clothes and fit models dress to show them. Everyone was everywhere. Maya couldn't even cower near a wall. She took off her jumper, which now looked ridiculous after all of the fab clothes she'd seen all day, and carefully folded it. She wasn't sure what she was buying time for. She held out the dress. Different, but cute. She shoved herself into it. There were no mirrors, thank the goddess. She was a hairy sausage. N'Zinga squeezed a cropped jean jacket over it. Maya's belly bulged out beneath it. Athena gave her a tummy poke.

"Well, at least we know what style we're aspiring to," said Luci. She snapped two Polaroids and added them to the bible.

"We sure do," said Athena, jumping into size 0 white hot pants.

The instant that Maya saw the Polaroids, she knew that Princess was right. She needed a complete overhaul.

"Athena, you are the assistant. Not the talent. I tell you what, Jez. I need to lose about twenty pounds myself. Let's lose it together," Luci suggested.

Athena folded both of her lips in and held her hands behind her back.

"You'd do that for me, Luci?" Maya tried in vain to bend her arms in the too-tight jacket.

"No, girl. I'd do it for me. It would help my career to get my humps and lady lumps in gear. Have you seen those bony white PR girls?"

Luci gave a little laugh with her mouth only and rubbed her temples. "The spotlight, baby. It adds ten pounds."

N'Zinga sucked her teeth. "Asses are luscious and womanly. Especially African asses." N'Zinga patted Maya's generous rear cushion. "And don't nobody want a bone but a dog."

"Well, unfortunately dogs run Hollywood." Luci kissed her reflection as Maya put on the jeans.

"That bitch is so extra," Athena said under her breath.

"You have a muffin top." Luci grabbed Maya's spare tire with both hands.

Maya's mouth opened but no words came out.

"What?" Athena's eyes went to her forehead in disbelief.

"Not for long, though!" Luci looked down at her own stomach, which was about the same size as Maya's although Maya had never noticed it before. As Maya reinvented herself, she created Jezebel. She decided that Jezebel was tough, sexy, fun, honest and smart. Jezebel was desirable, outspoken and did and said exactly what she wanted. Jezebel's man would never have been caught out there getting a BJ, and Jezebel would never have been caught out there in a dead-end job.

Maya spent the next few weeks in a whirlwind between the moxie coach(!), nutritionist, dermatologist, dentist, brow specialist, choreographer, manicurist, acupuncturist, personal trainer, interview specialist and a barrage of other experts in her rapidly growing entourage and beauty boot camp. They used phrases like flatter your body (while giving her too-tight clothing), bring out your individuality (while making her look more like everyone else) and new ideas (while repeating ideas that she had already seen in Sahara's fashion mag). Working out actually wasn't too bad. The dance workout devised by the fitness trainer was fun when she threw LL's scissor crunches into it. When she thought of the fat snapshots Princess's bible held of her at the bowling party, she worked out harder, while trying not to sweat out her new, brown bone-straight 'do. Maya and Athena tried on their new shoes, dresses, jeans, skirts and sweats every other day—leaving the tags in everything, just in case.

Chapter 15

"SOME GIRLS ON THE MIC
RAP LIKE VIRGINS AND GET REAL TIGHT
BUT I GET LOOSE WITH THE RHYMES I PRODUCE."
—*Roxanne Shanté*

Maya was in the shower and Athena was on a date when Maya heard her phone ringing, thinking that the Chinese food that she'd ordered from Ollie's had come faster than their usual forty-five minutes.

"Maya, hey what up?" It was Rob.

Maya turned up the volume on her phone. "Rob. What's up?"

He cleared his throat. "Uh, it's a beautiful day today."

"I'm not sure why you're calling with the weather report but I haven't been out yet." Maya balanced on one foot to dry her toes.

"Well . . . I was wondering if you wanted to see the city," he said.

"I think I pretty much already have." Maya snapped off her shower cap.

"Not Manhattan, the whole city. You know. Go on a hip-hop tour. You've been here for weeks and I know that it's been all work no play," Rob said. Was this a date? This couldn't be a date.

Maya walked out of the bathroom and sat down on her bed. "Uh—sure. Okay. Um, what should I wear?"

There was a brief pause on the other end of the line. "You always look good, Maya. Are you hungry?" Her heart beat faster. This *was* a date!

Yay. Sound casual. Sound casual!! "Uh, yeah."

"Cool, well we'll grab something in transit then." Cancel the Chinese!

"Should I wait for Legba?" Maya toweled off quickly.

"No, we're gonna roll out in Pimp's Hummer. Cool?"

"Cool." Maya hung up and sat on the bed not knowing quite how to react. This was great! Rob was taking her out on a date. She opened her closet. But why was she so excited? Because her make-him-fall-back-in-love plan was working—or was it something else?

Maya dialed Athena. No answer. "Hey 'Thena, it's me. I hope you and Ferrari are having fun. Guess who Rob invited for a *personal* tour of the city? Uh-huh. Your girl should use her powers for good. Call me when you get a chance."

What to wear? Maya put her entire new wardrobe on the bed and dialed Ollie's. No. Maybe she should pre-eat so that she didn't appear to be such a pig. Yes—good idea. She let the order—sesame chicken with brown rice—ride. She oiled her body with ylang-ylang, said to enchant the smeller's pheromones. Maya was obsessed with Rob's study music. She wanted him to see how hard she was trying, and it helped her delve deeper into her new persona. It was actually really good music.

Smokin! Maya sat in the lobby next to a curvaceous gold lamp feeling hot. Not heat hot, but Hilton hot in a three-quarter-sleeved purple off-the-shoulder chiffon top and dark butt-accenting jeans with super-high platform heels. No time like the present to learn how to walk in them. She still wasn't sure what she was feeling but Rob asking her out was a step in the right direction. What would it be like to be out on a date with him after all this time? (What would it feel like to be out on a date with anyone?)

When the bellhop announced that her ride had arrived, Maya was totally unprepared to see a blindingly white stretch Hummer limousine, triple the length of the usual monstrosity. It was a small bus. Totally oddball date car, Rob, but whatever.

"Jezebel, over here!" There were three photogs outside and for some reason they knew her.

"Just one shot please?" A balding middle-aged guy with a paunch held up another cam.

"Smile!" shouted another, and they snapped a flurry of photos.

Maya grinned and curtsied. How cool! Paparazzi. When Ill Verge opened the limo door to let Maya in she was mesmerized by strobe lights. Her eyes focused. There were several people reflected in the mirrored ceiling. Rob, Pimp, Athena, Paper Skirt Chick and a graying-too-soon light-skinned brother sitting next to Athena. Maya remembered him from the bowling party. Ferrari. The way that they all sat staring at her looked more like an intervention than a date. Maya looked over at Rob, who was smiling. Was this his idea of a joke?

"Hey Jez!" Athena said. She looked stunning, much more feminine than her usual sporty drag, giving much Michael Michele. "When I got Rob's text Ferrari was still with me so I figured he'd get a kick out of the whole tour thing."

"Good to see you again," Ferrari said. There was a shiny wooden floor with track lights and blue psychedelic lighting. A neon sign said Black Death. Ill Verge jumped behind the wheel as Maya settled in.

"Harlemworld!" Pimp shouted. "Dang, Jezebel, where you going, the VMAs? You look good!"

Rob gave Maya a sisterly pat on the shoulder. "J Lover. Glad you could make it."

Maya ignored him and turned to Athena. "This vehicle is sooo obnoxious. I'm officially embarrassed." What else to say? Why are you on my date? Maya bathed her hands in sanitizer.

"The Pimpmobile," Rob said.

Pimp leaned into the wet bar lit with fiber optics. "My land yacht. A pimp is only as tight as his flash. Holds eighteen." He turned around and resumed some sort of video game battle with Paper Skirt Girl on one of the large screens.

"Oh. Hey! We auditioned together," Paper Skirt Girl said. "You got the contract but I got the boys." Her eyes were glued to the game as her fingers manipulated her controller.

Maya had to regain her power. "I had paparazzi. Did y'all see that?"

"Oh, they weren't real." Rob looked glib. "Luci hires fakes for new artists 'til the real dudes get the hint. Creates a mood of urgency. Bait. Like the artist might really be interesting."

"Oh." Maya pulled out an emergency pack of cookies. She considered Granny Ruby's Spell for Sending an Ex to Hell. *Step One: Create a doll using a cherished object belonging to the target. Step Two: Stick exactly twelve pins in it. Step Three. Shove it into his exhaust pipe or bash him in the face with it.*

Rob rolled down a window. "So this is the Bronx y'all. Home of our own Black Death. This is where hip-hop was born."

Ferrari nodded. "Absolutely. Check it out, ladies. Kool Herc and b-boys like that made rap happen on these streets."

Athena hugged Ferrari, and he whispered something in her ear. Pimp and homegirl (wearing hot pants that might as well have been a paper skirt) were now feeling each other up. Maya gagged internally. Thank gawd the "land yacht" was big enough that they were about half a block away from her.

"So Jez, Ferrari told his friend Ezra how beautiful you are," Athena said.

"Really?" Maya looked at Rob. He was scrolling through his phone and didn't hear the comment. "Ferrari told his friend Ezra that I was beautiful?" she repeated.

Ferrari nodded again. "I was thinking that since we are going to be spinning through Queens, we could pick him up at his baby mansion in Jamaica Estates."

"Really?" Maya asked again. "Baby mansion?" Rob still didn't look up.

"Remember I was telling you how handsome he is?" Athena asked. Not really, but okay.

"It could be an impromptu double date," Ferrari said.

"I can't wait to meet him!" Maya declared.

Rob looked up abruptly. "I don't think there's time."

"There's plenty of time," Maya said. "After we pick him up don't we have to come all the way back home to Harlem?"

"Sorry, not this time," Rob said with finality.

Maya glared at Rob, who avoided her eyes.

"So we'll hit Brooklyn, the BK, home of Biggie and Jay-Z, Lil' Kim, Foxy; but first we'll hit Queens," Rob said, keeping it business. "Much underestimated in hip-hop but the home of—"

Maya put her hands in the air. "LL Cool J is hard as hell!"

Ferrari chuckled.

Rob pulled a notebook out of his pocket and scribbled something. "Yeah, and other unknowns like Run-D.M.C., Nas, 50 Cent . . . Then we'll wind it up in Staten Isle, home of the Wu," Rob said. "That's where Mi Amor lives too."

"Mi Amor?" Maya asked.

"The boy band on your label," Athena said.

"Ah. Mi Amor." Rob had gone back to his phone and notebook.

Maya moved over to sit next to him and nodded in the direction of the notebook on Rob's lap. "Your rhyme book. You still write?"

Rob nodded, looking very much like his twenty-one-year-old self. "Yeah. I put some rhymes on paper, record others on my voice mail."

"So kick something now."

"Nah, Maya." Rob actually blushed.

"Come on," Maya said, feeling suddenly very open. "For the good times."

"Word. Rob used to be off the chain back in the day," Athena told Ferrari.

Ferrari started beatboxing, and Pimp yelled from the front, "Uh-oh. Look at corporate boy taking it back!"

"You have to kick it now," Maya said.

"On GP," Athena said.

"Just this one time," Rob said, his face completely lighting up.

Maya looked on in admiration while Rob started rhyming in a stunning lyrical explosion. It felt good to be herself, kind of, for the evening. *Maya 2.0.* She felt something forming in her brain. Not the usual headache, but lyrics.

Hip-hop Infiltration: Notes

I watched a countdown of the greatest rap music videos of all time, for inspiration, or rather lack of. Of course every woman in every video sported bikinis and heels. No exaggeration. In every other video, no less than ten dudes threw cash at the screen. In fact, the videos that were surprising were the ones where people *weren't* throwing cash. LIST OF RAP ARTISTS THROWING CASH IN VIDEOS (these are just the ones in the countdown!): Cam'ron, Fat Joe, Jay-Z, Lloyd Banks, 50 Cent, Nelly, Diddy, Lil Wayne, Sizzla, Jim Jones, Hot Boyz, TI, Criminal, Damon Dash.

It appears that original thoughts are nonexistent in this non-brave new world!

Chapter 16

"I WILL BEAT A BITCH'S ASS."
—Kimora Lee Simmons

Yo Maya," started Rob's exciting message. "Big surprise. You're finally ready for the studio. The concierge has the info. Let's lay it down on wax." The studio was a nice reward as Maya had been writing up a storm, both rap verses and her own analyses.

Immediately after the date that wasn't, Maya almost couldn't stop her pen from moving across the page. She wrote from the heart, journaling a song of exactly how she felt about the whole Rob experience, now having had some distance from it. It wasn't that different from writing a poem. In fact it was a poem, just a poem dedicated to a specific rhythm. She wanted to practice it on Athena, but she couldn't get up the nerve. Besides, Athena had been busy with her new dude and writing her own lyrics to present to Rob and Shell when they finally got to the studio. That was the deal, wasn't it?

As soon as Maya received Rob's message, she sent an SOS to Athena. "We're finally doing the damn thing. The studio. Be there or be square." This was the moment that they had been waiting for. A chance to be immortal, to say something, to matter. Maya hoped that Jezebel was up to the challenge.

The recording studio was efficient-looking and low key. Maya rushed in to find Athena alone in a corner of the reception area, headphones on, feet up. She was practicing her rhymes. Maya gave her a double air kiss straight from Luci's repertoire.

"Hey you. How did you beat me here?" Maya asked, feeling a little harried.

Athena looked focused. "I had Ferrari drop me off as soon as I got your message. Did you tell Shell I was coming?"

Maya looked at the floor. "I didn't tell anybody anything. Just hopped in the car. I guess let's go find them and do our thing."

At the front desk a gum-cracking receptionist right out of central casting barely looked up at Maya and Athena as she grunted, "Yeah?" This seemed to be how a lot of people in New York communicated.

"Well I . . ." started Maya.

The phone rang; Gum Cracker picked it up: "Chung King Studios. Well lemme check that date. Um, only Studio B. Yeah. Okay. Sure." She glanced back up at Maya. "Yeah?"

"Well," Maya started again and Gum Cracker (assertive aggressive) answered the phone. Again.

"Chung King Studios . . . Yeah. Lemme direct your call." Gum Cracker looked up at Maya again and waved around her three-inch, three-color nails. "Yeah?!"

Athena waved hers right back. Only two inches and two colors, but a look of death accompanied the movement.

"We just . . ." Maya tried again, and the chick picked up her cell phone.

"Hello. Oh—hold up. Yeah Mali, so what did Tomas say then? Word?" The receptionist turned her back slightly and blew a gum bubble.

"Yo homegirl!" Athena got as close as she could to the counter without leaping over it.

"Yeah?" asked Gum Cracker.

"Check it. We got a session with Camp Hustla. Where?" Athena could get Over-the-Rhine on somebody in a heartbeat.

"Hustla? Why you ain't say that?" Gum Cracker jotted the studio info on a stickie. "Your peoples is already up there. Have a good session."

Besides the receptionist from hell, Maya now had several reasons to be uneasy. There was the dreaded ex and the protein diet sending her blood sugar haywire and her breath into ketosis, but most frightening were the new lyrics burning a hole in her pocket. There was maybe kinda sort of the slightest possibility that they could be passable. She didn't even have the courage to share them with Athena and now she was hoping to record them in her first studio session? Maybe not so bright.

The room was thick with rolling smoke—kryptonite weed and Egyptian musk incense. The dudes in the spot—assistants of assistants, people's 'round the way boys and wannabes—came alive when Maya and Athena entered. Maya was starving so she didn't notice anyone. Athena recognized a few of them as members of the camp and joined them in a game of video ball. The table in the back was filled with M&M's, Reese's Pieces, Hershey's and every other chocolate under the sun. On the side was a lonely bowl of celery sticks.

"Rob, why?" Maya knocked a fist on the goody table.

"Oh, we got all your favorites." Rob was texting somebody and didn't look up, as usual. She shoved a handful of M&M's into her face and immediately felt guilty.

"No." Maya chewed quickly then spoke with her mouth still full. "I'm trying to do this stupid fitness thing. Get rid of it. All of it. Now." Two studio assistants scurried to collect the chocolates. "And look at me when I'm talking please, Big Rob."

"Sorry, uh, Jez," Rob said. "What can you eat?"

"I don't know," said Maya, exasperated. "Call my nutritionist and ask for the rules. Bread is evil. No flour, no dairy, no sugar, no salt. Ever."

Rob handed his alternate phone to one of the assistants. "Right away, Jez. Wait 'til you hear the new Jezebel lyrics. I wrote them myself. Oh and warning, Shell's in session upstairs with Black Death and he's gonna pop by in a coupla hours."

Athena looked up from the game upon hearing Shell's name. "Oh—actually, we wanted to present the lyrics I wrote. Off the chain. I'm excited to show the camp what I can do." The Maya-Athena plan had always been to get Athena in the studio so that she could demonstrate her flow, and Shell would see her genius and give her a deal, immediately righting the wrong. Maya had kind of forgotten about this when she penned her own new lyrics.

"Cool, but . . ." Rob started.

Maya screwed her courage to the sticking place. "Well, actually, no, Athena. Um, as a surprise, I have some stuff that I want to run by y'all. Some stuff I wrote myself."

"When was this?" Athena's perfectly arched auburn brows moved closer together.

Maya teetered on the edge of her words. "I dunno; when I was in the tub maybe." She shrugged dismissively.

Rob intervened. "Well, Maya, I understand that, but if we don't go with my lyrics, then Athena's are probably more rhythmically sound and closer to who Jezebel is as a character." He went back into his texting.

"Exactly," said Athena.

"But y'all didn't even hear my lyrics," Maya insisted. "And I'm not a character."

Rob looked up. He saw the seriousness in her big eyes and small mouth. "You're right, but we're on the clock. I really want to crank something out before Shell comes in and slows everything down."

"Just hear me out." Maya looked at Rob, then back at Athena. *Auditory lingo. They should get that.* "It's my album."

At the tension the video game boys sat immobile, like roaches that think they're invisible if they don't move.

Maya's poker face was wack. Her forehead crumpled. Rob was whatever, but couldn't Athena at least believe in her once?

"Rob, let's just hear her lyrics and then we can file them away for a rainy day." Athena raised a brow at Rob.

All of the underestimation in the room pinched into Maya's side.

"You trying to get me in trouble, aren't you, Jezebel?" Was he flirting at a time like this? "Okay, let's get it over with. Time is money. What's the name of the song? 'Save the World'?" Rob stood up with a half smile.

"Actually no." Maya looked him in the eyes. "The song is called 'Angry Black Bitch.' It came from my heart."

"Really?!" Athena looked at Maya, then Rob. She sat down next to him on the leather sofa. The food-run flunkies came back in with several grocery bags and set up with the silence of ninjas.

"Cool," Rob said. "Drop your sixteen and let's get back on schedule."

"My sixteen?" Maya looked at Rob then Athena.

"Your sixteen bars," said Athena. "There's sixteen bars to a rap verse."

"Oh." Maya saw one of the game boys elbow another in her peripheral vision.

"Hey, hey, hey. What's good?" Shell appeared in the doorway. Everyone snapped to attention. Uh-oh. He was early. No one ever expected Shell to be early. Early! "Came to check on my pet project. What's the haps?"

Rob got up and sat on the arm of the chair. "All good, Shell."

"How are you?" Athena smiled her professional cheerleader smile.

Maya looked down at her lined paper, crumpled and rescued several times.

"We're figuring out the lyrics situation," Rob said.

"What's to figure out, Big Rob? What you wrote was banging." Shell pulled up a work chair and sat in the center of the room. "All the best female rap bangers were penned by a man."

Rob looked nervous. "Yeah, but Jez and Lady Athena both have lyrics they're presenting as Jezebel's first hit."

"We didn't hear my anthem yet. And we know it's gonna be hot." Athena slid her shoulders back and pouted her lips at Shell.

Shell rubbed his hands together. "Fresh—an old-school battle! Your producer ain't here yet, so before Kwamé arrives, let's see what you got. Who's up first?" All Shell needed was a bowl of popcorn.

Athena, ever the competitor, didn't need a cue. She smoothed her new, glossier by the ounce hair and paused for effect. Then she let it rip, dragging into a quick build:

"You slow, I'm blow
Man listen, you pissin'
I'm hissin', you listen
Combusting and dismissing
My style is like whoa, a mile of Hydro,
Nitro, Takin' bribes though
You're in dis ease while I'm a disease,
Spreading you? Please
All night long
Like Lionel Ritchie, bitch
His daughter's Richie Rich
You wish, you fish
You could dance like this,
Shake it,
I said dance like this . . ."

"Oh man!" Shell punched his fist as Athena started shaking it to the beat she left hanging in the air. "It's a wrap on that," Shell continued. "Let's do it, Lady Athena. That's what I'm talking 'bout."

Athena was beaming. "Let's move to the studio! I can coach Jez from my copy." Everyone in the room rose and starting moving toward the door.

Maya felt less doubted at her original audition. "But y'all didn't hear mine yet. Well, it's a work in progress, but you can get the gist."

Shell looked at his watch then at Rob while the team hovered near the door.

"Proceed," said Rob and everyone sat back down.

"Thank you, Rob," mouthed Maya.

"Yeah, okay, do your thing," Athena said. "There will be other albums so other lyrics are always welcome."

Maya was back in seventh grade. It was the day of the big storytelling contest. Top prize in each class was a trip to L.A. Maya had worked on Close the Door, a story about a couple who argued each night about their household chores. Homeboy came home from work and left the door open, insisting that it was wifey's turn to close it. Wifey said that it was his turn.

They bet each other that whichever of them spoke first would have to close the door. They sat like idiots on their sofa refusing to speak while thieves came in the open door and pilfered all their stuff. When a vagabond wandered in and began to rough up the husband, the wife screamed 'leave him alone.' Maya still remembered the last line of the story, 'I won cried the fool, now you have to close the door.' So did Maya win the contest, go to L.A. and get her seventh-grade fun on with the neighboring all-boys' school? No, because even though Maya Hopeless worked super duper hard on the story, she was intimidated by Athena's braggadocio and didn't even raise her hand. Athena won the competition and went to L.A. with the boys from The Hancock School. Maya went to gym with Miss Allen.

Maya looked at Shell, Rob and Athena and cleared her throat again. "This is called 'Angry Black Bitch.' " She stuck out her boobs—power boobs. She was fakin' it 'til she was making it. All swagger, moxie and big balls. She was looking at the floor, then she was looking at Rob, the catalyst. And then Maya, no longer hopeless, exploded:

"Yo! I never wanted me to sing this song,
Going on and on
Talking 'bout how you did me wrong
For oh so long
Flowing on 'til the break of dawn.
But I'm here now and the truth is the truth
Didn't get it before, but the youth is the youth
These men do you wrong
Then when you singing your song
They acting like you crazy
But my word is my bond
I wish to God it never happened
But it did so I'm strappin
And now I'm scratching this itch
Making a wish
Tellin' you who I is
Yes. The Angry Black Bitch
Say Word.

Who I is, yo?
The Angry Black Bitch

Yo. I never wanted me to sing this song,
Going on and on
Talking 'bout how you did me wrong
For so long
Going on 'til the break of dawn.
But I'm here now and the truth is the truth
I didn't get it before, but the youth is the youth

You say nothing succeeds like success?
I say nothing exceeds like excess.
So now who's the best?
Who's the mess?
Who wears the breasts?
Who's the one impressed?
Call me a bitch then
I'm a bitch in control
Just like I told you
The past took its toll
On your old soul
So, I say fold, motherfucka
Fold."

"Stop! Stop! Stop! Stop!" said Shell.

All riled up, Maya pushed her own stuff off the table and kicked the trashcan. "Ow!" She hurt her big toe. The last verse she kicked in Trini patois. She didn't even know where that came from, but she was delighted to see a drop of her spit hit Rob's nose.

Rob was immobile with an ambiguous expression on his face while Athena faced the wall.

Maya sank onto a table. Fine! She had done her best and it felt great.

"You *killed it!*" Shell screamed. "Bananas!" Was this good or bad? Maya looked at Rob. He was nodding.

"Yo!" The engineer got up and ran from his seat to the door and back again. Several other hanger-on dudes got up and high-fived Rob.

"Crazy!" said one.

"That bitch is wild," said another. They were completely bugging out.

Happy? Happy! They were rejoicing! This is what happened in the studio when the camp smelled a hit. Screaming. Especially from the entourage. The last thing they could afford was for the team to fall completely off. Then they would have to go back to their mom's basement or baby's mama's couch. Success was in everybody's best interest. Maya's face burst into sunshine.

"So?" Athena asked, sticking out her meager boobies.

"That's some deep stuff, Jez. Let's go for it." Rob shook Maya's hand like he was meeting her for the first time. " 'Angry Black Bitch' is a good look. Let's just work on that flow and breath control."

"Clearly, y'all got this thing on lock," Shell said. He gave Maya a strange hug, nestling her head in the crook of his arm and patting her head. "The East Coast is back! They say when you get the world's attention you better have something to say. And you do. Complete," he said, straightening up, and he left.

"Athena, we're doing my song!" Maya said, excited. She hugged Athena, but Athena sat wooden in the center of the hug.

Athena stood up. "Cool, Jezebel, I'll get up with you later."

Maya nodded her head. "Can't you be happy for me?"

Athena wouldn't meet her eyes. Whatever. She had no time for ego management. She was recording a song! Her song. Her truth. Her feelings. Her words! Athena stood by herself, momentarily disoriented.

Rob lowered his voice. "I guess this is where you tell me it's not personal."

"What do you mean?" Maya asked.

"Your song. Our song?" Rob pulled his Yankee cap down on his head.

"Oh, don't flatter yourself. It has a lot of meanings. Sociologist, remember? I wanted to make a song using the insult common in the vernacular."

"Blah, blah, blah. I got it." Rob and Maya stood looking at each other a beat too long for comfort, then Rob shouted to the boys, "Cool! Let's hit the studio and do our thing. Next room, everybody. Company move."

Maya moved closer to Rob as Athena shoved her things into her bag.

"Shawty, I'll walk you out," said the one maybe named Fats.

"Cool." Athena put her bag on her shoulder. As she walked with Fats, she looked back at Maya.

"Later, girl," Maya said. Athena nodded.

Maya felt emboldened. "Rob, do all of these people need to be here?" She was going to rock the opportunity.

"Who?" Rob asked. "The boys? We're fam."

"I understand," Maya said. "But I need to focus."

Rob smiled. "No doubt, Jez. The artist needs to focus. Go 'head into the studio and let me holla at them for a sec. They can stay here in the lounge."

"Thanks." Maya was grateful for the small victory. She would have to holla at Athena later.

There was now a beautifully laid-out spread of healthy snacks: sugar-free gelatin, apples, raisin-nut mix, hard-boiled eggs, protein bars, rice cakes, yogurt and yes, the tired celery sticks with dip.

At the center, on a mini pedestal, was an alluring hot chicken sandwich with Italian lettuce in place of bread. Melted Brie, Maya's favorite cheese, dripped from the sides. It smelled divine and her mouth watered. She reached in, hesitated and then gave herself over to temptation. She took a bite of heaven, feeling a bit like a vampire. Mmmm. Peppery garlic. Savory. Sweet and spicy honey mustard. Ecstasy. She discovered areas of her tongue that she never knew existed. Yeah . . . Maya balanced her blood sugar with her first taste of chicken (and broke the no-dairy-before-recording rule) and then headed for the mic.

Keyboards, mixers, monitors, screens and speakers everywhere. The producer, Kwamé, was the million-dollar man. The rapper's rapper and the producer's producer, the link between old school and new. Maya remembered his happy-go-lucky songs and videos where even the dog was sporting polka dots. The music he'd created for Maya was a hot combo of deep funk and updated soul grooves. He was attentive and supportive as she laid down her anthem.

"I feel like a real artist." Maya stepped into the booth and put on her headphones. "No, I *am* a real artist," she declared. Maya looked through the glass at Rob and Kwamé and winked at one or both of them. They could take it how they wanted to. Now that she was a carnivore she felt primal and predatory. She touched the padded walls. The booth had a solitary feeling, like it was just you and your soul in there. Damn. It felt good.

Recording "Angry Black Bitch" was a no-brainer. In her solitude with Rob, the engineer and Kwamé, Maya took a deep breath, looked Rob dead in the eye and spat it out. She spat for her anger at how the whole thing went down. She spat for injustice and she spat for her life.

And when Kwamé and Big Rob smiled respectfully and said good work, her job was done. Done, but just beginning. Exciting. Yay!

"You walked in a rapper but you're walking out an emcee," Kwamé said. When she got "home" in the morning's new hours, Athena was dead asleep. They would have to "get up" with each other when they rose. Maya tossed in her bed for forty agonizing minutes. She was exhausted but sleep would not come. She stumbled to the Heretix Celeb Care Package (condoms, lube, sleeping pills, Nō Dōz, dieter's tea and the like) and popped a sleeper.

The sound of her new track was playing in Maya's head, just between her eyes. It was her phone. Her brain came into dull focus. Oh—it was a ringtone, meaning that the phone was ringing. How and when did Rob do that?! Five A.M. She'd gone to bed at four. Unknown number, still ringing.

"Hello," she whispered, hazy with sleep.

"Yo, Jezebel. What up, Earth?" It was a heavy male voice.

"Who's this?" Maya asked, realizing that sleep was becoming more and more of a commodity.

"Get up, Angry Black Bitch, it's da Pimp," the voice said.

"Excuse me?" asked Maya. She still wasn't sure half the time when folks were joking and when she had beef.

"I heard your track, yo. You killt it!" he said. Oh. Pimp.

"Thanks." Maya wondered (a) when he woulda had the time to hear it; and (b) why he was calling at dawn's crack to share his approval. "Okay, g'night, Pimp. I mean good morning."

"Nah. We shooting our vid and need you to come lay down a verse." Pimp said "whassup" to one of the many voices in the background.

"When?" Maya asked.

"Right now, Jez. We need you to rep in our video. Basically Kronic wilded out on his SC. His PO wasn't having it so he got locked up in the Vue. We got a hole in the storyline, but Rob had an idea of how you could fill it." Huh?

"The Vue?"

"Bellevue, baby. You coming or not?"

Maya slowly opened her eyes. Seize the friggin day. "Most definitely."

"Good. And bring that fine-ass partner of yours. Hit Big Rob for the address." Pimp hung up.

"Wilded out on his SC?" Maya asked herself as she sent Rob a text through her sleep blindness.

"Sobriety companion," Athena said from under her covers. "A friend hired to keep him sober."

Maya looked over. "Athena, we should talk about . . ."

Athena's words tumbled out into a bulky pile. "Don't sweat it, Angry Black Bitch. A Black Death video? It's exciting how all of my dreams are coming true. For you. When you make it, we make it, right?"

"Aw. Athena. You're acting like I sold you down the river." Maya squinted and tried to see Athena clearly.

"Please. Nothing wrong with a little healthy competition, Maya. It's all good. I'm not tight witchu."

"You have no reason to be tight with me. If anything, I should be tight with you for not being supportive of me writing for my own album."

"What happened to *our* album, Maya? What happened to shifting Shell from you to me?"

"I know that you're used to everything coming up roses for you, Athena, and having to comfort your poor loser friend, but can we try a new dynamic where we both have it going on? You still want me to lock you in on that shot with Camp Hustla, right?"

"Oh, okay. You threatening me now?" Athena asked.

Maya wasn't sure, so she said nothing. She then figured she should react somehow so she shook her head.

"Whatever," Athena said.

"Pimp told me to make sure you were there," Maya said.

"Really?" Athena gave what Maya wanted to interpret as a small smile, but was more like twisted lips.

"Athena, we're sistas," Maya said and stumbled into the bathroom to get ready for her music video debut.

"Then act like it, Maya. That was my big shot!"

"Don't worry. We're gonna get you signed with the Boy Wonder. Promise."

"What happened to your 'hip-hop undercover' experiment?" Athena asked.

"What?" Maya called from the bathroom. She popped a Nō Dōz pill. "Oh. Yeah."

Chapter 17

"You say you proud to be black
and then stand tall,
But in the videos there ain't no sistas at all."
—*BWP*

Maya and Athena arrived on the massive set of the Black Death music video shoot, a sophisticated townhouse with a rooftop pool on a blocked-off street near Astor Place. In the scene being shot, an Asian woman—yup, Paper Skirt Girl (exhibitionist)—in a gold bikini danced while Pimp, Gunz and Nigg poured champagne on her behind and kicked lyrics to their new song, "Bottom Bitch." Behind them were two screens showing clips of their absent homies: Kronic, currently a resident of Bellevue Mental Ward, on the left and the late Thug on the right.

"My Bottom Bitch she never snitches.
On her ass I make my wishes . . ."

"Lovely." Maya picked up a Red Bull from the craft services table and guzzled it. "These aren't bad." Maya knew that psychologically if you wanted to make someone forgive you, you force as much interaction as possible. She had pledged to never use her knowledge to manipulate. It was unethical. But screw it. "You want to try some, Athena?"

"I'm doing good old-fashioned black coffee. I don't see how you can drink that on an empty stomach," Athena said, checking out the action. "This is hot!"

The woman was now crawling around on the dark parquet floor.

"Ugh, cluck-cluck," Maya said.

"Chickenheads are the official bird of popular music," Athena said.

Rob smiled when he saw Maya. How was he still going and looking crisp to boot? Maybe she was delirious. "Morning, ladies." Rob looked at his watch. "That's Dope Jones, the director."

"He's directed videos for every artist in the book. If the Jezebel project is up to his standards, maybe he'll do your video too, Jez."

A blower gusted cash around the scene as the "love interest" leapt into the air, catching hundred-dollar bills, some of which were stuffed into her panties.

"*His* standards?" Maya asked.

"Come on. It's Dope Jones," said Athena as the man himself approached. Wow. Hello there. Dope looked black Latin. He was short but very easy on the eyes, almost like a more exotic mini Cool J. Maya smiled.

Rob made intros. "Dope, this is Jezebel—the track you heard earlier—and this is her homegirl, Lady Athena."

"What up?" Athena said and Dope said hello back.

"Jezebel, it's a pleasure." Dope's eyes locked into Maya's. There was an energy between them.

Maya smiled and shook Dope's hand as he went in for a cheek kiss. Copacetic. Hands with a little pull to them. None of that manicured baby-soft nonsense most New York brothas had going. And she didn't even reach for the sanitizer.

Athena puffed her lips to make them pouty. "That 50 Cent video where he has the gun is slamming."

"Doesn't every 50 Cent video have a gun?" asked Maya, newly knowledgeable about such things. She threw up the with-it game face that everybody seemed to sport.

"Yeah," Dope said, "I guess so."

Hopped up on energy drink, Maya felt moxie-fied. "So, Dope, you're one of the first peeps to hear my song."

"And I loved it." Dope studied Maya like she was a science project.

"So, Jezebel, here's the concept. Even unmixed it was wild. You on some wild, crazy, bitch shit and so are we."

Maya's game face fell apart. "Nooo, I actually think that we're saying opposite things." She felt her eyes rounding.

"Exactly," Dope said. "And the contrast will be *outrageous*!" Dope smiled a million-dollar smile and licked his lips. Because he was so fine, it didn't look sleazy. "Let's take the last verse of your song and slow it way down. Kick it like you're on heroin."

"Heroin?" Maya asked.

"Flat and monotone," Dope continued. "A deep voice with that angel face. Outrageous."

Maya looked at Athena and opened her eyes wide. Dope was flirting with her! He kept his gaze on Maya. Rob looked like he swallowed something.

"Outrageous," Athena said.

"Yo Rob, lemme holla at you." Dope and Rob turned their backs in conference like the women were now out of earshot although they were standing right behind them.

"I have an idea for a cage scene." Dope's voice was filled with excitement.

"Oh, hell no," Maya said and Dope looked back. Damn. Too late to reel it in. Probably squashed all possibilities that Dope Jones could be the one.

"I'll do it." Athena said and lowered her voice. "Maya, this is Dope Jones. It's not like that."

"Do you think I would have you playing yourself?" Rob asked Maya.

Maya looked at him. "Dangerous question."

"I would never put you in harm's way," he said, looking more handsome than ever. Either Maya was feverish or the cute man factor was high this morning. Before Maya could react, four guys wheeled in a pink motorcycle with *Jezebel* spelled out in Swarovski crystals.

"That's me!" Maya screamed. Athena looked envious. Maya, on the other hand, was ecstatic. "Oh my goddess! It's gaudy, overdone and beautiful!" She whooped uncharacteristically. "Somebody made that for me?"

"Somebody did. Hours ago," Dope said, touching Maya's arm. "Because you're worth it." He winked and Maya winked back.

"Banging," said Athena, without a smile.

"Sorry I'm so emotional, guys," Maya said. "It's just I always wanted to try riding a chopper."

"You would look good riding a chopper," Rob said. Maya touched his arm, enjoying the competition for her attention.

Dope moved into general mode. "That's dope then. Jezebel, of course you'll be on the bike and Athena you'll be solo in the cage."

"Solo!" Athena jumped up, then regained her composure. "That'll work!"

"You gotta play your best players sometime," Rob said. "Let's get y'all both to hair and makeup." He slapped Dope on the back like men do, and walked off, with Athena and Maya following.

Maya and Athena got dressed in a room with an actual star (!) on the door. Athena stuck her nervous thumb in her mouth. Maya could see her mentally pumping herself up.

"Sorry, 'Thena, that you're not rapping."

"Who cares? I get to be the hot chick in the video. Do you know how much scrilla video hos are raking in these days? Awards, book deals. I might be on to something."

"You're not a ho," Maya said, and Athena looked at her for a moment, serious.

Then Athena was back to being Athena. "You damned right, 'cause pimping ain't easy, but hoin' is hell! And I better be rapping next time, bitch!" Maya smiled.

The hair and makeup people beat their faces within an inch of their lives. Glam lashes, luscious lips, the whole nine. They dressed Athena in a short-sleeved gold jacket with no shirt and matching hot pants, and they dressed Maya in a gold Balenciaga dress with a cropped jean jacket. Smokin!

Maya looked at her butt in the mirror.

"Oh," The video's stylist held out chocolate brown satin panties. "Put these on. Kendra Francis flesh-colored undies."

"Why?" Maya asked. "Nobody's looking between my legs."

"That's for sure," said Athena.

The stylist tried in vain not to show her annoyance. "These will keep everything smooth," she said.

"Fine." Maya looked into the dressing room mirror one more time before she headed to set. A bad mama jama.

Rob, Dope and a couple of other people in director's chairs sat up. Like everywhere in the music biz, the place was rife with hangers-on. Everyone traveled with no less than four old friends from the hood at any given time. Athena was Maya's only friend from the hood—only friend period—so that was that. It was a three-camera shoot. They were shooting Maya rapping on the motorcycle and then Athena dancing in a cage with the Black Death crew.

Athena licked a finger and held it up in the air, making a sizzling noise. "Sssssss!"

Dope Jones walked up to Maya. "Okay, Jezebel, so basically, you're gonna just sit on the chopper and kick your verse directly into the camera. Strong, cool, collect. Then we'll do a short lap on the bike."

"Lap?" Maya asked.

"Just kidding." Dope Jones wore a wry smile.

"I got your back," called Rob from his chair.

"And I'll take the rest, cutie," Dope said.

"Is there a helmet?" Maya asked.

"You don't need a helmet to sit on a bike." Dope helped Maya onto the bike. "Comfy?"

"Sure. How many times are we going to do it?" Maya asked. It was bigger than she anticipated.

"Until we're done." Dope turned his lips up into a smile. "Are you always this much trouble?"

Maya grinned and nodded. She couldn't think of anything else to ask, so it was time to do the damn thing and make her video debut.

"You good?" Rob shouted.

Maya held up her thumb.

"Playback! Roll cameras," someone said.

"Rolling," said a camera operator.

"Roll sound," someone else said.

"Ai, ai," a sound dude said.

"Action!" screamed Dope.

Maya looked dead in the camera and murdered her verse. *"It's the Angry Black Bitch / Who snitched? / Flip the ignition switch / Like this / What's my hitch? / Singing off pitch / Ditch the witness / I'm the wicked witch / A kiss? You wish!/You are/ Dismissed/So feel/My gist/So rich/ Squish."*

Gully. Then she looked into the cam and smiled like the Kool-Aid pitcher.

"Cut! Nah, Jez. It was hot up until the end. Don't smile. Ever. Keep it hard." Dope was even finer when he was in his element. "Of course bring the sexy, but I more or less need you just looking cold. You know, I would kill a man ice cold. Got it?" he asked.

"Would kill a man? Got it," said Maya, looking at Rob.

"Okay, going again," yelled the assistant director.

"Sexy, okay?" called Dope. "Action!"

Maya moved her hands on action and barely got out a few words when the director screamed "Cut!" again.

Maya rocked back and forth on the vibrating bike.

Dope caressed her arm. "Slowwww it down. Easy, girl. You a female acting like you don't know how to be sexy. With all that body. Gimme what you feeling down deep. That anger. It's very *Leave It to Beaver* right now. When you slow it down, it's crazy. It's like you channeling sex. Seduce us."

Sexy? Seduction? She had never seduced anyone in her life. Okay. Steam. Passion. Raw. She looked at Dope. He was a very handsome man. Maybe they could really kick it. She licked her lips and dropped her sixteen again, perfectly this time. Just for him. She could see Dope's face in her peripheral vision and feel his excitement. She thought about trying to please Dope, Rob and Athena and what they each wanted from her. Then . . . Somehow Maya's hand or foot pushed something it shouldn't have and she was moving.

Moving! On a motorcycle! "*Stop, Maya!*" came Athena's voice. Maya tried to steer the thing at first, then she just balled up into the handlebars trying to cover her head. FACES. People were yelling things at her and lights were flashing in her face. "Stop! Go left." "No, go right." "Watch out!" "Noooooooo!" IMPACT. Maya careened into a crowd of extras. THUD. Enough of them to break her fall. OW. Dope was down too, and yelling. FLASH. Blinded by a camera. She rubbed her head. Several people were trying to see if she was all right and folks were cussing each other out over fault. Three cameras close up in her bloody nose. Dope stood up and didn't even look at Maya as several people including Rob helped her up.

"That's a wrap on Jezebel," he shouted, storming off. All prospects of hooking up with him were most likely dead.

Maya insisted that her head was fine although the ringing in her ears was annoying. She sent the ambulance away. Could everyone just forget this happened already? Athena did. She was off shooting her scene. Rob called Shell's doctor to make sure Maya's Mensa brain was still intact. "Gotta keep you healthy for your infiltration," he whispered. Doc Hollyrock gave her a quick exam and a bottle of Vicodin in case she felt any more pain, although she told him repeatedly that she only took holistic medicine.

The icing on the cake? NYPD tried to break up the shoot because several extras called somewhere to complain that Maya did a Sharon Stone panty-less flash giving the cameras a shot of her secrets. Dope didn't have a permit for that. The team explained that Maya was wearing flesh-colored underwear but the coppers refused to leave until Maya showed them the drawers in question. Lewd Indecency. To say the least.

The next morning, they all awoke to the following news item on Perez Hilton.

RAP CHICK REVEALS SLIT
JEZEBEL CAUGHT WITH HER LEGS OPEN

HOLLY-WOULD, NEW YORK—Jezebel, the newest rapper at Camp Hustla, showed more than her ass recently as she careened forward on a specialty chopper with her legs wide open, flashing the crowd. She joins the spate of panty-less young stars partying hard and leaving their underwear at home. Each time, they leave us asking, liberated woman or overrated whore? The camp vehemently denies rumors that her bloody nose was linked to a cocaine habit.

Chapter 18

"STYLE, WHEN WE WANT
AND WE LOVE WHEN THEY HATE US."
—Foxy Brown

A couple of nights later, the Camp Hustla crew settled into the VIP booth at MocaBar, a cozy Harlem hotspot. Dark burgundy with low tables and eccentric Afrocentric art, the VIP area was a small elevated stage near the back adjacent to the DJ booth. Manifesta was spinning for Grown & Sexy Night. Athena was still riding high from her video ho premiere and Maya was just hungry. The Black Death boys were dispersed throughout, each already hanging over a hoochie or two. A couple of soap opera actors at the next table waved. Maya waved back and Rob got up to handle some business. They settled in and passed the menus.

"This is fine man central," Athena said.

"You look like you need a drink." A cute dark-skinned girl with a short 'fro leaned over Maya.

"Immediately if not sooner." Maya said.

"I'd recommend—" the waitress started.

"Actually, we'd like bottle service," said Luci.

"Of course. My name is Nerve. I'll be your server tonight."

"Shout-out to the Camp Hustla fam," came through the speakers over a smooth beat.

"Gimme a Sapporo," said Athena.

"Beer?" Luci smoothed the front of her pencil skirt.

"Last time I checked." Athena didn't look in Luci's direction.

"I'd like . . . a Cosmo," Maya said.

Luci waved her finger. "Not on our diet."

"Oh, come on. After the week I had?" Maya pouted.

"You need to get your drink on," agreed Athena.

"All I'm saying is let's check the chart." Luci found a lipstick case in her bag and unrolled a slip of paper that looked like a joint. It listed the caloric counts of alcoholic beverages.

"Light beer, twenty-eight calories? Coffee liqueur, one seventeen? Only you would have this, Luci!" Maya exclaimed.

Athena took it from Luci's hands. "Classic. For the vain and sexy."

"Cheers. Okay, so since we're not beer people, Jez," Luci said as she looked over to Athena, "we definitely want to stay in the cognac brandy family. Only fifty calories. So we'll have L'Esprit de Courvoisier." Luci crossed her legs.

Athena mocked her behind her back.

"Uh, we're out of that, but give us ten minutes and we'll get it." The waitress put a bottle of Korbel on the table. "Complimentary."

"What is *that*?" asked Luci.

"A bottle of champagne to get you started." The waitress bowed her head a little.

Luci pushed the bottle away. "That's not champagne. That's cheap sparkling wine masquerading as champagne. Champagne comes from Champagne, France. Please don't ever disrespect this table like that again."

"I'll take it." Athena snatched the bottle.

"No problem, miss." The waitress hurried away.

Luci turned to Maya aghast. "Ugh. Would she bring that to a white girl?"

"I guess not," said Maya.

"I think not," said Luci.

Athena popped open the bottle, splashing the floor, and took it to the head. Luci turned up her nose and Maya laughed at Athena's audacity.

"I'm dancing," Athena announced and made her way through the crowd.

The spot was a sexy den of sin. To their left a woman was giving a man a foot job. On the other side of their three-man wall of security guards, people were getting their definitive freak on, thumping, bumping and grinding in the bacchanal.

"Pimp, I love you!" shouted a girl in a wide yellow belt moonlighting as a thin yellow skirt.

Pimp was in deep conference with a slick-haired dude. "I love you too, baby," he said as Nerve and a second cocktail waitress made it back with the round of drinks, two bottles of Cristal, glasses and three platters of chicken wings. They poured the Cristal, waiting for Luci's approval before shrinking off.

Pimp sat down. "Champagne to my real friends and real pain to my sham friends," Pimp toasted. "Y'all represented in the video. It was hot." He hugged Maya and a couple of flashbulbs went off.

"Okay. Thanks!" Maya was somehow on her third drink. She pushed Pimp playfully and he left.

"Oh—there's one of my old clients from corporate," Luci got up.

"Hey! I have a surprise for you." Rob was carrying two tequila shots. He handed one to Maya, not knowing about the flutes of real and sham champagne.

Maya nodded at him. "Right on time." They clinked shot glasses. "This doesn't mean we're cool, Rob. Mr. 'I'm not gonna put you in harm's way.' " She downed her shot and plunked her glass down.

"Whoa," Rob said. "I see you doing big girl things."

A Jay-Z and Foxy Brown classic came on and everybody hit the dance floor as soon as Jay said, "I keep you fresher than the next bitch, indeed." Maya and Rob were the only two left sitting.

"So, Maya, whaddaya say?"

"About what? I could have killed myself on that bike. And again, that would have been less embarrassing."

Rob held out his arm. "Dance with me."

Maya didn't respond.

Rob tried a little Billie Dee. "What, are you gonna wait for my arm to fall off?"

Maya rolled her eyes.

"Come on. Don't be like that. We had a few laughs didn't we?" Rob reached over and tried to pull her up as Foxy sang, "Sleeps around but he gives me a lot."

Maya tried to hold back her smile.

Rob remembered that she did that sometimes. "One laugh, every now and then?"

Maya gritted her teeth. She didn't want to give him the satisfaction.

"I see you smiling in there."

Maya gave in, showing teeth and giggling. "Okay, okay. We had a good time sometimes, Rob. We were good together. Whatever."

"So you gonna dance for me?"

Maya cocked her head to the side. "Dance *for* you. This ain't no show or video or—"

"All right, all right, Freudian slip. I thought you were a Freudian. Can I live? Dance with me." Rob stood up.

"You forget that I don't dance." Maya was feeling his persistence. As the liquor hit her system, it felt good to be pursued. She crossed and uncrossed her legs.

He lowered his voice. She had to lean in to hear him amidst the chaos. "Yeah, *Maya* didn't dance but I see Jeze—Cleopatra doing all types of stuff. So dance with me. And make a brotha feel a little less guilty for one night, Cleopatra." Rob was still holding out his hand. Manipulative bastard.

Maya took his hand and followed him to the dance floor. She thought that she was a just little tipsy until she stood up. Whoa. Not tipsy. Noooo. Full on drunk. Whoooo. It felt great. They were playing Beyoncé, and at that moment all she cared about was the beat. She put her hands above her head and shook her butt from side to side.

"Whoa. Whoa. Whoa," said Rob. "Don't go whitegirl on me. Slow it down." He put his hands on her shoulders. Maya slowed down and they were grooving together, her full hips dazzling from side to side. "Listen to the beat. Yeah, that's real good right there. We're gonna just live inside that beat for a second right there." Rob's midnight eyes looked hypnotized.

Then the music changed and wouldn't you know it? Slow jam city. Maya pulled away. Dancing with him to Prince's "Adore" was just too much. Rob took both of her hands and refused to let go. "One more song."

Maya pretended to protest then immediately gave in. Loving it. *Until the end of time . . .* She held on and breathed into Rob's neck. *I'll be there for you . . .* She felt herself . . . letting go. Inhaling and exhaling and . . . wanting to make the stupidest move since she said yes the first time. But she couldn't help it. *Love's too weak to define . . . Just what you mean to me . . .* And she didn't want to help it. It felt too good holding him.

Rob smelled like that clean green manly soap. He was holding her closer than close and she was loving it. It. The situation. The surrender. *I truly adore you . . .* As they rocked back and forth she felt the bulge in his cords grow until they were full on dirty dancing. Damn. The walls were sweating. Hell, the floor was sweating. Her hands were moist and Rob's back in his husband beater tank felt wet. She smelled his smell under the soap, gripped his shoulders and remembered. She remembered how it felt when he entered her body. How he gave a guttural "oh God" when they hit their stride. She wanted to wrap her legs around his back. So she did. Right there on the dance floor. Rob gave a smile and kind of spun around. Not enough to be soap opera-ish, but just enough to let Maya pretend for sixty silly seconds that they were "we."

Fortune favors the bold, Maya thought. She moved her lips toward Rob's and stopped just before touching him. Damn, she couldn't do it. Thankfully, Rob leaned in. He leaned in and brushed his lips on hers. She felt all one million nerve endings in her lips shock her body awake. Rob leaned his forehead against Maya's and their eyes locked. It was hypnotic, dizzying. He moved his handsome head back and licked his lips. Aw yeah, LL style.

"I love this song," he whispered, kissing her ear.

"Um-hm," she mumbled, hoping that translated to "Kiss me, really kiss me. Please."

The music changed again; different. Faster now. They both let her feet hit the ground but they were still handling each other. Moving to their own rhythm. Holding each other tighter than they did when they rehearsed for their first dance. Holding on like the future of the free world depended on their electricity. Rocking. Grinding. He felt solid. Real. And then it happened. No, not *that.* DJ Manifesta was calling her name. *Her* name.

"Jezebel is in the house, y'all. I haven't had her swing by the radio hot spot yet 'cause she wasn't ready. I know y'all respect Manifesta 'cause I keeps it real. And I'm all about the music. So all I knew before today about Jezebel was she's a little scandalish, but I gotta give it up y'all. This track is straight banging. It is my sincerest honor to premiere for you 'Angry Black Bitch'!"

Her song was on! They were playing Maya's song. She couldn't let go of Rob to react until Athena came running up between them. She took Maya's hands and they jumped up and down, screaming. "They're playing our song!" Maya looked around. People were dancing. Loving it. The club was feeling her. The women were digging the words. The dudes were digging the beat. Maya and Athena were yelling and straight bugging. Especially when Athena heard the verse she didn't know Maya added.

"There's brick city chicks like Lady Athena
Know she's an angry bitch from the moment that you seen her
Lips puffed out bluest eyes fussed out
Let a mutherfucka step you'll be cussed out
Mind on your money. Yes your money's on her mind
Payback bitch! For wasting all her freaking time . . ."

"You're a beast!" screamed Athena. "This is hot! *Hot!* It's okay, 'cause the next one will be mine, right? Right?"

Maya's head was swimming too much to answer.

Luci started a telephone whisper in the crowd that Jezebel was on the dance floor and a circle formed around Maya yelling, "Go Jez, Go Jez." Maya was high on L'Esprit de Courvoisier, Cristal, premium Cuervo, Korbel and Rob's sweat. She screamed, "Go me, go me," fist pumping in the air. She didn't even feel Pimp's hands as he picked her up and passed her through the crowd. She was air surfing and life was crazy. Crazy beautiful. Rob stood by, heart full, watching what a difference a day makes.

"Prediction," Manifesta said over the speakers. "This is the new anthem!"

Thug's classic, "The Assassinator," launched and the energy shifted. Maya felt queasy. She was passed all the way to the front door and stone cold in her own perspiration. She didn't even notice the security hunk shadowing her. She found Athena in the crowd and grabbed her hand. When did Ferrari get there? She felt herself trying to act sober. Act sober. Athena understood. There was a line of people waiting for the bathroom. They got on it.

Luci saw them on line. "What are you doing?"

"Waiting to go to the loo," said Maya. Luci's international-ness was rubbing off.

"No babe, *you* don't wait." Luci held back the crowd as Maya and Athena headed downstairs. They opened a door, stepped inside and locked it.

"Maya—this is so much fun!!"

Maya was slurring her words. "Houston, we have a problem."

"It's the best night of our lives." Athena lit a cigarette.

"Remember that little ole *make Rob fall in love with me* plan?" Maya took the cigarette from Athena's hands and took a drag. She hadn't smoked since she was sixteen in a shed behind school.

Athena looked like a proud mom. "Yes! It's totally working. When you were dancing he was all about you."

Maya hacked smoke and Athena whacked her on the back. "It's more than working. On me! I think I'm all about him." Maya banged her head on the wall. "Ow!"

"You serious?" Athena wasn't sure how to react.

"It gets worse." Maya rubbed her head. "Athena! I want him, want him. Right now." Maya clasped her hands.

Athena smiled. "Well, it can't be right now, 'cause the club is kinda crowded and you're a celebrity now."

"Athena!"

"Listen, Pimpstress, if you brought me down here to get me to talk you outta hitting it with Big Rob, I'm the wrong one. Girl you are mad backed up. Your life is working. Do the damn thing." Athena fixed her extensions in the slanted mirror.

"Not that I needed your permission . . ." Maya was sliding down to the floor.

"Let's get outta this bathroom already and get you some." Athena pulled her up and put the cig out. "Wow. Look how thin you are, Maya."

They hugged and made it back up to the dance floor. They were walking over to Rob and Maya slipped on somebody's business card. Ouch. She was flat on the floor and laughing. The theme of the week. Camera phones went up. If you can't beat 'em, join 'em. "Cheese," she smiled, hoping that everyone wasn't catching a shot of any more flesh-colored evidence.

Rob picked Maya up and slung her over his shoulder. "Athena, where's her keys?"

Athena found a room key in her pocket. "She told me earlier, Rob, that she wanted *you* to take her home." Athena looked Rob in the eye making her point clear.

Luci rushed over. "Legba is outside."

"It's only a few blocks," he said.

"You just gonna carry her like that, player?" asked Ferrari.

"The night air will be good for her." Rob tightened his arms around her.

Athena reached up and touched Maya's hand. Maya squeezed and let go.

There were six looong city blocks between MocaBar and the Heretix, and Rob carried Maya all the way. He noted her lighter physique, unsure that he would have been able to carry Ohio Maya that distance. She babbled something about the world being upside down. In the lobby, the staff politely turned their backs and gave no reaction as if big brothas carrying drunk starlets-in-training walked though the lobby every day, and perhaps they did. Maya gave them a little wave. She resisted making any snide comments as Rob carried her over the threshold.

Rob put Maya in bed and slipped off her shoes. He looked afraid to come closer. Then in one swift movement he pulled the covers up over her and sat next to her. "Night, Maya."

"Night, Big Rob." Maya put her foot between his legs and moved it up and down in a move she caught earlier at the club. "Aren't you gonna undress me?"

Rob removed her foot and switched up his seating position. Uh-huh.

"They played your song, Miss Jezebel. How hot is that?"

"I knowwwww. Tonight was the best." She looked over at Rob. Damn. Captivating. Maya had made herself a promise she could not even utter that she would never allow this man inside of her body, inside of her self, again. And now she was smelling him and wanting to break her word. Wasn't the point of making him fall back in love revenge? But in this moment she felt nothing but pressure between her thighs, pressure that was asking, what's love got to do with it? Maya traced his lips with her index finger like a mini serpent. Oh. His lips were as soft as they looked.

Rob stroked his chiseled jaw and shifted on the bed. "You doing your thing. I guess I was too caught up to realize how talented you are." Rob sort of nuzzled her nose with his. "You're like a different person."

"That's 'cause I've been giving in to temptation," Maya said. "Tasting everything life has to offer."

"Oh, word?" Rob asked. He put his lips to hers and spoke into her mouth. "I shouldn't be doing this. We work together."

"Uh-huh," Maya said. Anything could be had with a little coaxing. The world was her oyster.

One of them moved and she was kissing him. He was kissing her. His lips were so . . . soft. She didn't remember this. Perhaps somebody's lips could get softer. He was holding her. It felt so . . . good. Kissing. Tonguing. Just to have contact. Contact. Missed this. Needed this. Wanted—

Maya nuzzled his neck and lifted up his shirt. Rob looked helpless and she kissed his chest down to his belly button.

"Ohhhh," he groaned as Maya tongued his navel. She started moving down, toward the tent in his pants. Yeah. She thought of Athena's mantra; *the penis is your friend*, and reached in to satiate her curiosity. "Do you still taste the same?" she asked.

"Ohhhhhh. Wait. Stop, oh stop . . ." he groaned. "Stop!" Rob was pushing her away, not in a no please seduce me kinda way, but pushing her away for real/for real.

"What?" She sniffed her underarms.

"Maya! It's not going down, okay? Let's just be business, okay? Where's your self-control?"

It took a moment for his words to travel to her ears. Much slower than the speed of sound. Wow. *Let's just beeeee business*. There was no greater moment of humiliation. Except perhaps the one that followed.

"Pleeeease. Please touch me, Robby. I've been celibate. Too celibate. And I miss you inside me. Be inside me. Pleease." Maya took Rob's hand and put it inside of her damp panties. "Look. Oooh." She wiggled around as he sat motionless. "Yeah." In spite of her better judgment Maya thrust her hips against Rob's motionless hand. "See the silk? Thong."

Rob slowly removed his hand and pulled the covers back over Maya. He curled up his hand and put it in his pocket. "Somebody has to be the grown-up. Sleep it off, babe." He kissed her on her forehead and left.

Ohhhhh. Maya closed her eyes and waited for death. Ohhhh no. Just going to drop dead and that will be that. "Good, Maya. Very good. Give the Ex as many opportunities to reject you as possible. That always works." After a moment or two of still being unfortunately alive she screamed into her pillow. She never understood what folks meant when they called something a sobering moment, but here it was. She had been blissfully drunk as a skunk five minutes ago and now she was dead sober. Ugh. Buzzkilled. She felt guilty and stupid for breaking her word to herself. Or trying to, at least. She couldn't even get failure right. She rolled over on her notebook and charted a lifetime of mortification: the sixth grade panty flash, bogus prom date, cheating groom, street harassments, being heckled at Pearl's, Shell's audition, motorcycle darling panty flash and finally begging the Ex for sex. Brava.

Eyes open. Next morning. Ow. Athena over aching head. "Do tell! Do tell!!"

Maya whimpered in response and rolled over. "I hate this conversation already."

"Why?"

"You're all joy and expectation. Where were you last night? You didn't come hooome. Ohh. I think I'm still drunk."

"Rocky has a brownstone up the block."

Maya opened her eyes. "Who the hell is Rocky?"

"Ferrari. I saw him sign his credit card tab last night at the spot."

"Oh."

"Soooo. Is that morning afterglow?" Athena was hopeful.

"No it's hungover puking all night glow." Maya realized that Athena was shining.

"Damn. That good?" Athena had a mile-long grin.

"I'm not sure who the bigger dick is. Me or him. You got a cigarette?"

"Do you one better." Athena reached under her pillow and handed Maya a joint and a lighter.

Maya took three deep drags in rapid succession. She needed no coaxing.

"Puff puff, pass," Athena said. "Nothing like a wake and bake to soothe the soul."

Maya got up coughing and staggered over to their unused mini bar. "Every time I think about him I'm taking another drink." She opened a mini Jack Daniels and took a swig.

"Swig on." Athena puffed the joint. "So I think I'm in love."

"With who?" Maya asked.

"Rocky, of course. It's perfect because he's an Aquarius and Aquarians and Sagittarians have the highest compatibility."

Maya's phone rang. "Hello?"

Luci was exuberant. "Get your game face on because, my dear, you are gonna be shaking your money maker on *Hip-Hop Resuscitator.*"

"What's *Hip-Hop Resuscitator*?"

"This is huge," Luci said.

Athena went ballistic. "*Huge*, Maya. Huge." Apparently it was a huge.

Maya and Athena spent the rest of the day multislacking and trying to catch the show on cable. They sat in their beds zoned out to the TV. It was good, if only for a second, to just kick it, get back to just them.

Athena was trying to figure out the remote that also controlled the AC, windows and probably the shower. "Maybe it's on at a different time here because I can't find it."

"Well, we'll be there soon anyway, 'Thena, so . . ."

Athena rapidly spun through the channels. "You don't get it, Maya, this guy is hardcore. You can't just show up cold without watching it."

"If I can handle Shell and my ex from hell, I can handle The Resuscitator." Maya said the name like he was the Terminator.

"Your funeral."

"I think I just saw my hair guy on some talk show," Maya said as Athena zipped through.

"Resuscitator. Found it! You're lucky." Athena turned up the volume. "That's BMOC. He won the white rapper competition and the man running things is Hip-Hop Ham. He's the resuscitator."

Hip-Hop Ham (perfectionist-aggressive) was yelling in BMOC's face on a huge stage: "Let's see if you're good just as a 'white rapper' or as an MC period. Rhymes is rhymes. So we're gonna put this hoodie over your head so that I can listen to your rhymes color-free."

Two women put a sheet over the guy's head and he launched into a song, kicking his lyrics.

"Ugh." Maya put her fingers to her ears. "I'm better than him."

"That's not saying much." Athena lowered the volume.

"That's what I thought," Hip-Hop Ham said as he socked dude in the face through the sheet. "You're a sellout to the music. Get offa my show."

"Wowwww. Why? That was a little extreme."

Athena was all in. "Had to. On GP."

Maya imagined a '70s Afro pick fist punching poor BMOC. "Fisticuffs. Goody. Always big fun."

"That's the end of that," Ham told the camera.

Chapter 19

"DON'T NEED NO HATERATION,
HOLLERATIN' IN THIS DANCE FOR ME."
—*Mary J. Blige*

When Maya and Athena arrived at the set of *The Hip-Hop Resuscitator*, there were about five to eight people waiting with cameras and recorders. They buzzed like anxious mosquitoes.

"Luci's fakerazzzi," Maya said.

"Over here, Jez . . ."

"Jezebel, this way . . ."

"What do you have to say about the fact that your man has broken up with you?"

"Old news," Maya said.

"Well, Jezebel, Pimp held a press conference this morning to say that he was through with your antics and he needed a decent woman. That was a follow-up to his announcement on *Jimmy Kimmel Live*." A robust woman with what could best be described as a beard thrust a mini recorder in Maya's face.

"What?! Pimp said . . . ? " Maya looked at Athena.

Athena opened her eyes wide. "Kimmel?"

A man held up four large photos: In one hand, Maya, legs open careening forward on the motorcycle, and wow, she did look underwearless. In his other hand he held a photo of Maya sprawled on the Moca floor and Maya butt-in-the-air at the bowling party. He also had a close-up shot of her nose bleeding.

"You look like a coke whore in that one," Athena said.

"What do you think of being dumped by Pimp?" An anorexic-looking brunette with mousy hair was holding out a tape recorder.

"Who told you that?" Maya was furious. How and why would Pimp make such a statement when they hadn't had any kind of real contact? Ever. She leaned in to one of the tape recorders and said, "I've been rejected by better people." At least get the man dumping her right.

Luci came out of the building. "Okay, that's it for today, thank you. No comment, no comment." She ushered Maya and Athena inside.

"Luci, can you next time at least make sure that your fake paparazzis are better informed?" Maya rolled her eyes.

"Those aren't fakes," Luci said. "Pimp really did break up with you last night on *The Jimmy Kimmel Show*."

"What? Are you serious? We're not a couple!" Maya looked back over her shoulder.

"I know, marv, right? Fantastic!" Luci clasped her hands.

"What?" Maya asked.

Luci realized how upset Maya was and exchanged her tone for a more somber one. "Um, well, I know, but let's focus on this show. Okay? It's important for your image."

"My image as what, a public buffoon?" Maya looked at Athena, who was nodding.

"Noooo. People love you. You're hot!" Luci smiled. "Athena, you are supposed to keep talent calm at all times."

"Maya." Athena leaned in. "The only reason I don't beat this bitch's ass every time I see her is Shell and my future deal."

Maya shook her head. "Why would they think I was involved with Pimp, Luci?"

Luci didn't reply. She was all business and busy with busy-ness.

They walked past a crowd filling the arena-style soundstage. Maya peeked in. A crowd of people who probably thought that she was an idiot. Maya heard snatches of their conversation. Everybody was buzzing about Pimp breaking up with her.

Maya whispered, "I'm a geek, Athena. People thinking I'm stupid is unacceptable. I have something extra to prove now."

"Okay, but if you start singing 'You're gonna love me' I'm out," Athena said. "No more complaining. This is the bombalicious."

"Where's Rob?" Luci was completely animated, speaking to someone on a headset. She turned to Maya. "Sorry, Jez, we can't get the interview questions before the taping. It'll be okay, though. Hip-Hop Ham is a teddy bear."

"That's not what I heard," Athena said.

"Big fun." Maya said, hoping Rob would stay missing.

A pimple-faced assistant appeared. "Can I lead you ladies to your dressing room?"

"That's why we're here, right?" One of Maya's new pet peeves was when people framed things as a question when they were telling you what to do. As a recovering passive aggressive, she got the vibe.

"It's about time," said Luci. "So, Jez, this is your first TV appearance."

Maya's other pet peeve was people stating the obvious. "Uh-huh," she said, starting to get nervous as they entered her dressing quarters. She was realizing a new fact about herself—being nervous made her bitchy.

"Here's the rundown. Hip-Hop Ham gives his State of the Union address, then they show clips of the oldhead who the show is dedicated to. A modern-day rapper or group reps the icon. Today that's Black Death. Occasionally, he does a showcase called New Jack City. That's where you come in, Jez. You're gonna kick just one verse of 'Angry Black Bitch.' Got it?"

"Got it, Luci . . . Um, can I go rehearse somewhere? Athena's Hip-Hop Ham horror stories are gettin' to me."

"Thank you, Athena," Luci scolded. "So long as you maintain that professionalism you're known for."

"Just trying to help," Athena said.

Rob walked in, solemn and focused on Luci and paperwork. Great. He wanted to keep it business? She was gonna be strictly business.

"Hey, Jez," he said. She didn't respond.

"I said hey, Jez," He took her arm and she yanked it back.

"And I said nothing," Maya said.

Luci turned to brief the stylist. "About time, Cortex."

"Shark on deck," came over the walkie and all of the crew in the room scrambled to get their stuff together.

"Maya, I want to talk to you about bringing you home last night." Rob looked like he'd been chewing limes.

"Oh yeah. Good looking out. Was that you? I don't remember nada." Maya waved his words away with her hand like Luci often did. She hoped that Luci and Rob would be very happy together. She was not gonna give him the satisfaction.

There was a knock at the door. "Yeah," Rob called out, and the host of the show entered. Hip-Hop Ham. Early thirties, the color of a Hershey's Kiss, more handsome in person and smiling warmly, he didn't seem nearly as intimidating as his reputation.

"Rob, what up, my man?" Hip-Hop Ham and Rob exchanged a pound.

"What up, Ham?" Rob pulled him in and gave him a hug like brothas do, double slapping each other on the back so that nothing seemed too *how you doing* about it. Maya remembered reading that Kory Floyd at Arizona State called this the "A-frame" configuration of the man hug: the bodies do not touch except at the shoulders, which only touch briefly, usually lasting for a second or less, thus preserving machismo.

Luci threw up both of her arms, "Ham—how goes it!!" She moved in for her patented hug-double-kiss.

"Luci, whassup?" Ham made a point of maintaining a professional distance between them. "A'ight, so who's my New Jack?" Ham glanced at Athena and smiled. "You look like hip-hop, baby."

"Ham!" Luci shouted. "That's not anybody. You're looking at the assistant."

Athena lowered her eyes and shuffled her sneaks a little.

"Actually," Rob nodded toward Maya. "*This* is Jezebel. She has a song named 'Angry Black Bitch.' Hot to death."

Hip-Hop Ham looked at Maya sideways then squared his eyes. "Her? I'm not buying it. I can smell a fraud. This thing is not a joke."

Ham walked out. Rob followed him and there were muffled sounds of a heated discussion.

"That went well," said Maya.

"Day-um," Athena broke damn in two before she saw how horrified Maya was.

"He's just temperamental." Luci pulled out her favorite weapon of mass distraction. Yapping. "So to finish up the breakdown of the show, the old-school emcee comes out and does his thing."

Hip-Hop Ham's decision came in that Maya was not going to be given *The Hip-Hop Resuscitator* mic until she was less green. She was free to rep her crew by sitting in the audience with them. She opted instead to rep her pride by staying alone in the dressing room watching the monitor as the On Air sign came up.

The crowd got quiet and an announcer's voice boomed: "One man's personal mission is to bring hip-hop back to life . . ."

Spotlight on Hip-Hop Ham. He picked up an old-fashioned gold rotary phone. "Yo baby, what's up, it's me. No I got it. I know we had a rough patch there, but I got you. 'Cause I love you babe. All right, Hip-Hop, talk to you later." The music for Grandmaster Flash's "The Message" came up loud.

"What's up, y'all? Welcome to *The Hip-Hop Resuscitator*!" The crowd applauded. "Tonight the house is packed as we pay tribute to the greatest DJ of all time, Jam Master Jay. We got clips and messages from the brethren, family and supporters of this beautiful community-minded legend. Then it's Shell the Boy Wonder and his clique Black Death for a live tribute."

A montage commemorating the life and legacy of Jam Master Jay played as his partners Reverend Run and the Devastating Mic Controller respectfully represented.

Maya was in the dressing room rubbing her eyes. The newly applied makeup fresh face she had earlier was now a raccoon in camouflage, Marilyn Manson, a hot mess. She searched the mirror for the L on her forehead. "Whyyyyyyyyy?!?!" she screamed.

As the timing in her life was always so picture perfect, the pimple-faced assistant (acute stress disorder) picked this moment to come back in. He looked more sorry for himself than Maya as he hemmed and hawed to fix his mouth to say something. Faustus Maya would have offered up a smile to put homeboy at ease.

New York Jezebel just didn't have the energy. She found that most folks here appreciated rudeness anyway and didn't understand or respect anything else. "Yeah?"

"Uh, I'm so sorry, but, er, we kinda need this space to prep for the next show."

"You kinda need it or do you actually need it?" Maya asked. Be direct, you prick. She had been rejected by better people in worse situations.

"We kinda really need it right now."

"Great, I'll just wander the halls." Maya stood up then sat back down. She didn't want make anything easy for anybody.

"You're down with Camp Hustla, right?" he asked.

Maya nodded. "That's the word on the street." Dammit. Shouldn't he know who she was? Could she not get at least a little respect?

"Look, why don't you wait in the Black Death dressing room until they're through?" Pimple Face led Maya down the now quiet hall to a room filled with empty booze bottles, crappola and the aroma of ganja tinged with man-size funk. It was like they lived here a few years rather than a few hours. Which part of her life should she cry about first? She sank into a pile of clothes on a leather couch.

"Yo!" A black as love brother, with dark sunglasses, a light beard and a fro popped out from under the clothes. He looked like he had been asleep for a hundred years.

Maya jumped. "Sorry. I wasn't . . . I didn't mean to disturb you. I, uh, I was . . . I was just kicked out of my dressing room because Hip-Hop Ham won't let me be his new jack." Maya bit her bottom lip to stop it from quivering.

"It's okay, Queen." He sat up and Maya realized that she was sitting on his lap.

Queen? Nobody had called her that in a long time. Maya started tearing up, fanning herself like a pageant winner.

"It's okay. Awww. Don't cry." Mr. Sunglasses hugged her. Hugged her hard. His hug felt good and his muscles felt better. Safe. She felt safe, protected in the arms of a stranger, who was not so strange at all. "I know, Queen. It's brutal. A game of gods and monsters. What's your name, ma?"

Maya moved over. Good question. What was her name? "My MC name is Cleopatra but Shell made it Jezebel. I don't know . . . I mean, can I live?" She looked at him for an answer.

"Well, the first thing you gotta know before anything, Queen, is your tag. C'mon. Your name drives your narrative." He moved a strand of hair from her eyes.

"True." Maya wanted to hold his hand.

He smiled. "The queen name, that's tight. Cleopatra? That's you."

Maya wanted to smile back. She just couldn't muster that right now.

She wanted to take off his glasses.

"You an artist?" he asked.

She needed to see his eyes. "Trying to be," she said.

"So yo, okay, advice for advice, Queen. You think if I perform it'll be stronger to kick it with my hood on the whole time like this?" Homeboy pulled his hood over his head to demonstrate.

"Not unless you wanna look like a ghost. People wanna see who's performing. They wanna connect. I think leave it off so—"

"So they could feel me. Yeah. I get it. Thanks. So what were you gonna kick in the showcase?"

She saw his eyelashes through the dark tinted lenses. Butterfly wings. "I wrote this song named 'Angry Black Bitch' . . ."

"Word?" He chuckled. "You?"

Maya felt vulnerable and defensive. She crossed her arms and her legs in front of her to form a protective barrier. "I know how it sounds but it's not like that at all. I wrote it from my heart."

"You don't got to apologize, sis. Poetry ain't always pretty 'cause life ain't always pretty. Where in *you* does that come from, though? 'Cause you damn sure don't look like no angry black bitch. Pretty eyes." He winked and rested his chin on his fist. He looked like that Rodin statue. The Poet? The Thinker?

"It's about how it feels to be thrown away. You know what I mean?" Maya asked, noticing his strong jaw and beautiful lips.

"I do," he said, clearly scoping her out.

Was this cutie trying to hit on her? For real/ for real? Maybe he was just one of those male groupies Luci was always warning about. Lurking and lying in wait to bail with your cash or your stash. "Ham thinks I'm a phony, and maybe I was, once, but I'm not now." Dude didn't say anything so Maya continued. She was rambling now but she didn't care. "Performing is my life. My love. I get that now. And my best friend is mad at me. And then my ex was hatin'. Nothing works."

"Yeah," he said, listening. "I feel you." *Feel you. Mmm. Kinesthetic.* "Look, Jezebel, me and you should talk more. I gotta take care of this thing with the show and then let's connect right after, okay?"

"Okay," said Maya. She should say something wise, smart, spiritual. Something for him to hold on to. "Um, later," was all she could drum up.

Sunglasses stood. Maya didn't want him to leave. He was oxygen. Especially today. He stretched his arms. Mm. He was the age of bronze. "And be ready to perform 'cause I got a little clout and I'ma see what I could do for you, New Jack."

"If it's not too much trouble." This is a good time for a smile, she told her face. Boldness. "How do we get in touch?"

"I'll find you after the show. Thanks for waking me up. Today is my birthday. Thirty-three. The Jesus year."

"Oh, cool. Happy—"

"Shhh! Don't tell nobody." He smiled and Maya smiled back. "Treat this like your thesis . . ."

"Thesis?" asked Maya. *How could he know?*

"Lauryn Hill. 'Final Hour,' " he said, and rapped as he went out the door, "I treat this like my thesis, well written copy broken down into pieces. . . ." He gave Maya one last look, nodded, and then closed the door behind him.

Whoa. Angels *do* appear just when you need them. Even in designer sunglasses. Cool. A real boyfriend prospect. Her mind ran ahead as women's minds do. They would make pretty brown babies together.

How would Big Rob deal with that?! Oh—stupid, stupid. She was so self-absorbed that she didn't even get dude's name. Who was he? Some entourage loser guy who wasn't one-true-love material? Hopefully he was at least a stagehand or somebody with ID, benefits and taxable income.

Maya turned up the monitor with Hip-Hop Ham on it. They panned the audience to reveal all of her life's usual suspects—Camp Hustla was representing. True to Shell's word he was bringing the East Coast back. Ham stood like the president making a pronouncement. "And now, ladies and gents. In honor of Jam Master Jay, in honor of Notorious B.I.G. and Tupac, in honor of Left Eye and Aliyah. In the name of all of our fallen soldiers and lost legends, I got something mad special for all of us. Take a deep breath and hold onto your seats. Our main lieutenant is back to fight the war."

Homeboy who was just kicking it with Maya was onstage in a black flak jacket and his dark glasses with a hood over his huge fro, nodding to his beat. The hoodie. He didn't take her advice, but something about the way he held himself spelled dignity. He stood much taller than he was, like a soldier, head up, chest out. People were feeling him. Then he flipped off the hood, showing his face like Maya suggested (yes!) and started his song. Something felt familiar. The camera panned Big Rob and Athena's faces frozen in the sidelines with the rest of Black Death. Shell was sitting next to them, wearing his biggest platinum diamond cross for the occasion.

Maya's future dude took off his sunglasses. The camera panned the screaming crowd. A woman fainted. Hip-Hop Ham was praying. Close-up on the infinite eyes that launched a thousand bullets, mixtapes and ghetto memorial murals. Tribute bands, releases and rereleases of anything he even breathed on. His likeness re-created in barbershop photos and bad art. The man who had outsold every living artist while he was dead.

WTF?! Yes. Thug. Or a photo-perfect look-alike. There had been a lot of those. Look-alikes. Wannabes. Hypers. Fronters. Try hards and posers. The perfectly carved face and thick neck was attached to a tattooed body that moved like the panther who had announced Maya and Rob's doomed engagement at that concert in Faustus a million years ago.

And now he was kicking a song named "Call It a Comeback." Was that Thug? Could that really be Thug?! The man who hugged her minutes ago could never be an imitation of life. All of the blackfolks in the audience looked pale and all of the whitefolks flushed with a dark blush.

"Yo! Where you been, Thug?" Grown men were full-on bawling as the man on stage spat the gospel as he saw it. "What happened, son?"

"I love you, man!" the crowd screamed separately and together.

"I love you, Thug!" women were yelling.

"Is dat really you, God?" Boyfriends were losing it and girlfriends were consoling them. Genders were bending.

The legion wanted answers but for now Thug would only give them lyrics, and he was kicking it, wrecking it, tearing it up. Hard. Testifying. Talk drumming with his lips. No dogs or hypemen this time, no mega screens or explosions, just one man and one mic. And his followers. Maya did something she hadn't done since her first communion on her last day inside of a Catholic church. She made the sign of the cross.

Thug finished up with "Resurrected from Exile." "I missed y'all more than you missed me," he said. There was more, but it was hard to hear him over the yelling. "A lot has changed but Daddy's home." He spoke/sang a gravelly line of the old Jermaine Jackson lyric. *"Your daddy's home to stay."* People were sobbing. "That's right, my b-boys and girls. There's a whole new school of people trying to do their thing. The right thing. Trying to tell our stories with new testaments, but we can't hear them through the noise. We gotta listen through the noise. So tonight it is my honor on the occasion of my return to present one such artist."

Maya looked at the door and two security guards were beckoning. She was caught in a split reality between the monitor and the door. She wanted to climb into the screen and hug him. Was he talking about her? Then he said it. Her name. Sunglasses, Thug, was saying her name. "I got nothing but love for y'all! Introducing Jezebel!"

And she was scrambling up, barely un-smudging her mascara and making it to the stage. On the longest walk in the shortest time, she was joined by Luci and Athena, who managed to make her look presentable as they rushed along. Tough act to follow was the understatement of the century.

As Maya joined Thug onstage, the gladiator took her hand and presented her to the lions without a shield. They applauded loudly, welcoming her as an extension of him. Cheering like they had the slightest idea of who she was besides the ass-in-the-air chick from *Best Week Ever.* They welcomed her because she was shining, illuminated by the prodigal son's halo, and each clap-clap-clap, every time someone's palms hit together, felt like a kiss.

The applause signs were redundant. The walls were respectfully thumping in and out. So Thug stepped to the side and Jezebel sang the shiznit out of "Angry Black Bitch," the whole song, until Hip-Hop Ham himself was mouthing the hook.

Rob watched Maya rip the stage with newfound respect. Rob. She wanted to step to him. She wanted to say, that's right, bow down and hail to the queen, but there was no need because it was already so. The dynamics of the earth had shifted. Maya Hopeless was no more, and the crowd, *her* crowd, was feeling her.

Thug stood in the wings, smiling only at Maya. The man that the media dubbed Thug the Criminalistic was cheesing. Cheesing, at her! And she was cheesing back. He was her knight shining in bulletproof armor. It had been so long since she felt such a deep crush for any man other than the one who she was dumb enough to let reject her again. Hm. Maya pranced, giving much booty, knowing that she looked fine, wearing her designer threads and new body. The only thing better than running into an ex when you know you look good is rocking it on national television in front of an ex (and being introduced by his idol) when you *know* you look good. Hell to the yeah!

Maya concluded her set to thunderous applause. Yay! She was unsure of what to do next. Uh, did she practice this part? Then Thug ran out and held her arm high like a prizefighting champion. *Maya Bumbaye.* Then he hugged her. Right there. Tightly. Whoa. She almost forgot that she was on live TV. Thug grounded her and they ran offstage into the frenzy of their waiting camp.

Maya was smiling so big that her face hurt. She knew that she looked like a dork but she couldn't stop. She was having a heart attack. A happy heart attack. She wanted to keep holding Thug's hand but they were quickly separated by the drama of the moment. Maya kept an eye on him as Athena and Luci hugged her, and Black Death fam gave her respect and dap.

"Hey Jez . . ." Rob tried to pull her to the side.

"Yo. Get official. Let's just be business," she said softly before turning her back and drifting into the team cluster.

When Maya walked out of the television studio the day had changed color and shape. Life was new and different. Its jagged rectangles were smooth ovals. Live TV satellite antennae formed her new skyline. The massive group of reporters waiting for Thug were hungry, questioning, taunting, leering, lunging.

"Who are you?" they shouted at Maya.

Behind the paparazzi, the cops held back a street-wide band of fans and supporters holding up Thug posters, photos, albums, anything they could get their hands on to make them feel closer to him. He made them feel closer to themselves. He had given his life and now they didn't have to. His life meant possibilities. In the midst of massive presidential security Maya saw news flashes in her mind as she walked with Thug, Shell, Black Death, Luci, Big Rob and Athena, flashes of old-school Thug spitting at the press in his former life, middle fingers blazing. Now he only looked forward, eyes like melting chocolate drops, and they made it to the car.

"Where have you been?" Maya asked as he helped her in.

"Hibernating," was all he would say.

In other news, a star was born. In the car they turned on the radio. Pandemonium. Everybody wanted to know who Maya was. Correction. Who was Jezebel? And how did she know this man? Had she been holed up with him somewhere? How did he know her? This man whom they wouldn't let die. Hopeful misguided youth and OGs, hip-hop, mothers of all backgrounds who had lost their sons, or were afraid that they might. Hip-hop was grown-up and earning an income now. Thug mattered to radio advertisers, clothing manufacturers, ringtone makers, college courses, magazines, TV, radio and corporations. They especially hated being out of the loop.

It had been pretty ridiculous for a long minute—the Thug sightings, the lame websites with ongoing evidence of his "faked death." A group called the Tru Believers even held monthly vigils to spread "the wisdom of Thug." These sites, groups and questions were mostly dismissed by folks with sense as wishful thinking. Like whitefolks' refusal to let go of Elvis. Sad. Pathetic even. Anyone with sense had pretty much let it go, let him go, and left the matter to conspiracy theorists praying that Thug was sipping mojitos in Havana with Assata laughing at the doubters, the haters and the never-caught shooters—and now here he was. Not in Havana. Not in Mexico or Egypt. But in a stupid-looking Hummer limo. Warm-blooded and alive. And they who were blessed enough to share his rare air felt more alive because of him.

Maya didn't get it before, what the media called the Thug Effect, when she first saw him on that stage at the Dandridge, but she felt it now. He had literally saved her life. He had taken her down from Rob's shoulders, rescued her and placed her on a national pedestal. And she was grateful. He took her hand and held her, and she curled up next to him in the fetal position.

Of course, that didn't happen anywhere but inside Maya's head. The whole episode of Thug's reemergence was so confusing that for a couple of days afterward everyone who cared about it even a little bit had what Maya diagnosed as some kind of Resurrection Syndrome, where they weren't sure what was real and what was fake, an inability to distinguish reality from dreams and the imagination. In actuality, she sat across from Thug in the gargantuan vehicle. Rob was the one sitting next to Thug, with Shell on the other side. Neither looked like they would ever detach themselves from him. It was annoying that Rob should even breathe in the same hemisphere. Gunz, Nigg and Pimp were also taking up space, as well as Athena and Luci, who sat on either side of Maya, but she was feeling Thug's energy so strong and so real, that she felt like she was curled up underneath him and attached. She was a battery and he was her charger.

Chapter 20

"WHATCHU WAITING ON?
FEEL ME, FEEL ME, FEEL ME."
—*Alicia Keys*

Immediately following the show, Shell summoned all relevant parties to a "family dinner." It was the first time that Maya had been invited to his famous town house, where it was said that even folks like Donald Trump, Martha Stewart and Ozzie Marvelous got down for soul food. Maya's mind was not on Martha, or even on Rob and the fact that she was supposed to break bread with him and pretend that everything was hunky-dory. Her mind was barely on the fact that Athena had been acting extra mad all week. Maya's thoughts, like everyone else's, were on Thug, the resurrected.

Maya didn't know what to expect as they all arrived in a clump at Shell's 65th Street residence. It eerily reminded her of leaving a funeral and coming home with your family to chow down as they all filed into his great room with its classical gold walls accented with ivory moldings and decorated with tasteful art. It was a calm and beautiful space, not at all the nouveau riche *Cribs* monstrosity full of *Scarface* posters, poker dog art and pissing David statues that she imagined. Shell held formal family dinners a few times during the year. A practice, Luci explained, started after Thug was "killed."

"The one on the left is the butler and the one on the right is the footman," Luci explained as two men took their hats, jackets and other accoutrements.

"I didn't know footmen really existed," Athena said. The footman or the butler was giving out coat-check tickets like they were in a restaurant.

"Athena, hold this." Maya handed her the ticket without waiting for a response. "I didn't want to bring my purse."

"Sure," Athena said. "I am Madame's assistant."

Maya smoothed her hair in a gilded foyer mirror.

"Y'all ever been downstairs to Big Rob's?" Luci asked, eyeing Maya closely. "It's huge."

"He lives *here*?" asked Maya.

Rob, it turns out, lived in the garden level of Shell's town house—or as they used to refer to it back in Faustus, the basement. It struck Maya that she had never asked Rob where he lived, but wherever it was, she assumed that he was cribbed up somewhere "of the people." She'd imagined him on the train all night ducking through dank subway tunnels. Shell's seven-million-dollar *Architectural Digest* home was definitely not of the people unless those people were on the cover of *Forbes*. Caviar wishes and hood rat dreams. Survivor guilt for making it out. So much for keeping it real.

Maya looked across the room at the man of the day. Thug's skin was flawless. It was hard not to stare. Maybe he was in the sol of Brazil or Ghana baking in fresh cocoa butter for the past couple of years. Okay, He wasn't ignoring her, right? Everyone wanted to steal a bit of conversation with him. The man was assumed dead until a few hours ago for goddess's sakes. Still, her old abandonment complex was flaring up. Maybe she'd just daydreamed a connection between them. Maybe he would have rescued any damsel in distress, not just her. Kind of like Rob's insert-damsel-here approach. She tried to catch his eye but played herself instead when Gunz or Nigg, she could never tell the twins apart, winked back and grabbed his crotch. Holy bizarro ghetto mating signal, Batman!!

Religion and politics are the two things everybody's mother tells them to shut up about. Thug wanted to discuss politics and religion nonstop. While Maya hovered on the sidelines, he spoke with Shell about Muslims and Afghanistan, Luci about white rappers, Athena about woman-hating videos, and his BD posse about everything from rap wars to Israel. He was different things to different people, switching up his swagger depending on who he was hollerin' at. His larger-than-life energy zapped everywhere except in her direction.

Was it possible to love him so soon? Or maybe she just wanted to love somebody and be done with it. It had been so long that she couldn't distinguish between crush, lust, love or infatuation. Either way, she couldn't keep her eyes off him. Luckily, no one else could either so she wasn't arrested for eye stalking. He was like an MIA veteran who wandered into the town diner one day asking for pancakes.

"Okay." Athena strolled up holding a glass of gin. "Word is that Shell had no idea that Thug was still alive and Ozzie Marvelous holed him up somewhere in South Africa healing after he got shot."

"I knew it!" said Maya.

"He is totally fuckable." Athena looked in his direction and damn near licked her lips.

"Who?" Maya felt her face getting hot.

"Hello! Thug the Criminalistic. I wanna make him a true believer in the Church of Athena."

Maya looked at Athena, then back at Thug, who was now kicking it with Rob, of all people. He almost glanced their way. She could definitely see Thug feeling Athena and her magnetic cerulean eyes. "Do you know I started writing rhymes because of that man right there? When I first heard "The Assassinator," I wanted to burn something down just on GP. His lyrics saved my life," Athena said. The thought of Athena or anyone else with Thug made her ill. She had first dibs. Thug wasn't just some conquest lay. She was feeling him for real/for real but that's not what came out.

"Athena, don't gossip about people in the room. Especially not my labelmates," Maya said, maybe a little too scoldingly.

"Oh, I'm sorry, Jezebel. I don't know all the new rules." Athena walked off. Maya let her. She didn't want anybody or anything screwing up the high she felt from the double whammy of a perfect performance and the yummy surprise of crushing on Thug.

As Maya pulled a drink from the tray of a passing waitress, two chubby pit bulls bounded into the room and started wrestling. Maya froze, trying not to breathe or make sudden movements. Damn! Dogs were her kryptonite. The two quickly tired of their game, and one trotted off to Shell. The other wandered up to her. Of course. What was the Girl Scout rule? Don't look dogs in the eye, or stare them down?

Terrified, Maya scanned the spacious suite for either Rob or Athena, both of whom knew that she'd been mauled in the tenth grade by Ralphie Scott's poodle. She saw Rob and Athena both notice her doggie terror, but neither jumped to rescue duty as they both had beef with her. Marv, as Luci would say. Good, Rob caught her look and was coming over.

"You look like you need saving," Rob said, standing beside her as the dog pawed at Maya's shoes. Although his presence was slightly relaxing, Rob made no move to pull the dog away.

Maya was stuttering. "Yes, uh. Please Rob. Move . . . dog."

"Too bad you've been igging me," Rob said.

"Rob, please . . ." He walked away. Jerk! He was definitely the asses' ass. Okay. She just wouldn't look down. Don't look down. Don't . . .

"Don't tell me that you're afraid of Pookie." Thug. Finally. Maya looked up into his broad shoulders. To the rescue?

"Uh, no, I just . . ."

"Here." He reached down and stroked the dog. "Try it." The dog rolled around on his back, paws in the air. "That's right boy, it's me. Uncle T. What up, dawg?"

Maya was beyond frozen. At least now she could breathe. Thug! What to do? Respond! Maybe if she kept him talking she wouldn't have to touch the beast.

"So what up, man?" It was Pimp.

"Chillin', man. Chattin' up the young lady. Talk more later, Pimp?" Thug looked at him with punctuation.

"A'ight, man." Pimp was clearly annoyed that Maya took precedence. "Sloppy seconds," he said, walking away.

Maya was glad for the interruption. It gave her a beat to remember how small talk went. "Sooo, why do you call yourself Thug?"

"Why I call myself Thug?" His darker than black eyes flashed. "I thought my fans were up on me."

Fans? Maya was quiet. How to process this? Was he thinking she was just some chickenhead groupie? How cocky and rude! However, if all he wanted to do was to use her, she would let him. She looked at his lips. Over and over again.

"Wowww, not a fan." Thug was simultaneously taken aback and impressed.

"Well, not until you rescued me." Maya squared her shoulders with his and unclasped her hands. Body language that said open and available. He was not that much taller than she was.

"You rescued yourself, baby. I just happened to be there." The now docile dog folded himself at Thug's feet.

"Well, thanks for that." Maya looked up at another posse dude approaching. Oh, come on, people.

Thug held up a hand and homeboy walked away. "You wouldn't think an angry black bitch was looking to be rescued anyway."

"Yeah, well . . ." Maya was all out of game. *Okay. Breathe.*

"But I'll take cred. I discovered you like Diana Ross discovered the Jackson 5. Like the Europeans discovered the Indians." He laughed at his own joke. "So how'd you get your name, Miss Questions?"

Listen and respond. "Uh, you first." *That's good. Show interest.*

"Charge it to the game." Thug sat on the floor in a way that black men never feel comfortable enough to do. Okay, should she keep standing or sit or what?

"So what is your real name?" Maya asked, one eye on Thug, the other on Pookie. Keep standing. Maya hated to keep on with the name thing but it was all she could find in her conversational bag of tricks. You would think that someone who studied human interaction would do better.

Thug shook his head. "You don't know nothing about me?"

Maya hated arrogance. "Everybody's not a fan, you know." *Change it up.* "Sometimes people are friends."

"Sometimes." He let it go. "So you never been to a Thug concert or nothing?"

Why did he keep harping on this? "Well, yeah. With my ex. We went to one."

Thug was back on familiar territory. "Yeah? That's what's up. Where?"

"I don't remember." Probably not best to get into memories of the concert where he got "murdered" and people were trampled to death, not to mention the announcement of her doomed proposal. "Um, so . . . happy secret birthday, Thug!"

Gong. A dinner bell. *Gong! Gong!* Shell the Boy Wonder took his seat at the head of the table in the next room.

"Robeson," Thug said.

"What?" Maya tried to find Athena in the room with her eyes so that she would see them talking and know that Maya had dibs.

"My first name." Thug smiled and put Maya's hand under his on the dog's back. Hm. Thug's hand felt hot and Pookie's hair was softer than hers.

"Robeson? Really?" Maya was pleasantly surprised.

Thug nodded. Some posse members were shooting dice under a Bearden painting.

"Somebody must have expected great things from you." Maya actually stroked Pookie's back, feeling more confident now. "You look like your name would be Robeson."

"Yeah? What you know 'bout Robeson, huh?" His smile was pure light.

Okay, Maya, she coached herself, he's smiling. Quit while you're ahead. Be like water. Wax on, wax off. Shut the hell up!

"Black coffee, no sugar, no cream, that's the kinda girl I need down with my team," Thug sang. "Heavy D called it."

"Here boy!" The dog and Maya looked up. It was singer BaTricia Simone. Bizarre. Like they were all together again.

BaTricia was sporting an any-minute pregnant belly. "Pookie don't like strangers. He sees *a lot* of 'em. Disposables." Pookie bounded over to BaTricia and followed her as she waddled out of the room.

Okay. Maya walked with Thug to the table, sunning herself in his rays until gold hand-lettered place cards announced that they were to sit separately. Thug was sitting at Shell's left hand with Rob at his right.

Maya was stationed between Athena and the glamorous Luci in a ghetto that Luci called BabyMamaville. Luci undoubtedly was the one person besides Shell dressed for a formal dinner.

Shell had changed from his cap and jersey into a black velvet suit with an amber ascot. He stood up. "If it's true that you can measure a man by the strength of his family, call me King Kong. Let's toast the rebirth of Harlem's finest. To Thug."

"To Thug," everyone repeated.

"To life and rapture. Long live Hustla," Shell chanted.

"Long live Hustla," they all repeated. They had passed the surreal life hours ago.

"C'mon, man. Speech," Rob said to Thug, and the table of about sixteen people chanted, "Speech, speech, speech, speech."

Thug stood, in that humbly uncomfortable way award winners do, pleading that they are totally unprepared, and then giving Oscar-worthy monologues. "It's an honor to kick it with y'all tonight. Lots of new faces and places, so humor a brother. Let's reintroduce ourselves."

Maya, fresh from washing her hands (puppy germs), wiped her silverware on her napkin and saw one of Shell's babies' mamas, not BaTricia, the other one, notice. They passed the giddy mood around the table and introduced and reintroduced themselves—performers, execs, models, Glam Squaders—and prepared to partake in a sumptuous eight-course formal meal. Not semiformal. Not kinda formal. Wedding formal. Victorian formal. Just when the day could not get any weirder, they flipped into the absurd watching Nigg, Gunz and Pimp dine on a white damask tablecloth with white-gloved white servants and solid gold flatware.

The embossed ecru menu announced:

1st course—Fresh Bruschetta
2nd course—Brie, Sun-Dried Tomato & Romaine Salad
3rd course—Sweet Potato or Chicken Noodle Soup
4th course—Shrimp Cocktail
5th course—Linguine with Olives
6th course—Lemon Sorbet

7th course—Beef Tenderloin, Lamb, Salmon or
Baked Chicken with golden mushrooms
8th course—Ice Cream, Bean Pie or Peach Cobbler
garnished with sprig of mint

"Fish, fowl, beef or mutton?" Maya's personal server asked.

"Beef, please." Maya couldn't wait to taste tenderloin.

"Fowl, please," Luci said. "Clues. They're serving burgundy in a merlot glass. And watch what Shell does when they pour his white wine."

Maya and Athena watched as Shell swirled his glass and smelled it.

"So. He looks like a connoisseur," Athena said.

"Amateur." Luci sniffed. "You should never swirl white wine."

"Who cares?" Athena blew a kiss. "He can wife me up any day."

"Luci, you're such a snob." Maya felt more comfortable every day expressing her true thoughts.

"Snob just means Seeking New Or Better." Luci folded and refolded her napkin.

Maya, Luci and Athena were the only ones waiting for everyone to be served to start chowing down. Pimp stuffed food in his mouth just as Shell began the grace, spearing into it with a clenched fist like he and the food had beef. Athena on the other hand was proud to show off that she still had her Beardsley manners, even if she didn't get to use them much on Maya's Oodles of Noodles. The medium rare gourmet was too much for Maya's unpracticed, veggie-trained palate. She spat the beef into her napkin and saw Rob peep it out. He smiled. Whatever. The attentive server took it away and brought back a well-done cut that turned out to be quite yummy.

Maya stole a glance at Thug. Cutie pie. And where did he get such great table manners? The eight-course meal reminded Maya of her family in Trinidad, who prided themselves on being more British than the British and made asinine jokes about being glad that their ancestors caught the boat. The selfsame ones who made her practice walking with a book on her head and wore large hats to avoid turning black although they were already the color of tree bark. Her Trini family would have had a fit at the boorish behavior. Soup slurps and table elbows. Licking spoons and interrupting cell phones. Food in teeth, talking with mouths full and Pimp telling his personal waiter, "Dang, man, fill up the glass. Mines don't need to breathe." This was Thanksgiving on acid.

When little bowls of water with lime appeared on doilies with dessert, everyone who had been to one of Shell's family dinners knew to wash their fingertips in it. Because the formals began after Thug was gone, he didn't always get the new post-ghetto protocols quite right. Maya saw him sip from his finger bowl. She followed suit before Luci could make a snide comment and soon everyone was doing it. Sometimes good manners is having bad manners to make others feel comfy, Granny Ruby used to say.

Shell threw Maya a smile. "I know how to pick 'em, right? Jezebel is gorgeous."

"That she is," said Thug. "A real Cleopatra."

"Ripe," Pimp added.

Pimp aside, Maya bloomed. No one had ever reveled unprompted in her looks. She didn't even consult her usual *Field Guide for Self-Deprecating Responses*. Compliment: You look thin. Response: I'm a whale. Compliment: Your hair looks good. Response: It's filthy. Compliment: Cool shirt. Response: It fell out of my closet.

They finished off with champagne (what else?), Shell's own personal brand of vodka and cigars.

"Castro Cubans," Luci pointed out as a couple of the models requested doggie bags.

"Probably to barf in," Athena said.

Maya didn't get a chance to speak with Thug again that night, but they made eye contact several times. She wasn't tripping though. For now, that was enough. It had to be.

The day after. Maya woke still seeing through the dazzling kaleidoscope. The orangy red light streaming through the decorative brambles formed purple streaks that looked like butterflies on the bed. She fingered the laminated *Hip-Hop Resuscitator* backstage pass and House of Shell cloakroom ticket on the night table that proved yesterday happened. She picked up her iPhone and punched in Thug. Nothing. His name wasn't there. Resurrection Syndrome. Maybe she *had* fallen into a hallucinatory state and imagined the whole thing. Then she remembered that in the three private minutes they'd shared when they dropped her off at The Heretix he told her to call him Robeson and typed his name and number into her phone. R-O-B-E-S-O-N—there he was! Robeson also known as Thug. Should she call? Send a text? A fax? Telegram? SOS? Who would have thunk it? Her brain was buzzing so much with the whole thing all night that she'd had to take a sleeping pill to crash. (She tried melatonin but her adrenaline was on fire and it wouldn't work.) Thug was a man she wanted to love. Maybe he was even her true love.

"Can you believe—" She turned around. Athena wasn't there. Again. Whatever. Athena had been spending more and more nights away. Maybe she should call her, smooth things over and make sure that they were all good. Maya was about to press "A" (her shortcut to Athena) when her phone rang. It was Luci.

"Jez, wake up, wake up, wake up!" Luci was singing into the phone.

"I'm up, Luce—hey!" Thank the goddess that Luci had become a friend. There were many things that Athena didn't get that Luci saw dead on.

"Can you believe your life? Today is the best day in the world." Luci was always so happy for her. That's a friend.

"Luci. I . . . I think that I'm in love."

Luci was adjusting the phone on the other end. "Oh? With whom, do tell!"

Maya paused, testing the name with her tongue. "Thug," she said and meant it.

"Thug!" Luci exclaimed. Maya suddenly felt dumb. Who probably wasn't in love with Thug? It was like having a New Edition poster above your canopy bed. "Really? That's perfect. A publicist couldn't ask for more."

"Uh, yeah, well . . ." She hated when she forgot that Luci wasn't just her buddy.

"So guess what, Jez? What do you think could be better than Thug coming back to us?" How was Luci so bouncy with no sleep?

"I don't know." She wished that she hadn't told Luci her private thoughts. Maya wanted to get back to her busy schedule of replaying her every interaction with Thug, Robeson, her future baby daddy.

"Remember how Rob and I said that it could be a year at least before we could get you on Manifesta's radio show?"

"Yeah."

"Well, dude, Jezebel is gonna be on the show *today*!" Luci paused waiting for Maya's response.

"Today?" Maya turned over on her side. She was exhausted. She had to ask the kitchen to mix her green teas with Red Bull.

"Yes, with none other than our boy, your boy Thug. Manifesta requested you both."

"Really?!" Maya jumped up. She was way more excited about seeing Thug than being interviewed by Manifesta. "Oh my goddess!"

"Top of the show. It starts at 2:00 P.M. So Legba will pick you up at twelve-thirty, okay?" Luci was damn near orgasmic.

So was Maya. "Okay!" Awesome. "What to wear?"

"This is pretty big, so hair, makeup and wardrobe will be by at ten-ish." Professional hair and makeup for a first date. Slamming!

Maya looked at the Piaget clock on the wall. "But it's nine-ish now."

"No rest for the weary." Luci gave a last *yay*, and hung up. What a development!

Maya turned on her laptop. A reminder popped up. Overdue. Draft preliminary Hip-Hop Undercover report. She fully intended to get a jump on it, but instead her fingers went to Search and typed in Robeson Thug. The computer exploded with entries. Four point six million, to be exact. Sites about his legacy. Blogs. Podcasts. Questions. Answers. Songs. Clothes. Music videos. Documentaries. Movies. His pictures. His poems. Poems inspired by him. Lead prophet of the rap canon. Debates about whether he was alive or dead. Well, that case was closed. Time to get her man.

Notebook
of
Love

THE DARE EXPERIMENT
HIP-HOP UNDERCOVER
BY MAYA GAYLE HOPE

Notebook of Love

Who got next?

You ever seen a cypher?

Brothas and sistas in a tight circle passin' the rhyme over a beat?

Much of hip-hop is about the cypher. I know you might have learned about the "cipher" in school, and that's part of it, but I'm talking about the *cypher.* The three hundred and sixty degrees that we travel cosmically to rhyme over a bangin' beat. The way you pass the rhyme to the next man or woman.

Love is a freestyle in a cypher. Passing adoration back and forth, round and round, giving and taking. Vowing never to break the cypher.

Love.

Did I say yet that this experiment is about learning and evolution?

If I knew I could not fail, I would dare to greet every woman, child or man I encountered with love. I would love my enemies and my friends. I would love myself and that which created me with an unabashed, overwhelming, flooding, flowing love. I would love life.

I would love like I have never been hurt.

If I knew that I could not fail, I would dare to have the courage to be me, without explanation or apology. I would have the nerve to receive more love than I ever thought possible because I would give more love than I ever thought possible.

LOVE DECLARATION: (Repeat five times every morning, noon and night to reinforce your love.) *In this instant, I love me, without explanation or apology. I greet every woman, child or man that I encounter with love. I love myself and that which created me with an unabashed, overwhelming, flooding, flowing, freestyle of love. I love my life, and I vow never to break this cypher.*

LOVE ACTION STEP: *Make a list of people and situations that you need to forgive as an action of love for yourself.*

Chapter 21

"KEEP IN MIND THAT I DON'T HAVE ALL DAY
GOTTA HURRY UP BEFORE THE NIGHT SLIPS AWAY."
—Lady May

Thug and Maya each wore headphones and sat in front of microphones. Manifesta wore a tight black T-shirt over her big boobies, a baseball cap pulled low over her asymmetrical cut, calf-length jeans and boots. Two station engineers were also in the room, as were the video cameras that had become virtually invisible to Maya. Ill Verge, Shell's special security man, stood guard.

An all-bass prerecorded male voice boomed, "99.6 on your FM dial from the broadcast capital of the world, WKTR." Rob, Luci and Athena were on the other side of the glass. Maya was glad Athena was there, although she was unsure if it was to support her or to watch Thug and Manifesta. (Who would turn that down?) She had to make a point of talking to Athena privately, today.

Aside from Funkmaster Flex, Manifesta was known on the street as the ultimate hip-hop radiohead. Not bad for a woman. She came up scratching and spinning for The Fresh Females, a clique of girl emcees back in the late eighties. Even when people had beef with her, they still respected her flow. She could unleash nasty gossip in one sentence and break down the musical structure of a melody in the next. With her club gigs, magazine, radio show and TV specials, her love for the craft often met glitz, but she was known for keeping it hood. Manifesta *was* hip-hop.

"Taking hip-hop back to hip-hop, DJ Manifesta kicking it *live* from the NYC. Everybody today is talking about one thing: one man with one heart. Our very own *All My Children*–style back from the dead story. Except this is life in living color. Nope, you haven't seen a ghost. Thug is alive and guess what—he came to one place first. Not Larry King or Barbara Walters. Thug is here with the female MC he introduced to the world, Jezebel.

"So what up, man?!" Her radio voice was much smoother than her tone when she confronted Maya at the bowling party.

"I'm good, Manifesta" he said.

"So where *were* you? Holed up somewhere listening to Manifesta Live?" Manifesta poured champagne to grease her guests. Maya took hers. Thug didn't.

Thug chuckled. "Something like that."

"So I guess you're not gonna tell America where you were hiding?"

"I wasn't hiding, Manifesta." Thug's tone flipped a little, showing hints of the volatile man they remembered. "You got the tail wagging the dog. I was in plain view. That's the best place to obscure anything. In plain view."

Maya downed her champagne and one of Manifesta's assistants refreshed her flute.

Manifesta clasped her hands at the promise of drama. "Okay. Now we didn't always get along when Thug was alive the first time. Anyhoo, that's H_2O under the radio bridge. Man, I'm glad you're back. To what do we owe the honor of your return?"

He settled back in his chair. "My peeps needed me. I'm raising an army. Declaring a war. It's time to step up. Man up. Fo' sho'. For all of us. For hip-hop. And I'm back with a strategy."

Manifesta smiled to put him at ease. "Okay. Sooo, let's talk about how many times you've been shot. Did that last time when you were dead almost kill you, at least?"

"That it did. Five bullets entered my body." Thug leaned into the mic. "I'm not here to glorify that, though."

"So Thug, are you saying—"

"Pardon the interruption, Manifesta, if I may—I wanna take this time to announce my new name, Robeson."

"Robeson?" Manifesta asked, and Maya nodded vigorously, feeling him.

"Robeson. Thug is staying dead." Thug looked at Maya. "Robeson is my real name. My birth name, and I'm reborn." Robeson. A name full of life.

"Okay." Manifesta circled her prey. "That's what's up. Robeson! You heard it here first, folks. ROBESON!!" *KAPOW!* Sound effects of multiple bombs exploding always preceded Manifesta going in for the kill. Maya noticed Thug flinch slightly at the sound.

Manifesta zeroed in with a dramatic pause. "Soooo, who murdered you, man?"

"You." Thug nodded his head slowly several times. "And everybody listening to this show. Everybody who watches the news. Everybody who was glad that it wasn't them. There's a war happening and I was left out on the front lines alone—to represent life in the ghetto. Who speaks for the ghetto? Robeson does."

"Oh. Okay, okay." This was heavier than Manifesta wanted to take it. Her TV audience was down for more journalistic matters. Her radio audience wanted it gully.

Thug wasn't finished. "Wasn't just the shooters. The government surveillance was crazy. There's hip-hop police in every major city and undercovers in the culture. I had to re-up in exile and come back. Walk in my kicks for a minute."

"Sure but—" Manifesta started.

Thug wasn't finished. "Then after Imus, everybody was blaming hip-hop. Acting like we invented the violence and misogyny in America. Acting like the biggest consumers of black culture wasn't whitefolks. I had to come back. To save the music. To save you."

Maya was surprised to see the assured Manifesta look a little uneasy. Manifesta's engineer gave her a flying birdie hand signal. It looked like keep it light. "I'm not sure I'm the one that needs saving. Sooo, um, what's up next on the music tip?"

Thug gave Rob, as the label rep, a peace sign to show respect. "I'm gonna just do my thing."

Manifesta leaned forward. "Your former comrades Black Death were by the station last week. When is the reunion album?"

"You know, Manifesta, I'm probably just gonna kick it solo for a minute. Go on tour. Take it back to the people. Maybe Black Death can open for me."

"Really?! Open for you?" Manifesta didn't like getting in the middle of intra-squad beef as much as she used to, since more than once gunshots had rung out at the radio station, but this was more than she could have hoped for. "Like warm up the audience?"

Thug shrugged. Shrugging. Not good for radio, but she could probably use that clip for her TV show. Manifesta winked at the camera guys. Thug looked at Maya and his face relaxed.

Manifesta was a dentist yanking a stubborn tooth. "So, um, did you have access to news when you were . . . away?"

"A man like me is gonna stay informed."

"So were you in South Africa with Mandela?"

"Not this time, but maybe in the future." He smiled at Maya. She was hanging on his every word.

Manifesta picked up the vibe between them. "Or were you . . . into . . . something else?" Manifesta stared at Maya. Thug once again didn't respond. "Okay. Well . . . Any message for your legion of fans?"

"Yeah. I don't need followers. I need generals."

"Well I know the main general, Shell the Boy Wonder, is glad that you're home."

"We'll see." Thug was ruffled at the thought. "I'm not even sure I wanna still do the label thing. Cats need to be taking it independent. The old-guard label system needs to be obsolete. Cut out these vipers and middlemen."

Manifesta pepped up, a vulture smelling blood. "You calling Shell a viper?"

Thug was silent for far too many beats. Radio is not silence-friendly.

"Sooo, uh, tell me about the beautiful chick beside you. Jezebel. I played her single in the club and folks lost their minds."

"Oh, her?" Thug smiled at Maya in a way that people could feel through their radios. "She can introduce herself. She ain't being called

Jezebel no more though. She's switching it up. Call her MC Cleopatra. Cleopatra X."

Manifesta cocked her head to the side. "Wow, people add on new names these days before we can even learn the first one."

Cleopatra! Cleopatra X. *Thank you, Thug.* They gave each other permission to have their true names. Maya looked at Rob. The bastard was still her manager, and she was learning how to play her position. Rob nodded. Thug touched her hand. It was official. Her heartbeat multiplied.

Manifesta leaned into her mic with a rare sugary anti-diatribe. "Lemme describe the vision in front of me. Homegirl Cleo is fine. Like in that back-in-the-day Cleopatra Jones way. She's bringing chocolate sistas back 'cause she's a burnt sienna honey with eyes as big as mangos. Like on a clear day Thug could see forever in those eyes."

Maya felt her face blush. "Thank you, Manifesta."

"Then lemme tell you what she got on. Some crazy all-white one-shoulder shirt with a miniskirt. Slammin," boomed Manifesta. "You should see the faces on these two." The cameras in the perimeters zoomed in. "So Jez . . . Cleopatra X, I checked out your blog, home-girl, and you are a wild thing."

"My blog?" Maya looked through the glass at Luci. Luci nodded. Maya wasn't even aware that she had a blog. How could she have a blog and not know it? "Yeah, um, well, I'm just happy to be here with Thu—Robeson. Glad that he's back. Now we can all start living again." She downed the glass of champagne in front of her.

"Like I always say, your life starts now." Manifesta was clearly digging Maya. "So who are you?"

Cleopatra X née Jezebel née Maya looked into the umber eyes of Robeson né Thug and wanted to be whoever he expected her to be. Whoever he needed her to be. She wanted to live inside his heart. True that. When Manifesta turned on her microphone Maya was under the baobab tree with Robeson Thug. "Manifesta, I started writing rhymes, because of this man right here. When I first heard 'The Assassinator,' I wanted to burn something down just on GP. His lyrics saved my life," she said, definitely not peeping Athena looking through the looking glass. Then she spun a story, a yarn from her soul, of who she had become: Jezebel Johnson.

The important stuff was real: How she felt ugly and poor and abandoned and never fit in and how her life pissed her off but she never had the balls to change it. She moved her Granny Ruby from the big white home behind the lighthouse in Trinidad to a crude, wretched dump in Over-the-Rhine, but Granny Ruby's stories were true. She moved herself from Miss Beardsley's Academy to a group home but the anguish she felt was real. What? Same difference. Kind of like changing the names to protect the guilty.

But there was another part to Maya's tale. The part that outlined the facts of her existence. How and where she grew up. That part was true too. It wasn't her truth but it was a truth she knew very well because it was Athena's. It all just flowed out—growing up fatherless in the Nasty Nati in a fam full of street pharmacists half-pimping her beauty. Momma on the dole and Daddy (never met) in jail. Testing, thankfully, with a genius IQ to make it out. Heart wrenching. And when she was done, everyone in listening distance—except perhaps Athena, who was looking at the floor—loved her.

Maya, Athena's family and Granny Ruby were a hit. They were winding in the labyrinth together. The phone boards lit up. They listened to Maya and her dissipated nerves share things Granny Ruby used to say, and felt her. Manifesta and her listeners loved Maya as Thug felt comfortable to open up as well.

On the way out of the station, Maya caught a glimpse of herself. Hmph! She was more beautiful than she thought she was, especially because Thug was holding her hand. Even though he was technically a Just Met, it felt perfectly natural. She hadn't looked Athena in the eye yet, nor did she have the desire to do so. She promised herself to make time to explain the whole thing later.

Rob's shirt was damp with sweat. "Robeson is righteous, dawg. I'm all for it." Rob and Robeson Thug slapped palms although Robeson Thug's face said that he didn't give a damn what Rob thought, or need his approval.

"Pants on fire," whispered Athena into Maya's ear. She had to lean around a security guard to do so. Maya kept looking straight ahead.

"Yay!" Luci pointed up to the loudspeakers in the lobby of the radio station. "Angry Black Bitch" was playing. Maya felt the goddess' generosity.

"We need to meet," Rob said.

"Me?" asked Maya.

"All of us. We moved up the tour. Restructured it. Let's grab something to eat, then—"

"Sorry, Big Man. I'm taking Cleopatra somewhere first." Thug looked at Maya.

Rob bit his lip and Maya reveled in the moment. Yeah. That's for leaving me to get mauled by Pookie, she wanted to say.

"Okay." Rob looked Maya dead in the eye. "No doubt. Uh, call me if you need me, a'ight?"

"Sure," Maya said, not looking at him at all.

"She's gonna help me lead my revolution," Thug said.

"There ain't no revolution, Blackman. We all gotta do for self," Rob said, trying to bond with Thug over a joke and a head nod.

"I see you part of the problem." Thug pulled Maya ahead.

Athena's words were not yet ringing in Maya's ears as they walked into another sea of aggressive people with cameras, recorders and mics, and went their separate ways.

Chapter 22

"ME, THE ROX, GIVE UP THE BOX?
SO YOU CAN BRAG ABOUT IT FOR THE NEXT SIX BLOCKS?"
—*The Real Roxanne*

Bulletproof." Thug handed a piece of paper to Legba as they settled into the car.

"Huh?" Maya was fluttering on the ends of Robeson's lashes as Legba squired them away from the radio station. She watched Athena, Big Rob and Luci summon a cab. Hmm. She was living in a dream she'd never had.

Thug waved a hand in front of her face and she looked at him. "My old car. It was a Phantom. Bulletproof. It's been in a garage for the past three years."

"Oh, okay." Where were they going? Was it rude to ask? Damn he was beautiful.

"Cleopatra." Thug's lips said her new name.

Maya gave him her complete attention. "Yes, Robeson." She burst into a doofy laugh despite her best effort to appear sophisticated and edgy.

"Thank you." Thug was smiling too. What he was thanking her for? He kissed her hand. "I wanna show you where I was. Where I've been. Everybody's been asking, but I want to show *you*."

"Oh, okay." Where were they going? She wasn't prepared to fly.

Thug had a touch of the devil in his eye. "Can I blindfold you?"

"Blindfold me?" Maya tried to return the sexy look but this was becoming too Scorsese.

Robeson nodded. "For security purposes."

Maya looked at the back of Legba's head. It would be okay. She took a breath. "Yes." She leapt from the ledge as Robeson took his black-and-white scarf from his head and tied it over her eyes. Blind trust. Foolish, but she was already soaring above the soft earth. Flying. She could see nothing. Legba drove for another hour or so while they listened to Thug's music. Maya giggled uneasily.

"Your giggle is sexy." That voice could lead her anywhere. When they exited the ride onto concrete she was spun around three times, then walking in the daytime darkness. Thug greeted people right and left. None of them commented on the fact that the most famous back from the dead man in the world was leading a blindfolded woman. She saw twisted headlines and news stories: "That's when Maya knew things were terribly wrong. If Woody had gone straight to the police, this would never have happened." They were buzzed into a heavy metal door and were riding in an elevator that smelled faintly of piss.

A corridor. A zillion locks. Another metal door. Footsteps echoing. Trust, trust, trust, but why?

"Ready, Cleo?" Thug untied the blindfold. "Welcome."

Okay. Wow. Vision. His space was . . . breathtaking—a loft, all decorated in shades of black and white. Huge black-and-white photos of people with different color ebony skins. A large open space divided into a living room, library (?!), kitchen, studio and bedroom. There were heavy black drapes everywhere.

"Where are we?" Maya asked.

"A converted housing project. I blew out my fam's three apartments to create this space."

"I've never seen anything like this." What does one say after being blindfolded and taken to a secret location? "This is . . . different, Robeson. Did you use a decorator?" Ugh, lame. Oh well.

"Decorator?" Thug laughed. "Nah, baby. This is all me. This is where the kid's been resting his head for the past three years. Like I said, in plain view." Thug laughed again, louder this time, like the idea of pulling the wool over everyone's eyes got him pumped.

Maya was nervous not only about her safety (the man had been convicted for sexual assault and goddess knows what else) but about her body. He was quite possibly the biggest musical star of their generation and had been with every flavor of flawless women—some of whom were framed in artful nude portraits on the austere walls. Great.

"The people who live in these projects, Cleopatra, are down-and-dirty, hand-to-mouth, poor black, brown, red and yellow people."

Maya followed him into the space. "So how did you hide from them?"

"Your man was never hiding, baby." Maya pressed rewind on the words *your man*. Wow. And she thought that *she* was jumping the gun. "They all know I'm their neighbor. They just kept it low. No bribes, no payoffs, no threats. Just the code of the street. They brought my groceries 'til Fresh Direct came out. They tended to me when I was sick and served as my cooks, my handymen. Whatever I needed."

"Why?" escaped from Maya's mouth.

"Honor among thieves, baby. They cared for the man they know cared for them. No matter how many albums I sold I let it be known that I was one of them."

Maya assembled the pieces in her mind. Deep. This iconic man was a neighbor in the projects and they kept his secret.

"Don't worry. I wasn't just taking. I gave money for books and medicine; you know, shared a little love with people who ain't got none."

"Heavy." Books lined shelves and were stacked in piles around the room. Enough to open a public library. Maya scanned the shelves. Morrison. Ellison. Abant. Angelou. Hughes. Shakespeare. Proust. "It's like a professor lives here. I feel at home."

"Check this out." Thug ran across the floor and jumped up on the top of a huge sofa.

If you're jumping, jump. Maya slipped off her Manolos and caught up with him. She climbed to the top of the couch and followed Thug's pointing finger past the exposed brick wall. She expected to see brothas duking it out in an alley.

Maya put her hand over her mouth. "A bird's nest!"

Little blue baby birds were being tended to by their mama. The nest was awkwardly lodged between two buildings and Mama was feeding them bits of something. The tiny birdies looked up, beaks open, awaiting sustenance.

"Blue jays," Thug said.

"It's a miracle." Maya felt herself tearing up at the perfection of it all.

"It is," said Thug. He took Maya in his arms. They sat in silence on top of his leather sectional watching the blue jay show, each grateful for all sorts of things, and dozed off.

Maya felt drool on her face. She also felt eyes. She opened hers and wiped the dribbles away. Embarrassing. Thug was still holding her and watching her like she was the nest. It was pitch-black outside now and being in his arms was nourishing. Warm. She felt . . . safe.

"Hello," he said.

"Heyyyy." Maya raised her brows. She felt silly although she was unsure why. She shifted her weight, trying to give Thug some relief. "Aren't your arms and legs asleep?" She spoke away from him in case her new diet was making her breath foul.

Thug took her chin and turned her face toward him. "Baby, I've been shot so all of that is nothing to me."

"Oh." Maya tried to see the birdies in the darkness. "What did that feel like?"

"What? Being shot?" Thug lifted up his shirt.

Maya nodded. He took her left hand and traced his tight abdomen and chest. There were at least eight scars. Some were raised keloids visible through the tattoos, others were flat and barely perceptible. His body was a journal of his life. Words, pictures, scar tissue and muscles. He was a book that she wanted to devour. Her hand grazed his nipples and he flinched. She wanted to rest her face on his sturdy chest.

Thug pulled his shirt down over Maya's hand and stroked her bone-straight press and curl, any promise of ringlets faded with the day. His touch was tender.

"We should get some dinner," he said. "The choice is yours. Chinese or my home cooking."

She felt herself dissolving into him and feeling easier about the whole thing. "Home cooking, huh?" *A man of many surprises.* "That depends. What can you cook?"

He jumped up. "I'll show you."

Maya didn't want to separate so soon. "Sounds good," she said.

Thug headed toward the kitchen. Maya started to walk to the bathroom until she remembered that she didn't know where anything was. It felt so natural for her to be in his safe house that she'd forgotten.

"Master bath over there, guest bathroom to your right," Thug said, reading her mind.

"Which should I use?"

"It's on you, Cleo X."

Maya headed past a California king–size bed to the master bath. She wasn't planning on being a guest. Ooh. Her blood sugar dropped. She didn't want to be a diva, but she had to eat. Now.

"Here." Thug walked over and handed her a Ziploc bag of baby carrots. "These should tide you over." Timing. Ziploc? Hilarious.

She pictured Mr. Criminalistic Eternal Thug Menace holed up ziplocking fresh veggies far from the roar of the crowd. It was too close to Tupperware! Maybe Ziploc bags were the great equalizer. Who couldn't use a stay-fresh pouch?

"Um, you don't have a plastic cap, do you Robeson? I want to take a shower."

"What? Your hair can't get wet?" he called out.

"It can, it's just . . ." It had been weeks since Maya had handled her own hair. "I don't know what Rob and Luci have planned and I need to stay presentable."

"Scared that the kitchen'll revolt and get to turning back?"

"Shut up!" Maya laughed and closed the bathroom door. John Coltrane's tones were filling the space.

"You know Napoleon thought that it was sexier when Josephine didn't wash," she heard Thug yelling. "Look in the closet for towels."

She looked at his black-and-gray bathroom full of stone and slate and found that she had no desire to hyperventilate. She peeped the glass—no nosebleed. Yay!!! Okay, what are you doing, Maya? Why do you need to take a shower? To be fresh. Just in case. Just in case.

Maya was in the shower trying to figure out the five nozzles when the door opened. Uh-oh. She wasn't sure that she just wanted to go for it like that. Not right away.

"Just leaving a T-shirt and shorts." Thug closed the door behind him.

Maya walked out of the bathroom and into Eden. Incredible. There must have been about twenty-five candles lit all over the space. Good, maybe he wouldn't be able to get such a good look at her in the dark. Maya felt like the most unsexy schmo in a man's extra large T-shirt and boxers, her hair somewhere between a 'fro and a cold wave. Taking a shower was a brilliant plan.

"How'd I get so lucky?" Thug asked.

She was grateful for the reassurance. "What did you make?"

"I did a reheat but it is my cooking, I promise. Spaghetti and tofu meatballs. You don't eat meat, do you?" The food was laid out on the coffee table. It looked divine in a big bowl next to bread and a salad. Thug pulled Maya next to him on the sectional.

"I, uh, do," Maya said anxiously.

Thug looked up. "Why?"

"Well . . . I didn't use to. I was raised vegetarian."

Thug furrowed his forehead. "In a group home?"

Whoops. "Uh, yeah." Maya wanted to explain but she didn't know how. "No. Well, my Granny Ruby was very influential in my life."

"I respect your flow but no more meat, okay?" Thug handed her a square black Japanese style plate. "Life. It ain't easy."

"No," said Maya. "It's not." She didn't explain to Thug that she now loooved the taste of chicken, beef and fish too in case it was on his hit list. She didn't want to kill the vibe but technically she was not supposed to be eating bread or pasta. So now what? She'd promised her nutritionist and Luci that if she was ever going to eat anything "off plan" she would call and inform them. Bump it. This whole shebang was off plan.

"What do you want, Cleo X?"

She dipped wheat bread in olive oil. "Same as you. Ultimate happiness." Yummy.

Thug and Maya indulged in scrumptious food, conversation and wine and when they were finished eating they were drunk, mostly on each other. What now? Ask him to kick some rhymes? Maybe talk more about the neighbors? Or ask him about his beef with Manifesta and everybody else Athena said he had beefs with? It's better to be thought a fool than to open your mouth and prove it, her father would say. Maybe she should just—

Thug leaned in and gave Maya a minty kiss. Actually, he put his lips to hers and sucked her tongue deep into his mouth. It was like whoa. *Then* he kissed her. Kissed her. Kissed her. Mm. She felt his lips on hers. Her tongue had a direct connect to her spot. She hoped she knew what she was doing. It had been so long.

Her heart pounded against his chest. She put her hands on his shoulders. He put his on either side of her face and kissed her nose, her forehead and her cheeks. It was all so . . . sweet. Maya was not used to sweet. Both Big Rob and the therapist had been completely aggressive. This man was about doing work. She could feel her pulse thump-thumping with the music. His music. He smelled like manhood. It had been too long. She was the damsel in the romance novel surrendering to Fabio and she couldn't wait. She started to pull off the T-shirt.

Thug placed his hands solidly on top of hers. "I like to lead."

"Okay." She was officially wet. She waited for his next move. He put his hands on her backside and alternated between kneading and caressing as he continued with The New Kiss. Mmm. Triumph. This brother was about making love. Tongue. Kissing. Mouth. Lips. Throat. He kissed his way back down to her feet and back up to her lips. The ones on her face. Maya tried to roll over on top of him. She licked the dragon on his arm. She wanted to make love to his tattoos, and keloids too.

"I told you I'm in charge. I'm a grown man." That he was. The grown man took her hands and placed them up over her head. She wanted to turn this grown man out. Seal the deal. "Patience," he whispered, then stopped and looked at Maya. Most people kind of look generally into someone's face but he was really looking *at* her. Into her eyes. Into her soul. Into her. She liked seeing herself reflected in his irises. She was gorgeous there.

Breasts—ooh. Breasts over shirt. Then breasts under shirt. Left, then right, then left again. Still kissing. Lingering. Lingering. Particularly enamored with that left breast, he started sucking. *Oooooooooooh.*

Hard meet wet. Wet meet hard. They dry humped like kids playing spin the bottle until they were on the brink of ecstasy and there was nowhere else to go clothed but . . . asleep, spooning. When Maya woke up his mouth was down there, between her legs, over her shorts. He was an expert in tactical slow torture. He said he liked to lead so why were their clothes still on? She couldn't take being rejected again so she waited for his cue.

"OOOOOOOOOHHHHHHHHHHHHHHHH!!!" His tongue. Flicking through the shorts. She orgasmed, hard, vise-gripping her knees around his head.

Thug wriggled his way out and kissed Maya on her closed eyelids. "Trust me. I want you. I haven't had a woman in years." He kissed Maya's cheeks two times each. She nodded. "That's the problem with us as a people. We always want instant gratification. So what are you? Narc? CIA? FBI?"

She read online about his bouts with paranoia. She couldn't tell if this was that or a joke. "All of the above," she said. After that they knew instinctively that anything that happened between them would stay between them. They turned off their phones and lost track of time after Maya sent Athena a text saying "I AM FINE. C U SOON." Athena texted back "CALL ROB. ASAP." Not.

Thug didn't answer his rings either or knocks from the neighbors. They breathed together . . . woke again and again ensconced in each other's smell . . . mind funked . . . played with his guitar . . . cornrowed each other's hair—his Gram taught him how . . . read Rumi *want to merge with you* poetry in a bath of milk, myrrh and rose petals. Fit for Cleopatra, he said. Then they played video games—not the ones named after him (too violent)—and did an IM battle rap competition online called scrypting to a jazzy neo-classical soul backdrop of

Mos Def, Public Enemy, Talib Kweli, Common Sense (his playlist); Me'Shelle, Lauryn, and Dwele (hers). Phew. Music was definitely the food of their love. They were chocoholics, indulging in hot fudge.

Maya asked questions: How does it really feel to get shot? (Told you, painful.) Didn't you get lonely? (Yes.) What's the deal with the rape conviction? (The charge was assault, not rape. Like in Central Park, somebody violated her. It just wasn't me.)

He wrote Maya the beginnings of a poem: "Did I ever love before this night?/ Did I ever love before your sight?/ Did I ever kiss before I kissed you?/ I am bathed in your sweat./ I'm why God made you."

They ate some more, losing crumbs in the sheets. Thug's bed became their entire universe. They were the original woman and man, helpmates. His life story rolled out between nibbles. Mostly the same stuff she already read. Mom was an artist (paint and photos). Dad was an addict (heroin, died of AIDS). Two stints in group homes (while Mom was getting it together). Army then AWOL then prison. (Gave Sam two years, then Sam took two more.) Then a cat named Pimp from his group home invited him to join a rap group.

They turned on the news. Sal Masakela was talking about "the star-crossed hip-hop lovers on the run" who "disappeared after a hostile radio interview. They could be anywhere. Kind of a post-millennial Bonnie and Clyde. Several friends overheard them plotting."

Maya sat up on the bed. "That's crazy."

"People fill in their own blanks, Cleopatra." Thug massaged her freshly manicured (by him) feet.

"Angry Black Bitch" music. Maya's phone. She looked at Thug.

"I turned the phones back on." The time and date said it was three days later but they still didn't fully know each other in the biblical sense. BOBBY blinked on the small screen.

She could barely muster a hello before Rob screamed, "Maya!"

Maya paused. "Yeah?"

"What are you doing?"

"Uh, drillin'."

"Where have you been? I was worried about you. We've all been worried about you."

"My bad." Maya turned over on her side to give Thug better access to her soles.

"You over there wherever fiddling while Rome is burning. We have to meet, Maya. Immediately."

"What?" She loved hearing the anxiety in Rob's voice.

"Right now!"

"For?" Maya looked over at Thug. He looked like a calendar poster in his black satin boxers. Yummy.

"Concert prep. Meet me in my office ASAP."

"Handle your business," Thug whispered, kissing Maya on her back. She half-stifled a purposeful moan.

Rob lowered his voice. "You don't even know what diseases that man has."

Maya rolled her eyes even though he couldn't see her. "I haven't done anything like that." Not for lack of trying.

Rob breathed out relief. "Shell moved the tour up. Before we go, I need to talk to you 'bout testing yourself on real people."

"Testing myself?"

"You real or fake?"

"You don't have to put it like that. I told you I'll perform wherever, whenever."

"Cool. My office. See you there." Rob hesitated, then hung up.

"What's up?" Thug asked.

"Rob wants me to meet him in the subway."

"You don't got to jump 'cause he says jump. Who is this man anyway?"

"Shell's right hand. And my manager."

"New Jack City."

"I'm a new jack too, baby. Come."

"Subway? Nah. I don't think so. People still want my blood. I went underground not just to protect me. A lot never made the headlines. We not going."

"Please." Maya poked out her bottom lip. She didn't ask herself why she was asking his permission.

Thug gave Maya a long look. "Fine. Go. Accept your death first and then go."

"What does that mean?"

"It means we're all gonna die, Cleopatra. Me, you, everybody. We're born to die. Once we accept that, we're free to do anything."

After Maya showered and dressed, Thug handed her a pair of his sunglasses on her way out. "All good things, baby . . ."

Maya had to force herself to leave him. The soul-to-soul connection was like whoa, but she wanted, needed a body-to-body connection. She was honored by his respect, but wanted to be pleased by his power. She would have to gather the years of Athena's love lessons and make it happen sooner rather than later. Didn't revolutionary brothas need loving too?

THE THUG PLAYBOOK

Tactical Rules for Survival & World Domination

1. Hell and heaven is right now. Life means what we make it mean. You choose.
2. Kings only roll with other royalty, even if that means going it alone.
3. Fortune favors the bold. Act now. Seize the minute.
4. If your enemy thinks that you are weak, play weak. When ego gets the best of them, pounce. However, the only true enemy is the self.
5. Be elusive. Lay low, fall back and assess when necessary. Retreat is not defeat. Re-up, then come back.

Chapter 23

"I'M THE QUEEN OF RAP AND THERE IS NONE HIGHER
ALL YOU SLUT BAG WHORES SHOULD CALL ME SIRE."

—Remy Ma

Maya walked down the A train platform in dark sunglasses trailed by the security guard Thug insisted on sending with her. He had given one of his neighbors a couple hundred bucks to run out to grab her a new outfit, so she was looking quite ghetto fabulous. Thug allowed her to leave without the blindfold and Maya realized that the whole time they were still in Harlem.

"Maya!" Rob was behind her on the platform.

"You rang?" She felt less anxious seeing him now that her soul was somebody else's. He was irrelevant. "Aren't you supposed to call me Cleopatra or Jezebel?"

"Fuck that." Rob threw his arms around her in a great bear hug. "I'm glad you're okay."

"Suffocating." Maya shoved him away. She looked around and noticed that people were recognizing her. Her face had only been plastered with Thug's throughout the mass media for the past four days.

"You okay?" Rob's face was inches away from hers.

Maya took a step backward. "Yeah. Fine. Let's get started."

"You know, Maya . . . I realize that you might want to make me jealous, but . . . But this is not necessarily the best way to, uh, go about it."

She translated his mumblings into English. "Are you serious?"

"I'm just saying . . ." Rob looked flustered.

"You're just saying what? My relationship with Thug has nothing to do with you."

"Your relationship?" Rob stormed away from Maya and came back. The security guard moved closer.

"Yeah. My re-la-tion-ship, nigga." Maya had never dropped the N bomb in her life and surprised herself when she hit him with its ugliness. "The world doesn't revolve around you, Big Rob. You wanted to meet? Let's meet."

Rob paced back and forth. They had become just another couple beefing in the subway. Rob looked limp and impotent and Maya was loving it.

"I'm just saying you can't disappear for three days like that. We're on a schedule. We got papers on you. It's . . . It's . . . It's unprofessional!" Rob was as emotional as Maya had ever seen him. Aw. Maybe he was genuinely worried. She didn't like seeing him hurt despite everything.

"What did you want?" she asked.

He took a breath. "Your last test before you go on tour—"

"My last test? I'm already on green light. Manifesta, Hip-Hop Ham, Shell and Thug all signed off."

"Told you, Maya. Two hip-hops. There's the commercial garbage lighting up your radio. People greenlight that, too. Then there's true school street hop. You keep it true, we sell more music. Where do you want to be?"

"All I can be is me." Maya turned to walk away.

"Punk out then." Rob knew he had her with that.

Maya stopped. She turned and bowed mockingly. "What's your final test, master?"

Rob held out his hands over the grime of the NYC public transit system.

"And?" she asked.

"Kick your rhymes, Cleopatra X," he said mockingly.

Maya watched a man reach into his pants and adjust his privates. "Here?"

"These are your buyers. A lot of hot acts start off down here. We're underground. Literally. Kick it."

"There's no music. And isn't that illegal?"

"Illegal?" Rob laughed. "Like I said, punk out. You can have the glitz without this. The phone's been ringing off the hook with endorsement offers."

"Really? Who?" Maya was intrigued.

"Liquor and cigarette companies mostly." Touché. Rob was smiling inside his snide face.

"I wouldn't do that—"

"Because you're of the people? Prove it." Rob had her by the cojonés. Well, ovaries, really. However, it was mega seeing him jealous.

Why did she need to prove anything to him? She had just made the best love of her life, even without penetration, but she still wanted, no, *needed* to prove to him that she was good enough. Good enough not to be left.

See, I am a keeper, she wanted to say. Instead she asked, "What do you want me to do, Rob?"

"Just stand here and kick it. You make it through a whole song and you pass."

"Okay. Um, well, are you gonna bring a crowd over or something?" Maya kicked a beer bottle away from her "stage."

"Nope."

"Well, fine. I'm gonna test out something else since people are already feeling 'Angry Black Bitch.' "

"That's whassup. Street test to get a vibe." Rob touched Maya's shoulder, then stepped back. His eyes softened and so did her heart. Maya couldn't believe she was doing this but here she was.

She cleared her throat like subway beggars and solicitors did, and let loose:

> *"I'm a tell you how to love me so listen close*
> *Now the Sunrise rose goes grandiose . . ."*

A couple of girls nodded their heads. *Isn't that the chick on the run with Thug*? a man asked. *Yeah, yeah. Angry Black Bitch Cleopatra*, his woman said.

"I was a dirty duckling; Living hard and struggling
But that ain't nothing but a thing 'cause now my hope springs . . ."

An old lady who looked like Granny Ruby opened a mini green Bible and starting competing with Maya, verse for verse in fire and brimstone. "Let he who is without sin cast the first stone . . ." Her skin was the color of baked chickpeas and her mighty yellow rainhat almost pushed her tiny frame off balance.

"Eternal as the day is my maternal journal
The fires of hell in this life are not infernal . . ."

"Shut up, you dumb bitch." A pre-teen boy elbowed his friend. Was he talking to Maya or the old lady? Maya could barely hear her voice over the preacher woman but she continued.

"You got me bubbling, bubbling, bubbling over you
'Cause the joy that I'm feeling is mad overdue . . ."

Two women laughed and Maya continued even as a man struck up a tune on a small harp.

The preacher lady had her own rap: "Pride goes before destruction; a haughty spirit before a fall. Better to be lowly in spirit and among the oppressed than to share plunder with the proud."

A train rumbled in as one roared out and a rat scurried past, its skinny tail leaving a trail in the dust. Maya was terrified and her skin crawled but she continued anyway, even as she spotted a police officer in her peripheral vision. He was coming toward her but she would not be moved.

"Over? Not hardly, 'cause I'm just beginning
No wedding ring needed, we got that zing and—"

"Do you have a permit to perform?"

Maya was unsure of what to do. She had practiced falling to the ground in nonviolent protest but that was for important causes. What was the cause here? Proving something to your ex?

"Hey, Puff Daddy." The officer was in her face. "Answer me. Do you have a permit?"

Rob started to intervene.

Without missing a beat, Maya dropped:

"Permit? Shit. Don't ask me how I spit.
Ask me 'bout my clique 'cause I commit to keep it brick."

The people on the platform, including Rob, guffawed and clapped. Rob's perfect teeth flashed in the background. Even the stone faced bodyguard cracked a smile.

The cop was bright red. "I'll be back with a female officer. Stay right there."

"I will be right here,
Copper, never fear, pop a
Mint in your mouth, uh, if you're talking non stoppa!"

Maya was embroiled in a battle rap with the officer, who rushed off with the arriving train as the "audience" erupted with hoots, hollers, applause and giggles. Maya felt like herself. Just . . . like herself. In the way that Prince with his deliciously random funkadelic self is just don't give a rass Prince. No frontin.

As soon as the cop was out of view, Rob was upon her. "Come on!" He grabbed Maya's arm and they ran up the stairs, hitting every other one. Yes, in heels! Her security man followed close behind. Rob lifted Maya over the turnstiles and dashed outside to the waiting Bentley.

What a rush! Maya wrapped her arms around Rob's neck and they cracked up laughing. Maya couldn't believe it herself, but she was loving her life. Telling off a cop then finding your driver in a luxury car on the curb rocks!

Delirious with chuckles, endorphins and adrenaline, Rob and

Maya tried to catch their breath. "So, uh, you sure you still wanna do this?" Rob already knew the answer.

"I'm already doing this!" Maya's eyes were shining. "Maybe we *can* be friends, Rob." She kissed him on the cheek and he kissed her back, on the cheek.

The back window of the Bentley rolled down. Thug. "Hey baby." His poker face was solid.

"Uh, hey." Maya climbed out of Rob's arms and took a step backward.

"Let's get in," Rob said.

Maya scooted over Thug's lap and Rob went to the other side while the big man got in the front.

"What up, Robeson?" said Rob.

"What up, Big Rob?" They exchanged a pound, giving each other the gas face.

"Drive," Thug said and Legba was off.

Maya's energy sitting between Thug and Rob was bigger than the car. "Baby!"

"Yeah," Thug and Rob said in unison.

"My bad," said Rob.

Okay. That didn't just happen. Maya talked fast for distraction purposes. "Guess who just kicked it freestyle on a subway platform?" "Yep, *moi*, and it was gangsta!" She slapped Thug's leg for punctuation.

"Word?" Thug looked over Maya's head at Rob behind her.

"Yo. We leave for the tour in a couple weeks, man." Rob told Thug.

Thug nodded, looking straight ahead.

Legba dropped Maya off at the Heretix. Thug gave her one of his special kisses on the golden sidewalk with Rob watching before she went in. She tried to get him to come up, but he had a war to plan. When she got to her room her key didn't work. The concierge gave her a note from Shell. She opened the small envelope with the Camp Hustla insignia. "A platinum suite for my new platinum artist. Congrats Ms. Cleopatra upstart!" A bigger suite—two bedrooms!

There was a page ripped from the week's *Billboard.* The single "Angry Black Bitch" was number two on the Billboard Top 100. Thug (with no new music), Gwen Stefani, Beyoncé and John Legend were one, three, four and five. Incroyable!!! She was a bona fide star! Why didn't Rob say something? If he had, she wouldn't have performed in the sub—Aha!

Maya bounced into her new living room. It was gorgeous, but she was tired of moving. It looked like the last suite, but now she walked into a living room instead of the bedroom. Her stuff was all unpacked. Creepy.

She felt big. Expansive. Larger than life. And look at the digs! She opened the other, smaller, bedroom. Athena was chilling with BaTricia Simone and two other chicks who pepped up upon seeing her.

"Athena, hi." Maya wasn't even aware that BaTricia and Athena were social. "Guess who's platinum? Us!"

Athena was kicked back on a buff leather chair with her feet up.

"Rob texted me that you resurfaced."

"Hey Cleopatra." BaTricia rubbed her pregnant belly.

"Hey BaTricia." Maya didn't waste her time acknowledging the no-name chicks. She used to be the type of person to say hi to everyone when entering a room, delicatessen or post office. Lately, however, there were far too many hangers-on for her to waste her time doing so. "Well, I . . . I was hoping for some alone time, Athena, so we could talk."

"Oh—now that Jezepatra is free, I'm supposed to drop everything?"

"Um, can we talk privately?"

Athena acted like this was all a great inconvenience. "Okayyy. Be back y'all."

"Cool!" said one of the no-names. "Cleopatra X, I'm Mocha and this is CJ. Can we have your autograph? For my little cousin."

Sycophant. Maya didn't reply.

" 'Angry Black Bitch' gets me pumped every morning. I listen to it with my latte macchiato," the other one (control freak) said. BaTricia rolled her eyes.

Maya managed a "thanks" before leaving. She had critical personal business. She and Athena stepped into her room.

Maya sat on her bed. "Athena, I don't want beef. We're sistas."

Athena stood at the door. "Sistas, huh?"

"What are those people doing here?"

"You mean my friends? This is my spot too."

"Fine. I don't even know what we're fighting about."

"Come on, Maya. You were a Ph.D. student. You can't be that stupid. The plan was to get me put on. Instead you stole my life. You got put on with my talent and now you're living my life."

"Athena—" Maya wanted to say that wasn't true. She didn't get put on with her talent. "So I'm not talented?"

"I didn't say that, Maya. I'm just saying that this was my dream. *My* dream."

"Yeah, after cheerleading, then hair styling, modeling, dancing, NASCAR racing and goddess knows what else. You get to find yourself and I don't?"

Athena contemplated this for a second. "I'm sorry. I'm just gonna keep it real and tell you your shit stinks. You're eating *meat*—"

"It's a free country."

"And drinking up a storm."

"And you should talk, Athena?"

"Whatever. Just check yourself, that's all I'm saying."

"We're still girls, right Athena? I'm mean, we're still us, right?"

"I'm still me, homie," Athena said.

They stared at each other. Then Maya offered an olive branch. "Missed you, 'Thena."

Athena burped. "Is that why you stole my life in the Manifesta interview?"

"I'll do better, Athena. I promise." Maya wanted to hug Athena but somehow it didn't seem like the right moment. "So how's tricks?"

"Girl, you're the one screwing America's Most Wanted. Let's hear about that." Athena sat on the bed.

"Yeahhhh. That's my boo." Maya couldn't explain that they were bigger than sex, for now. That they were waiting, although she wasn't sure for what.

"Don't worry, I'm gonna give you Mama's seduction tip sheet." Athena was all over it. "You got yourself a bona fide roughneck and if you're not careful, you'll be in over your head. That's a special brand of loving right there."

"True," Maya said.

"So where does the great Thug hang?"

"In his spot." Maya felt affronted by all the questioning. It felt like an invasion of privacy, which was strange. This was Athena.

Athena held out her arms, like come on, out with it already. "In his spot, which is where?"

"Can't say."

"Maya. You're joking, right?" Athena held a palm to her heart.

Maya's shoulders went up slowly. "I gave my word."

"Oh. Him you gave your word?" Athena looked hurt.

Maya smiled to soothe the blow. "So, uh, we're rolling out on tour. You'll finally be on stage."

"I know. Ferrari's gonna try to visit me on the road."

Maya raised her eyebrows. "Is he still around?"

"You don't know *what's* going on in my life, do you?" Athena cocked her head to the side like there was something else she wanted to say.

Luci caught Maya up on all the camp gossip over a soul-food dinner at Baton Rouge Restaurant near 145th Street. They gave each other permission to take a diet break and grub out on Southern fried chicken, candied yams and mac and cheese. They'd each already lost about fifteen pounds and were looking, in Luci's words, fantabulous.

"You hooking up with Thug was the best thing you could have done. Smart maneuvering. Absolutely marv." The waitstaff maintained a polite distance while giving them dedicated treatment, although patrons kept interrupting the meal to tell Maya that they recognized her.

Luci broke it down: The original plan was Jezebel opening for the Black Death reunion tour, headlining Pimp. The new concert plan was that Jezebel would still open. However, the headliner was now Thug aka Robeson. Uh-huh. Stealing Pimp's comeback thunder. Black Death would perform about three songs before he came out as the main event. Payment structure remained the same, but respect had shifted. Whenever that happens in the hood, beef is never far behind.

"And what's up with the blog? I would never say half the stuff that's up there." Maya blotted oil from her macaroni with a napkin.

"Sorry. Most of our artists are semiliterate so we usually take care of it, but knock yourself out if you wanna take that on."

Luci explained over red velvet cake that she needed to get the album recorded on the road. In addition, Ozzie Marvelous had reissued everything that Thug ever touched. His Midas touch and intro of Cleo X had put Camp Hustla and the East Coast back on the map for real/ for real.

With hip-hop reigning for so many years on the West Coast, then the Midwest and now the Dirty South, the East Coast was largely viewed as tired and washed up. Camp Hustla still loomed large mainly because of its back catalogue and multiple businesses, not its music. With the reemergence of Thug and the development of Jezebel/ Cleopatra, Black Death and Shell the Boy Wonder were assured that the hit machine was back. Cleopatra X was assigned a permanent security detail.

Chapter 24

"Bitches and niggas every day
are practicing to do my shit.
Bitches every day are eyeing this number I spot."
—*Wendy Williams*

Deliverance was coming. That was the name Thug and the boys came up with for the tour. Pimp had wanted to call the tour The Plague but he was outvoted in favor of the name proposed by Thug the Criminalistic, who was now being called Thug the Immortal. Hardly anybody except Maya called Thug "Robeson." "Robeson Thug + Cleopatra X + Black Death = Deliverance. Save Yourself," the ads said.

The game plan was to jet down to Atlanta and pick up the tour bus and roadies there. Riding anywhere in anything with Black Death was like babysitting kindergarteners. Pimp, Gunz and Nigg (Kronic was still in the looney bin) bounced off the walls while Maya and Thug curled up in the Gulfstream's bedroom, leaving Luci, Athena, Belle the flight attendant and entourage to fend for themselves. As for Rob, when he was in the dog pound he was just like the rest of them. He sat in a corner playing *Suicide: The Official Black Death* video game on a large flatscreen.

Tour, as the tour manager was called, was reading a tabloid. The joke was that it didn't make sense to know his name because Rob micromanaged and took care of everything anyway. "Theopatra Embarks On National Tour" the headline on his paper said. "Theopatra" was the Bennifer, TomKat, Brangelina, Jayoncé nickname that the press had created for hip-hop's new reigning supercouple.

There was originally mad beef over the concert rearrangement but now everything was all good. Mostly. Black Death refused to rehearse, meaning that the show would be a surprise to everyone. With all the ego drama, Madame Cleopatra was bumped down to her one hit song, which she over-rehearsed with Athena and her four dancers to within an inch of its life.

The jet's romantic bedroom had wine-colored brocade walls. Maya had stopped by Turning Heads before they left for a bikini wax to make things more enticing for her man. Three zips of hot wax, four bloodcurdling screams, a new birth control prescription and she was ready for natural love. Miles high in the sky, Maya lay on the circular bed swaddled in the burgundy velvet covers that matched her lace babydoll and sexy boyshorts. If this wasn't a hint, she didn't know what was. Maya reached over to the side table and took a swig directly from the bottle of Krug Clos du Mesnil Champagne right before Thug came out of the bathroom and got in bed. He was wearing old gym shorts and a scruffy tee, but he was still flawless. Thug passion. A man couldn't be more enticing.

"Damn." Thug nuzzled his face in Maya's neck. "Somebody smells good."

"Ylang-ylang," she said, arching her back to make her neck and other areas easier to access.

"All this for me?" His gravelly voice sounded deeper.

Maya nodded.

"I think you're trying to seduce me, Mrs. Robeson," he said, running a hand down her legs and between her (already parted) thighs.

Maya giggled suggestively, waiting to follow his lead.

"Damn, I love you." Thug kissed her face.

Maya stroked his hair. Mmm. Rugged. She never thought that she could love anybody else like she'd loved Rob, and she still wasn't completely sure. She was trying to love Robeson like she had never been hurt. Difficult, but he had to be carrying baggage too. Isn't that life? Being that she definitely was no longer in love with Rob (he actually disgusted her), the space in her heart was open.

Robeson nibbled on Maya's lower lip softly, but forcefully. She would have thought this would be grating or annoying, but it was incredibly erotic. It told her what kind of lover he was, what kind of lover he would be. "Full, raw and unedited," he said. "That's how I love you. Yeah. You know why I came back, right?"

"Yes," she said, incredibly turned on. Maya rolled over and sat on top of him. "For me, baby." She decided to go for it. Athena always said that speaking to men dirty seemed to drive them crazy. "I got something for you, Robeson," she said.

Robeson held Maya's neat waist and centered her on his manhood. "What you got for me, Cleopatra?" He slid his hands down (good) and started molding her butt (better!).

Maya was feeling her champagne courage. She started slowly moving her hips around on top of his body.

"Yeah, baby," he said, so she moved faster, feeling his enjoyment.

She steadied her mind. Okay. Dirty talk time. She cleared her throat quietly. "So, um, you like that fat ass, Robeson?"

"What?"

"I said, you like that big, fat juicy ass?" She bounced up and down. "Everything is nice and tight. Ready for you."

He moved his arms from her butt back up to her waist. "Cleopatra, why are you talking like that?"

Uh-oh. She felt him softening. "I just thought—"

Thug sat up. "You just thought what? That you'd act like a whore?"

"I figured that it was okay if I was being *your* whore." Maya searched his face for meaning. Was he angry?

He put his arms around Maya and regained his composure. "It's okay, but I don't want to dirty you up like that. You're a goddess, Cleopatra," he said. "A queen. I just want to kneel at your shrine."

Maya nodded. Was it too much to want him to enter the shrine for worship?

Robeson leaned in and kissed Maya straight through to her soul. Their tongues encircled each other, and locked. His lips felt sooo good.

"Even our kisses are poetry," he said, caressing her breasts through the lace. He was driving her to the brink of insanity. "Sistas say y'all wanna be respected. A man try to respect your nappy head and he gets shot down." He laughed.

"You should talk," Maya said. She grabbed his hair in two handfuls.

"Ow," he said, and they laughed together.

Maya and Thug pulled the covers over their heads and talked like kids do until they fell asleep. They were awakened by the pilot announcing that they were flying over Virginia. Thug stumbled out to get food from the kitchen. Moments after he left there was a knock on the door.

"Come in," Maya called.

Luci peeked her head in. "Safe to enter?"

"Of course!"

"Well I didn't know if you were buck naked in here!"

"Hardly. How's the zoo going?"

"Chile, puh-lease." Luci did a neck roll.

"That well, huh?"

Lucy laughed. "I actually just had a quick question. I'm trying to help Rob and Tour get the reservations straight. You and Robeson are rooming together all along the way, right?"

"Yup."

"Okay. That's it. You crazy kids have fun now."

"Later, Luce."

Luci strolled back into the main cabin, triumphant. She snuggled up under Rob. "How's it going?"

Rob's eyes were glued to the screen. The objective of *Suicide: The Official Black Death* video game was to gun down as many Haters as possible. "Chillin', Luce, what's up?"

"Maya wants you to tell Athena that she'll have to pay for her own room because she's shacking with Thug the whole tour."

Rob pressed Pause and looked at Luci. "Oh man. You serious?"

"Yup," Luci said coyly.

"Maya said that?" he asked, incredulous, and Luci shrugged. Rob went back to his game. "It's messed up, but that'll save some bank."

"Marvy." Luci sidled back to her fashion magazines victoriously. "Let's clean up the riffraff."

Rob finished his game (*snuff a bitch 10 points*), then sat down next to Athena. She sat on the side listening to Gunz, Nigg and Pimp's stories about growing up in New York in the '80s. They never let her feel a part of the crew. She was just entourage, hovering always slightly on the perimeters.

"Yo, crackheads used to be roaming the streets like night of the living baseheads, yo!" Pimp held his hands in front of him and demonstrated.

Nigg (loud but harmless) stood up. "Yeah. People used to wild out. Run in the street naked. Straight bugging."

His brother Gunz (quiet but deadly) laughed like a madman. "'Specially Kronic and old-school Thug, forget about it. Crunk is not the word."

"That sounds bugged." Rob paused. "Athena, uh, this is gonna sound kind of awkward coming from me but—"

Athena looked up. "Spill it."

Rob scratched his neck. "Don't kill the messenger, a'ight? Cleo X wants you to pay for your own room. She's staying with Thug, which works for the budget, but, well . . . We're staying at The Siegfred ATL. The rooms are four hundred a night . . ."

The Black Death dudes, beef lovers from birth, hyped it up. It was as if they were performing a mini play and Athena was the butt of it.

Nigg: "Ohhhhh, she played you!!"

Gunz: "That's wild, yo."

Pimp: "Athena, I wouldn't take that if I were you, Boogie . . ."

Athena stood up. Her eyes looked crazy. "'Nuff said. Good looking out, Big Rob."

Pimp stumbled up and opened his eyes wide. "That's cra-zy, ma."

Athena went into the bathroom and slammed the door.

Meanwhile, Maya decided that tonight she was going to finally get her man—mind, soul *and* body. Enough was enough. Was it wrong to want a little kinesthetic healing? She understood that he was abstaining out of respect. With all due respect though, she was overdue. Her self-control was nil, and she had been looking at the crew boys more and more, although they never would have been her flow before. Not to mention one jerk of an Ex who shall remain nameless. The rest of the flight was all about Cleopatra, Robeson and the art of seduction. Since Thug liked to lead, she would let him do so, laying traps of a woman's good graces to snare her Thug. She would present her entire being as an invitation. Thug was a contrarian who liked a challenge, so a closed door approach was hopefully the way to go. Contrarians want what they cannot have, going contrary to what is expected. Again, she realized that it was unethical to use her field's knowledge for personal purposes, but whatchugonnado?

Thug had fallen back to sleep. Perfect. Maya sent the team a message to leave them on board even after the jet landed and took a hot bath, cleansing every orifice and oiling her pulse points. L'Occitane Rose & Reine, Luci promised, would make any man's knees buckle. Athena's lifetime of notes had only gotten her so far, and although technically she hadn't seen Luci with anyone, her tales of international exploits and intrigue were the stuff dreams are made on.

Maya tightened up her bikini wax with Thug's cordless razor and buffed the instrument clean. What? He'd never know. She smelled like passion. She pulled her hair back in a loose ponytail that could dismantle at the most opportune moment. She was excited knowing what was in store, seducing herself as much as she planned to induce lovemaking from her own personal Thug.

Maya put Vaseline on her lips and powder over the dark circles under her eyes. She wanted it to be a long night so she hid three condoms between the pillows. Maya slipped on a red see-through backless and almost frontless La Perla teddy. (She wasn't sure what distinguished a bodysuit from a teddy, but this was most definitely a teddy).

Maya replaced the room's lightbulb with a red one. The better to see you with, my dear. She wrote seven words on slips of notebook paper and trailed them around the bed. Tactical procedure: Know your target. Words are the bait to capture a poet, just as diamonds are the bait to catch a thief. Her gingerbread trail of words would lure him into her chamber. Maya caught a glimpse of herself in the mirror and leaned so close that she almost fell into her image and drowned. She was on fire. It was time for the original man and woman to indulge in a little original sin. No excuses.

She shook him. "Baby, somebody left you a note."

"Who?" Thug looked at the floor and back at Maya, who was wearing her most angelic expression as she walked back into the bathroom. "What you up to, Cleopatra?" Thug made his way around the bed, reading the words out loud: "The heaven U Give is a Pyramid." She knew that he would get it immediately. "Thug is a pyramid, huh?"

"Solid, ingenious and everlasting," Maya called out.

"Hey," he said softly. "What's up with the light?"

Maya reentered and sashayed across the room as if she were looking for something that wasn't there. "The bulb blew and this was all I could find," she replied. "Relaxing, huh?" She wove her hips like a serpent winding between the trees of its choice. The apple she offered was herself. Just the sound of his voice drove her crazy. Her body had never had this kind of physical reaction to any man.

Thug seemed to lose his words, so he repeated hers. "The heaven you give is a pyramid. Solid, ingenious and everlasting."

"Uh-huh." Maya rose. She threw her arms around Thug, who stood in the room's center and squeezed, subtly thrusting her pelvic region toward his. "I'm so glad you're here, pyramid."

"Where else would I go?" he asked, confused.

Maya strutted around the bed, stuck out her butt and her breasts and sighed. "You're right. We're with each other." Thug's eyes were stuck to her as she climbed back into the nest, padded with silky sheets. She leaned back on the pillows and opened her knees as if by accident.

"Okay, baby, good night," Maya said. Thug sat down next to her bathed in the embrace of the red light. She reached up and put her lips to his, knowing that instinct would lead him to give her a soul-baring French kiss. Maya pulled away and got under the covers.

"You going to sleep?" he asked.

"Mmm-hmm," she said. "Try not to make too much noise, okay?"

Maya closed her eyes and felt Thug doing his trademark pace around the room. Rustling. And then he was back in bed with her, lying close. Naked. He put an arm around her, his hardness pressed against her. Agonizing.

Thug kissed the back of Maya's neck. Then he was moving quickly. Kissing her everywhere. Face, nose, lips, down to hips and toes and back up again. Now we're talking. He tugged at a bow and Maya turned up a hip.

"Those have to be untied," she said quietly. It was hot watching Thug's manly fingers unlacing and untying the delicate red bows.

He got on top of her. Contact. Oooh. Damn.

"Oh Robeson." Maya was breathing with her entire body. Take no chances. "We have to stop," she said. "You were right. We shouldn't do this." Catnip to a contrarian.

"What?" he said, already sweating like a runner.

"Your whole respect thing," she repeated, breathy, gripping his firm backside. "We have to stop."

"Fuck that," he said. "Of course I respect you." Bingo.

Maya handed him a condom and Robeson Thug entered her body with the purpose of quenching them both. He started strong, roughneck style. *Yeah.*

"I think I was created just for you," Maya whispered.

"You want some Thug Love?" he asked.

"Yeah." He felt so good. Buckwild.

"You want some Thug Love?" he repeated, his rhythm tight.

"Oh yes!" It was crazy amazing. It was lyrically smooth. It was damn. Her world was rocked as her man laid it down! She loved looking at their bodies intertwined in the red light, getting hazy over which limb belonged to whom. After that, they were walking on sunshine, and to everyone else's annoyance, couldn't keep their hands off of each other.

Chapter 25

"THE ART OF WARFARE
IS SPRAWLED ACROSS THESE PAGES
TRANSFORMING BLOODSHED INTO BEAUTY
AND RAISING THE PHOENIX OF FORBIDDEN EXPRESSION—
THE REAL WAR IS IN US."
—M.I.A.

Bloody hell! I don't see the value of artists being in camera-free zones," Luci said over afternoon tea at the finest hotel in downtown Atlanta. "I'm not going. Hip-Hop battle what?"

Maya handed her the honey. "Luci, can't we just chill off-zone for one night?!" The answer remained no as Luci emphasized that the impromptu nature of the whole thing was not her style. Instead, she was going with Black Death to investigate a Janet/Jermaine soiree. Athena had been acting extra funky and Maya was hoping that Luci could be a middleman to defuse the tension.

"Besides, Jez, I don't wanna intrude on a double date."

Maya placed her tea cup on the table. "What double date? Me and Robe—"

"Uh-huh. And Athena and Big Rob."

Maya dropped her spoon on the Persian rug and leaned over to pick it up. "What do you mean Athena and Big Rob?"

Luci shook her head and put her sandal on the spoon. "Girl, lemme just say that the walls have ears and the streets is watching. Lady Athena is getting her piece of B.R. and, speaking from experience, she's gonna have a fun ride."

Wow. "Oh. I feel you, Luci. I guess. Ugh." Maya rubbed her near-flat stomach. This couldn't be true! Maybe that's why Athena decided to get her own room in a separate hotel?

"You okay?"

"Tummy ache. I'm gonna head up, Luci." Maya stood up.

"Cool. Feel better, Jez." Luci lifted her cup to her lips.

All those times Rob and Athena were whispering? This was jacked-up! *Girlfriends Rule #1.* Kaput. She already pretty much suspected Luci was hitting it, but Athena was her girl from third grade to the grave. She could have at least said something. Whatever. Maya had the real prize so if somebody wanted to indulge in her tired seconds, let her. Rob and Athena could be the poor man's Theopatra. Athrob. That was jacked up.

There was a crowd of about 150 people on a grimy lot in backwater Hotlanta. Most were guys in their twenties and early thirties with some girlfriends and female cliques here and there. A congregation like this would have made Maya hella nervous back in the day, although upon closer inspection most were middle-class brothas and sistas looking for a good time in the warm night air of the South.

About once a month or whenever the mood struck, they gathered for Hip-Hop Battle Reenactments. These were similar to Civil War battle reenactments where people dressed like Union and Confederate soldiers to reenact the war. In this case however, folks reenacted hip-hop lyrical beefs: Foxy Brown vs. Lil' Kim. LL Cool J vs. Kool Moe Dee, Canibus or whoever. East Coast vs. West Coast. Shell vs. CEO. 50 Cent vs. Everybody. Different teams took turns repping their rapper. Individuals could also chance it and throw in a freestyle rhyme although in most cases that was suicide. Better to leave the lyrical fusion to the masters.

"I think we're near Morehouse," Rob said, and Athena nodded.

Theopatra, Athrob and Ill Verge were rolling deep. Maya and Thug were undercover in baseball caps and dark glasses. The thing no one ever tells celebs is that this actually draws attention to you, so people were mumbling about who they might be from the moment they entered the scene.

"Durrrty South! Welcome to tonight's Hip-Hop Battle Reenactment!" the host screamed. The crowd applauded and homeboy continued in his salty twang. "Tonight we're reenacting one of the greatest battles of all time. Nasty Nas Escobar vs. Jay-Z Jay Hova. We're playing for pride and fighting for bragging rights. Y'all know the rules. ATL—set it off!" The host rocked a white Camp Hustla hooded sweatshirt with a green barbed-wire design, a shiny LED dog tag and matching belt buckle with Wise scrolling across the small screens.

"I'm psyched. Jay and Nas is my favorite battle." Maya had played their rhymes over and over again on Rob's study pod. "Whassup with the mini hubcaps on dude's tennis shoes?"

"Shoe spinners, baby." Thug was magnetic. This was his thing. He had battled everyone from every camp, even and especially his own.

"Wannabe Jay-Zs to my right, wannabe Escos to my left," the host announced. The Nas team was made up of three guys and a woman. For Jay-Z, four dudes stood on their side of the stage. "Nas' team won the coin toss."

The first kid stepped up. "Okay. y'all. My piece is from *Stillmatic.* Not on the album, just mixtapes." He moved his arms and body in punctuated movements trying to replicate Nas as he kicked the verse:

> *"And bring it back up top, remove the fake king of New York*
> *You show off, I count off when you sample my voice . . ."*

"This is so much fun!" said Maya.

Thug kissed her on the cheek. "It's a knockout. Nas wins every time."

Rob looked at the kid onstage. "You can't assume that."

"Why I can't?" asked Thug. "Nas won every time for real. So why he won't win a reenactment?"

"It's the political warrior versus the party king," Maya said.

"This boy is good!" Athena was all into the show.

Rob kept his eyes on the show. "That's your opinion, Robeson, which you're entitled to. In my opinion, just like the two hundred mil in sales' opinion, Hov kills it."

Thug held Maya tighter. "The best rappers of all time is a short list, my man. And I'm the only one in this dump actually on that list. So if I say Nas wins, well, let's just say if I was just a manager, I would trust my opinion too."

Rob avoided looking at Maya, although she was the skinny elephant between them. "No beef necessary, playa. We all chillin' and we all entitled to our own opinion."

"Fuck opinion, kid, I'm telling you the gospel truth." Thug kissed Maya again, this time keeping his eyes open and eyeing Rob with a smile. He looked back at the show. "Everything is at stake."

Maya looked at her man, then back at Rob.

Rob took off his jacket. "I'm going up there."

"Up where?" Maya asked.

"I'm repping." Rob stepped up. "Repping for Jay-Z." Rob waited for no affirmation from the group to move forward.

"Repping for Jay-Z? You don't even know him like that," Maya called after him.

Athena was already clapping. "Hot to death! Do it, Big Rob!"

Maya rolled her eyes as Rob chatted on the sidelines with the host.

"This mothafucka is funny," Thug said. "Mad 'cause he ain't us, baby, right?"

Maya answered, "Right," before her brain could catch up with the beef reenactment beef. She was too busy looking for energy between Athena and Rob.

Mr. Shoe Spinners was amped. "Okay, last-minute entry y'all!! We got a man right outta New York to rep Hov!"

Right outta New York. What a phony.

Dude was about to say something else but the music came up loud and Rob went into Jay-Z's "Takeover," a song that Maya was very familiar with. One of her faves on the study mixtape. She hadn't seen Rob rhyme for real/for real in years and was hypnotized despite her best efforts not to pay attention. He was a magnificent peacock strutting his majestic feathers as he dominated the stage with Jay-Z's tight lyrics. Gorgeous. He spent a lot of time looking in Thug's direction.

> *"A wise man told me don't argue with fools*
> *'Cause people from a distance can't tell who is who . . ."*

When his performance was over, Rob looked at Maya and finished with, *"Because you know WHO did you know WHAT/With you know WHO but just keep that between me and you . . ."* The crowd was feeling Rob, bobbing their heads, giving him shouts like, "Yo you did Jay-Z serious justice!" Maya didn't know that her eyes were smiling until Athena yelled, *"Big Rob!"*

"Uh-oh, Nas people, what you got?" the host shouted. As the Nas team mumbled among themselves, Thug disentangled from his woman and moved toward the stage.

Maya pulled Thug's shirt. "Robeson!"

He put a finger to his lips. "Don't ever stop your man from going into battle. You feel me?"

Maya touched her stomach to appease the butterflies.

"This is getting good," the woman screwing her Ex said. Maya reminded herself that she didn't care. Rob was community property.

Thug plowed through the crowd and made his way to the other side of the small country fair wooden stage. POW! Thug leapt out on the platform with no intro, permission or warning, and the crowd gasped.

"Yoooooooo! It's Thug. I mean, Robeson! Respect!" the host yelled.

The audience guffawed and patted each other on the back, not believing their luck.

"Gimme the mic, son," he told Rob, igniting a chorus of "dayums" and "oh shits." When Rob didn't move, Thug snatched it from him. Rob stood still, then moved off stage backward.

Thug did what he did best, held court. He stood silently for a full minute, the calm before the storm, letting the audience work themselves into a frenzy. Then he spoke. "Yo, I didn't get along with either of these brothas in my first life but life moves forward and I respect their hustle. That being said, I'm on squad Nas tonight. 'Ether' is the best battle rap of all time. Besides any of my own of course." With that he launched into a verse, wrecking shop with Nas' words and his own deadly flow:

> *"I've been fucked over, left for dead, dissed and forgotten*
> *Luck ran out, they hoped that I'd be gone, stiff and rotten . . ."*

"You killin' 'em, Thug!" People were feeling Thug's gift to them, awed that he granted them his presence.

Maya's eyes spelled love. "Go, baby!" She bathed Thug in a moony gaze, which highly annoyed Athena, but she had no rights Maya was bound to respect.

Yeah!! They, his audience, shouted, whistled, clapped and stomped. *Preach!* They felt his truth through the words of a former rival and the power of the moment. The movement.

Knockout. No other man was still standing and the mic was on fire. To add insult to injury, he blew it up with his own verse in Nas' honor.

> *"I say God is my nigga*
> *My scrilla*
> *The killa*
> *How could you be trying to win when I already won?*
> *How you trying to win when I'm repping God's son?*
> *Fall back, Lil Rob, 'cause the job is done."*

When Thug finished, the crowd stood at silent attention, agreeing altogether that applause was superfluous for a king. The wind howled in gratitude. Thug held his fists in the air prizefighter style.

"Where's my belt?" he yelled. He was Tyson with Holyfield's ragged left ear dangling from his teeth. Rob put his fists in his pockets and walked back to their area. Athena patted him on the back. Maya stepped between them. When did they get this close?

"Run it, baby," Maya yelled out in the lone night, causing people to peer through the darkness.

"Yo, is Thug's bitch here too?" someone asked.

"Yo, Cleopatra, if you here, we love you!" a female voice yelled.

"I love y'all too," Maya yelled back. The crowd applauded as people craned their necks to find Cleopatra X. Maya cast Athena a glance.

"Lemme get next," Athena said and moved toward the stage.

Thug dropped the mic to the ground, threw some cash on it and walked off.

"Shut it down! Thank you, Robeson! We, uh, needed a new microphone anyway, right?" *Yeah*, the crowd responded.

Athena ran up on the stage.

"I guess so much for rules tonight," the host said. "Are you anybody?"

"All's fair in love and war," Maya said from the audience.

"I'm with them, and yeah—I'll rep for Brooklyn," Athena said. "Y'all gon' need to listen close to hear me with no mic."

Maya smiled to herself. Puh-lease. *I'll rep for Brooklyn?* Athena was a bigger fake than she was. *Pants on fire.* At least she was a real fake. Athena asked the crowd if she should kick "Supa Ugly" or "Blueprint."

"Yo, Team Jay-Z, y'all got a little girl standing in for y'all?" a tall dude in a Spelman jacket yelled.

"Ya momma's a little girl, beeyotch," Athena yelled back. "Knuckle up!" In response to the shouts and performance suggestions (some valid, some rude) Athena looked dead at Maya and announced, "Supa Ugly." *Was Athena talking to her?* Athena looked at Maya again with an exclamation point, and set it off.

"Kick your little lies; I kick my real facts
Like you sneaking out the back at the Source Soundlab . . ."

"Oh y'all feelin' it?" Athena reveled in the crowd's positive response. "So I'm gonna switch it up. This next little ditty is called 'Blueprint 2.' "

"What is this, a concert?" Maya asked and yelled a Nas rebuttal lyric before Athena continued. "And your manuscript just sounds stupid when KRS already made an album called *Blueprint* first!"

Athena cleared her throat:

> *"Can't y'all see that THEY'RE fake, the rap version of TD Jakes*
> *Prophesizing on your CDs and tapes . . ."*

Athena thrust both hands in the air. The crowd gave up a roar. When she turned around, however, she saw that they were not entirely roaring for her. Cleopatra X was behind her.

"Here comes the sun!" Maya announced. "Cleopatra X in the building." She was Bush at a gun convention and her fellow shooters went wild.

"There is no building," Athena shouted.

Maya turned her head sideways. "Am I hearing what I'm hearing? Who got love for Cleo X?" The response was clear. Everybody. Then Maya picked up the fallen mic, Thug's cash blowing in the wind and spat the lyrics for Nas's "One Mic":

> *"Yo, all I need is one mic, one beat, one stage*
> *One person fronting my face on the front page . . ."*

The crowd went bonkers at the free unannounced concert experience. They would be telling their friends about this for months. The host ran back on stage. He was literally on top of himself with joy.

He could barely speak. "Do I even need to say it? The winner by a knockout is team Nas!" but Maya couldn't hear him. No one could. Because Thug was by her side and Maya was kicking it bonus freestyle with Thug chiming in:

> *"This is the bonus freestyle*
> *Your shit is known as B Side*
> *I'm an extra credit pro*
> *Athena—you da ho*
> *And Rob, he business be nada*
> *'Cause for shizzle my checks bought all of y'all's Prada."*

The applause meter cracked. Athena and Rob had to give it up. This was HOT.

"Star power, baby!" Thug screamed.

Maya wrapped it up with "Check us out tomorrow night. The Deliverance Tour! *Deliverance!*"

Shoe Spinners was crazy appreciative. "Hot to death!! See what goes on at the Reenactments, y'all? Big things—tell y'all's friends. Yeah! The Jay-Z versus Esco battle stayed on wax and ended with peace so can I get all of the participants back on stage for a little making up?" The first dude to rap, the one who kicked *Stillmatic*, joined the host on stage. Thug and Maya stood on one side holding hands and Athena and Rob stood in the crowd, still only tolerating each other. None of them moved or blinked. It was the Apollo gone mad. "Righteous," said the announcer as the fans surrounded Maya and Thug.

"Back up!" Ill Verge, who was the master of undercover security, lived for moments like this. He presented himself and held up an arm that resembled a log. "Bacdafuckup!"

"It's all good, man." Thug held Maya in front of him. "We can sign a coupla 'graphs."

"I'll wait in the car," Athena said.

"Y'all good, yo?" Rob addressed his inquiry to Thug, as usual avoiding contact with Maya. Blackman to Blackman, it was the right thing to do. This tactic just made things a little tricky as he was Maya's manager mainly, since Thug pretty much managed himself.

Thug was chewing on something that looked like a stick. "All good. Don't need securing."

"Then I'll be in the car too." Rob held up a fist and Thug put his to it. Rob walked away with Athena and Ill Verge breaking his Management Rule #1, never leave a charge alone, unmanaged and unguarded. At this moment however, he didn't give a shiznit.

"Hatefest," Thug said. "'Cause we straight whupped them!"

"Robeson—shhh! Later, Athena," Maya called. "Good show."

Athena kind of waved her hand.

"Probably upset because poor black-ass Cleopatra is getting a little shine."

Thug nodded. "I warned you how friends and lovers become haters. It's all good. We Bonnie and Clyde for real now."

Maya and Thug signed bellies, bras, sneakers and, in one case, a crying baby.

"People want my signature!" Maya said, incredulous.

"Every thing you touch from now on is platinum." Thug kissed her on the chin.

After the last fan was hugged, Thug took Maya's hand and they walked toward the parking area since Athena and Rob weren't waiting out back where they would normally be.

Just before they got to the ride, Thug slowed down and picked something up from the ground. It was a battered rose. "A rose growing in concrete, babe, that's us."

Maya took her gift and kissed her man. "Awww. Thank you, baby." Tonight was their night.

"Lemme holla at you for a second, Cleopatra. You have fun with me?"

Maya answered before the sentence was even out. "More than I ever have in my life."

"Then we should get married," he said as casually as ordering a side salad.

"Um . . ." Maya still didn't totally get his sense of humor. "Married?"

"Yeah. Why waste time?" He was serious.

Soon much? This was beyond moving fast. Maya touched the Chanel sunglasses on her forehead. She already knew she loved him, but everything was still so new.

"When it's right, it's right," he said.

"Maybe." What was there to wait for? She and Rob waited and that still blew up in her face.

"And your life is already threatened just from being with me. The only way to keep you safe, my queen, is to keep you close."

Could this be true? Or was it just paranoia?

Not knowing what else to say, Maya kissed him.

"I ain't sayin' it gotta be this minute, Cleopatra, but soon."

Maya nodded, glad for the momentary reprieve. "Yes, baby, soon."

Blog. Cleopatra X. Atlanta, GA Tuesday 2:26 A.M.

Title: On The Road

Hey Party People,

Whassup!? Your girl Cleo X likes to keep it real. This is the first blog that is really from me. My label is going to be peeved with me exposing the truth but I just wanted to let you know that now I'm speaking to you directly. When I penned "Angry Black Bitch," I was a chick with a broken heart. We've all been there. Well, I just wanted to let you know that there is hope. If you dare, your dreams can come true. Just keep on keeping on. Today I was out at the Battle Rap Tournaments they have out here. So many talented people doing talented things and for a second I was asking why me? Wondering why with so many deserving I was reaping. Well, I'm not questioning it anymore. Just living it. Do you. Peace.

Chapter 26

"MY THUG LOVE GOT THE WEIGHT
OF THE WORLD ON HIS SHOULDERS
SO EVERY CHANCE I GET I TRY TO
GRAB HIM AND HOLD HIM."

—*Mia X*

The Battle Reenactment was the perfect warm-up for the first Deliverance Tour concert since Maya was the only one at sound check. Thug was catching up on sleep since he stayed up all night dealing with Maya's increasing insomnia and high tolerance for sleeping pills. Black Death were dispersed throughout the ATL doing what young rich punks do in a hot city—shopping and macking. Athena just decided not to show.

Nerves, nerves, nerves. Maya had pre-show nerves. "You got this," Thug told her as Rob watched from afar. Yes. She was feeling the fear, but she was doing it anyway. She would let the show be one big affirmation.

"Stand up, stand up, stand *up*!" Athena introed Maya by giving shout-outs and hyping up the crowd. She started to launch into a line or two of her own lyrics but Maya and the dancers came running out.

"Here comes the sun, y'all. Queen Cleopatra X is here!" Experiment be damned. This was real. Maya's show consisted of Maya, Athena and four okay-looking female dancers. (Shell said that it was customary to hire dancers slightly less attractive so that the star is never upstaged. Sounded good to Maya.) Maya freaked it, performing her signature hit—well, her only hit—"Angry Black Bitch," wearing a black and gold tube top and mini-miniskirt. The crowd *loved* her and she loved them back.

"Whoo-ha!!" Black Death bum-rushed the stage and pumped 100 percent anabolic steroids and testosterone straight into the veins of the room. ADD was the entry fee to be in the group. No less than fifteen guys on the stage at any time. You couldn't tell who was group, who was fam and who might have just wandered up there. They ran up against each other with pure vehement violence. They were supposed to do two songs, which morphed into four then six: "Fuk Wit Me," "Dead Niggaz," "Bottom Bitch," "Fukumentary," "Ma Pride" and "Deathwish." There was strange order in their disorganization. Most important, the crowd was primed for the main event and if Thug felt upstaged by their multiple songs, he didn't show it.

Clank. Clank-clank. Clank. Thug's show opened with the sound of shell casings hitting the ground but against Shell's wishes Thug had removed all of the obvious gunshot sounds. "Shouldn't the whole 'I've been shot' thing be played out by now, man?" he asked Shell.

He was wearing jeans and the Che Guevara T-shirt Maya bought him on one of her shopping sprees.

Maya and Athena watched from the wings. "Good show," Maya said.

"You, too." Athena looked straight ahead. "As long as I get on stage, it's all good."

The crowd listened with rapt attention as Thug let loose. A reel of news footage covering Thug's "death" and funeral played throughout the show and he gave straight energy. The show was a banger! Male fans gave loud vocal love and female fans threw bras and panties. ATL represented. And who knew that celebs were fans of other celebs? There was a boatload of them in the audience and the master showman didn't disappoint. He was unwillingly sexy and everyone wanted a taste.

Thug closed with a very elder-statesman political speech about stepping up as brothas and sistas. "I'm not just a soldier of fortune. I'm on active duty and I need y'all to be too. Don't leave me out on the front. It's about tactical procedures. Our new civil rights. Seize the damn day!"

"Punch somebody in the grill, Thug. Like you used to do," a kid down front yelled.

"What's up with Malcolm NeXt?" somebody else called out. "Martin Lutha Bling!" The audience chuckled. Thug blazed middle fingers and his crowd, as indignant as their leader, continued as if they were all playing a game. "Yo yo, what about Al Sharp-gun?" "Yeah. Jesse James Jackson!" Sometimes Thug seemed fazed by the reactions and other times he didn't, but he stayed on his message: "Urban people unite."

Maya and Thug left each show horny. They got hot watching each other spit lyrics and champagne stumbled into their hotel room on some that's my *boo* ish and sexed each other crazy.

Then they lay in the dark and Thug fell asleep. Maya took a sleeping pill to catch up with him and dreamt of violent, incomplete images. Hexagons and odd, awkward shapes dancing with ugly-ass words.

Every day Maya turned her computer on meaning to work on her undercover report. Instead, she sent a blog into cyberspace and her fans responded by the hundreds feeling her for her "openness and realness." It was dope to connect with those who made her feel loved, adored, and worthy. She felt more love from her fans than real people she'd known. She shared her life and her thoughts but she didn't keyboard the one question she most wanted answered: *Is he really my one true love?*

Blog. Cleopatra X. Miami, FLA Thursday 4:00 A.M.

Title: After the Concert

Okay. I gotta bring the fire. Last night was inspirational. Let me tell you about the Black Death show. Adrenaline was overflowing. I'm not violent, but watching their show makes me want to punch somebody in the face. Black Death is the bomb and of course my baby, Thug, was incredible. Thanks for showing us so much love. My set was off the hook!!! You inspired me to hit the studio on the road. Shout-out to my girl Lady Athena for hyping up my crowd.

Blog. Cleopatra X. Dallas, TX Wednesday 3:48 A.M.

Title: On The Road

Insomnia, insomnia, insomnia . . .

Thanks for keeping us sold out. I am feeling so much love—the love of my fans, my friends and my man—that I have already written and recorded my whole album in studios on the road in the past week and a half. Crazy, I know, but I hope you feel it. Twelve songs with three Robeson Thug collabos. It's true when they say musicians never sleep. I woke up yesterday at around 3pm!! My new album is *Pyramid Scheme* by CLEOPATRA X: "Angry Black Bitch," "Mad FameUs," "Village of the Dayumed," "Uglee Duckling," "Donwanchu," "I Wuz Robbed," "Po Po's Gun," "Cluckers," "The Devil's Destini," "Booty Scratch Dis," "Jezebel-ed," "Robeson My Robeson."

Chapter 27

"I USED TO BE AFRAID OF THE DICK.
NOW I THROW LIPS TO THE SHIT."
—*Lil' Kim*

"Yo Rob—Big Man. Whassup? Corporate is going crazy. We need a video, man."

"Told you I'll see what I can do, Shell."

"What are y'all doing for the Cleo birthday bash?"

"I dunno. Luci is handling it."

"Well, check this out, Rob. Get some cameras. Tape the party. That's our video. It'll be perfect, live from LaLa Land, right?"

"We're already taping for the reality show, Shell, but that's not the right video to take her in another direction. I thought we were investing in this thing, man. You promised."

"Yeah, Rob."

"Good. Holla."

After the ten-hour drive from Atlanta to Miami, Maya announced that she would no longer be taking the tour bus with Black Death. "Waking up with peanut butter on my feet was the last straw," said her text to Shell. The label obliged by agreeing to fly their top artists, Cleopatra X and Robeson Thug, to every tour stop in the private jet. Luci opted to join them in the friendly skies while Rob and Athena chose to keep it real by rolling out on the bus with the team to Miami, then Dallas and now L.A.

Los Angeles. The city of angels . . . and devils. The place where dreams are made and then pummeled to death with blunt objects. L.A. is the perfect place for anyone to have a birthday. After all, aren't we all just a little reborn when we visit Hollyhood? Maya's thirty-third birthday and Jezebel's twenty-second. Maya had been having a private freak-out over turning thirty-three. Like everybody else she was thirsting for eternal youth, but now that she was here it wasn't so bad at all. Especially because she was now only twenty-two. Again. The plastic sunshine looked ready for its close-up too and it was clear that fame was the top religion in the land as they exited the jet to find paparazzi waiting on the runway. Reporters from *Hip-Hop Weekly* to *Rolling Stone* trailed the tour and met them at every stop, *but on the runway?*

"I don't think that's legal," said Luci. "But I do like their style. To your right, Cleo. Give attitude. Give them hips."

"Look!" Maya shrieked. There was a dead seagull behind the photogs, its long beak splayed against the pavement.

"Aw man. Plane musta hit it," Thug growled, groggy from the night before.

"What was it doing this far away from the ocean?" Maya shielded her face, trying not to see its death.

"Cleo, Robeson, over here . . . Over here . . ."

Luci, part-time publicist, full-time den mother, decided that the Cleo X birthday celebration would be at BiSex, the new Sunset Drive hot spot that boasted male and female strippers and a dance floor. In addition, the luxe "burlesque" club jointly owned by several celebs had a full-scale Italian restaurant serving the finest cuisine, three bars and a wine lounge. Maya's red carpet party was in full swing by the time she arrived at midnight poured into a gold and Grecian white Cavalli minidress that showed off the bigger boobs she'd sprouted from her BC pills. Even though it was 77 L.A. degrees, she had an old-school fox stole just to drag on the floor behind her. She took the carpet like a pro, posing and smiling for some shots, giving massive 'tude for others, working hips, tits and ass. Her highlighted blowout was super snatched and accented by a shiny fairy princess tiara.

"I love y'all too!" She waved at the screaming fans and unfortunate losers on line as the velvet ropes parted. "The best thing about fame is the shorthand. No need to prove you're the cat's pajamas—people already know it. Look at the PETA protestors trying to hate on my flow," Maya said to Athena.

"A few months ago you would have been one of them," Athena said.

"I feel them," Maya said. Haters. "But this thing has *been* dead. I'm just making sure that he didn't die in vain. Tonight is about feeling only the love." She blew a kiss to a multitude of young girls near the PETA people.

Dane Norris, the principal owner of BiSex, waited by the door to meet Maya and personally seat the Camp Hustla posse in three VIP booths right in front of the circular stages: one for the Cleopatra X squad, one for Thug and Black Death and the third for entourage, fam, associates, groupies and hangers-on that they picked up on the road. Dane (borderline deranged) was the son of some shipping magnate and clubs were his latest pastime. The fantasy lighting was a rainbow of the mixed colors of a Serengeti sunset, or at least what Maya imagined a Serengeti sunset would look like if it was designed by Luci. There were multiple shiny gold poles everywhere.

"Look. WE'RE NOT JUST MENTERTAINMENT." Athena pointed to a plaque behind the main bar.

"Cleopatra X, welcome!" Dane pressed a moist palm to Maya's.

"Ewww." Maya pulled out a tiny bottle of Purell from her cream Marc Jacobs clutch, turned her back and slathered her hands in it. Dane scowled; Maya flared her nostrils and sat down.

"So Dane, who's here?" Luci looked around as if they might not stay at their own party if the answer was wrong.

Dane bobbed his oily head like a dashboard doll. "The panty-free party girls will definitely be here."

"Good. They're a must. Who else?"

Dane pulled a piece of paper from his pocket. "Either promised or already in the house we have the Ashleys, the Michaels, the baby moguls, the socialites, celebutots, haute magicians, the Grammy girls, the athletes who want to be rappers, the rappers who want to be actors, the famous for just being famouses, the entire cast of *Entourage*, the Jessicas and every Jennifer you can think of."

"Perfect!" Luci declared and took her seat next to Maya, signaling that the party was acceptable.

Maya leaned back in the Head Bitch In Charge seat and surveyed the crowd. "International hotties plus my man. Happy happy birthday! So I guess Rob's a no-show, Athena?"

"Who knows and who cares? Bring on the man skanks!" Athena settled in next to her. Now that they were both getting the opportunity to perform—Maya as the headliner and Athena as her hype woman—they'd been getting along a little smoother.

"Uh-oh. Trouble in paradise, Lady Athena?" Maya waved at Thug at the next table with his crew, who were wilding out as usual. He blew a kiss back.

"What are you talking about?" Athena looked through a drink menu.

"Hmph." Maya rolled her gold-dusted eyes. "Rob."

Athena looked confused.

"Cristal to start," Luci told a musclebound bikini-clad waiter. "So Cleo, a little bird told me that Ozzie Marvelous might show up tonight so you can finally meet. You know L.A. is his hometown."

"He gives me the creeps." Athena shivered.

Luci shrugged. "You are probably just not used to men who are not out on parole."

"That would be incredible," Maya said before Athena could reply. "I want to thank him for everything. OMG. I just thought of something . . . I have been sober for almost forty-eight hours." Maya covered her lips in mock horror.

"Why?" asked Luci.

"Accidental."

In the next booth, Black Death and posse were receiving lap dances from a multiracial group of women—black, white, Latin, Asian—who somehow all looked exactly the same, with long blond hair, big bouncy boobs, puffy lips, tiny noses and cinched waists.

"That's right!! I'm an equal-opportunity pee-ump," Pimp yelled, and slapped one girl's ass. Maya, Athena and Luci turned around in disgust as another chick in an itsy-bitsy, teeny-weeny, no room for polka dots bikini raised and lowered herself on the crotch of his Camp Hustla brand jeans.

"Ugh. Thank you," Luci said to the waiter returning with their bottles and glasses.

"Anything else for you, Miss Cleo?"

"Don't call me that. I'm not a psychic." Maya looked at Enrique Iglesias' long-lost twin brother and the bulge in his tight royal blue swim trunks. Wow. His height and Maya's lined them up perfectly so that every time he came to the table, she was speaking directly into his blessed manhood. She couldn't bring herself to face "him."

She turned to Athena, brown girl blushing. "Can you please tell him that I'm fine?"

Athena wrinkled her nose, but she got it. "She's fine."

Luci tossed her head back. "Didn't you promise a specialty drink called the Cleopatra X?"

"Yes ma'am. I'll look into it."

"Thanks," said Luci. "And I'm not a ma'am!"

Athena clocked the guy's butt as he walked away. "He thought you were. You know, thirty-five is the new forty-five."

"Cleopatra, nice touch with the whole Prince thing," Luci said.

"What?"

"The whole talk to my assistant thing. Genius." Luci clasped her hands together like she was plotting world domination.

Maya shook her head. "Oh no—I just, um . . ."

"She just didn't wanna be yapping into his Richard like it was a mic," Athena corrected, but she didn't look in Luci's direction.

Several of the aforementioned famous people dropped by the table to congratulate Maya on her success, creating a serious logjam around their table. Each guest brought more drinks and the ladies indulged. Then the Cleo Cocktails hit: 1 oz. Bourbon, ½ oz. Peach Schnapps and 1 dash Angostura Bitters. Stir with ice and strain. Fill with champagne. Delicioso!

"Is the mic on?" Dane Norris was onstage. The music went down and the lights came up. "Tonight the stars are out to celebrate one of their own. Cleopatra X." A spotlight shone on her table and Maya beamed back. "Hip-hop's latest wunderkind, or should I say enfante terrible, brings to mind one statement when I see her in that dress. It's all good in the hood." Everyone laughed and Maya nodded. "It's my sincere pleasure to introduce Shell the Boy Wonder."

"Shell is here?" Maya stood and looked around.

A screen popped up behind Dane. Shell's image waved. He was flanked by two women who looked liked they danced at BiSex when hooking got boring. "What's up, Cleo X? Who's better than you? Couldn't let your birthday go by without giving you a what-up. So what up, love? Happy Bday. Keep making it do what it do, baby." The screen folded back into the wall.

"Heartfelt," said Luci, clapping.

"That's it?" Maya asked.

"That's it? I can't believe that Shell put that together just for you," Athena said as Maya powdered her forehead. "You know how busy he must be?"

"Thank you, Shell," Dane said as his sweat glands went into overdrive under the hot lights. His hair was plastered to his scalp and his metrosexual tight tee was glued to his chest.

"Rob would have loved that," Athena said.

Maya put her drink down hard. "Oh would he, Athena?"

Thug strutted up to the stage. "Happy birthday, baby!"

"Awwww," Luci said along with everyone else, then they gave him a standing O just for being Thug.

Aw. Maya put her hands to her mouth and sent him a smooch.

He kissed back at Maya and continued. "I also wanna take this opportunity to say something more. In this room, I see some of the most influential heads in music, movies, TV and finance. What kinda change could we make if we galvanized our power, nahmean? And if the press helped instead of slandering . . ."

The spotlight on the stage dimmed and the two cameras that were shooting Thug moved off into the audience toward the pole dancers.

"We see those commercials. Fifteen cents a day and we laugh or turn the channel. But it could be that simple to feed and educate our babies right here." People started ordering drinks again. The music got louder until it was full on blasting. Thug was screaming into the mic. "So what are we gonna do, America, Hollywood? Black people? Huh?

What's the damn deal? Step up." Thug was standing in darkness and his Camp Hustla peeps were probably the only ones still listening. His increasing political rants had been turning off even the most devout Thug lovers.

"Yo Thug, stick to rapping, man," somebody yelled. "You a genius at that." Thug held up a middle finger.

"A'ight y'all. I'm ghost."

"If you listened to him, you might learn something," Maya yelled into the crowd. She stood and gave him a one-woman ovation.

"Your man is cute, Cleo." Luci watched him head back over to his booth.

"Yes, he is. My man." Maya winked. "Y'all can have Rob but don't get it twisted. Oh Athena, did Luci tell you that we've been invited to a Hef party tomorrow night?"

"No." Athena looked at Luci.

Luci struck a pseudo pouty-lipped *Playboy* pose. "We're gonna have a ball. I have a fantasy of being Hef's black girlfriend." The DJ was spinning Camp Hustla's music catalog as male and female exotic entertainers showed their skills.

"Before I was a cheerleader, I spent a minute as an exotic dancer," Athena said.

"I never understood why strippers call themselves dancers," said Luci. "If you're a stripper say you're a stripper. You're not a dancer."

"I was a dancer." Athena stared at the side of Luci's face.

"Dancers don't have a cash register in their drawers," said Luci.

"Just checking on you." Thug was behind Maya. He had been slightly on edge since the backlash against his recent political manifestos. There was a general shut up and rap attitude growing in and out of camp, and the media wasn't being kind either. People missed the old gunshots-and-weed Thug.

"I'm fine, babe," Maya said.

"Well, don't be sweating these dudes too hard. You're taken," he said as a server placed a tray of chicken, beef and shrimp shish kebabs on the table. "You not eating meat, right?"

"I'm all about you, baby," Maya said.

Thug kissed her on the forehead and went back to his rowdy booth.

Luci gave Maya a high five as soon as he turned his back. "Nice deflection, Cleopatra, and an A for dick control."

Maya giggled.

"Watch this." Athena stood up. "It *is* dancing."

"What is?" Maya asked.

Athena mounted the pole behind them, one of many sprinkled throughout the club for antics such as this. She climbed, gripped the pole and slid down upside down in her $500 Chloé jeans and belly shirt. "Gymnastics," she yelled as the people closest to them applauded.

"Gym-Nasty-Icks," Luci said.

The main show started. A bald black cowboy wearing a ten-gallon hat, brown suede vest and pants with boots and chaps danced around doing lasso tricks. A few women ran to the stage. The difference between New York City and L.A.? In New York, people would have been too cool to react.

"No Cowboy Curtis didn't," said Athena.

"Mmmmm. I think he's cu-uute." Maya was already slurring her words.

"Gay. Not that there's anything wrong with that." Luci toasted him with her champagne flute.

"Nooo." Maya poked out her lips.

He whipped off his pants and pumped one-armed push-ups.

"Look at that perfect tush," said Luci. "I should hook him up with my brother."

Luci scrolled through her messages. "Oh—Marv! This just in, Cleopatra, the crew from *Cribs* is shooting you tomorrow."

"*Cribs*?"

"Yep. People are desperate for video on you. We gotta give the fans something."

"Oh yeah?" Maya was entranced by Cowboy Curtis' gyrating hips. They were into the second bottle of champagne, mixing Cleo Cocktails in between.

Athena put her feet up on the empty chair. "But she has no crib."

"She does now. Faux. We're putting it together down to the food in the fridge and the maxi pads in the closet. Soon Cleo will be able to point to a bed like everybody else and say, 'This is where the magic happens.' " Luci smiled, proud of the brilliance of it all.

The cowboy was now in his skivvies. He held the mic near his crotch and gave it a hand job. "So who's coming to the stage? Who dares? Birthday Girl?" he asked.

"Yes! You should totally go up there," said Luci.

Athena shook her head. "That's not her, Luci-fer."

"Maybe it is." Maya held up her glass.

"Go for it." Luci nodded at a cameraman in the corner.

Maya bounced up and danced toward the stage. "Whoo hoo!"

Athena and Luci chanted, "Yes, yes, yes," and Maya turned around to bow. Cock-blocked.

"Where are you going?" Thug spoke in a low voice.

"To the stage!" Maya yelled, raising her fist high.

"No. You're gonna sit down." Thug pulled Maya's arm. "You're drunk."

"Nooo!" Maya screamed like she was being abducted. "Get offa me!"

Thug squeezed Maya's hand. "Nah, baby."

"It's my birthday!" Several people turned around as Maya wrestled her hands out of his.

"OHHHHHH." Black Death relished any sign of trouble in paradise. Although Maya said very little to Thug about his biz, they had come to see her as their Yoko Ono.

She hid her face in his chest. "I thought I was whispering."

Pimp stood up. "Told you, Thug. Bros before hos."

"Money over bitches!" yelled Nigg.

"I'm not a bitch!" Maya yelled back. "I am Angry Black Bitch but I'm not a bitch."

"Handle your bitch, Thug," Luci screamed as a joke.

Thug's face crumpled and he put his mouth to Maya's ear. "You're lucky I don't drag your ass out. I'm trying to look out for you." He paced around. "If this was old-school Thug I would beat your ass. Right here. You lucky," he said. "I'm Robeson now." Before she could reply he headed toward the door.

"'Bye, baby," Maya called softly after him. She didn't know whether to be concerned or turned on.

"If you can't save ya girl, how you gonna save hip-hop?" Pimp screamed.

Maya scrambled to the stage and the (probably gay) cowboy lifted her up. She held on to her tiara and whipped her hair on the slow beat from side to side as Thug watched from the door. If he wanted her to stop, he could come make her. She rubbed her breasts on the pole. Although the cowboy wasn't attractive close up, it felt good to be bad. There was temptation in every corner and she felt like she was losing her soul. Maya finished to big applause as several female dancers dressed as Catwomen took over.

She glided into her seat fanning herself. "Hot!"

"You're on fire!" Luci gave Maya a high five. "Oh good. These chicks are much sexier to watch than homeboy."

"I can outdance them," Athena said.

"Ego alert." Luci chuckled deviously and kneed Maya under the table.

Maya missed the beginning of the entire exchange. "Big deal. I got up there. It doesn't make me Fred Astaire." The Cats Gone Wild humped and kitty clawed across the stage in neon sparks. The lights grooved angry slashes across Athena's face. Fueled, Athena marched up to the main stage, shimmied up a pole and slid upside down. She stayed onstage almost a full five minutes as the cats removed their suits paw by paw.

When Athena returned, Luci and Maya were over the entire conversation. The Camp Hustla posse surrounded a pink multitiered cake singing "Happy birthday, Cleopatra. Happy birthday to you." Somebody tried to get a chorus of "speech, speech, speech" going, but Maya was busy drunk texting Thug: "WHERE R U?" Then, in true L.A. fashion, everyone moved on immediately and had another drink.

"Sooo Luci?" Athena began.

"So Athena," Luci replied.

"I just danced my ass off and you have nothing to say?"

"Why do you care?" asked Luci. "I don't."

"Meoww." Maya made the international catfight squeal.

"How dare you?" Athena was livid and Maya was confused.

"How dare who?" Luci burped over Athena's shoulder.

"'Thena, calm down." Maya kept texting, checking voice mail and re-texting. A message from Rob: "Happy Bday M."

Athena stood up. "Don't tell me to calm down. I'm sick of being underestimated! Luci's a Taurus. She can't help it, but *you*, Maya!"

"Don't call me that. Cleo X or Jezebel." Maya uncrossed her legs and stood up.

"Bathroom," Athena said. Luci started to stand and Maya shook her head.

Maya made a point of turning her back and walking ahead of Athena to the ladies' room. Ill Verge shadowed.

When they walked in, that starlet who recently moved from TV to film was doing coke with her young friend, who was married to that old rocker. The friend starting hooting. "Hey—Cleopatra. I love 'Angry Black Bitch.' Wanna line?"

"No. Just privacy," Maya said.

"Okay. Happy birthday!" The girl grabbed a handful of paper towels and looked at her starlet buddy. They giggled and rushed out.

Maya and Athena waited for the door to close. Maya saw her security man in the crack. "Don't let anybody else in here, okay?"

Athena didn't wait for his affirmation or confirmation. "Listen Cleopatra. You make me sick!"

"What are you talking about?"

"What am I talking about? What am I talking about? I'm talking about when I'm gonna get put on. I'm talking about how you wouldn't even be here without me!"

"Um, Athena, you're drunk."

"Twelve songs and you ain't let me shine on one?"

Hm. Good point. "But Athena, I put you up in a fat crib. You're performing on stage. You're screwing my ex. What more do you want?"

"Screwing your ex? Are you crazy? What more do I want? I want cokehead actresses worshipping me. I want a back-from-the-dead rapper boyfriend making bank. I want my life you took. I want—"

"You want *Fame*?" Maya tried to lighten the mood. "Well, Leroy, fame costs, and right here is where you start paying for it."

"Fuck you."

Athena's words slapped Maya in the face. "You need to calm down, Athena. Now."

"No. You calm down. I'm over being your plus one."

"Athena. Don't do this."

"Don't do what? Tell you that you used my talent, stole my life? You user-ass no-talent-having bitch! You're a loser, Maya. A loser who—"

Red zone. Red zone. Red zone.

"Loser?! Loser!" Maya was outside of herself looking down, Maya, SHUT UP, she was saying. But it wasn't her. It was Cleopatra X or Jezebel or somebody. "Bitch!? Me? You know what? I never used your talent, Lady Athena. From the beginning, this was me. All me."

"What do you mean?"

The words tumbled from Maya's mouth like acid rain. "Let me spell it out for the learning impaired. I didn't use your wack-ass rhymes at the audition. I used *my* shit. My hot shit. My real shit. My nonstinking shit. Shell bought me. It was me he wanted all along. Lady Athena and her itty bitty titty committee was never a factor. You're here as a freaking favor. I'm being benevolent."

"Liar!" Athena turned paler than her normal buttermilk color. Then her lips were moving with no words. Or maybe Maya had gone deaf from drunkenness.

"That's right. I win. I have the prize. The man every woman on the planet wants *and* the platinum album."

Athena was flailing her arms. No words.

"You look like a seven-armed Hindu goddess," Maya observed. "The goddess of nada."

Tears. Athena started wailing in the way that only the truly inebriated can. Bawling. Screaming. Drenched. "That's a *lie.* You are a liar, Maya Gayle Hope. Shell bought my lyrics. He wanted me."

Maya was beyond calm now and playing her position to the fullest. "No, baby. I'm the star. And I am fabbing fuckulous." She looked in the mirror and fluffed her hair for volume in a way that Athena never could with her weaves. She winked at Athena's image in the background.

"Bitch!" Athena lunged at Maya. *Ow.* They hit the freezing bathroom floor and Maya's tiara went flying. *Splat.* Although Athena was the experienced fighter, Maya still had her by at least four inches and twenty pounds.

"My crown!" Maya squeezed Athena's arms, her fiberglass nails drawing blood, and threw her like a rag doll. Athena grabbed Maya's hair and punched her in the face.

Full-on fighting. Vaseline your face and take off your earrings fighting. They had never had a fistfight with each other. Not through stolen crushes, lost favorite shirts or test copying.

"You ruined my Cavalli!" Maya ran out of the bathroom and through the back exit with a handful of Athena's extensions. Athena chased her. Tackle. Ill Verge pried Athena off and she ran into the crowd of waiting photographers.

"Cleo X, over here. Why did Thug leave early?" one yelled.

"Hear you don't talk directly to waiters. Is this true?" a reporter asked.

"Why should I?" Maya screamed, looking like a shredded banshee in stark contrast with the massive billboard above her head of her with Thug. They had taken three hours of loving pictures and the one chosen was snapped when Maya had bent over to adjust the Choos on her fishnet-clad feet. Her artfully torn denim halter dress, which matched Thug's jeans and denim bulletproof vest, said "Hustla, baby" across her behind, which pointed up in the air, apparently her trademark.

Athena held out her bleeding arm as the reporters converged like vampire bats. "See what Cleopatra X did to me?"

"What happened?" they asked.

"She's a savage bitch, that's what happened."

It wasn't only Maya's birthday. It was a field day. "Aren't you part of the entourage?"

"No. I am a rapper. A solo artist. Lady Athena. A-T-H-E-N-A."

It was Christmas for the paparrazi. *Flash. Flash. Flash. Flash.* It looked like daylight.

"I can't believe that you would play me on camera. Do what you feel is real, Athena." Maya spun around to Ill Verge. "Stop following me!"

"Orders," he said as Luci rounded the corner. She grabbed Maya's arm as the burgundy Rolls pulled up to the curb and pushed Maya in. Ill Verge jumped in front and they sped away. Maya saw Athena's face in multiples through the flashbulb reflections, tinted glass and the bright L.A. lights. She opened her palm. Athena's ocean wave weave with a springy natural design.

"Budget hair," Luci said, and tossed it out the window.

Chapter 28

"I'LL BE THERE FOR YOU, IF SOMEBODY HURTS YOU,
EVEN IF THAT SOMEBODY IS ME."
—Beyoncé

Maya stumbled around Bungalow 138 at The Hotel Bel-Air. If she had been a metal rock dude or Courtney Love, she would have trashed it. She yelled down to a family of swans in the pond beneath her window. "The problem is not being drunk. You looove being drunk. Breaking up with your BF is the problem. Where's Robeson?" she asked them. "Doesn't he know about my abandonment issues!"

She plunked down onto the curly flokati rug, picked up the phone and dialed something.

"Yo." It was Rob.

"You're Bobby. You're not Robe," she informed him.

"Hey, are you okay? Luci just told me what happened."

"Wrong number." She hung up. Oi. "Athena should have been here to stop me from drunk dialing. I need a Vicodin for my pounding head. The bottle is somewhere." The video doctor man after the motorcycle incident gave it to her in case of further pain, right? Right. She popped two into her mouth. Gag. Big. Slimy. Gross. The phone was ringing. Rob. She didn't answer.

Oooh. This was a good time to do the one thing both Rob and Luci made her promise for her own sanity that she would never do. She Googled herself. "Cleopatra X, Jezebel, rapper." Click. Wow. OMG. Five hundred ninety-six thousand hits. Crazy.

"I'm so Googleable!" Click. Fan sites, gossip and of course all of the updates on her own website where people could find photos, a tour calendar, buy her song or pre-order her album. Click. Fab!

Click. Uh-oh. Hater sites. Many. A Cleo X page set up on a site called *Am I Annoying*. Click. Big mistake. Why she might be annoying: Bad weave, girly voice, awful clothes, zero style, and lyrics written by Shell? "Haters and liars!" Click. Site after toxic site.

ONLINE POLL

WHAT DO YOU THINK CLEO X WILL DO NEXT?

Streak naked at the Super Bowl 20%

Run for president 5%

Overdose 15%

Wrestle a crocodile 10%

Embarrass herself in ways we can't yet imagine 50%

Click. Hateful, scornful and dangerous to ingest. Click. One site listed her in a disgusting litany of women that Thug had sexed over the years—models, rock stars' daughters and the like. Click. Another site hinted that Thug was two-timing her with that slutty ex-VJ. Click. Crazy. People were already writing about tonight. Oh no! LL Cool J arrived at her party after she left? "Screw you, Perez Hilton!" she screamed. "And you too Bossip! E-hoodlums." At least Touré and *Aint It Cool News* were being kind.

Click. The Smoking Gun listed the items that she "demanded" from each tour stop in their Tour Rider section: Dehumidifier for her voice; air purifier; Do Not Disturb sign honored by housekeeping upon peril of firing; carpeted dressing room with a private toilet (& new seat); large sofa (fine fabric, no leather); tub of Red Vine licorice; Madagascar Aveda candles; oxygen (3 bottles with masks); peppermint tea with honey from Vermont (made with pure water); room temperature Evian with bendy straws only; Cleo requires warmer than usual room temperature of 80 degrees at all times & 100 orange tulips. News to her! All she had requested was the red licorice and new toilet seats. She thought that venues were providing the tulips because they liked her. *Bendy straws only?* Luci or Rob or someone had these people thinking that she was some kind of horrible demanding diva bitch.

"I need a candle." Maya rummaged around in a bag, found a $150 La Dolce Vita candle and tried to light it but her hands were shaking too much.

Blog. Cleopatra X. Atlanta, GA Friday 3:49 A.M.

Title: melting on my bday . . .

Dear Blogary & Fans,

Yo . . . My life is a freakin clown fest. Good-bye affirmations. Must sprinkle more glitter. Melt up. Melt Up. MELT UP. PEACE. And to all everybody's saying my man shouldn't be talking no politics. SCREW OF. OFF. pants on fire/?

Maya stood at the bathroom counter, washed her hands ten times and popped a sleeping pill. "My face is stretching sideways. Mirror Mirror on the wall. Picasso made me fairest of them all!" She took out one contact and her eye squinted. "I would make an exquisite corpse. Maybe next show everybody close one eye." She took out the other contact. "I can't see anything," she said. Except her eye watering. Except pain. Stinging eye pain. She dropped to the floor clutching her face. Owwww! PAIN. There was the shadow of a man there over her.

"Rob?"

"No baby, it's me, Robeson." Duh. Why would it be Rob?

"Robeson, something is stabbing my eye."

"It's okay," he said. "I got you."

Robeson dressed Maya and carried her down to a taxi, left hand covering left eye. "I didn't even get to give you your bday poem," he said.

"Eyeball in my palm," she said before giving the brave 5:00 A.M. solo photog a middle finger with her right hand. "Leave me alone!" Vomit. Blackout.

"Shell here. Who's on?" Via four-way conference call, Rob, Luci, Shell and in a rare appearance Ozzie Marvelous tried to figure out the best way to handle the Cleopatra X situation.

"Rehab? Recovery is hot right now."

"The stomach pumping was a good angle."

"So was the drunken blogarrhea."

"The puked on reporter might even sue. That could extend the story for months."

"Maybe we should send Thug to anger management for spousal abuse?"

Never mind that Maya wasn't his spouse or the fact that she'd scratched her own cornea, the shots of him carrying her with her busted eye and black and blue marks on her shoulders from the Athena squabble said it all. The Cleopatra X situation was all anyone could talk about. Camp Hustla had to push the concert back but it was cool because they had to add at least twelve additional shows. With all the hoopla, the Deliverance Tour was outselling everything.

"Big Rob, why are you so quiet?" Shell, Luci and Ozzie Marvelous asked him again and again and again.

PRESS RELEASE

LOS ANGELES—Platinum-selling rapstress Cleopatra X is fine after a minor scare post–pole dancing birthday bash. The reported altercation at hot club BiSex, where Camp Hustla former posse member Lady Athena attacked Cleo X, was all a part of a stunt filmed for her upcoming music video *Angry Black Bitch*—a mash up of Cleo X stripping and concert footage, said to premiere on BET late tonight. The camp denies that the fight with Athena was a lovers' spat. Many other boldfaced names were in attendance at the twenty-second birthday party of the rapper with a reputation for being a wild child.

Cleo, as she is known to her legion of fans, was hospitalized for exhaustion and denies any rumors that Vicodin and sleeping pills found in her system are related to a painkiller addiction that may have started after her highly publicized motorcycle crash. The camp, citing issues of privacy, also will not comment on re-

> ports of physical abuse between Robeson Thug and Cleopatra X despite cameras catching an altercation between them at the club, except to say that Cleo's former relationship with Thug's band member Pimp had nothing to do with it. The bizarre, rambling messages on her site were due to dehydration, sure to be quenched by the major soft drink deal in the works.

Thug and Maya sat in front of a poster of themselves advertising Deliverance. Luci had arranged a press junket—twenty-six interviews in six hours—to address the situation after Maya's twelve hours in the hospital.

"Robeson, I'm sorry." Maya nestled her head in the crook of Thug's neck. He was in a not-so-bad mood. She didn't mind his mood swings because she had her own. She was learning all of the selves that they were. Athena had decided to leave the tour and Maya felt like Thug was all she had. "You love me?"

Thug gave Maya a long hug. "It's all good, baby. It is what it is. A mixtape. Nothing means nothing. We tie it down with stories."

Rob and Luci came into the generic-looking hotel suite and gave it the once-over.

"No Black Death?" Maya asked.

"Nobody's going to ask about music, unfortunately," Rob said.

Luci piped up. "The questions will be things like, did Robeson sock you one because he's jealous of your relationship with Pimp."

Maya took Thug's hand. "But I never had a relationship with Pimp. Baby, you believe me, right?"

Everyone in the room started chuckling.

Maya smoothed her hair. "What's so funny?"

Thug looked at her. "Pimp is gay, baby."

"Hello!" Luci crossed her arms. "If you didn't know that, I must be good. Why do you think I had to create a fake relationship between you two?"

"So Luci, if you went through all of that to squash rumors that

Pimp is gay, why would you insinuate that Athena and I are lesbian lovers?"

Luci went to the door. "Learn the game. Women gay good, men gay bad. Have some water. The first reporter will be in about fifteen minutes. Everybody will ask the same ten questions that we already answered on the press release. You two will pretend to be shocked that anyone would ask such personal questions and appear to keep trying to talk about your current projects. Easy breezy?"

Chapter 29

"IT'S SAD TO SEE HOW ONE WEEKEND
COULD BE LIKE DAMN."
—*Angie Martinez*

Maya wasn't sure how much her notoriety had trickled down in the small town. She stood on the steps of The Dandridge Pavilion and Convention Center on Three Birds Avenue in Faustus, Ohio, with Rob, Tour, Thug, Pimp, Nigg and Gunz amidst heavy security. In Faustus style, the biggest stars ever to face these burbs faced locked doors when they arrived for their sound check.

Thug pulled his hoodie strings. "There a breeze whipping up."

Maya nodded. "Ohio River. It's unforgiving."

"Feels eerie being back here," he said.

"Yeah," Maya agreed. That was an understatement.

"Oh. This is near where you're from, right?"

Maya nodded, distracted. "Kind of. You know, Robe, I can't believe that she's not calling me back. I left fourteen messages."

"Then she's not your friend."

He was right. Any friend who wouldn't check to see how you were doing after a drunken breakdown is no friend at all. Maya figured that since the next stop of their tour was Faustus, it was perfect for Athena to go home to the Nasty Nati, or drop off the face of the blasted earth if that's what she wanted to do.

Faustus. It was foreign and so irrelevant to life as Maya now knew it that she'd completely resisted this leg of the tour. However, Thug had something to prove by returning to the scene of the crime, as it were. He had to conquer Faustus, and truth be told, so did Maya. Although not quite the local girl makes good that her parents would have hoped for, Maya was, for all intents and purposes, home, whatever that meant. She remembered watching *The Wizard of Oz* as a kid and not understanding why Dorothy wanted to go home. *There's no place that's home.*

"Mayor George Davis is sending someone over ASAP." Rob closed his phone.

Thug was mad jumpy. "We just gonna stand out here like this in the meanwhile?"

"Faustus was your idea, man," Rob said. "This is how we roll down here." A brigade of cars honked as they heard that Thug, Black Death and Cleo X were standing in the open on the Convention Center stairs. Fans yelled their greetings as they drove past.

"Theopatra!"

"Thug, I love you."

"You look beautiful, Cleo!"

"Black Death!"

"Thug, you're a lucky man."

"Cleopatra, you got it made!"

"Man, Thug, you must be wearing horseshoes!"

Maya remembered standing on these stairs and being harassed in different times. These days, haters were few and far between, or public haters anyway. By the time Mayor Davis' man arrived with the keys, Maya was feeling the Faustus love. It just would have been so much sweeter to be feeling it with Lady "I Dare You" Athena.

Rob pulled Maya to the side when the entered the arena. "No place like home. How does it feel?"

"All good," Maya said.

"You know you can always talk to me, right?"

Maya shrugged and looked over her shoulder. She was feeling on edge. "Why would I want to?"

"I just don't wanna witness the devolution of Maya, that's all."

"Then just manage Cleopatra, Rob, and mind your business," she said, grabbing a cig from a roadie and taking a drag.

"Not before a performance." Rob snatched the cigarette and Maya shoved him, loving inside that he was sweating her.

After sound check, Maya wanted to show Thug around, illustrate the pieces of her former life, but she was afraid that the chemical combustion from combining old with new would be like the levees breaking. Mad unpredictable. Plus he knew her as Jezebel from the Nasty Nati, not Maya from Faustus or Yellow Springs. So she left her man with his peeps to make his peace with the city that nearly killed them both. She would go it alone. This time she rolled in a new Hummer instead of on an old bike. Since she knew the town, Maya considered not using a driver but she was sorely out of practice.

There was no answer at her old apartment so she had no idea whether Athena was there or not. She half expected to see herself open the door. What would she say to herself if she did?

She stopped by Desi's Desserts hoping for a hero's welcome, but Salma was home tending to her child and Desi knew nothing about pop culture. He didn't even give her a free cupcake. She wanted to spin by Pearl's Café and flaunt her success at her old job but Christianne wasn't worth it.

"Where are we staying?" she asked the driver (ostrich complex), a blond guy in his twenties.

"Wendy's Luxe Bed and Breakfast. It's not as lavish as what you're used to, I'm sure, but it's the best we got here in Faustus. We get an underground hip-hop station from Kentucky," the driver said, turning on the radio.

The female voice coming from the speakers was very familiar.

"Oh," he said, starting to switch the station, "you don't wanna hear this."

"Leave it," Maya said.

It was Athena rhyming over a jacked-up beat, her voice low and rumbling, but very on point.

". . . Soon you gonna face the music, Cleopatra,
Your pyramid, yo, is crumbling at ya
Stacking thin paper don't mean I won't catch ya
You dumb beyotch, pretending you rich
In a minute we all gonna know who you is . . ."

When it finished, the DJ came on. "This is Sway and that was the new dis record from Lady Athena, the goddess of love. That's the way to beef. Put it on wax. Cleopatra X, where you at, homey?"

"Hip-hop is one competitive sport," said the driver.

Maya felt slammed in the gut. Athena was more than a friend. They were family. More family than family, or so she thought. They never had a beef they couldn't talk about, a fight they couldn't recover from, but like Thug said, it's the ones closest to you who know how to hurt you the best.

"You coming out with a response?" the driver asked.

"Hell yeah," she said out loud but her eyes were already watering. She put her head on her lap and cried, feeling like a complete victim. *Why would Athena do this?*

"Stand up, Faustus. Cleo X is home! Nasti Nati stand up!" Without Athena, Maya had to be her own grandstanding hype-up-the-crowd chick, and she needed to shut down the grumbling about Athena's new song.

The Faustus show was thankfully uneventful. Rumors had been brewing for weeks that the shooters would return to the scene of the crime to finish the job on Thug once and for all, so security was airtight. There were probably almost as many undercovers as fans. Private security forces made up of everyone from the Tru Believers (a Thug fan group who had held fast to the dream of him being alive) to the Guardian Angels to the Fruit of Islam were said to be in the ranks.

Maya had her own personal *this is crazy* moment looking into the wings at Thug and Rob watching her show. Her show! All because she was dared, and accepted the challenge. Last time she was on this stage, well the only time she was on this stage, she was in Rob's arms with Athena and some dude watching Thug be carried away.

A blonde cluster of Miss Beardsley girls (hyperactive) was down in front. Maya knew them from their hiked-up uniform skirts and glitter-glossed lips. The spoiled brats who looked exactly like Hitler's perfect youth put their hands over their heads and sang about being Angry Black Bitches. Little did they know that Cleopatra X was one of them. Kind of.

"Cleopatra—I usually don't do this."

Deep. Living well is truly the sweetest revenge because when they exited the stage door, the most shocking fan waiting for an autograph was Athena's old boss, Christianne from Pearl's Café. It was downright confusing as she held up a CD.

"Like I said, Cleo X, I don't usually do this, but your work moved me. Spoke to me. Who doesn't feel bitchy, you know? We even have your picture in the window of my café." Christianne was speaking as though she had no idea that Cleo X was Maya. Maybe she didn't. Apparently, fame was stronger than protocols, people. Maya signed the CD with an evil smiley face. No words.

When Maya went into the bathroom, a younger woman with long braids seemed to be walking along with her, kind of shadowing her. Maya stopped and spun to confront the would-be attacker the way Thug taught her to. "If this is beef, let's get it over with."

"Um, my name is Lola Ochun and I'm a first-year Dunbar undergrad." The girl hesitated.

"Oh. Autograph?" Maya pulled out the green Sharpie she carried now in her pocket. "Ochun?"

"No. I just wanted to say that, uh . . ." The girl had a dark green Africa on her shirt.

"Yes?" How cute that someone could be so shy to talk to her.

"People like you and your posse set black people back fifty years! You're going to need your soul one day and you won't have it," she shouted and took off running.

"What did you say?!" Maya was about to run after her. "How can you say that? How dare you?" How. How? Jeez. Maya remembered when she used to think like that. "Damn."

Notebook of Truth

THE DARE EXPERIMENT
HIP-HOP UNDERCOVER
BY MAYA GAYLE HOPE

NOTEBOOK OF TRUTH

Yo, keep it real.

What is real?

Truth and choices
Many voices
Not talking 'bout Rolls Royces
Hoistin' me up to the top of my list
The sun kissed sista with her game on grist
Don't get it twisted
Yes. I am unassisted.

Truth and choices
Many voices
What you choose is up to you
So save your boo hoo
Save your "what am I gonna do?"
'Cause my sympathy is sparse
No spare parts.

Takin' control of my vision
Yes I've been tempted,
But I've been winning . . .

Keep it real. Keep it true.

TRUTH DECLARATION: (Repeat five times every morning, noon and night to reinforce truth.) *When we dare to live our truth, we are unafraid of the consequences of our choices. On this day I make choices that are healthy for my mind, my body and my spirit. I choose to love me now.*

TRUTH ACTION STEP: *Today I take responsibility for everything that has transpired in my adult life and I take full responsibility for the choices that I make today and tomorrow.*

Chapter 30

"Keep a G on stash.
No, I don't mean cash."
—Marie "Free" Wright

Maya and Thug were moving into their new duplex after spending the last couple of weeks chilling. The penthouse at the Harlem Heretix was purchased and deeded to them by Ozzie Marvelous himself as a gift for rescuing Camp Hustla. Along with the usual moving-in mess, there was also a ton of swag—free clothes, accessories, furniture and gifts sent from designers, wooing managers, and potential sponsors worldwide. The irony was that now that Maya could afford to buy what she wanted, people sent her everything free.

"What's this, babe?" Thug held up her tiny jumping broom. He had been in a great mood all weekend, playing and bugging out.

Maya took the broom from Thug, feeling the soft kente cloth and rough bristles between her fingers. "Oh. That's mine."

"I know, 'cause it ain't mine. What is it?"

Maya tossed the broom into the trash, "Another life."

Maya always pictured herself married to the man she moved in with but life happens and she couldn't have seen this coming. The penthouse was designed in blacks and whites like Thug's old spot, with a sundeck and heated rooftop pool. Yeah, it was odd living in a hotel but almost half of the residents at The Heretix were co-op owners.

Thug finished off a bowl of oatmeal and rested it on a box. "I told you to toss everything. We don't need your stuff or my stuff. Let's just have our stuff, babe."

"Baby, we talked about this already." Maya smiled to herself the way you do when you're trying not to go mad. *Our stuff.* It was so romantic. So claustrophobic. Maya didn't want to toss herself in the trash and begin to exist only when her man discovered her. She needed the self she used to be and the stories she chose to tell to explain to herself who she had become. Huh?

"You know why I came back?" Thug asked as he did once a day.

Maya shook her head.

"To find you, babe." He held her face and kissed her lips.

Minions helped them unpack and rearrange. The place had to be show perfect by morning. That major network was broadcasting Maya's reality TV special as *Cleopatra X-Posed*, a two-hour special that was going to be hosted live, from their home, by Manifesta. "Millions of fans get to watch live with Cleo X herself and Robeson Thug from their new love nest."

Maya grabbed a powdery doughnut and watched Thug explain to the helpers where stuff went. The knot in the pit of her stomach had been there for weeks. Her infatuation for her boyfriend waxed and waned like morning haze and she was left trying to figure out what she felt for real/for real. Sometimes she lay beside him knowing somewhere in her being that he might not be the one. Other times he touched her and sent a spark through every layer of her life and she knew for a fact that she could never be without him. She looked at him now arguing with the movers and didn't want to ask the question that kept coming to mind. If there was a teensy weensy chance that Robeson was not the one, then who? Maybe there wasn't one. Maybe Maya wanted Robeson to be the one so that she could be done with it.

Maya heard her voice saying, "Baby . . . What if we take a step back to get to know each other." *Was that out loud?*

"Why, babe? I thought we knew everything already." Thug sat on a box and it caved in.

Maya made no move to help him up. "We do."

He took off his Thug-brand sneakers and chucked them in a corner. "When it's right, what difference does it make?"

True. A Magic 8 ball would be great right now. Did she have the right to break up with somebody like Thug for no reason? Reply hazy, try again.

He started kicking the door. What now? *Kick.* He was so loud that she couldn't hear herself. *Kick.* She loved him but this was too much. *Kick.* She didn't want to become one. *Kick.* She wanted to be a strong twosome. *Kick.*

Maya let him have at it for thirty seconds, then grabbed his arm. "Baby! Why're you doing that?"

"Maya," he said, wavering a little.

She was quiet for a second. Did she hear what she thought she heard? Couldn't have been. "What did you call me, Robe?"

"Maya Hope. That's your name, right?" His voice was solid now. Accusing.

Maya the Guilty sucked in air. This she was not expecting. There was nothing else to say except, "I can explain."

Thug was pacing. "After what I been through? You lied to me?"

She tried to stand at a focus point as he moved back and forth. "Not you. Everybody."

"That makes it better?" He wouldn't look at her.

"You lied to the world about being alive," Maya insisted. "Charge it to the game."

"That's different." He dropped to the floor and started doing push-ups.

"Don't hate me, Robeson." She wanted to knock on her head with closed fists.

He jumped up. "No, baby. You don't get it. I loved you not your ghetto bio. Are we real? Is this real? Or are we one of Luci's publicity stunts?"

"I'm your Cleopatra. That's who I am. For real." She didn't want to ask, but screw it. "Who told you?"

"Your man Rob got twisted last night. We got into it and I was gonna wreck shop. Then he dropped the bomb on me."

"Oh." It figured.

"Rambling. Saying you loved him first."

"So Robeson, baby, you wanna break up with me or take a break or something?" Her voice sounded almost hopeful.

Robeson put his arms around Maya and squeezed. Circulation impaired. "You can't get rid of me that easily, babe. We ride or die. You my everything."

Maya was suffocating, smothered by expectations. She couldn't be somebody's everything. You want a mate who wants you, not needs you. You want love that is deep not dense. She didn't want somebody to lose himself inside her. If he was completely inside her, where would she go?

"Where do y'all want this stuff?" A guy held up a box.

"Figure it out! That's what we're paying you for, right?!" Maya snapped. "Is helpful help too much to ask?!"

"There's always people everywhere." Thug pulled Maya into their barren bathroom and climbed into the empty four-person tub. It looked bottomless. She stepped in between his legs and they both sat staring ahead at the purple and gold tiles.

"What were you gonna say, Robeson?"

"Nothing. I'm done. I been trying to offer strength and people don't want it. Putting my neck out there and they don't want it." He smoothed her hair. "Just don't leave me, okay? Listen to your heart."

Maya laughed a little. "Leave you?"

He grabbed Maya's shoulders. "I mean today, Queen, okay?"

Maya tried to listen to her heart and could only hear the soft hum of the AC. She was sure that he didn't know how tight he was squeezing, that it actually hurt. She leaned forward. It had been a rough week. He almost had a fistfight with a dude who said with all his preaching he should have stayed dead. Nobody wanted to listen to what he had to say. They only wanted to dig up his old work and blame him for the actions of grown men.

"You're okay, Robeson. You are. I promise."

"You promise? Who? Maya or Cleopatra?"

Good question.

"People never ask what would have happened if Malcolm or Martin woulda lived and they didn't turn out to be who we wanted 'em to be," he said. "Suppose Malcolm wanted to take Betty and the kids to hang out in Africa and chill?"

Maya shrugged. "You're on point, baby."

"What if Martin was tired of fighting and he told Coretta that martyring wasn't for him no more? What if old boy just wanted to play golf? Or what if he stayed in the game but switched up his flow and told us to get our own shit together. People wouldn't have been feeling none of that, right?" The look on his face was turning her to stone.

"I guess not, baby." She lifted up his shirt to rest her head on his chest, and did a double-take. Her face. With Egyptian Cleopatra's gold beaded headdress. "Robeson, is that . . ."

"You," he said. "Got it last week." How could she not have noticed this? Maya laid her head on top of her image and held him.

"Malcolm and Martin and Mandela and them is just men," Thug continued. "Like me. I'm just a man. Speakin' the truth. Ain't nobody else darin' to. And I'm tired. Real tired." He sat up abruptly. "Cleopatra, come with me to Ghana."

Left field. "Robe, I—"

He was excited. The storm was breaking. "We could just chill out, you know, retire." He pushed Maya up, jumped out of the tub and threw newly unpacked things back into the Louis Vuitton toiletry bag like they were leaving in five minutes.

"But, Robeson," Maya chose her words carefully. "Baby, you can retire because you've lived. I just started living. I wanna make this Cleopatra thing work."

"I feel you, babe, but there might be bigger things for Cleopatra and Robeson to do. Nahmean? Wanna leave before it's too late."

Diagnosis: Mania. The clock on the wall turned to noon, then 2:00 P.M., then seven and she was still holding her man, beating the demons away from their luxury suite. The ultimate test of any skills of human analysis. Good thing she had being a rapper as a backup plan because she sucked at this. At that moment, she wanted most of all not to console her man, but to call Rob and let him off the hook. To say "I understand."

Chapter 31

"IF YOU LOVE ME THEN THANK YOU.
IF YOU HATE ME THEN FUCK YOU!"
—*Lady Sovereign*

Six hours to live TV," someone yelled. Handlers and groomers were abuzz. A long day was planned, with the TV show and then the first New York City concert at the Garden. Maya was in the makeup chair of her new grooming suite, next to the guest bedroom. It was a full salon, equipped for hair, nails, massages and facials, and a barbershop.

"I got something I need to take care of, babe." Thug gave Maya a bear hug, then he held her and smooched her lips.

"Baby, you're smudging me." Maya never asked Thug where he was going even though he required a minute-by-minute report of her comings and goings. Now that she realized that she had been too clingy with Rob she made a conscious effort to adjust that for Thug. The multi-lightbulbed mirror reminded Maya of old Hollywood. Thug's face echoed three times over her head in the tri-fold glass reflection. Mirrors also covered the other three walls.

Thug gave her another hug. "Okay, babe. I'm out. What's the word for today?"

"Never let your enemy know what you're thinking," she called after him.

"You got it. I'm ghost, babe," he called out, and Maya was glad that she loved him.

Maya tried on twelve outfits before finding one that made everybody happy: Escada Couture Swarovski Crystal jeans ($10,000), a

Natas Davidus greenish-black snakeskin tight tee ($1,500) and Styleaholics Jewelry ($3,000). Rock star! Her blondish highlighted hair, which had grown to mid-back, was in big waves with bigger extensions glued in between. The glue was burning her scalp, but not more than the vat of face-shrinking moisturizer lathered on under her thick layers of makeup. Beauty is suffering, the makeup artist said.

Hours later Maya flashed her bright red nails, individually designed with matching crystals. The pedicurist worked on her feet, which were soaking in champagne. "I feel like I'm getting married," she said.

"Hello, hello, hello!" Maya's new BFF Luci floated in. "How much fun are we having?"

Maya's eyes were glued shut as the lash lady did adjustments. "What up, Luce? Question. Do you think I need Botox?"

"Presenting!" Luci waved her arm like a game-show model.

"No visitors, please. I really want to meditate before the show." Maya peered through a half open eye.

A man marched in with the reverence of the pope, bringing a gush of cold air with him. Ozzie Marvelous! He looked younger than she remembered with dark glasses and a rat-tail ponytail. He reeked of Sulfur 8, the anti-dandruff conditioner, but his suit looked like Armani himself stitched it on him that morning. The pedicurist and eyelasher respectfully stepped away.

Maya pried her eyes open. "Well, sir, uh, we finally meet. Thanks for the crib." Maya nervously popped five Super Mints in her mouth.

"Well, thanks for the sales," he said, the faint sound of a rattle under his voice. "I told Shell and my daughter Luci that I had to meet you tonight."

"Your daughter?" Maya grinned. She didn't do that much these days. Luci blushed. "I feel like I should ask you the meaning of life or something," Maya continued.

"Why's that? You would know much better than I do. From what I hear you're too smart for your own good." He smiled. "Anyway, have fun. It'll be over before you know it. I wanted to do this thing aboard my yacht, but they told me you get seasick."

There was something very fatherly about him, if your father was a calculating old European man with a brassy voice. Maya looked through his gray-green eyes into his heart. Darkness.

"Good luck now." He kissed Maya on the cheek, his prune lips cold and stiff on her face. She shivered. He was warm but repellent, like a beautiful headache.

"Hey, your boots match my shirt," Maya called, but he was already slithering out the door.

"How sweet was that?" asked Luci.

"Ozzie Marvelous is your father?" Maya asked.

"Maya!"

She swiveled around the other way. Rob.

"Oh—for a second I thought you were Robeson."

"No," said Rob. Ever since she and Thug became an item Rob had this faraway look whenever their eyes met. Like he was guilty of something. Or like she was.

She wanted to say it was okay but her patience had become paper thin. "Well, what's taking him so long?"

"I, uh, don't know, but somebody else very much wants to see you."

"You sound very door number three. I need to focus. Just a minute to clear my head before the show," Maya said. "Is it the contest winner?"

"Can Lady Athena join this party?" Athena floated in sporting her natural hair in a very short early Braxton. She stood by the door, fresh and clean-looking in a short white sundress and super-high heels. Her grooming suite now felt pretentious. It had been so many moons.

"Hey!" Maya shouted, her heart opening up before she remembered that they had beef.

"You look beautiful, Maya."

It was sooo good to see Athena's face. Maya missed her partner-in-crime completely but her own game face was finally intact. She remembered that they were enemies now. "Who invited you?" she asked.

"Manifesta," Athena said.

"Well, it's my house." Maya noticed that Athena was letting her freckles show through her makeup and she had to keep reminding herself to be angry. "So I heard your song. 'Pyramadness'?"

Athena nodded. "It's been getting good regional airplay."

"Should I be happy that my ex–best friend's song slamming me is doing well? What's the protocol?"

"I had to do what I had to do, Maya."

"I feel you. I was doing me so you had to do you."

Athena nodded again. "Gonna ball 'til I fall."

"I like the haircut," was pretty much all Maya could think of to say next.

"Come on, Maya. We both know it's not a haircut. I just released my weave into the wild to roam with the other animals. For now. Guess who's engaged!" Athena held out her left hand, accentuated by something big, blingy and shiny.

"Hot damn! Okay, now I'm blind. Ferrari?"

"Who else?" Athena was smiling.

"I had no idea that it was this serious." It felt unsettling that Athena should be married before she was, but then Maya remembered that she was comfortably in love with her own dream man. "I's married now," Maya said, pushing her lips up into a grin.

Athena picked up the line from *The Color Purple* where Shug, the good-time singing whore, shows her judgmental preacher daddy her ring, and they said it together: "See, I's married!"

Maya was glad for the relief of laughter. "Ooh—I saw Christianne in Faustus. She asked for an autograph."

"Say word!" Athena's blue eyes looked gray in the grooming suite's special light.

"Word," Maya said.

Athena shook her head at the thought of it. "Well, Rocky is producing my music independently."

"Really? Who's Rocky?"

"My husband-to-be, Maya."

"Yeah, of course. Rocky." Maya repeated the name to imprint it on her brain.

"Rap is dead. It completely played itself out so from now on I'm gonna sing," Athena said.

Maya let the dig against her music go. "Sing? Really?" She also chose not to mention that when Athena sang she sounded like a bag of cats being flung into traffic. The Athena reunion was throwing her off-beat. She needed privacy.

"Today is September thirteenth, the first day of Rosh Hashanah. Rocky's Jewish, but I had to be here." Athena looked like there were more words hiding between her lips.

"Okay, then," Maya said.

"Cool." Athena hesitated.

Maya swiveled her chair around, signaling the end of the conversation. "I'm glad you're here, Athena," Maya told her reflection.

"Me too," Athena took the hint and turned to leave.

"You need anything?"

"No, Maya. I'm good. When I make it," Athena began.

"You make it," Maya finished. They still needed each other. No matter what.

Athena swiveled out and Rob swiveled in. There was no time to gather thoughts. It was a lost episode of *This Is Your Life*.

Rob shifted his weight from one foot to the other. Maya closed her eyes and leaned back in the chair. She didn't mind meditating in front of him.

"Maya."

She opened her eyes, exasperated. "What now?"

"I thought you should hear it from me. After tonight's show, I'm leaving the fam."

Maya frowned. "Why?"

Shell and an assembly of security and handlers pushed Rob to the side. "Hey, lady! This is Peaches." A handler placed a pale, yapping, red-eyed dog on her lap.

"What is this?" Maya asked, holding her arms up like she was under arrest.

"Where's your man?" Shell was uncharacteristically miffed.

Peaches, now yelping, was plotting an attack.

Rob pushed his way through the entourage. "She's terrified of dogs, Shell."

Before Maya or anyone else could react, Luci scooped up Peaches and pulled Maya's arm. "Va va and voom, Jez. We're on."

"We should wait for Robeson," Maya said.

"We'll send him in as soon as he gets here," Luci said. "And don't worry. Peaches is on Prozac."

They were broadcasting live from the living room suite. Maya was propped up on the white fur couch that she hated. She planned to have all of the furniture switched out tomorrow. Somebody put Peaches on her lap. Manifesta wore white sweats from head to toe. Maya peeped out her visual language and noted that she had cast herself as an angel, and where there's an angel you need a devil. She was kind of glad that Robe hadn't shown yet. Homegirl loved to put him through the wringer.

"Last looks," Luci called, and hands converged on Maya to primp, powder and straighten. Everyone rushed everywhere. Maya waved at Manifesta and she waved back. Shell, Rob, Luci, and Athena watched from the sidelines in director's chairs with the rest of the posse and Manifesta sat on the side. Black Death was at the studio.

"Good luck, Cleo X," Rob called from the sidelines.

"Action!" someone yelled. Maya kept one eye on Peaches and tried not to be undone by a pooch.

"Taking Hip-Hop back to hip-hop DJ Manifesta's live. Welcome to *Cleopatra X-Posed.* Little did we know when we first met Jezebel at Harlem Lanes what a big star Cleo X would become. This is her newest crib that she shares with the man she loves, and most of us do as well—although to some of us, he is the man we love to hate. Robeson Thug." Manifesta turned away from the words scrolling through the teleprompter. "Female emcees are usually breasts and booty with no skills. Their posters sell better than their records. Most of them don't write for themselves and are created by some male Svengali. This week something different, the interview we've all been waiting for. Cleopatra, formerly Jezebel."

That was Maya's cue. "Hey. Whassup America!"

"Sooo, tell us about yourself," Manifesta said.

Her story tripped the light fantastic off of Maya's tongue. "Well—my government name is Jezebel Johnson. I raised myself because my parents were . . ." It was suddenly uncomfortable to tell Athena's story. "Let's just say having to strive for myself I had to define myself."

"How do you respond to critics who say that songs like 'Angry Black Bitch' spread negativity?"

"I would dare them to walk a mile in my kicks." Maya adjusted her diamond Camp Hustla pendant. Athena coughed, prompting Peaches to start barking—short, nippy, angry barks. Someone handed Athena water. "In my case, it's poetry. Listen to the lyrics, not just the beat."

"Fascinating, Cleo. Well, we're going to take a quick pause for the cause and see you back here in two and two. Don't forget the reality special follows this live interview." The show went to commercial and Manifesta sat back and closed her eyes. It was all very Zen.

Maya felt calm just looking at her as three to four hands poked, prodded and adjusted her own clothes, hair and makeup. The handlers were invisible now. She had become used to the personal invasion. An assistant fixed Peaches' bow.

Maya reached out to stroke Peaches, who snapped her jaws. Peaches growwwwled and then started yipping. "Somebody take this dog!" A roadie handed Peaches to Shell. "Thank you!"

Shell yelled from the wings, "Yo Manifesta, check it—don't forget—the deal was that at least once per hour you'd show the Angry Black Bitch video."

"In five, four, three, two . . ."

Manifesta killed the Zen, opening her eyes and mouth instantly upon *action*. "And we are back. Let's talk to Lady Athena—part of the Cleo X posse."

Maya looked at Shell. "Lady Athena?"

Shell looked at Rob, who seemed confused as well. Luci rubbed her hands together as she did when she was nervous.

"Lady Athena has been burning up the mixtape circuit and getting some radio love with her independent single 'Pyramadness,' where she insinuates that Cleopatra X is wack. Lady Athena, what prompted Pyramadness?"

"A squad is family," Shell interjected from the sidelines. "And we take care of each other. All kinds of deals might be in the works." He eyed Athena meaningfully. "It's all love, right?"

A camera swiveled around to Athena. "No doubt, Shell. Nothing but love/love." Athena stood up, fully feeling her moment. "I know y'all know who I am, America. You seen me on stage doing my one-two thing or heard my voice on the tracks keeping the beat hype."

Maya sat up taller and pulled the attention back to herself where it belonged. "That's right, my *second* in command, the best *background* hype woman in the business." Like Thug often said, if you're larger than your enemy, flex. Only if you're weaker do you ever play weak.

"So where *is* your man?" Manifesta asked. "Maybe somebody told him that rich and famous brothas don't date dark-skinned sistas?"

Maya bit her lip. She exchanged looks with Athena.

"Haaa!" Manifesta laughed with her head back. "Just jokes. So let's talk influences. Who's your favorite rapper, Cleo X?"

Her brain was sizzling. How dare Athena? How dare Manifesta? And where was her man? "My favorite rapper? Besides Cleopatra X? Robeson Thug." Maya smiled, tilting her head to a three-quarter angle. Photos came out extra fly when she posed this way.

"But are you influenced maybe by Rakim? You have a similar cadence." Manifesta smiled baring all of her teeth.

Rakim? Maya was drawing a blank. Which one was that again? Her contacts were shifting. Something was wrong. Brain freeze. She could barely remember her own name. Anxiety attack. She had never choked on a test. Never. Not chemistry, or semiotics. Until now. "I am totally influenced by Rakim, Manifesta. How did you guess? So anyway . . . Thank the goddess that we are broadcasting live from the gorgeous living room of my fabulous new home!"

Manifesta was circling. Prey. "What's your favorite Rakim verse?"

Yeah. Rakim was one that she really liked too. Creative and lyrical? Or was that Slick Rick? Dammit. The room got hotter. Maybe if she spoke faster this would be over sooner. She looked to the sidelines.

Shell was clutching his pearls. Well, he wasn't wearing pearls but if he was he'd be clutching them. "My favorite verse? So many to choose from. Everybody has a favorite Rakim verse. Yo Rob, what's your favorite Rakim verse?"

Rob joined Maya on the couch spotlit for Thug. "Oh, like everybody else, it would have to be '7 Emcees,' the most famous lyric of all times."

"Word." Maya was grateful for the rescue, though it annoyed her that he was in Thug's seat. Rob caught the hint and stepped back off-camera.

"Recite it for us, Cleopatra X." Manifesta leaned in and held her mic under Maya's chin. Unnecessary. She knew that Maya was miked.

"Sure—um . . . Where do I begin?" Maya looked around for Peaches, a lifeboat. Something.

Athena tossed her a line. "I'll take seven emcees put 'em in a line . . ."

"Right," Maya said. "Take seven emcees put 'em in a line . . ."

"And add seven more brothas who think they can rhyme . . ." Athena added. Maya was lost but she didn't want to repeat like some idiot savant without the savant.

"Well it'll take seven more—" Rob raised his arms like people do at carnivals to get people to join in. "Before I go for mine."

The crew, including Shell and Luci, all chimed in. "And that's twenty-one emcees ate up at the same time."

Maya's nose was bleeding back into her throat. She stood up. "Yeah—that's it! That's the bomb, yo—yes! Word up! That's whassup."

Manifesta folded her hands calmly on her lap. "Of course viewers recognize Shell the Boy Wonder, super manager, producer, entrepreneur and business magnate."

Shell flashed a Camp Hustla hand signal to resettle the universe.

Athena tapped a beat on her leg. "Rakim is a genius."

Maya glared at her. How dare she jump back in uninvited? "And let's not forget how sexy LL is," Maya added. Everyone in the studio, er, living room inhaled like she missed a loop.

Shell jumped in. "Clearly, Rakim's style—among others—has helped make Cleopatra X the powerhouse she is today."

"Check out a preview of our reality special and we'll be right—" Manifesta began.

"And when we return we'll go straight to the video for Cleo X's hot single 'Angry Black Bitch.' One love, Thug," Shell called out.

Maya waved Athena over and Rob went into a mini-conference with Luci and Shell.

"What was that?" Maya asked.

Athena overemphasized scratching her head. "Uh, what are you talking about?"

"I'm talking about why are you trying to play me, Athena?"

"Nobody was trying to play you. I was trying to help you, Maya."

"Don't call me that here, a'ight? The name is Cleopatra X. You killin' me. Just gat me right now."

"Um, no, chica. You're killing me. Some getaway driver." Athena raised her voice into a falsetto to mock Maya's voice. "When I make it you make it, right Cleo X? And I came here to make up with your sorry ass."

"Back in ten," someone called out as Athena walked back to her director's chair. Maya stared at the monitor. It showed her stripping at BiSex, barfing on the sidewalk, fighting with Athena, crashing into the crowd on the motorcycle, butt in the air at the bowling party and a whole host of other crazy images. Wow. If you put it together like that . . .

"Excuse me." Maya got up and stood in the corner. Damn. This was jacked up. Jacked up.

Action. When they resumed Manifesta was again wearing her broadcasting face. "Let's get down to business, Cleopatra. You are a part of Camp Hustla and you're label-mates with Black Death? Correct?"

"Correct," Maya said. Good. Familiar territory.

Shell flashed the Camp Hustla signal again and Maya flashed it back.

"It's a fact that you and Pimp used to be a couple before you hooked up with his former bandmate who stood us up tonight, Thug." Maya rolled her eyes. "So how do you feel about the new Black Death music video 'Rape the Game' where Pimp pulls cash from a woman's butt cheeks?"

"What?" Maya looked over at Rob, then Shell. She had been so caught up her own thing that she had no idea what Black Death was up to other than their show. Luci shook her head.

Shell stood up, "What the *hell* is this?"

"Live TV!" Manifesta said.

Shell stepped back into the wings, uh, dining area. Luci was a kitten watching a birdie.

"Umm." Maya searched her brainbase for the appropriate response. Her phone vibrated and she looked down at a message from Rob: NO COMMENT.

"As a woman, how does that make you feel?"

Maya thought about the heavyset guy in the Black Death fam who always had one of his women on a leash.

She took a deep breath. "It . . . I . . . It . . . makes me feel terrible."

Shell called out, "That's enough—are you playing the videos again or not?"

Manifesta was of singular mind, "And you come from a pretty rough lifestyle, don't you?"

"I guess," Maya said quietly.

"You guess?"

"No, I do. I do."

"Your man was shot many times over beefs with rich, famous black men that occurred when he was already rich and famous. Do you feel that the violence is an accurate and necessary portrayal of ghetto life?"

"Well . . . it's human nature to want to tell your story."

"Yeah, but just because you have something to say doesn't mean people need to hear it, right?"

"Sociologically speaking, well . . ." She was at a loss for words.

Maya looked over at Athena. "Actually my homegirl Lady Athena has some interesting thoughts on this." Maya waved her over.

Shell stepped forward. He now had a microphone. "That's right. We're a camp of many players."

Athena joined Maya on the sofa. "Tupac said that the Viet Nam war ended so early because the pictures of the war zone left Americans feeling like something had to be done. He wanted to do the same thing with his violent ghetto images."

Manifesta returned her look to Maya. "But Tupac died over ten years ago. From violence."

Shell waved his arms.

Maya leaned back. She closed her eyes, then reopened them. "Yes. Urban violence is being pimped for cash. Instead of journalists and Viet Nam, we have pay-per-view poverty. I guess if the Klan wanted to make its case it could have invented some of the voices of rap."

Manifesta's assistant director gave her a signal. The DJ looked down at her phone and read a message. She seemed juiced. "So you're pretty critical of your industry, huh?"

Maya crossed and uncrossed her legs. "Most times people only criticize something when they love it. And I am passionate about this music. These people. Words. Beats. It runs deep." She affected her Trini patois:

> *"Like a nation of slaves swimming home in my veins.*
> *They don't beat us now with sticks now it's just poli-tricks."*

Rob, Shell and Athena applauded and Luci gave her a thumbs-up. *Kapow!* Sound effect of bombs dropping. A National Honor Society photo of Maya in thick glasses and a cap and gown appeared on screen. Shell jumped in front of it.

"So who's this, Jezebel?" Manifesta snapped and the screen switched to fuzzy cell phone video of Maya protesting as an activist.

"I, uh, I, uh . . ."

"Your name is Jezebel Johnson from the Nasti Nati jungle, right?"

Maya was choking. She looked around for a glass of water. "I, uh, I, uh . . . Break please?"

"Cut!" Shell yelled.

Manifesta stood up. "Why is it, Jezebel Johnson, that you didn't even exist before this year?"

"I—"

"Why is it, Jezebel Johnson, that you bear a striking resemblance to this woman? One Maya Gayle Hope, daughter of college professors, an M.A. from Dunbar University."

"I—"

"Didn't you go to one of the poshest boarding schools in Ohio?"

Maya fanned herself with her hand. "Yes, but . . . a partial grant—"

Shell screamed, "Commercial break! Cut!"

Manifesta unfolded herself up to her full height. She was just warming up. "Aren't you a charlatan, a fraud, a Milli Vanilli, a Mensa member?"

"Enough already!" Athena yelled.

Manifesta was relentless. "Answer the question, Maya."

"Okay! Okay! Fine then. Athena is the talented one. I suck at everything!"

Athena jumped to Maya's side. "Not everything! Fuck you, Rob—did you do this?"

Rob stepped up. "Me? It was probably you."

Luci shook her head. "Everybody knows how jealous you are, Athena!"

Manifesta continued, "Isn't this some undercover experiment to expose and embarrass hip-hop like in 2005, when you did a report online infiltrating Goob's Donut Haven to expose their shoddy ingredients?"

"I—"

Shell regrouped. "All of the answers will be on the new Cleo X album. Just check the Camp Hustla website for the whole scoop."

Manifesta drank in the chaos.

"Stop it," Rob said. He took Maya's hand and started to lead her out.

Shell found his light. "See Jezebel Cleo Maya or whoever she is tonight in her farewell performance! All proceeds benefit Boy Wonder Kiddee Charities."

"We'll be there, Shell! Back in two minutes."

Commercial break. Mass confusion. Everybody lost it, pointing blame and fingers. Shell blamed Luci and Rob. They blamed each other. Athena blamed everybody. Maya blamed herself. The fight moved into the hotel hallway.

Shell whispered to Maya, "Yo, don't stress. I like your hustle. Whoever ratted you out couldn't have done you a better favor. This will be *huge*. Comeback album in six months." He looked at his phone. "We're selling through the roof!"

Maya wanted to spit on him. Where was her man?

The camera followed Maya and company down the hall.

"And we're back. How do you feel, Maya Jezebel?" Manifesta asked.

Rob put his hand over one camera and Manifesta shifted focus to another one.

Shell winked at Maya off camera and then screamed in her face. "How does she feel? Like a liar! Like a hypocrite! Who ratted on Jeze-Maya? A hip-hop mystery—was it Lady Athena, her bitter hype woman who she has beef with? And whose album we'll be releasing immediately?"

"Yay!" Athena whooped. Maya looked at her. "Sorry," she said.

"Shell, knock it off." Luci screamed.

Luci ripped off her pink diamond Camp Hustla pendant. Everyone was thoroughly confused. "Punk!"

Shell pushed Luci off camera. "Or was the squealer Big Rob, emcee in his own right relegated to lowly road manager? Or Pimp the cuckolded lover, in a lonely act of desperation? Et tu Brutus, you Judas?"

Rob put a hand on Maya's shoulder. "Chill. The girl's been through enough."

"How do you feel, Maya?" Manifesta's camera caught every nuance.

Stupid question. She had flown too close to the sun. Manifesta had tossed a bucket of water and Maya's waxy wings were melting.

"Whether 'tis nobler in mind to suffer the slings and arrows of outrageous fortune or to take arms against a sea of troubles, and by opposing end them," she said. There was a general *huh?* Maya buried her face in Rob's shoulder, looked up into his eyes and felt how through it all he was there for her.

Devastated.

They were finally at the elevator, followed by Manifesta and her cameras. Athena pushed the button. There is nowhere to go from the penthouse but down.

"You want the truth?" Maya asked quietly.

Manifesta threw her hands in the air. "Finally! I dare somebody to tell it."

Maya looked down at the bridge she was standing on and ignited it. "Fine." She took the microphone and looked into the camera. "It was me. I ratted me out."

Shock. Let the chips fall where they may.

Shell started yelling, "The scandal of the decade. Camp Hustla dot com! Camp Hustla dot com! Rob, Cleo X, Athena, Luci—you're all under contract. Cleopatra X will perform tonight as planned. Boy Wonder complete."

Maya imagined a spinning tabloid cover: "FRAUD." Arrangements, assurances, agreements, pacts, pledges, promises, dares, deals, covenants, contracts, transactions and treaties. Pants. On. Fire.

When the elevator finally came, the doors opened into another hell. Ill Verge. Eyes bulging and green Hustla jersey covered with blood.

"Thug's been shot!!" he screamed.

"What?" Nothingness. Fade to white. Brain not processing. *Thug's been shot.* Move! They fought for spaces in the elevator. *Thug's been shot.* Rob took Maya by the shoulders and placed her in the center. *Go!*

Manifesta and her team dashed for the stairs. *Thug's been shot.* The words played and replayed like a scratching record.

A joke or scheme from Rob. Maybe Shell was trying to get her out of the situation. Maya looked at Shell. No wink, no smile, no nudge, no nothing. *Thug's been shot.* Nineteen, eighteen, seventeen, sixteen . . . Lobby. Open. Running. Characters and cameras poured out of the lift and stairwell in a rough heavy stream. Thug was holding on in half of the H of the front door, standing on the yellow bricked road. Gunz or Nigg was standing over his brother. Panic. Shell ran into the street. Pandemonium. Screams. Black crimson everywhere, and spreading. Falling inside. Thug's head was in her lap. Where was the blood coming from? Flowing.

Thug looked up at Maya and smiled. "Whassup, Cleopatra?"

"What's up, Robeson?" Maya asked. He closed his eyes. She shook him. Sirens. Yelling. Bleeding.

"Unconquerable." Thug looked glassy and tired. His lids bounced up and down, long lashes fluttering like bloody butterflies. "Blood gotta have blood."

"Where's the ambulance?" Athena screamed.

Maya kissed his forehead, leaving a lip print of frosted gloss and blood. "Don't go to sleep, okay?"

Sirens. Screaming.

"Tired." Thug closed his eyes. "Be you, baby. Free," he said. Then he wasn't moving. At all.

This was too fast. He was in a black cherry sea. Floating. Free? Isn't death freedom only for a slave?

Ambulance.

Finally.

They pried Maya away from Thug's body. Athena took one arm and Rob took the other, and they parted the red sea with her body. Scarlet footprints. Ruby handprints. Rob gave Maya a crimson hug, whispered something in her burgundy ear.

"My shining black prince." Maya could see only red.

She held Thug's hand in the back of the ambulance softly repeating his rhymes in case by some small chance he could hear her. His eyes remained shut and she was separated from him by paramedics, tubes, beeping machines and blood. At the hospital, they would only allow Shell and Maya in the intensive care unit, Shell as his brother and Maya as his wife. Shell informed her that Nigg was dead. Nigg and Pimp were beefing over billing and pulled out on each other. Thug was trying to break it up. Pimp fired off rounds on Thug and Nigg, and ran off.

Too numb to cry, she hovered over the hospital sink, washing her hands over and over again. Trying to get the blood out. She watched Robeson swirl down the drain.

"I don't know what to say," Athena said as she stood in the corner of the waiting room.

A clean hand on Maya's shoulder. Luci was the only one blood free, snapping pictures. "Be valiant," she suggested to Maya, giving advice as either a friend, rep or maybe both. "Valiant women go forth and fight the good fight. Be very Jackie, Coretta, Betty."

"Valiant?" Maya adjusted the fifteen-carat canary yellow diamond ring on loan from Jacob the jeweler and punched Luci dead in her grill. She felt a crack on contact.

"Spin that," Maya said as Luci ran out, holding her jaw. As Maya started to run after her, Athena grabbed her and held her tight.

Thug was shot twice in the head and once through the arm. All bullets went in through the skin, and, by a glorious miracle, out through the skin. He opened his eyes only three hours later, and Maya was by his side. Touch-and-go the doctors said, but she was by his side.

Chapter 32

"NOW DON'T YOU UNDERSTAND, MAN, UNIVERSAL LAW
WHAT YOU THROW OUT COMES BACK TO YOU, STAR."
—*Lauryn Hill*

Dry. It was a hell of a week, but Thug finally stabilized.

Maya came home to their penthouse that he had lived in for one day plus one hour. Alone. Where was Athena? That was the only way that this monstrosity could feel like a home. No, Athena was married now. She had to tell Luci . . . No, that's right. Nobody was coming to rescue her. There was no Luci, no Ill Verge, no Legba, no anybody. Ozzie gave them one month to move out of the home that had been "gifted" to her and her beloved. He had to distance himself from the violence. She was a princess without a tower or a prince. Her bank account was empty. She actually owed Shell money. Videos, parties, jet rides, wardrobe, everything had been charged against her uninsured contract. This after she turned down offers from every other manager in the book just to be loyal.

Maya sat down on the stupid fur couch. The place was less homey somehow without the cameras, entourage and junk that had become as natural as air. Thug's sneakers were in the corner. "At the end of everything, there's nobody," she said as she lit a white candle.

She looked through the mail. How did fans always find them? Get-well cards mixed with birthday wishes and demo CDs. A letter from her mom.

The card cover featured a roughly scrawled quote from Kurt Vonnegut: "We are what we pretend to be, so we must be careful what we pretend to be." Inside: "Maya, call your mother."

Great. Her mother was one of two people left in the free world who didn't follow entertainment news. Her father was the other.

Maya dialed home. Yellow Springs. She couldn't remember the last time that they had voice to voice contact. Since she slept all day her body was too off kilter to contact most people because of the time difference. They were on Greenwich Meridian. She was on M.S.T.—Musician Standard Time. She sat on the bed amidst the black wardrobe of mourning clothes that designers had sent, just in case, listening to her mother's phone ring.

"Mommy!"

Emmaline paused. "My child. To what do I owe the honor?"

"My boyfriend was shot. Here in New York."

"Oh Maya . . . What happened?"

"Shot," she said. Maya listened to her mother repeat the story in the background to her father.

"Oh, yes. That was him? Did they catch anybody?"

"Kind of."

Well, why don't you come home?"

Bing. Text from Rob: B UP IN 3.

"Mom, I have to go. Text message from Bobby."

"Oh, are you two back in touch?"

"Kind of. Love you much."

"Call back as soon as you can," her mother said.

"Will do." Maya hung up. "What the hell does he want?"

She cracked the front door and went to take a dump. Maybe the foul odor would wash him away. Her head was too full to deal with Rob.

Even when she was caring for her man in the hospital, Maya couldn't stop her bratty brain from bouncing back and forth between thoughts of Thug and Rob, and somehow she blamed and hated Rob for that. Which man, which hip-hop was really hers? And which life? Big, fine, fun and do for self? Or rough, rugged, teaching and each one upgrade one?

Sitting on the crapper, she knew in her beat-down soul that Thug had a piece of her but he was not The One. It had been Rob all along. She would never give him the satisfaction of knowing that, though.

She sat on the toilet counting marble tiles and then washed up. Rob was waiting when she came out, his curly hair wild and unkempt.

"I came to see if you were okay." He stood, then sat back down again on the fur sofa.

"I'm a trouper. Isn't that what you whispered to me when my boyfriend was shot?"

Rob put his arms around Maya and held her. "I just want you to be okay." He hugged her. Tightly.

If she had tears, here's where they would have flowed. Here's where she might have been bawling, screaming, fainting if she was a good girlfriend. Instead she hugged Rob back. And held him. And rested her head on his chest.

Big Rob. Bobby.

She breathed him in, expecting caramel.

Sandalwood and musk.

Drakkar Noir. He had worn it his entire adult life. Every frat boy's first cologne. She told him once that it made her weak. After they broke up, it made her sick. She reached up, put her lips on his neck and thought about her lips on Robeson's forehead. Rob turned his head and their lips were touching.

Touching.

Maya wasn't sure who started it, but sixty seconds later they were kissing.

Tonguing.

Four minutes later they were ripping each other's clothes off.

Falling.

Rob lay on top on the fur couch. Kissing her. All she wanted was him inside of her. Thank the Goddess that she was wearing her purple satins.

Bitten.

He felt her urgency. She reached into his boxers. She had forgotten. Dark and smooth, not too veiny, with neat foliage.

Packin'.

He kissed her down to her waist and stopped.

Waiting.

His hands and his mouth pulled off her panties. He put a finger insider her. "We should stop."

"No," she said. "Never."

Rob stood back and looked at Maya lying on the white fur.

Beautiful.

Completely naked. Bikini area waxed smooth. He stood up, lifted her in the air, put his mouth to her nectar and drank.

"Rob . . . Ohhh. Ohhh . . . I can't take that. I can't take it. Stop!"

He held her legs on his shoulders. She wriggled and screamed. He would not stop. stop. stop. as his tongue flicked and probed every millimeter between her legs.

When she was near collapse, Rob put her down on the white couch and held her. "I'm sorry," he said. They were kissing again.

Maya curled up on his lap. Then sat on him. Slowly.

Home.

"Home," he whispered as he entered her body.

She was holding his shoulders and riding him, wild and bareback. Their rhythm was a song. Bucking/Sucking/Hot/Angry/Yearning/Searching/Bargaining . . .

Love.

"Maya, I love you," Rob whispered as he held her booty and pumped her up and down on top of him. A sex thing, she told herself. Men say anything in the heat of passion. The room was starting to smell vulgar.

Passion.

Rob lifted Maya up and bent her over. Damn. In. Damn. And out. Damn. In. Mmmm. Out. He held her close, caressing as he went. In and out.

She moved faster—oh—and faster—oh—faster. "Rob, I can't take it." She wanted to explode.

"Take it," Rob said, slamming gently into her. Over. And over. And over again. "Maya, am I the best you ever had?"

Over. And over. And over again.

There should be another word besides—YES!!—or if she spoke another language—YES—because when he used to ask she would be lying when she said—YES—or faking and now he deserved some special acknowledgment—Yes—A new, different term. "Yes! Yessss! Yes!!! Rob! YES!!"

She was turned out. Falling. In. Turned out. Out. Bitten.

"I love you, Maya," he said again.

She climaxed. Seconds later, he did too. Maya stayed in position, feeling him soften.

"Harmony," he whispered.

"Harmony," she repeated and held him. Tightly.

"Maya . . ."

"Shhhhh." She didn't want to him to speak. Their bodies had said it all.

"I know that the timing is jacked up, Maya, but I love you. I never stopped. I will always love you."

"Ssssshhhhhh." Maya looked into his face. She tried to turn off her sociological mind that said that this was just communal grief sex, the lovemaking people do after a tragic event to feel life. God, she was a horrible girlfriend.

Maya focused on a point on the floor. Was that Robeson's sock?

He wrapped his arms around her. "I'm your soul's mate."

The talking was making it worse. She tried to kiss him, to shut him up. He kissed her back and continued.

"You feel our symphony, Maya? I wasn't ready before but now I am. I knew it when I walked into that hotel room and Jezebel was you. Why else would the universe do that?"

She didn't know. He was right. Totally improbable, but there she was. She couldn't think about that now. She put a hand between his legs. He took her hand, kissed it, and he kept talking.

Maya saw/felt/heard his truth.

"I hear you," she said.

"I'm sorry," he said.

"I feel you. You love me, Rob?"

"Of course, but right now—don't love me, Maya. I'm just gonna be here for you. I'm just gonna hold you."

Maya felt Rob's sweat on her body and she wanted to sit in his soul. But she couldn't . . . "You had sex with my friends. I mean Luci, I don't care. Y'all had whatever going since whenever but Athena? Athena?"

"Athena? Maya, I would never do that. She would never do that. And Luci? Come on." His eyes were true but she couldn't hear him.

She saw her sorrow, sadness, anger, denial, bargaining but there was a B-side. Revenge. Red, ripe, delicious revenge, even in her grief. She tasted its bloody sap on her tongue and needed a place to spit it out.

Maya hugged Rob, felt her heart beating against his chest, and said the only thing she could say in the situation. Eight words. "I'm /just/ sorry/Rob/what/can/I/say?"

"Maya . . . Please don't do this." He ran his fingers through the length of her hair and smoothed it back.

She pushed him away. "No. Don't do what, Rob? Be business? I'm/ just/sorry/what/can/I/say?"

"Maya, we love each other."

"It's too late." Maya stood up, signaling an end to the conversation, his wetness between her legs.

She handed him a box of Wet Wipes. "I think the makeup artist left these."

Best served cold.

Silence.

Finally.

No words.

He stood, dressed quickly and left with no more words.

No more words.

Maya walked calmly to her huge purple and gold bathroom, bent over the lovely custom bidet and vomited up what was left of her self-respect. She was heaving air. Air. *I won, cried the fool, now you have to close the door.* Revenge didn't seem so great. She was a heel. She was the worst girlfriend in the history of girlfriends. She took a solemn vow to wear black for the rest of her life. To sing the Ballad of Maya Hopeless.

Knock Knock, Knock Knock! He came back!

"Rob!" Maya ran to the door and opened it stark naked.

The only way she could approach him ever again was naked, with her heart in her palm. Instead of Rob it was an oldish porter. He handed her an envelope and then quickly turned away, trying hard not to look back at her nude body. Maya opened the envelope carefully to avoid spilling a pillar of salt on the expensive floor. Damn. Damn. Damn. A plane ticket to Ghana and a blue-boxed princess cut engagement diamond attached to a flawless platinum ring that was who-knew-how-many carats. (Where was Luci when she needed her?) Wow. Rob was serious. For real/ for real. Maya put the ring to the mirror and pulled. It split the glass. Her first ring was a chip that couldn't cut butter.

The door knocked again. Maya hid her naked body behind it, peeking out only her head. Rob. He looked past Maya. "I think I left my keys." He moved quickly to the side of the sofa. "Got 'em." He threw the keys up and caught them. Maya held out the blue box, smiled and waited for him to address his re-proposal. Now they needed to talk.

"What?" he asked.

"I was bugging," she said. "For real/for real." Maya hugged him. Tight. Rob put his lips to hers and they were back to two hours ago, before she let revenge rain on their parade and stupidity reign on her queendom. Rob sank into the fur couch and kissed her belly button. Maya dropped to her knees and unbuckled his jeans. He put a hand on her shoulder in anticipation just as the door opened one more time. Neither Maya nor Rob heard it, caught up as they were in their own thing.

"I checked myself out."

They looked up.

Thug.

Maya was kneeling, naked, in front of Rob in her man's spot while her man, head heavily bandaged, leaning on a cane, stood in front of them. Damn.

"Yo, you okay? God." Rob asked as he buckled his pants and stood.

Maya jumped up and grabbed her jacket, hastily shoving herself into it. "Robeson!"

"Where the fuck is my ring?" Thug asked.

"Your ring?" she repeated.

"My fucking ring, Jezebel."

Neither Rob nor Maya knew what to say.

Thug started laughing. "Matter fact, keep it."

"Robeson, I'm . . . I'm just sorry," she said.

"Yeah. You are." Thug peeped the Tiffany box and plane ticket on the table near the door. He grabbed the ticket and walked out. "You not the queen I thought you were," he said as the door closed. Maybe they were damned from the start.

Chapter 33

"I SEEN A RAINBOW YESTERDAY
BUT TOO MANY STORMS HAVE COME AND GONE
LEAVIN' A TRACE OF NOT ONE GOD-GIVEN RAY"
—Lisa "Left Eye" Lopes

Maya was wrestling with her soul. With Luci's snapshots and Manifesta's video of Maya holding Thug's body, Maya was past "Angry Black Bitch." She had joined the ranks of those famous for being famous. People couldn't get enough of her blog confessional about the whys of her lies, her desire to be loved and her quest for courage. Who couldn't relate to wanting to be more than you are? The fan love was deafening. Even the stalkerazzi and the media were being kind.

She gulped a glass of whiskey down. How could she do that to Thug? (Never mind what she had done to Athena and to herself.) When the original cheateration went down she knew for sure that Rob was lower than scum. Is that how Thug saw her? Is that who she had become? Some Jezebel sucking on the next man while her man was bleeding his way back to breath? She felt cypherless.

Thug had left the country with no contact info. He was a man who knew how to get lost. Maybe she should go to Ghana to find Thug, put out a public love letter. She hadn't made one gesture. Who was she? She couldn't find herself anywhere. She wasn't Maya Hopeless, Jezebel or even Cleopatra really. She took out her notebook and put pen to paper to re-create Maya. She started from scratch with the facts:

I am a woman.

I am thirty-three

I am a poet from Yellow Springs, Faustus and Trinidad.

The stage is my altar.

That was a good start, but it wasn't enough. Maya was fighting for her soul. In her drunkenness she imagined Scratch, the albino, trying to strangle her. He wrestled her, ripping at her clothes. Shade/sweetness/struggle.

The devil was scratching at her door, gnawing at her from inside her own belly, shouting that her bill was overdue. She spent many nights in a feverish sweat, praying, screaming, lighting candles and chanting incantations.

I am what I am.

I am what I am.

I am what I am.

I am.

She finally passed out and dreamed a simple dream: An old man with raggedy clothes and a rich face was rowing a boat across the Ohio River. He picked Maya up and took her on a solo journey. As he dropped her off on the riverbank, he said two words: "Stamp Paid."

The facts of who she had become spoke for themselves. She was a deceiver who went under shallow cover and lost herself because she wasn't found to begin with; but are we our best moments or our worst?

She was two fiancés and one best friend in the hole. To have a friend, be a friend, Granny Ruby used to say. She picked up the phone and dialed.

"Hello, Athena." Maya hesitated. They had spoken almost daily but had yet to see each other since the hospital. "It's me."

"Hey babe. Just thinking about you," Athena yelled.

"I can hardly hear you."

"We're at a game," she shouted.

"Athena, are we still us?"

Athena didn't skip a beat. "Everything's okay, babygirl. Shit happens and we keep keeping on."

"Are we good though?" Maya asked. "Copacetic?"

"Yeah honey. Most def."

"For real/for real?"

"Yes Maya. For real/for real. You still gonna be on my album, right, Cleopatra X?"

Maya laughed. "Of course."

"Then we're good. I'll be by tomorrow for a playdate."

Maya baptized herself in a fresh shower and felt free. Nobody would be grabbing her soul today. She wasn't all bad. Like the ancient poet Rumi said, she was the mirror and the face in it. All debts were stamped Paid. She had killed her bad luck, found her calling and was sharing her words and herself. She was in a position to make an impact. Maya had fought the devil in her own hellish illusion and won. She couldn't be a part of Thug's army and revolution because maybe she had her own to lead. Life was the grandest social experiment of them all. Oh, and she had chosen her true love.

After she had the Heretix take away the minibar, she sat with her Tiffany rock, pictures of Robeson, snapshots of the trampled audience from the first Faustus concert, her CD, affirmation cards and her thoughts of Rob.

Her true love prospects over the past year were an eclectic bunch from the hypothetical, imagined and nonexistent to the real. The sidewalk dudes and Craigslist bunch, Dr. Akawaaba, Pimp, Dope Jones, Robeson Thug and, of course, Rob. No one had seen him in days. No one knew where to look except her.

She called for Legba. He was reinstalled to her team when Shell found that her career hadn't peaked out yet. She asked Legba to take her by Thug's old spot. Crazy. It was like she had dreamed the whole thing. There were several families squatting in his space like the loft never existed.

Next stop. One two five. Maya headed underground into Rob's "office" sporting Adana sunglasses and a lavender Bongi Gray Couture minidress. She found him on the subway platform listening to music and watching the trains go by. He gave a full-on smile as Maya sat down and put her head on his shoulder.

"What are you listening to?" she asked.

Rob held her hand and they watched the uptown A pull into the station. "I Ain't No Joke," he said.

"Ahhh. *I used to let the mic smoke. Now I slam it when I'm done and make sure it's broke.* Classic. The King."

"That's right."

"Rob . . . We need to talk."

"Aw man. The worst thing you can say to a brotha is we need to talk." He latched his fingers through hers and tried to play thumb wars.

"I'm serious." She let go and fiddled with the latch on her Fendi Spy bag, a birthday gift from Luci.

"Not to interrupt your moment but I've been meaning to tell you something too. I'm proud of you, my papaya Maya."

"I know. So you gonna let me finish or not?"

"Sorry. Go 'head."

"Okay." Deep breath. "Rob. I love you. Big surprise, right?"

Rob put his arms around Maya.

"When we were engaged you completely screwed me over, but you didn't dump me at the altar. I was the one who made a decision, the best decision, not to go ahead with the wedding."

He kissed her on the lips and she kissed him back softly.

"I had to change the story I was telling myself, Rob, to change my definition, because we're different people now."

He smoothed her hair, tangling his fingers in it.

She breathed him in. Sandalwood and musk. "Okay. Lemme finish. I want you to be happy. So happy, Rob. Even if it's not with me. I can't do this, not right now. I gotta do me."

"Oh."

They sat quietly. Rob clasped his hands and put his fingers to his lips. He crossed his arms. "You going back to Faustus?"

"Hell to the no."

They laughed.

"Rob, I don't want you to be my man right now, but I do want you to be my friend, my manager—"

"Nah." He looked at the tracks. "To the manager part. I'm taking a five. Gonna focus on something more creative for me."

"Good! Maybe I'll roll with Luci then. She offered."

"Take you up on the friend part, though." He paused. "So you're going to Ghana?" he asked.

They both smiled at the wonder of Robeson Thug. Maya hit Rob on the leg. "Nope. Not yet, although I definitely wanna check out the homeland."

"No doubt," he said. "I'm surprised you and Luci still speak."

"There's no devils. And I'm not perfect so I can't ask anybody else to be." Maya's heel hit something.

"You know she's the one that snitched on you," Rob said. "She figured she could get you good publicity mileage out of the scandal."

Maya nodded. "It's all good." She bent over and picked up a tiny iridescent green stone frog. It was the same color and size as her good luck rock that she lost before coming to New York. In the subway's fluorescent light it appeared to be glowing. She closed her fist around it.

"See you at Athena's wedding," Maya said.

Rob held out his fist. Maya pounded hers on top of it and put her sunglasses back on. As he watched Maya walk away from him in the humid New York City subway, she actually became bigger, not smaller, on the horizon of people's faces.

Back in the Bentley, Maya sat behind Legba and put her feet up on the hand-stitched seat. She had become comfortable with the silence. They passed a newsstand, a litany of covers sporting her face and, more important, her story. *Essence, Vibe Vixen, Jewel, Honey, Bonfire, Mode, Sparkle, Poise, Runway, Glamour . . .*

Legba looked into the rearview mirror. "So you realized your desire and kept your soul."

Maya looked up. "Excuse me?"

"Realized. Made real. We always want what we already have."

"I guess." Since she was not used to Legba talking, she was not used to listening to him. The DVD screens showed a rough cut of Maya's new video, a low-key vibe with her kicking poetic lyrics onstage in the Den, a small Harlem café. She watched the audience as they applauded. The woman onstage was smooth and sophisticated, both teaching and having fun.

They stopped at a traffic light and Legba turned all the way around to face Maya. "You know at home we Caribbeans have tings like dumplings and pepper pot and metegee where you throw in everything and cook, and the mess that comes out is beautiful."

"Yeah." Maya pepped up. "Granny Ruby used to make something like that. Stew, right?" She shook her head. "Yeah. Like a mixtape."

Legba un-pursed his lips. Maya thought all this time that was just how his lips were. "Yes, daughter. But not a mixtape that you purchase. Or a mixtape that one of them boyfriends or girlfriends give to you. Is like a mixtape you already have."

"No doubt." Maya looked across into the backseat mirror at her one true love, then enjoyed the magnificent view as they whizzed along the FDR Drive.

Notebook of Joy

THE DARE EXPERIMENT
HIP-HOP UNDERCOVER
BY ME

Notebook of Joy

"Some of y'all might call it getting crunk or getting hyphy. I'm calling all that pursuit exactly what it is, trying to get joy." Wearing a vintage-green wrap minidress, wooden bangles and Cleopatra X brand high-tops, Maya sat on a stool kicking it with her crowd as Hip-Hop Ham grooved back and forth. "I hope that you enjoy my new flow," she said.

"It's *The Hip Hop Resuscitator*, baby," he said into the camera. "And we've added live music to the mix. Today we're hanging with a woman I thought would be a one-hit wonder for sure, but she's still doing her thing. Cleopatra X and her all-girl band, Goddess Wishes." The studio audience applauded.

A jazzy beat started. The drummer set it off and Maya kicked her electric poetry over a tight beat:

"Homemade/Sweetness/Doubled
Yes—always this much trouble
Nappy from the git, but I've never been a ho
Don't take my word, your soul also knows
Maya begat Cleopatra in her own likeness
And lived for five hundred years just like this . . ."

The crowd fed on her words and energy, the golden highlights in Maya's long wavy 'fro dazzling in the stage lights. From her vantage point on the stage, Maya could see every smiling face clearly, and for those very few clueless folks that weren't feeling her, that was their prerogative as she did a Yeve Thunder

God move, a dance that she learned on her last trip home to the motherland. The stage was her altar indeed.

JOY DECLARATION: (Repeat five times every morning, noon and night to reinforce joy.) *Every moment is an opportunity for joy. I am committed to my wellbeing and I inhale joy with every breath.*

JOY ACTION STEP: *Take yourself on a joyful solo playdate. This need not involve money. Go on a solo picnic and dare to indulge in the harmony, beauty, moxie, love, truth and joy that is you.*

DISCUSSION QUESTIONS

1. What would you say this book is about?
2. Which character(s) do you most identify with?
3. Talk about the concept of one true love.
4. Discuss any parallels between characters and real-life figures.
5. What does the novel say about ideas of family?
6. What do you think of the commercialism in the story?
7. What does the story say about entertainment and pop culture?
8. What does this book say about fame? Popularity?
9. What does the novel say about truth and reality?
10. Did you actually use any of the inspirational pages that divide the story into sections?
11. What does the novel say about identity?
12. Did your opinions of any characters change during the story?
13. Are there any villains in this story?
14. What are your favorite moments?
15. What did you think of the use of poetry and song lyrics in the novel?
16. The author does not consider this a hip-hop story but a human story. Do you agree? Disagree?
17. What does the story say about happiness?
18. What fairy tale themes or references do you find in the novel?
19. Did you find any biblical themes in the story?
20. The author wanted to do a version of *The Wizard of Oz*. What parallels do you find?
21. *Faust* is a popular German legend about a scholar who makes a deal with the devil and succumbs to a life of temptation. *Dare* is a retelling of that story. How did temptation play a part in the story?
22. How does the author use language and imagery to bring the characters and story to life?
23. Did the book's characters or style remind you of any other books?
24. Does this book have a message? Or touch your life in any way?
25. Maya makes a list of ten things she'd do if she knew she could not fail. What is on your list?

Please visit Abiola Abrams's website at www.thegoddessfactory.com.

CPSIA information can be obtained
at www.ICGtesting.com
Printed in the USA
LVHW110112020120
642281LV00001B/1/P

9 781416 541660